FALCON

First published by Romaunce Books in 2023
Suite 2, Top Floor, 7 Dyer Street, Cirencester, Gloucestershire, GL7 2PF

A catalogue record for this book is available from the British Library

Falcon
978-1-7391173-4-4

Cover design and content by Ray Lipscombe
Printed and bound in Great Britain

Romaunce Books™ is a registered trademark

Nina stanger

FALCON

Everybody wants Clelia...but no one can really have her.

Foreword

by Helena Kennedy

Nina Stanger was an unusual woman to find practising at the English Bar in the late Sixties and early Seventies. Beautiful, Bohemian and fiercely clever, she brought glamour to the group of left-wing lawyers who championed civil liberties and defended in the political cases of the time.

She was born in Bromley, in Kent, in 1943; her father was an accountant, her mother a schoolteacher. After studying at the London School of Economics, she was called to the Bar in 1965. She was soon involved in some widely publicised cases. She defended the Holborn squatters and the squatters in 144 Piccadilly, who were arrested after they occupied empty buildings to draw attention to homelessness.

When the Old Bailey was bombed in 1972, she was one of the lawyers who defended the Price sisters. She also acted in many of the cases arising from student unrest in the universities and indeed met her future husband, the Oxford politics don and writer Steven Lukes, when she acted for the students involved in the occupation of the Indian Institute in 1974.

The Seventies also saw the resurgence of the Haldane Society as a meeting place for progressive lawyers. As an organisation it had gone through a moribund period but was revitalised by a new generation who wanted a serious discourse about the role of lawyers of the Left in making the law accessible to those who were disadvantaged. Stanger was an active member and her contributions to debate were delivered with great precision and dry wit, informed by her passion for civil liberties rather than rigid ideologies, which she deplored. She had an exquisite voice which she used to great effect, especially with judges, and abundant blonde hair which looked glorious even under the barrister's wig.

Although Stanger continued to practice throughout the Seventies, her marriage in 1977 to Lukes transformed her life, as it did his. Their partnership led them to diversify many of their interests. They travelled extensively to the United States and Canada, Brazil, Argentina, Mexico, Peru, South Africa, China.

I first met Nina Stanger in 1971 when she had just represented the protesters against the Miss World contest and was part of the legal team defending in the Angry Brigade trial (a group of anarchists who in the late Sixties and early Seventies attempted to bomb establishment targets). Women at the criminal bar were still few in number and here was one with the sort of practice which interested me. I sought her out, eager to be reassured that survival was possible in that chilly, male-dominated environment; she not only provided warmth and wisdom, which I came to recognise as her hallmark, but was also a constant source of encouragement in the years which followed.

Whenever we met, she was full of news, political and cultural, as well as stories about the legal systems she had witnessed. She also co-founded the British Kurdish Friendship Society in 1975 and with a handful of others put the issue of Kurdish oppression on the agenda.

The birth of her three children followed and then in 1987 her husband was offered a post as Professor of Political and Social Theory at the European Institute in Florence, and she could think of no more idyllic place to live. She embraced the move to Italy as a great adventure, even though she had herself just that year been admitted to the New York bar – she and Steven had previously planned to go and live in America.

Although she continued over the years to take cases on an intermittent basis, her main focus became her children, her husband and Italian life, which enthralled her. She became immensely knowledgeable about Renaissance art and history, which seemed so appropriate as she had always looked like a Fra Angelico painting herself. She also made a comparative study of English and Italian law and not only organised conferences on the subject in Florence but acted as a consultant to Italian lawyers about British practice.

When I last saw her two years ago at a political seminar in Siena she was as vibrant and beautiful as ever. Amidst proud and tantalising descriptions of her children, she made me promise that I would resist all attempts by government to interfere with jury trials in Britain. Having seen the inquisitorial system at close quarters, she was highly critical of it.

Her descriptions of her life were wildly funny but delivered as always with careful pacing and a wonderful turn of phrase. She was well abreast of the political scene in the UK and incisive in her commentary about the key players. As we parted, she told me of her plans to return to practice but only after she completed a novel which had been taking form in the months before.

Nina Vera Mary Stanger, barrister born Bromley, Kent 6 August 1943; called to the Bar 1965; married 1977 Steven Lukes (two sons, one daughter); died Galliano, Italy 30 January 1999.

Baroness Helena Kennedy KC

FALCON

by Nina Stanger

Yenathios was wildly excited. He could barely contain himself while Albert was pouring the hot chocolate, and desperate for him to withdraw so that he could tell Clelia.

"The patriarch is coming, His Beatitude Petros VII of Alexandria. He's coming to bless our monastery, and I will take part in the ceremony! I shall meet him! It's such an honour!"

"When is he coming?"

"Next week! You must come to the service, so that even if you aren't able to meet him, at least you will see him!"

"Are women allowed?"

"Of course they are! They attend all the normal services at the church, they bring their children to be baptised. During the service with the patriarch, he will bless some of the children of the community, and they have already been chosen. I shall take part in the service wearing a magnificent gold robe."

"I've only ever seen you in black."

"That's why you have to come and see me in gold!"

"I would love to, you must tell me where and when."

"Every day I have to go and take part in the preparations and the rehearsals. It is so exciting!" Yenathios was so excited that he could hardly concentrate or teach properly, but it was risky trying to go to Clelia's room before nightfall. He decided to run back to the monastery and return under cover of darkness. Only when he was lying in her arms could he relax and calm down, and eventually, in the early hours of the morning, try and get some sleep.

"Tell me," asked Clelia. "Are priests obliged to be celibate, as in the Roman Catholic Church, or are they allowed to do what we do?"

"It is better for them to marry than to burn," he replied, "but if they do marry, this precludes them from ascending to higher office."

"So you don't intend to marry?"

"But I do intend to go on making love to you."

"As long as they don't know."

"Why should they ever know? What's it got to do with them? Although I easily could, I wouldn't want to be called upon to explain the difference between sacred and profane love."

When the day of the great ceremony dawned, they rose early, and Yenathios ran off through the forest to return to the monastery and prepare himself.

Clelia arrived early at the church in order to get a good seat. When she entered the church she was overwhelmed by its beauty, the power of the incense, and the very small number of chairs. The chairs were arranged around the edge of the church and the columns, leaving a wide open space in the centre of the church where the congregation stood. More and more people were pouring into the church, and the excitement was tangible. Many carried children and babies, and elderly people hobbled in assisted by younger relatives. Clelia found it preferable to move about and inhale the intense spirit of anticipation. She listened to the happy babble of conversation, drank in the beauty of the gold encrusted icons, and gazed mesmerised at the enormous number of candles everywhere. They were set out on tables before icons of the Virgin and Child that were covered with mosaics and gold leaf, shimmering rubies, amethysts, sapphires and emeralds, candles rising in tall masses that almost stretched to the top of the gold-covered altar screen, some in green, others in ruby-red glasses, all blazing with a mysterious, ethereal light that glittered and reflected in the gold and jewels that shone everywhere the eye could see. The sad face of Christ Pantocrator gazed silently down upon them.

Above the sound of the chatter and laughter rose the beautiful languorous music of the invisible choir singing in Greek. The acolytes, young boys dressed in light gold wispy garments, moved among the congregation placing enormous bowls of white lilies around a raised red velvet cushion that stood in the centre of the nave. Priests in magnificent gold robes moved in and out of the side doors of the high altar screen but the central doors remained firmly shut.

In the midst of all the crush and confusion, Clelia saw Yenathios, in a magnificent gold robe lining up the children and reading out their names in a high singsong voice. He was partly reading the names and partly singing the blessings, and then he lifted high a very small baby, raising him high up to heaven, and after displaying him to the congregation, blessing him, and then retiring with him into the inner sanctum for baptism.

There was still another day upon which Yenathios had the chance to meet the patriarch. In order to ensure that he arrived in time, he had borrowed a horse and tethered it in the forest near the wall of the Elmsmere Estate. Thinking that he had plenty of time, he remained with Clelia slightly longer than he intended, then ran through the garden and climbed over the wall. "With the help of my God, I shall leap over the wall," he said to himself. It was only on arrival on the other side that he discovered that the horse had gone. Hot, sweaty, and in a terrible state of panic, he ran through the forest and arrived at the door of the monastery just as the patriarch was being led out to the waiting Rolls Royce.

One of his aides noticed Yenathios's late arrival, and had the temerity to point it out to him.

The patriarch turned towards him. He smiled benevolently, and placed his hand on Yenathios's sweating shoulder. "Do not worry about being late, my son," he said. "For it is written in the Scripture, that even he who is late in Heaven will still receive his wages."

Embarrassed beyond belief, and not daring to hope that this would apply to him, Yenathios bowed his head to receive the patriarch's blessing. As the patriarch placed his hand upon his head, he gazed in silent wonder at the immense silver cross that bedecked the patriarch's ample chest, the black robe spread out before him. He looked up into the merry, smiling eyes. He was convinced that the patriarch knew everything, but was betraying nothing.

Yenathios reported all of this back to Clelia as they lay in bed that night. Clelia considered this.

It was six o'clock, and drinks were being handed round in the drawing room at Eaton Square. They were mainly being handed around by white-gloved waiters, but one tray of drinks was being tottered around by a young girl in a long, slinky, low-backed evening dress on absurdly high stilettos.

The boys were greatly amused by Clelia's bravado, and were taking bets on when she would topple over, and whether the tray would go down with her. From time to time she would glance back at them, as if to smile, "So far, so good!" There was a buzz of conversation, and the sound of animated amusement at her efforts.

Nigel was deep in conversation with a friend from the Foreign Office. He was watching Clelia closely, but making every effort to give the impression that he was not. He marvelled at how she could balance so well on Veronica's high heels, and he could not keep his eye off the black seams that went all the way up her legs until they disappeared somewhere inside the slits of the elegant long skirt. James had obviously been detained at the House, and no-one knew if he would make it at all to the party.

After spending some time laughing and joking with the boys, Clelia snaked her way carefully across the room to Nigel. He pretended not to notice, and went on talking. Clelia pushed the heavily laden tray towards him.

"Would you like another drink?" She smiled.

Nigel turned to look at her. She had obviously enjoyed free rein with Veronica's make-up box, and had spent a long time in front of the dressing-table mirror. Nigel was not sure how successful she had been.

"Have another whiskey," she said. As he reached out to take it, Clelia said softly and urgently, "Nigel, please ask James if you can take me out to the theatre. He won't allow me to go anywhere. It's so awful having finally got to London if I can't go anywhere."

Before he could make any reply, a commotion at the door indicated that James had arrived. Accompanied by his personal private secretary and with George and a number of others in tow, he swept elegantly into the room, and immediately started greeting people and shaking hands. As he moved about smiling and chatting, he suddenly came upon Clelia going about with her tray of drinks. He looked at her in total amazement. "What on earth do you think you're doing?" he said. The whole room came to a shocked silence.

Clelia quaked before him as he gazed at her in astounded

disbelief. "Veronica gave me permission," she said in a low, timid voice.

"Perhaps she did," said James, not wishing to accuse her outright of lying in public, "But I certainly never did, and I never would, and you know that." By a gesture of the head he indicated to a waiter to remove the tray from her trembling hands. "Go to your room at once, and remove that ridiculous stuff from your face. Never, ever, let me see you like that again."

The room echoed with the soundless shock of all who stood there as Clelia, head bowed, made her noiseless exit. They all watched her as she moved silently through the doorway and crossed the hall.

Nigel felt a desperate desire to go to her, as they all did, but no-one dared to move.

As she approached the staircase and reached the first step, the lowered head glanced back at the room, but very quickly turned away.

"Now then," said James cheerily. "Let's all have a drink, it's been a very long day!" The conversation gradually started to pick up, and the party resumed.

In among the crowd, George found his way to Nigel, and moved in close to him. "Damn lucky I didn't ask him if I could take her out to dinner. I was going to."

"I know you were. Well, don't."

"How can he treat her like that in front of everybody?"

"He's very severe. He's very correct and proper. He doesn't like this relaxation of morals that's going on all over the place. So you'd better watch out that he doesn't notice you, and what you get up to."

"But I was really looking forward to taking Lolita out to dinner. She never gets the chance to go out."

"You don't think you've got enough girls buzzing around to

keep you busy for the time being?"

"I can't help it if girls chase me. It's not as if I go looking for them."

"Please don't do anything to upset him at the moment. You see how

things are. I'm having my work cut out in trying to persuade him to let her go to school."

"I thought it was the law that you had to go to school."

"He thinks a private tutor is better. He doesn't want her to become infected with new-fangled ideas. I think it was all right when he kept her in the country, but now he's finally allowed her to come to town, I think it's essential that she should go to school and study properly. She's been taught very well, she knows an awful lot, but she's very cut off from everything."

"What hope do you have of persuading him?"

"I don't know, I'll have to work on it. But all my efforts will be destroyed if you mess in. It's fellows like you that he's trying to keep her safe from."

The boys on the other side of the room were equally distressed on Clelia's behalf at the harsh treatment she had received. It had all been innocent fun, and they could not understand why James had chosen to humiliate her like that in front of everyone.

It was a long and tedious business, but Nigel finally managed to get James to consent to Clelia's going to school. Through his contacts, Nigel fixed it up with St Paul's.

Clelia was insanely excited at the idea, and Nigel drove her down there for her first day. She was overjoyed by all the subjects she had to study, and by being in a classroom with other girls. She excitedly gave a breathless report to Nigel of the events of the first day.

It was the evening of Queen Caroline's Ball. Nigel was amazed that James had given his consent to allow Clelia to attend, but it had been on the strict instructions that Nigel was to remain with her throughout the evening. This really was asking a lot of any man. It was all very well accompanying a young debutante to a ball, but keeping any control over her once they arrived there was truly impossible. As soon as they entered the ballroom at the Grosvenor Hotel, Clelia was whisked away by her classmates and taken off into the ladies so that they could adjust her make-up for her, contrary to James's strict injunction that she was never to wear any ever again. Then, when they finally emerged, they all went running past Nigel, screaming and shrieking with excitement in order to introduce her to dance partners.

There was absolutely no difficulty in that, since a number of the boys in James's private office had been frenziedly drawing lots as to who was to dance with her. There was a very complicated rota that they had worked out as to who would dance with the other girls while the lucky boy was dancing with Clelia. They were keen to get her drunk as soon as possible so that her behaviour would be really outrageous. They were hoping for everything, but in intense rivalry with each other, jealously watching each other's every move.

Nigel realised at once that it would be impossible to compete with any of this, and went off to the bar for a double scotch. It was to be the first of many.

From time to time Nigel would wander back into the ballroom. He found the noise from the band overwhelming. Amidst all the wild dancing, running and shouting, he occasionally caught glimpses of an excited Clelia, her cheeks flushed and glowing, an expression of ecstasy upon that beautiful face, dancing with a wild abandoned fury as though she were a maenad at a bacchanal. But he found the orchestra, the noise, the clatter and the unending supply of boisterous energy unendurable, and quickly sloped off to the bar again. He was joined by a number of drinking companions, all in the same frame of mind. One of them, Archie, was good enough to go into the ballroom from time to time, between rounds of drinks generously supplied by Nigel, and give him a running report on how things were going at the battle front. Nigel had managed to point out Clelia to him, when she was taking part in a particularly mad rush in the Dashing White Sergeant, and Archie did his level best to keep up with her movements after that. From time to time he would describe what she was up to, although most of it was indescribable.

As the raucous evening wore on, and the whooping and screaming of the riotous dancers became ever more ear-shattering, Archie carne running back from the ballroom and reported breathlessly, "You must come and see this. She's dancing on the table. There's an enormous crowd round her, chanting and swaying. I'm not sure how long she'll be able to stay up there. They're all hoping – well, that strapless dress – it looks as if – well, you'd better come and see!"

Nigel reluctantly put down his glass and followed Archie. The scene was as he had described.

There she was, on the top of a table, and all the boys around her were chorusing and shouting. She certainly did not have any shoes, and he was not sure if she had any stockings. The white strapless ball dress, upon which all attention centred, really did look as if it was not going to last another minute.

Nigel did not know whether to intervene and drag her down or run away and pretend that this disgraceful display was being enacted by a stranger. He found himself rooted to the floor and watching in fascinated horror. The boys were all screaming at her to pull her dress off, and it almost looked as if she were about to oblige them. There was a terrible scramble around the table, so it was impossible for him to fight his way through the crush. He could hardly scream at her to come down because the noise of the dance band was so unbearably loud and his voice could not possibly be heard above the roar of the shouting boys.

Intoxicated with the power that she was exercising over all these rampant young males, Clelia continued to dance and tease as though in a hypnotic trance. But she was keeping a keen eye on all of them, to see the effect that she had on each of them. It could not then fail to be the case that her wandering eye alighted upon the horrified face of Nigel gazing up at her. This was her real moment of triumph. Pulling her ball dress as low as she dared, she stretched out her arms to him across the sea of exuberant boys. "Darling!" she cried, "Come and rescue me!"

He moved forward towards her, and she launched herself across the crush of boys towards him. A whole crowd of them fell in a laughing, tumbling, writhing mass onto the floor, with a wave of hands groping out to grab whatever part of her they could.

As they slowly emerged from the floor, Clelia managed to emerge from the melee, and flung herself, sweating and exhausted into Nigel's arms.

He wasn't sure how he got her home, but it was a great relief to sit in the quiet of the drawing room at Eaton Square trying to recover from the destruction of the evening. The lights were turned down low and Clelia reclined, happy and tired, on a velvet settee. Nigel helped himself to another whiskey from the drinks cabinet and sat down at the other end of the settee.

Clelia chattered on gaily about how delightful it had all been.

Lying at full length, she moved slightly towards him and rested her feet on his legs.

"Whatever happened to your stockings?"

Clelia burst out laughing. "I really don't know!" As she continued to chat in her animated way, he seemed to notice that her toes were wriggling about in the region of his crotch.

As he tried to move himself slightly further off, the persistent toes followed him, and continued their tenacious caressing of his private parts. Was she aware that she was doing this, he wondered. She was chatting about the events of the evening. Perhaps she had drunk too much, she certainly was unused to alcohol. Nigel tried to remove her legs from his thighs, but they soon returned.

She was laughing excitedly about the dance on top of the table. "I think they really did think that the dress was about to tumble down!"

"They were certainly hoping for it."

"But that's so silly, they obviously have no idea how firmly it is fixed on, there's no chance that it will slip off."

"I've always wondered, how is it fixed on, and able to stay up like that without any straps?"

Clelia immediately carne very close to him, kneeling on the settee beside him. Her beautiful breasts loomed very close to his face. "It's all done with whalebone. Look, I'll show you. Feel here, there are all these hooks, they hold it very tightly in place." She took his hand and placed it on the bodice. As she did so, she opened the first line of hooks. "Feel here, where the whalebone is. Tightly holding his hand, she moved it inside the first layer of white silk, and began to undo the second row of hooks.

He looked at her breasts, and suddenly realised that in another moment the dress would be off, and the naked breasts would come tumbling out before him. As he thought this, he suddenly became aware that he had an erection, the first for twelve years. In a desperate state of panic that he would be caught here with Clelia, he got up quickly from the settee. Hastily putting down his glass, he said, "I must leave. Goodnight." He walked quickly from the room. Clelia heard his footsteps echo through the dark drawing room, the silent hall and the empty house. She heard the front door close, she heard him descend the stone steps of the house, she heard the engine start up, and she heard the car drive away into the silent night. She remained for a long time in the drawing room. "I wonder what it was that made him leave like that," she thought.

Gordon was irritatingly insistent. "We've been invited. What's the point in not going?"

"It's miles away, what's the point in driving so far for a few drinks when we can have a good drink in the Club?" asked Nigel.

"The Club!" snorted Gordon, "This is going to be a real scorcher of a party. Really swinging! There are going to be all kinds of girls, dancers, strippers, you name it! This will sear the pants off you! You don't get anything like that in the Club!"

"Is that what I really want?"

"You haven't had a woman in years! Now you can make up for it, and in one evening have one for every year you've missed them!"

"Is that what they're promising, is that why you're so desperate to go?"

"This is the party of the year, the decade! You've heard that new phrase they use, blow your mind! This is what the Swinging Sixties is all about. We can't miss out!"

Without a car it would have been awkward for Gordon to get there, so he was delighted when he finally persuaded Nigel to undertake the long journey to Hever Castle in his Morgan. Despite the depth of his scepticism, Nigel found that he was not entirely immune to contagion from Gordon's feverish anticipation of the delights awaiting them at the journey's end. Two hours in the car in such close proximity with one so infected with such a frenzied desire to partake of the new, unleashed immorality that was breaking out everywhere did, despite his natural reserve, have some degenerative effect even upon Nigel, at least in some very minor degree.

It was still light when the car pulled into the car park of the castle, and Nigel lined it up along with all the other cars that were already there. They strode off towards the sound of the music and drinks.

"This is just the kind of jazz I like," cried Gordon, "Whaaar! Dig that trombone! Bill Harris, such crisp sensitivity, 'Jan-Cee Brown,' just listen to him, listen to the way he places the notes!"

The glorious scent of the flowers in the early evening had a liberating effect upon them. Gordon was so eager to break free of any restraint that even Nigel felt a strange re-awakening of something indefinable that had been closed down or turned off for such an age that he had felt for some long time past that it no longer existed within him. Tonight he feared that he would be exposed to the presence of women in a way that he had not been for a very long time.

Moving along walkways through the beautiful lawns and gardens, they soon found themselves at the side of the castle on a terrace overlooking yet a further burgeoning parterre and the lake. Trays of drinks were being offered around.

Gordon grabbed a glass of champagne and then disappeared into the twilight. Within minutes he was back at Nigel's side. "Down there, down there, you won't believe it, but it's just as I said."

"What is it?"

"I can't describe it." He was breathless with excitement. "Those women, the ones I told you about. It's true. It's there, where that fantastic music is coming from. Bring your drink, come." He strode on ahead, almost pushing his way past the partygoers dancing and swaying to the music, and those who were simply eating and drinking from the proffered trays. They descended the steps, and came to a very crowded area on the lower terrace.

A slightly raised section had been roped off, and behind it women in leathers, which had been cut open at all the appropriate places to be maximally revealing, were striding around with enormous horse-whips offering to whip anyone who dared to step inside the ring. A number of men had torn off their jackets and had climbed into the ring. The sound of the whips resounded as the pacing women struck out at their willing victims. As the dusk descended over the scented gardens blazing torches were lit around the raised arena, and the music swung out, wilder and louder.

Gordon was desperate to go into the ring. As he tore his clothes off he wanted Nigel to hold them for him. At Nigel's refusal he managed to find someone else and climbed almost naked into the ring.

Nigel was pushed out of the way by a crowd of active voyeurs, and decided to return to the upper terrace for another glass of champagne. As he pushed his way up the stone steps he passed the sweet smelling wallflowers that were so dark that their velvety petals appeared almost black in the dusky night.

Suddenly, he was almost knocked over by an excited crowd of young people who laughed and screamed their way down the staircase. He clutched at the wall to steady himself as they ran by. Someone in the crush seemed familiar. but it couldn't be Clelia, could it? They had all disappeared too fast, he couldn't tell. The dance floor on the terrace above was full of swaying bodies crushed together and dancing to the bossa nova. He wound his way around the edge of the constantly moving dancers to try and get to the table overloaded with every kind of drink. It was a laborious process to avoid being knocked over by the gyrating dancers who constantly swung into his path. He only managed to get through when the music ended in a triumphant climax, and everyone fell exhausted into their partner's arms and applauded the music much too loudly. Then the band started to play a slow, lilting, sentimental tune that he half recognised but couldn't remember the words, and the dancers swung into action again. A woman in a sequined dress got up at the microphone and sang out:

Pack up all my cares and woe,
Here I go, singing low,
Bye bye, blackbird.

Nigel tried to push past the throng at the bar to get to the drinks, but the swell of the crowd was intense. He saw a glass floating by and snatched at it.

Where somebody waits for me,
Sugar's sweet, so is he,
Bye, Bye Blackbird.

Nigel swayed to and fro in the crush. Canapés with caviar came by and he grasped them, crushing them into his mouth.

No-one here can love or understand me,
Oh what hard-luck stories they all hand me.

Some more champagne followed to wash down the canapés, and Nigel grabbed an extra glass just in case.

Make my bed and light the light,
I'll arrive late tonight,
Black bird, bye bye.

Nigel slowly managed to extricate himself from the swaying mass as the darkness of night descended, and flares and flaming oil lamps were placed about the terrace and the gardens. Sounds of excited revellers were heard from everywhere in the grounds, and the music from a number of different bands floated everywhere and mingled in the deep blue sky above. As he tried to walk towards the overloaded white tablecloths that groaned with a cornucopia of meats, lobster, salmon, salads and fruits, again the whirlwind of exhilarated young people came flying along, precipitating aside anyone in their path.

One of them had golden curls piled up very high on her head, and wore a glistening golden micro-mini skirt with matching top supported by very thin shoulder straps. The absurdly high ankle straps must have been her own this time because she was able to run in them.

He seized the naked arm as she flew by and pulled her out of the group. The others whirled away into the crowd. Nigel held on very tight until she had stopped spinning. Then he put his arms round her and drifted off into the dancing mass with her, holding her tight.

Clelia placed her arms round his neck and they swayed in time to the music, holding each other tight.

"I wouldn't have thought that James would have allowed you to come, and certainly not dressed like this."

"He's down below, running about by the side of the lake, how can he not let me come?"

"He's down below?" asked Nigel in surprise. "I didn't think he permitted himself to go to parties, and certainly not one like this."

"I think it's a bathing party, except that none of them is wearing bathing costumes. Luckily, it's a very warm night."

Nigel contemplated the very idea of this as they danced

together.

Clelia placed her head on his shoulder.

"Are they?"

"What do you think?"

He did not know what to say.

"And what do you think they are all doing up here?" she continued. "Where?"

"Here, around us. You don't think they are dancing, do you?"

Nigel looked at the swaying mass of people who crushed against them. The music was very loud, and the dance floor was very dark. "What are they doing?" he asked in a voice of disbelief.

"You know what they're doing, only you can't do it."

"Can't I?"

"No, you can't!" Her mocking eyes challenged him, and she tried to pull away from his grip. But there was nowhere to go in the middle of the crowd. She placed her lips on his cheek and drawled, "You know you can't!"

He found the provocation unbearable.

Her hand was caressing his cock, and she was unzipping his fly. As her hand slid inside his under pants and grabbed hold of him, he placed his hand under the miniskirt to discover the flimsiest of underpants which could easily be pushed aside. Pulling her very tightly towards him, he held her hard. He quickly manoeuvred her into position and lifted her onto his cock, to his own amazement shooting suddenly inside her. Clelia gasped as they staggered about, held upright by the enormous press of the throng. The sensation was unbelievable. He was angry with himself for coming so fast, but it was the first time after so long. He had no idea where he was as he lifted her down and hastily did up his trousers. The music and dancing around them continued regardless. He wondered how many others clasped together in the melee were actually doing it. Was this what the Swinging Sixties meant? Had he been waiting for it all along? He grabbed her by the head and kissed her very hard on the lips.

With his arm tightly round her, he guided her from the dance floor towards the dinner tables. After pushing about they finally found places and sat down together. An army of waiters served them from the buffet. They ate salmon with mayonnaise, salad tossed with vinaigrette, and drank champagne. The waiters then served strawberries and cream. Nigel was very anxious that in the vast mass of guests no friend or acquaintance should approach him, and he was keen to leave the dinner table before Clelia's boisterous friends discovered them. He saw that by now, the carefully lacquered curls were beginning to unravel, that the make-up around the eyes and the eye-liner was becoming a little bit smudgy, and after at least three glasses of champagne, the eyes were becoming a bit glazed.

He helped her from her seat, and as he guided her gently along the walkway towards the gardens, he noticed that the tottering on the high-heeled ankle-straps was becoming ever more unsteady. The party was in full swing and there were jubilant guests getting very drunk and having immense fun. Nigel was aware that the grounds were vast and that they contained very little lighting. He realised also as they gradually descended into the gardens that a lot of people had had the same idea, and that there were couples lying under all the azaleas and rhododendron bushes. With Clelia leaning more and more heavily upon him, it was difficult to avoid tripping over all the legs sprawled out in the dark.

He finally found a place under some trees where the nearest whispers were more than a few yards away, and he laid the almost comatose Clelia down on the grass. He desired her so intensely that he was unable to control himself or think clearly. He was desperate to make love to her as quickly as possible.

Without a thought for anything, he pulled up her spangly top and undid her bra. He felt the beautiful breasts burst out into his mouth, although in the dark he could not see them. Kissing her frantically, he pulled up the miniskirt and tore off the flimsy underpants. He pulled his trousers down and climbed onto her, and found himself transported into another universe. The music faded into the distance, the noise of the party disappeared from the face of the earth and the sensations of the comingling of their bodies was so overwhelming that he lost all sense of reason, and could exist only through the intensity of the pleasure. He had never known anything like this in his life before. He tried to prolong the experience, but again, it exploded much too fast.

He lay for a moment shuddering with sensuous gratification, then quickly pulled up his trousers. He could hear the sounds of moaning lovers quite near, and he was anxious to get Clelia to the car. Trying to get her to stand up was an enormous effort, and pulling her and dragging her took up all his strength. After a lot of whispered cajoling, he managed to get her to put her arms round d his neck. The spangly shoulder bag kept falling off and had to be retrieved. Nigel took hold of it and stuck it in his pocket. Half carrying her, half dragging her, and avoiding all the centres of crowded activity as best he could, he finally got her to stagger with him to the car, where he pushed her into the passenger seat. Jumping quickly into the driver's seat, he pressed the ignition, and the engine roared into life. Driving smartly out of the car park, he made for the road to London as fast as he could go.

Driving through the night, Nigel finally reached Piccadilly, and drove up to the Albany. Throughout the journey Clelia had slept. Now he sought to rouse her. He was worried that she would attract the notice of the porters if she had to be carried to his rooms. It was an effort to get her to stir, but finally he managed to wake her sufficiently for their entrance to the Albany to be relatively unremarked upon.

They went up the stone staircase, Nigel keeping a firm grip in case she fell. Finally he managed to get her through his own front door, and escorted her to the bedroom. As soon as she lay down on the bed she fell fast asleep. He removed the ankle straps. Then he carefully removed the rest of the clothing, what little there was. Holding his breath, he stood gazing at her. He had never seen anyone so ravishingly lovely. He removed all his clothes and climbed into bed beside her. But there was no hope of waking her, so there was nothing to do but fall asleep.

It was late the following morning when he finally awoke with the sunlight streaming in through the windows. Clelia slept peacefully beside him and he had no intention of disturbing her. He wandered off into the kitchen to make some coffee, returning from time to time to gaze at her. Finally she opened her eyes. He knelt down at the side of the bed.

"Darling, would you like some coffee?"

"Yes, I'd love some. Where are we?"

"At home."

The beautiful green eyes gazed around the room.

"My home. The Albany."

She looked at him in wonder. He hastily went to get the coffee. As he handed her the cup, and as she adjusted her position in the bed to take it from him, she suddenly realised that under the sheet she was naked. Her eye fell upon her clothes on a chair at the side of the bed, and she gazed at Nigel kneeling beside her in his silk dressing gown. She took the coffee and drank it, and he took away the cup and saucer.

He immediately took off the dressing gown and climbed into

the bed beside her.

Clelia regarded him with astonishment. "How did we get here?"

"From the party."

"When?"

"Last night."

"What party?"

"At Hever Castle, where we met last night. When we did this." As she continued to gaze at him, he flung himself quickly on to her. Now he could make love to her in the sunlight and see everything that he could feel, and he could do it openly without groping about in the dark. It was even more sensational than the night before.

"Have I convinced you that I can do it?"

Clelia laughed. "Did we really do this last night at a party?"

"Oh, so you think it was with someone else? You still think I'm incapable? Then we'll have to do it again." He was ready, willing and able.

Clelia reached out to the spangly shoulder-bag that dangled from the back of the chair. She felt about inside it and produced something that looked like a home-made cigarette which she placed to her lips and lit.

"You're not allowed to smoke!"

"It's not a cigarette," she said as she inhaled very deeply, "Here, try it. Inhale very deeply, and hold it in for as long as possible."

He followed her instructions, and felt an intense burning sensation in the chest, causing him to choke.

Clelia took the reefer from his hand, and inhaled deeply. Then she handed it back to him, and told him to try again. They continued in this manner until the reefer was consumed. "How do you feel?"

"Hmmm, not bad. Not bad at all. So you were stoned last night. That explains things."

They lay together gazing at each other. "You know," said Clelia, "I've always loved you."

He stroked her cheek. "James must never, ever know about this."

"Of course not."

"Listen. We'll make love again. Then I'll take you out to lunch, and we'll go to the theatre. You'll stay here tonight with me. But at the end of the weekend, when I take you back to school, we'll have to behave towards each other as if this had never happened. We'll have to go back to how it was before."

"Why? We haven't done anything wrong."

"I didn't say we had. But we have to go back to how we were."

Clelia cast her eyes down, but said nothing.

"What did you say about James's view of you?"

"Nothing, really nothing."

"You did say something. It's something you don't want me to know."

"No, it isn't, really."

"Now you've said it you've got to tell me what it means. There are lots of things I don't know, but you mustn't treat me like a silly little girl. Obviously it's important or you wouldn't try to conceal it from me like this."

He looked at the trusting, expectant face, and stroked the adorable long golden curls. "James has always thought ... but I have never said it, I've never mislead him on this ..."

She waited.

"Susan has never thought this, I can tell by the shameless way she flirts with me at dinner parties ..."

"Yes?"

"Well, it's just that some men don't like women, they prefer men."

"What is that supposed to mean?"

"It's difficult for me to explain. They are not like normal men."

"He thinks you're like that?"

"If he didn't think that, he would never allow me to be your guardian, he would never allow you to come and stay with me at the Albany. I've never alluded to it or suggested it; perhaps he got the idea from the fact that I'm not married, and he's never seen me with a woman."

"Haven't you?"

"Not since university, I haven't had anyone until you. Perhaps that's why he thinks I'm one of those inverted type of men, who have these unnatural desires, who desire other men."

"But what exactly is it? I don't quite understand. Who are these men?"

"Men who are afflicted by it."

"You make it sound like an illness."

"Well, it is an illness. Men who are like that are not normal."

"Is there a cure?"

"Yes, I suppose so, if they are prepared to undergo it. Now can we talk about something else slightly less distasteful. If you work terribly hard at your A Levels, and follow my directions, I can get you into Oxford."

"But won't I have to do the entrance exams? That would mean staying on at school for part of next year. Would James let me?"

"I'll go and talk to people. I'll see what I can do. But you really will have to work very hard."

"But will I be able to keep up with the work at Oxford? What will I have to do?"

"You'll have to go to a tutorial once a week and write a weekly essay."

"What on earth will I write about? I don't know anything!"

"The tutor sets the essay, and if he's sensible he sets the books related to the subject matter of the essay."

"But do I have time to read all the books in order to write the essay?"

"The tutor, if he is sensible, will say, for example, 'Focus on chapter three, because that's where the main argument lies.'"

"But how do formulate your view on it if it's already written? You've just read it in the book, what are you supposed to do? Are you not meant to copy?"

Nigel laughed. "Obviously you're not meant to copy. You have to work out the argument for yourself, and then write out your own argument. At the tutorial you read out the essay to the tutor. He asks you questions."

"Will I know any of the answers?"

"On your essay, on what you've written, on the argument you have produced. It's designed to make you think, to work out your own argument on a subject."

"So you don't copy out, but what do you say if you say the same argument?"

"You work out the argument, but you write it out in your own words. There was a tutorial I was at where the tutor congratulated the boy who read out the essay, and then said, 'That was very good, I wrote that!'"

"And had he?"

"Yes, it was from a published set of his own essays."

"Surely the boy knew?"

Nigel laughed again, and gently took Clelia's hand. "In another tutorial, where a boy was reading his essay, the tutor suddenly jumped up and ran to his bookshelf. He seized hold of a book and opened it, and said, 'Now your next sentence is …' and he read out a sentence from the book!"

"And was he right?"

"Of course, he knew where the essay had been copied from. When I was teaching in Harvard, the students never read whole books, they wanted me to give them page numbers. I once set a subject based on a short essay by Simmel. The students said to me, 'Do we have to read all of it?' I said yes, it's only thirty pages."

"Did you ever have a student who copied something?"

"Yes, and the internal tutor wanted to be very tough with him. I didn't want to be so severe."

"Why did he copy?"

"Obviously he was in difficulties. In the end it was alright. We discussed it, and he produced another essay that he had worked out for himself."

"Did you enjoy teaching?"

"There's no such thing as teaching. You can't teach anyone. You can

enable them to learn, and to use their minds and work out things for themselves, but you can't teach anyone anything. You can create the favourable conditions in which someone can learn something, you can encourage, promote or foster the conditions in which someone can learn, but then it is up to them to take advantage of the situation."

"But if somebody doesn't teach me …" said Clelia sadly.

"Don't worry," said Nigel. "If you follow my advice I shall guide you and instruct you."

Clelia was very excited to hear about Guy.

"Why do you want to know about him?" asked Robin.

"Everyone in my class is very excited about him, they talk about him all the time. Tell me about him."

"He's not in any way interesting. He's one of these superior aristocrats who've got it made for them. He doesn't have to do anything, it's all there for him. What else do you want to know?"

"What does he do?"

"He goes around looking good-looking. He's very languid, suave and urbane. Rather foppish. He swaggers about in a very proud, superior way. Very superior. In fact, he is a peg too high for me in some of his notions, and I wouldn't object if someone would take the opportunity of taking that proud boy down a peg or two. Does this help you?"

Clelia laughed. "I think I'd like to see him. Everyone in my class has. They say he's very beautiful."

"And totally narcissistic. Handsome is as handsome does. He's actually not very nice. You'd do better to meet his friend Henry Aubrey. He is an extremely nice person, serious, mature, studious, like you. He's someone you would really like, and if he has any defect at all, unlike Blandford who has thousands, his only defect is that he's rather paranoid about getting top marks. He always watches very carefully to see what marks his nearest rivals have, and gets into a panic if there's any chance that anyone else will beat him at the top. It only happened once, when Guy beat him by two points in the Final Order. He nearly went crazy! But apart from that, he's really nice. He also features in your collection of eligible young aristocrats who have lots of money, although he doesn't have as much money and his title isn't so ancient. Also he's not the son of a duke, so if you're determined to become a duchess, you can't do it with him. But he is a hell of a lot nicer, and just as clever, if not more so."

Clelia laughed again. "How do you know about my collection of aristocrats?"

"Because I'm one of the assistants who has to do *The Times* cuttings service with all the details of their wealth. Anyway, I've seen your collection of genealogies, I admire how well you've done them. I'm also well aware that you've got a whole collection of very nice young men, all of them with titles, and every single one of them nicer and more worthy of your attention than Blandford."

"Some of them are a bit too young."

"But a lot of them are not. I'd much rather introduce you to someone else. In fact, I think it would be a big mistake to meet Blandford, and I refuse to introduce you to him."

"Why?"

"He's at Oxford, and he's supposed to live in college. Instead, he comes down every Friday night and goes to parties. I've seen him a lot, and he behaves very badly. He's always on the look-out for new girls, and he invites them to his father's palace just outside Oxford for the weekend. Who's going to say no to that? You can imagine what he does when he gets them there. After that he's not in any way interested in them, and many of them have come crying miserably to me, asking me to phone him for them so that they can get re-invited. They don't understand that their conduct with him marks the end of the relationship. Once he's had them of course he's not interested in them anymore, any fool knows that. But you try and tell them!"

"Does he come down to a party every week?"

"Yes, more or less. Do you want me to take you along?"

"Yes, I'd just like to see him, so that I know what everyone is talking about."

"I'll do it only if you promise me that I can also introduce you to Henry, so that you can see the difference."

"I agree."

As Clelia approached the room she could hear the sound. As soon as she opened the door she was almost knocked over by a wall of music bursting out at her.

Guy was playing the saxophone and Rupert was playing the double bass. Rupert had had very few lessons and had more or less taught himself, but he was accompanying Guy very well, who was showing off and playing at breakneck speed. As Clelia discovered during the course of that glorious afternoon, Guy was an acid-toned, exciting saxophone player who, despite the constant showy display and fooling around, had an edge of seriousness to everything he did, even when he was running scales at break-neck speed or softly, gently phrasing out a blues.

Guy proudly showed her how he learnt the pieces. He had a book of music manuscript paper, and he laboriously wrote out each tune from the record. "Sometimes I have to play the record hundreds of times to work out the notes. Then, once I've written it out, I practise it until I know it, and to get it perfect, I play along with the record. Let me show you." He showed her in the book how he had carefully written out Yardbird Suite, and then put the record on the turntable. As the alto sax of Charlie Parker swept over the room Guy played along with him, and Rupert accompanied them.

Clelia was tremendously impressed. "Do you play in a group at the university?"

"I should do, but it would require too much practising. I have too many other things to do. But I would like to get back to full time playing." He took up a record of Sonny Rollins. "Listen to this, this is Sonny Rollins on tenor sax and Clifford Brown on trumpet, 'Valse Hot.'" He placed it on the turntable.

The music swelled out into the room. Clelia listened, enraptured …

"Now listen to this, it's really good, this recording has just come out right now, 1963, I play along with this." It was the re-formed Benny Goodman Quartet with Lionel Hampton, Teddy Wilson and Gene Krupa. The music raced away and Guy raced away with it, Running Wild. At the dramatic climax he played madly, flung down the saxophone and caught her passionately in his arms, burying his face in her breast, then kissing her intensely on the mouth. "We're going to have a wonderful weekend," he assured her. He ran back to the records. "'Running Wild,' you loved it, didn't you. Let's see, let's see," cried Guy enthusiastically, sorting through his records. "Hey, listen to this, boogie woogie." He put the record on. "'Pinetop's Boogie Woogie.' This is the man who invented it. Let's dance! We have to follow his instructions." Suiting the action to the words as he grabbed hold of her, he followed the singing voice.

Stop! Don't move a peg.
When I say Git! Everybody do a boogie woogie.
When I say hold yourself this time,
All get ready to stop.
Hold yourself! Nobody move.
Now, everybody mess around!

Guy certainly knew how to mess around, and hardly needed any instruction to do so. The singing voice continued,

When I say Git! Hold yourself! Mess around!
When I tell you to hold yourself, you get set,
And don't move a peg.
When I say Git!
I want you to shake that thing.

It was fast and exciting. As soon as it ended Guy ran to choose another from his collection of boogie woogie. While they listened to it, Guy's happy face gleaming with excitement, from somewhere in the distant background the sound of shouting voices could be heard. It was coming from the courtyard. Guy went to the window.

"It's them," said Rupert, grimly.

"Who are they?" asked Clelia.

"You'll see," said Rupert.

There was shouting, laughing and screaming in the corridor, and the door burst open. A crowd of boisterous boys and girls burst into the room. One of the girls with a blonde beehive hairdo wrapped herself round Guy and smacked a noisy kiss on his lips. Clelia at once recognised her as Gloria from the party in London. The others all swarmed about the room and took it over.

"What on earth are you listening to?" cried Gloria contemptuously, her arm still tightly round Guy's neck.

It was Memphis Slim singing, "Whiskey and Gin Blues." The voice on the record sang out, *Play 'til 1952!*

"My God! How antique!" shrieked Gloria. "How out of date! We don't want that! Look what we've brought you!" She held up a bag of records. "It's all the latest! Put one on, Gemma, put on Elvis, let's dance." They tore the piano and vocal of Peter Chatman off the turntable and put on one of the records they had brought with them. The music burst out of the record player as loudly as possible, and Guy and Gloria, with their arms tightly round each other, lead the dancing, while everyone else joined in.

Clelia watched in amazement.

"Don't be left out," cried Rupert, and seizing her by the hand, he dragged her into the wild abandoned melee. It was very noisy and they all danced madly until they became very hot and exhausted.

Gloria demanded that they should go downstairs and have drinks, and they all burst out of the room and raced down the corridor, Gloria dragging Guy along with her.

Rupert and Clelia remained alone in the silent room.

"Horrid, aren't they," said Rupert.

"Do you think so?"

"You do too, but you're too polite to say so, you don't want to offend Guy, but those are his friends."

Clelia remained silent.

Rupert sat down next to her and took her hand. "Don't think any more about Guy. Marry me, I'm much more suitable. Anyway, as you can see, she's really got her hooks into him. If she considers you a serious rival, she'll scratch your eyes out. She's already seen off scores of other girls. Harry me, don't think that I'm too young for you, really, I'm very mature." The earnest face looked eagerly into hers. The face pushed forward and tried to kiss her.

Clelia turned her head away, and smiled. "I do like you very much."

"Don't like me, love me. I love you."

"Do you?"

"Yes, you know I do. Also, I don't have all the burden of inheriting the title. That's what Gloria is really after, she wants to become a duchess, that's all it is. Guy is a terrible fool not to realise this." He looked at her seriously. From the anxious expression on his face she could see that he was tossing about in his mind as to how much he should tell her. He was torn between the desire to win her and his loyalty to Guy. He desperately wanted her to give up Guy, but he couldn't bear to betray him. "You saw for yourself how it was, how trivial they all are," was all he could muster.

They went out into the garden. Guy and his friends were racing around, laughing, having fun, chasing each other, playing hide-and-seek, falling about on the grass when they found each other, tumbling together like young kittens, and generally messing about. They were all enjoying themselves immensely, and paid no attention whatsoever to Rupert or Clelia.

"Will they stay all weekend?"

"I'm afraid so."

They went to the library, where Rupert enthusiastically showed her around.

Clelia was stunned by the extensive collection of antique books. They spent most of the afternoon reading from the books and poring over the illustrations. As they discussed things Clelia was impressed with how many ideas and interests they had in common.

Rupert took her for tea. The drawing room was teeming with Guy's friends still riotously fooling around, and pushing past them and reaching over them as they grabbed sandwiches, scones, cakes and crumpets. Guy was in the thick of them, laughing and joking and enjoying himself.

Rupert watched them with ill-concealed contempt, but did not make any comment. After devouring and guzzling everything in sight, the noisy crowd finally ran off outside to play badminton. Their shrieking voices could be heard from the far distance.

Rupert screwed up his courage. "Perhaps I should tell you …"

"Please do."

"Gloria may be very crass and lacking in any taste, but she's no fool. She keeps Guy's diary."

"What do you mean?"

"If there's someone he really wants, she doesn't stand in the way. She arranges it, so it's subject to her control, to some extent, and she can make sure that it doesn't become serious. If she's concerned, she can make her move to get rid of whoever it is. You look upset. Have I shocked you? I didn't intend to, I just told you so that …" His voice trailed off and he looked very upset. "Perhaps I shouldn't have said anything." He looked very worried. "You mustn't think anything bad about Guy, it's just that …" Again, his voice trailed away.

The riotous friends continued dominating everything for most of the weekend. Clelia spent most of the time with Rupert. Gloria noticed this, and seemed contented enough by its implications to leave with all the others after tea on Sunday.

Suddenly the place fell completely silent. Guy took a shower, changed his clothes and came to find Clelia sitting with Rupert on the terrace.

"I couldn't do anything about them," he explained, "You can see that they are all totally out of control."

"It's not as if you tried," commented Rupert.

"I want to thank you for looking after Clelia," said Guy, "but now they've gone …"

"I can just buzz off. Thank you very much!"

"I wasn't going to put it like that."

"But buzz off just the same! Very nice of you!"

Guy smiled. "I've hardly seen Clelia all weekend because of them."

"You've hardly seen her because of you! You could have told them to buzz off, not me!"

Again, smiling, Guy took Clelia firmly by the hand and led her away into the garden, leaving Rupert standing speechless on the terrace.

When they were alone, Guy explained, "There really was nothing I could do. But Rupert looked after you. We'll spend tonight together."

"Why, just because you don't have anyone to spend the night with?"

"No, not at all, I want to spend tonight with you. I couldn't do anything about them, I didn't invite them, they just turned up.

I invited you here so that we could spend the weekend together. We must, at least, spend what remains of it together. Darling, you do agree?"

"Clelia, please don't go. I haven't offended you, have I? I had no idea that crowd was going to turn up, and take up the whole weekend. Once they were here, there was really nothing I could do about it." He placed his arm around her waist and led her back to the music room. The room was in chaos, and had not yet been tidied up since the visitors had wrecked it. Still holding her tightly, he looked through his collection of records. He chose one, and placed it on the turntable. Then he placed his arms round her and they swayed about gently to the music. The voice of Ella Fitzgerald sang out the old classic by Cole Porter:

Every time we say goodbye, I die a little,

Every time we say goodbye I wonder why a little,

As they moved to the music, Guy placed his cheek against hers, and placed her hand on his heart. The voice sang so plaintively,

When you're near, there's such an air of spring about it,
I can hear a lark somewhere begin to sing about it,
There's nothing finer, but how strange the change
From major to minor.
Every time we say good bye.

"Don't say goodbye to me, darling, I can't bear it when you're not with me. Please don't go."

"I have to get back to school, I have A Levels to study for, you know that."

"We've hardly had any time together, it wasn't my fault that those people came."

"I have school work to do, homework, when am I going to

do it?"

"Stay here tonight, I'll drive you back very early tomorrow morning."

"It's quicker on the train, and there's a train at six."

"Stay the night here and I'll go with you on the train tomorrow morning," he pleaded with her.

"I have to go home, I have to do homework tonight. Tomorrow morning there wouldn't be time to go home and get my books and change into school uniform. The door slams closed at ten past eight. Anyone who is late has to come half an hour early for a whole week as punishment, and has to sit in the entrance hall while all the other girls go by, and has to hang their head in shame."

This made Guy laugh. "Then I'll drive you to London tonight, we'll stay the night in the house in Charles Street, and go to your house very early."

"I won't be allowed to."

"Who won't allow you? We can do as we like."

"Maybe you can, but I certainly can't. It's all right for boys, but girls can't behave like that."

"They can if nobody knows. Why should anybody know?"

"James will know. He's very strict. He knows everything."

"When can I meet him?"

"He has a very full diary."

Clelia was quite insistent that he took her to the station to catch the train.

"You'll come again next weekend?"

"Yes, of course."

He leaned in through the window to kiss her, and the train almost imperceptibly began its gentle glide out of the station.

As it slowly moved away she looked across the fields at all the dreaming spires gleaming in the late afternoon sun. "I wonder if I'll ever be able to come and study here," she thought.

James came hurriedly into Nigel's office.

Nigel immediately indicated to his secretary to leave the room. "You look concerned. What is it?"

"It's Clelia."

"Why, what's the matter?" As he asked this, Nigel's heart missed a beat. He had not seen her since their weekend together.

"She's gone off, and I'm very concerned."

"She hasn't gone off with that young aristocrat you're so keen for her to marry?" asked Nigel anxiously.

"Blandford? No, he's quite charming, came and had drinks with me the other day. No, she's gone to Rome. I allowed her to go because she was going to see mother. Naturally, I thought she was going to stay with mother. It seems that she did call by, but she isn't there. It's been ten days now, so I'm getting worried. It would ruin all hopes of this marriage coming off if she's gone off with a man."

As he said these words, a knife stabbed through Nigel's heart. "What man?" he gasped.

"I'm not saying she's gone off with a man. She hasn't been in touch."

"Isn't she supposed to be at school?"

"That too." He lowered his voice. "I'm very bothered about these rumours that are still circulating. Of course, the press can't publish anything, or at least I hope they can't. I could get an injunction to restrain them if necessary. But these anonymous letters keep arriving. So far I've managed to keep them from Susan. But these girls, their behaviour is so risky, provocative, thoughtless, it's as if they don't recognise the danger, not to them, but for me."

Looking at his ashen face, Nigel's mind went back to that

night at the party. What had they all been doing at the side of the lake, and in the lake itself? It may have been dark, but there had been so many people present. Denying everything now was very difficult. "I'll do everything I can to help you. I'll get the Committee to serve D notices on all the newspapers so that nothing can be published."

"No, don't do that. That will make them all the more determined that there's something to hide."

"I'll go to Rome and bring Clelia back."

"Would you? I hope it won't be necessary. She knows I'm concerned, perhaps she'll phone me. I'll let you know."

As soon as James left, Nigel found that his peace of mind left with him. He lost all ability to concentrate on his work. He anxiously phoned the house in Eaton Square for news, But Arthur never had any. James was hardly ever there. While Susan was away filming. Nigel could imagine who James was with.

The days passed wretchedly. Then one morning, as he wearily phoned yet again, Clelia's bright, breezy voice was at the end of the line.

"Where on earth do you think you've been? Haven't you got your A Levels coming up? How do you expect me to get you into Oxford if you go jaunting about?"

"Sorry, darling, just had to have a break. Had to go and see Mumsy."

"You were hardly ever there. Anyway, thank God you're back. Listen, I have to see you urgently."

"I've got all my homework to catch up on."

"This is very important, it concerns James."

"Oh no, what is it?"

"I can't possibly tell you over the phone. It is very serious. We have to meet somewhere private. I can't come to Eaton Square."

Clelia considered where it could be. It was decided that it would be the Albany. "You'll be safe, darling," she cooed. "I've got a boyfriend."

Nigel felt a sharp blow to the chest, but said nothing. "I'll collect you in fifteen minutes on the corner of the Terrace."

As his car swung into Eaton Terrace, there she stood, casually on the corner, sporting a golden suntan in her bright blue mini skirt and black sling-backs. She was idly tossing around a tiny shoulder bag as he banged the horn to attract her attention. He tried his best to disguise his ill-temper as she climbed into the car. She was all sweetness and light. He drove as fast as he could to the Albany, and they hurried up to his rooms. Nigel immediately poured himself a whiskey. As he handed her a gin and tonic, he said, "You 're going to need this."

"Is it bad?"

"I'm afraid so."

She sipped the drink and looked at him nervously.

"You remember the night at Hever Castle?"

"No, I don't."

"At least you remember James beside the lake? Well, a lot of other people do, and they intend to publicise his antics both there and elsewhere. The girl in question is having far too many affairs with far too many men, some of whom are totally inappropriate. She is becoming increasingly indiscreet."

"They won't dare to publicise it!"

"Any minute now it's all going to explode in his face, and it will destroy the government, too. I'm sure that's why they want to do it."

"James hasn't done anything wrong!"

"I'm sure he hasn't, but he has been remarkably careless for one so astute."

"Oh, poor James!" Clelia burst into tears. "After everything he's worked so hard for! Are they trying to blackmail him?"

"If only it were that, then at least he could pay them off. No, it's much worse, they are out to destroy him."

"Oh no, oh no!" She covered her face with her hands but was unable to stem the flood of tears.

"I may be unable to do anything to save James, but I want to do something to save you."

"What do you mean?"

"Don't you understand?" he said fiercely. "If he goes down in an avalanche of disgrace, I don't want you to be swept down with him. If his reputation is destroyed, if he is cast out of society, who will marry you? He's been trying so desperately to get you married into the upper ranks of the aristocracy. Your whole upbringing has been based on that. If he is discredited, they'll never marry you."

"Do I have to get married?"

"Of course you do, and as soon as possible. That young man, whoever he is, you've met him, haven't you. Instead of running off to Rome with a boyfriend, you should have been using all your skills to get him to propose to you."

Clelia looked shocked.

Nigel seized the phone and banged it down on the low table in front of her. "Phone him! Phone him now and get him to invite you to dinner. Then get him to propose. When he's engaged to you, he can't break the engagement off once the scandal explodes around James's ears."

"I can't just phone him!" cried Clelia desperately through her tears. "I don't know where he is. I haven't been in touch with him."

"Of course you damn well haven't been in touch with him!

You just went off, didn't you. You weren't in touch with James, were you!"

"James was never at home."

"You weren't in touch with me! I was always at home. Waiting for your phone call, you never phoned me. You didn't give a damn how worried I was, did you? Concerned about you, caring for you, losing sleep over you, while you! All you can think about – who is your boyfriend?"

Clelia looked down. She clasped her hands together. "I only said that because …"

"Who is he?"

"Because you said that we had to behave as if nothing had ever happened between us, and I didn't want you to think – "

"Don't repeat back to me something that I said!"

"But you said that in future we – "

"I told you!" he said furiously. "Just because I said something. Don't ever say it to me again." He was hovering over her menacingly.

Clelia cowered down on the couch.

"This boyfriend, does he mean anything to you?"

She looked nervously up at him.

"When did you meet him? Have you known him for a long time? Did you know him at the time when we had that weekend together?"

How bitterly she regretted that she had ever mentioned a boyfriend. "No."

"So you met him after we had our weekend together? You hardly know him. You've known me all your life. How can you go with someone you hardly know?" He gazed at her. "You know how much I've always cared about you. You know how concerned I have always been that you should get a proper education. How concerned I am now that nothing should go wrong for you, that the disaster of James should not overwhelm you!" He pulled the glass out of her trembling hands and shoved it onto the table. He leaned forward and started to tear at her blouse, tearing the buttons off as he tried to open it too fast.

Protesting feebly, Clelia tried to stop him, but he quickly got her down on the floor and pulled up her skirt. It was pointless to struggle since she could see that he was utterly determined to have his way.

"You should have been with me, not with him," he said through gritted teeth as he sank deep inside her and ploughed ever deeper in a frenzied passion. "I care about you more than anyone, don't ever forget it."

But once was not enough. He pulled her up roughly and dragged her to the bedroom. She took her clothes off quickly before he could tear them off. He tore his clothes off and grabbed her in the bed. "Suntan all over!" he cried, staring at her naked body. "Where were you, on a nude beach?"

"It was a private beach."

"Whatever it was, it isn't going to happen again. You are never to see that boyfriend again."

He kissed her desperately. He had never realised that he was capable of such determination, such raw, naked passion. Nor could he understand how he could not have known that he was.

Afterwards, Nigel insisted that she made the phone call. "You have to phone him, you must meet him. If he is engaged to you, you will be alright. Otherwise it's a disaster."

"I think it's a mistake. It really isn't suitable. I don't think he will propose to me. He will never do it as fast as you want."

But Nigel forced her to phone.

After holding on for a while, Guy came on the line.

"Darling, where have you been? I've been trying to phone you. We've been invited to a party at the Ascombes' in Berkshire. But it's at the weekend, I can't wait til then. How about dinner tomorrow night? I'll drive down and pick you up at Eaton Square."

"There," said Nigel. "Now it's up to you. But you are on no account to do anything with him. I absolutely forbid it. If you were to, he would have no respect for you. He would use you up and move on to someone else. Then all this would be pointless and you would be disgraced. You have to be a virgin up until the moment when he actually marries you, it's completely crucial."

"I know all about that, James has always insisted on that and completely drilled it into me."

"Well then, make sure you stick to it, and now come back to bed."

They met at the house of James's solicitor in Kensington. The solicitor, Sir Charles Cowdray, had gathered together a small team of experts to give advice. James's whole research team was also there, although they were not directly involved in giving advice, but were there more for moral support and as a sympathetic presence. Valerie was away filming, so Clelia was there instead, chatting to Robin and Richard, and feeling intensely worried. There was lots of coffee, and plates of sandwiches were constantly being brought in. Sir Charles was in deep conversation with James and Nigel as they were drafting the personal statement that he was going to make to the House.

The door of the room suddenly opened and Guy marched boldly in. Clelia was amazed to see him, and immediately ran up to him. He flung his arms round her and embraced her.

"Darling, how are you? I came as soon as I heard the news."

"How did you find us here?"

"As soon as I heard what had happened I drove down. I went to the house in Eaton Square, and I had to fight my way in past a huge crowd of paparazzi. Vincent gave me this address, and I came at once. I made absolutely sure that no-one followed me. I've come here to take you away from all of this and look after you."

Despite the fact that he was deep in conversation with James, Nigel hadn't failed to notice Guy's grand entrance and the fact that he had remained with his arm tightly and protectively round Clelia's waist. Extracting himself from the group of advisors he approached them. "Who are you?" he asked.

With an elegant grace that became him naturally, Guy immediately introduced himself, and added brightly, "I'm Clelia's fiancé, she's going to come and live with me, I'm going to look after her."

Nigel looked at him in amazement. "Since when have you been engaged?"

"We got engaged on Sunday."

"I haven't heard a single word about this. I am Clelia's guardian, I haven't given my consent to this. She is certainly not going to live with you."

"I had no idea that Clelia had a guardian, this was all fixed up with James when I had drinks with him a few weeks ago."

"I know nothing whatsoever about that. Since all of this business has erupted, James is in no position to look after Clelia, and he has charged me with the task of doing so. He has made me her legal guardian. Will you kindly take your hands off her?"

Their raised voices could now be heard by James on the other side of the room, and he looked up from the draft statement he was reading and noticed Guy. He immediately got up from the couch, walked across the drawing room and extended his hand in greeting towards Guy. He grasped him warmly by the hand and smiled affectionately. "How completely charming of you to come! It is so nice to have one's friends supporting one! These dreadful lies, these rumours, you mustn't believe a word of them."

"Of course I don't, Sir, that's why I came," said Guy. "I haven't even read them, but I know the trashy papers fill up their pages with untruthful rubbish."

"I'm so glad that you've come to stand by Clelia. I'm going to give a personal statement to the House denying all these lies, and then that will be the end of it all. You will come to the House and support me, won't you? You'll sit with Clelia in the Strangers' Gallery and hold her hand." He looked at Clelia's anxious, white face. "It's going to be all right, darling, don't worry so much. I'm going to quash all these lies and that will be the end of it. Come on, Nigel, I need your advice on the draft statement." Smiling happily at Guy, he returned to his place beside the advisors, and continued with the reading of the statement.

"Now, about this so-called engagement," said Nigel. "Does your father consent to it?"

"Well, it only happened on Sunday, and since then I haven't had the opportunity of speaking to him, he's been quite busy."

"Ah! So he doesn't even know about it yet. Then it's completely premature to suggest that you are in any position to look after Clelia. Aren't you at Christ Church?"

"Yes."

"Don't you live in college?"

"Yes."

"It's term time. You're not even supposed to be here, you can't come down 'til the end of term."

"I had to come down as soon as I heard this terrible news."

"Well, we are coping with the problem, you know, and we

are doing our best to resolve it. It is nice of you to come, but I shall be looking after Clelia, and now I think it's time for you to return to college."

"I can't go back to Oxford tonight, it's too late. I thought I'd take Clelia out to dinner, so that she can relax and feel a bit better."

"You don't need to worry about that, I'm taking her out to dinner. She can't stay out late because she is studying for her A Levels."

"But she can't return to Eaton Square because the house is being besieged by the paparazzi, and it would be very bad for her if the press connect her with all of this, she would have awful problems at school. My father has a house in Charles Street, just off Berkeley Square, and she can stay there tonight with me. I can't see why you should have any objection to that, and tomorrow morning I'll drive her to school."

"Tomorrow morning I will drive Clelia to school," said Nigel very firmly. They both looked at Clelia's anxious face. "Will you excuse us just a moment," Nigel asked her. "I just need to have a private word with your would-be fiancé."

"I am her fiancé," said Guy equally firmly. They moved away slightly so that they could talk privately, and Richard and Robin, who had been listening with intense interest, moved across to comfort Clelia.

"Listen, I want to know if your intentions are honourable," said Nigel haughtily.

"Of course they are," replied Guy equally haughtily.

"Then what on earth do you mean by offering to take her off to your father's house for the night. I know exactly what you young men are like. That's why she has a guardian to protect her, and I'm amazed you didn't know that. She can't do anything without my consent, and that includes getting engaged to you."

"I came down from Oxford tonight especially to offer her the protection that she needs, from publicity, the press, and it's obvious to me that she can't go back to the house in Eaton Square."

"If she has to go anywhere tonight, I will arrange it, not you."

"But you are very busy as one of James's advisors. He specifically asked you to help him with the statement that he has to give to the House. You don't have time to make the arrangements for Clelia. I do, and as her fiancé, I am the one who should be looking after her."

"But it's no good just asserting that you are her fiancé, you can't be until I give my consent. And besides, it hasn't been announced in *The Times*."

"It will be very soon."

"How can it be, your father doesn't even know about it. Has he even met Clelia?"

"Yes of course he has, he spent a very delightful time with her when she came for the weekend, and he likes her very much. I can't understand a single word of your objection. Why on earth wouldn't you give your consent? Don't you want Clelia to be happy?"

"That's the thing I want most in all the world," said Nigel sadly, moving away to speak to Clelia.

Guy wandered over to a sideboard on which were displayed copies of the *Daily Express*, *Daily Mail* and *News Chronicle*. Apart from the salacious articles, they all contained photographs of the model in question in various stages of undress. As Guy started to peruse them with interest, he was joined by the other boys, who had spent the evening going through all the details.

"Bloody good looking, don't you think?" asked Robin in a low voice.

"Mmm," said Guy appreciatively, turning the pages. "Did

your opinion of James go up as soon as you saw these photos?"

"You bet!" said Robin.

"Did you ever actually see her?"

"Of course not, but you can see why he's crazy about her."

"But he denies it all?"

"He has to, doesn't he," said Richard. "It's all terribly unfair. If this were France or Italy, his popularity rating would shoot up, a scandal like this would do him good, enhance his reputation, not damage him. He's an excellent minister with a brilliant mind, and he's made it to the top against all the odds and without any help. It's been fantastic working for him, and now all our jobs are on the line. It must have been spite by someone to expose him, I'm sure lots of other men do it, they just keep it quiet."

"You've no idea how it all came out?"

"Absolutely none. But the girl herself seems to be a bit careless, using the apartment he paid for as a base for her call-girl activities behind his back."

"It's also her indiscriminate choice of other boyfriends that caused the problem. In retrospect, it all seems so unwise, but how could he have known about that, particularly considering how infatuated he was."

They all looked across at James, sitting elegantly on the couch, deep in conversation. It all seemed so unreal. He looked so confident and in control.

They also noticed Nigel deep in conversation with Clelia.

"You seemed to be having fun with him," laughed Robin. "Who the hell is he, I find him totally obnoxious."

"That's Nigel Rawlinson, he's one of these high flying civil servants heading straight for the top. Congratulatory First at Balliol, that sort of thing. Very close friend of James, practically lives at the Eaton Square house," explained Richard.

"I don't understand what he's got to do with Clelia. I fixed everything up with James two or three weeks ago, and he was absolutely charming. This fellow was never mentioned at all," said Guy.

"Well, it wouldn't do you any good to get on the wrong side of him, he's going to be pretty powerful quite soon, and whatever happens to James, he will be unaffected. He's completely neutral in this. The friendship is purely personal. The other thing," warned Richard, "is that we at Eaton Square do not take kindly to any bad behaviour in relation to Lolita."

"Is that what you call her!"

"All of us, and that includes Nigel, are very concerned that she should be treated well by anyone she's ill-advised enough to get involved with," said Richard.

"That's meant to be me, I suppose. So you've been bad-mouthing me to him, have you? Is that why he spoke to me like that?"

"Not at all, I never mentioned you. Why would I mention you, I didn't know you were supposed to be engaged."

"None of us knew," said Robin. "Is it true?"

"You think I was just making it up?"

"Weren't you? How can you possibly be engaged? What about Gloria? Isn't she supposed to be preggers?"

Guy looked shocked. "Is that what they're saying?"

"It's what she's saying. Apparently she's going to see your father about it, so that he can organise a shot-gun wedding."

"I've never heard of any of this."

"Well, you would be the last to know. Did you think she was on the Pill?"

"Aren't they all?" asked Guy in surprise.

The boys laughed.

"For your sake, they'd better be," said Richard.

"Is Clelia on the Pill?" asked Guy.

This time both boys looked genuinely shocked. "You mean, she hasn't told you?"

"No, she won't say. She says she's a virgin. Is it true?"

Both boys looked silently at each other. "Is that why you got engaged to her?" asked Richard.

"Of course not."

"I think it is, Guy. You intend to seduce her and then abandon her. The only thing that bothers you is that she might be left pregnant, so you want to make sure she's on the Pill. If that is your plan –"

"It is not!" said Guy fiercely.

"If it is –"

"I told you it isn't!"

"Well, why do you need her, then. You've got quite enough girls as it is without corning into our circle and raiding here as well. She's sweet and innocent, we don't want her life ruined by you. She's young and impressionable, why don't you just leave her alone? Aren't there enough girls in Oxford for you?"

Before Guy could reply Robin noticed the time and switched on the radio.

A voice spoke out, "This is the BBC Home Service. Here is the nine o'clock news." Everyone in the room fell silent. "Miss Virginia Ashcroft, the young model in the case concerning the Minister for Foreign Affairs, the Right Honourable Mr James Crespi, is reported to have left her London address and is believed to have gone abroad. No forwarding address has been given and her precise whereabouts are unknown."

"Oh, that's wonderful!" cried Clelia. "She's gone! It's all over!" She immediately burst into tears, and Guy rushed to her and flung his arms round her. Everyone in the room burst out talking excitedly.

"It's wonderful news!" cried James in delight. "The nightmare is over. Perhaps I don't need to make a statement at all!" The excited talk filled the room with noise. Everyone was intensely delighted, but Sir Charles sounded a note of caution, since things were still uncertain. "Whatever happens," cried James. "I shall be going to Ascot tomorrow with the Queen Mother!" Everybody clapped and cheered.

"What about us?" cried Guy, ecstatically kissing Clelia. "Shall we go, too?"

Clelia shook her head sadly. "Can't. School. A Levels."

"Yes, that's right, work must come first. But Guy, you can come, do let me invite you. You can come in the royal carriage."

Guy was very happy to accept. Richard looked at Robin, and they both shook their heads.

Nigel and Clelia sat in Fortnum's waiting for their friends to turn up and drive in convoy with them to the engagement party in Bracknell. It was a perfect day for a garden party. The drive down had been very pleasant, and Liza and Adam were over the moon with each other. For Clelia it was a welcome break in the constant grind of Greek translations. For Nigel it was a chance to meet some old friends whom he had not seen in yonks. It was not something he would normally have done in the busy round of work and cabinet meetings.

The garden was shimmering in the sunlight and the elegant white table cloths were flapping gently in the breeze. All the women wore hats in the latest fashion. Liza wore a crown of roses and a thin organza dress that floated about her in the gentle early summer air. A string quartet composed of Liza's student friends sat on the green sward playing Vivaldi.

Guy had driven down from Oxford, and was very happy to see Clelia.

She spent most of the time paying court to Nigel and his friends, but when she felt the coast was clear she would slip off to spend a few minutes with Guy.

"Is James coming?" he asked her.

"Yes, of course, he's been looking forward to this party as a relief from all the gloom."

"You didn't decide to drive down with him?"

"He has to hide out to avoid the press, they really are making his life a misery. He doesn't want to make any comment on the endless scandals and love affairs of Miss Ashcroft, but they won't accept no for an answer. He has to stay in different places, so I don't see him that often."

The sound of a Rolls Royce purring gently into the grounds caused them to turn round and look. They recognised the powder blue car, that along with all his other elegant accessories, had been James's trade mark for some time now.

James, in a new Italian suit assisted Veronica down from the car.

Veronica, sophisticated as ever in one of her spectacular creations, walked across the gravel drive to the lawn, leaning decorously on James's arm. A light puff of air almost caught the beautiful hat she wore, and a slim, bespangled arm idly reached up to restrain it in time. As they reached the party, they were surrounded by friends and well-wishers, who loudly expressed their annoyance at the continuing publicity being given to the never-ending saga of Miss Ashcroft.

"I'm sure it will all die down," said James confidently. He picked up a glass of champagne and raised a toast to Liza. "You are looking so lovely, my dear!"

"If only that wretched woman had stayed in Spain!" cried one outraged guest.

"Perhaps she wasn't paid quite enough," muttered another.

"We've heard enough detail about her supposed activities," cried a gloating third. "It's all so degrading. Why can't the press move on to another topic? It's not as if nothing else is happening in the world."

As they drank the wine and ate the refreshments, and loudly voiced their support of James, they became aware of a number of cars entering the estate through the wrought iron gates and slowly moving up the drive.

"Some late guests," said an early guest.

"Liza, it looks like the photographers you ordered," said another, as a large group of men carrying cameras and television equipment began to walk towards the party on the lawn.

"We didn't order any photographers," said Liza, "My brother is going to take the photos."

The photographers and camera men marched ever nearer.

James looked up and saw the phalanx of men advancing resolutely towards him. An expression of panic broke his habitual smooth smile. He grabbed Veronica by the hand as she was about to bite into a sausage roll. She looked up and saw the men starting to swarm onto the green sward towards the marquee. More of them were arriving at every moment.

"Into the house!" cried Liza, "they won't dare to follow!"

"Not a bit of it, " cried Adam. "Outflank them! This way!" He rushed ahead as James dragged Veronica after him.

As soon as they saw James running, the newsmen made for him as fast as they could, pushing startled guests out of the way, knocking over chairs, sometimes with guests still in them, and climbing over tables laden with food and drink where necessary. An all-out panic struck the guests in their desperation to get out of the way of the advancing mob while at the same time a frenzied determination struck the newshounds that this time their quarry should not elude them. Through the chaos, panic and hysterical screaming, they could catch glimpses of him and Veronica running away as madly as they were chasing him.

Adam reached back for James and was pulling him by the hand as they outflanked the barbarians and arrived breathless and frantic at the side of the powder blue Rolls just in time for the chauffeur to start up the engine and make a dash for the driveway and the wrought iron gates.

Suddenly realising what was up, the newsmen started streaming from everywhere in the mad dash to get back to their cars and follow, determined not to let him get away this time.

Thrilled at the excitement of a chase, and not to be outdone in the insanity stakes, Guy seized Clelia by the hand and dragged her with him. "Run, run!" he shouted. They raced to his red Triumph and leapt in arriving at the car before any of the hacks got to theirs. Guy roared the engine and raced across the car park nearly knocking down two of the running men. He roared through the gates only seconds after the blue Rolls had shot through and set off at high speed down the road. The chase was on, with Guy putting his foot down without any sense of the survival instinct alive anywhere within him.

The cars of the hacks tore off after him.

"Fantastic, fantastic!" he kept shouting above the noise of the engine as he rounded corner after corner on the wrong side of the road and with total disregard for other road users. "Don't you see, we'll lead them on, and they'll follow us and James will get away."

"Please don't go so fast!" cried Clelia in terror. "You'll hit something and it will be our bodies that will block the road, nothing else."

Guy was in his element testing his car to the utmost, constantly checking where the hacks were behind him and where the Rolls was in the distance in front. He had decided precisely where he would lead them, and where he would turn off from the road at a point when the Rolls would be hidden from their view. The beauty of it was that the roads were so narrow that by swinging dangerously to and fro he could stop the cars from overtaking him, and slow down at the most dramatic moments causing them almost to hit him. Breaking suddenly he lurched forward and took a sudden turn to the left, racing away very fast. He almost whooped with delight loud enough for them to hear, but managed to restrain himself as he saw to his joy that they were following him. Now he really had to get away, otherwise if they caught him they would kill him. Now he raced even more dangerously than before.

Clelia sank down almost to the floor and clung on for dear life.

Guy drove like a demon risking everything. He knew all the roads and short-cuts, and twisted and turned until he was sure that no-one had kept up with him. Then he made a straight bee-line for his father's estate. Once he had arrived at the leafy beech forest he could relax and calm down a bit.

"Have you any idea where James would have gone to?"

"Absolutely none," replied a white faced and shaken Clelia.

He pulled the car over in the shady forest. He did not ask if she was alright. He took a small box out of his pocket. "We won't stay here, but it is the family estate," he said, thrusting the box into her hands. "I think this is the moment."

He watched her closely as she opened the box. A diamond ring glittered before her. He was anxiously looking to see if she liked it. He could see she did. He swung the car smartly into action and drove off at high speed.

As the cars of all the newsmen and paparazzi roared off down the road, Nigel rushed around in a panic desperately trying to locate

Clelia among the injured and asking anyone he could find what had happened.

One boy standing in the carpark was holding forth to an enraptured crowd and giving a blow by blow account of the invasion and the retreat. He was describing with great excitement how the chauffeur-driven Rolls had roared away across the car park. "And then immediately behind it, the red Triumph took off like a rocket and shot across the green, cutting off the intervention of the hacks and the paparazzi. They all frantically ran over to their cars, and some of them fell over in the rush. But Guy had the edge on them as he soared away, and they madly tried to follow in his wake. Two of them nearly had a prang at the gate, they were so desperate to get out. I doubt that they will catch James, Guy will head them off."

"Was he on his own?" asked Nigel.

"No, of course not," was the confident reply. "He had his fiancée with him."

Nigel withdrew from the audience. How on earth would he contact her now? Perhaps he should stay at the party, maybe she would ring the house. He moped about miserably, trying to avoid conversations and groups of excited gossipers. It really was most unfortunate. He dreaded that Celia would be dragged into it. So far the press knew nothing about her, but if they once latched onto her, who knew what they might make of it. What if they found out that she was in some way connected? With Guy driving off like a madman, and negligently throwing himself in the thick of it, there was every risk that they would find out. Any publicity would be sure to scare Guy off, or at least put him under pressure from his family to call the engagement off.

Nigel found himself hovering near the telephone. But it never rang. Gillian was rather too interested in him, and he feared that if he did not leave, he would get trapped into offering her a lift to

London and inviting her out to dinner. He had intended to spend the evening and the night with Clelia, not with anybody else. Using a suitable moment when Gillian was otherwise engaged, he slipped quietly out of the house and went to the car. He drove as fast as possible back to London, and went to the Albany. He was sure that Clelia would phone him there. From time to time he phoned the house at Eaton Square, but there was no news. He tried to impress upon Arthur the importance that Clelia should phone him, but after a while it became too embarrassing to keep phoning back. Now there was nothing to do but wait.

The afternoon stretched into evening. The long evening slowly drained away. The intense late evening sun burned through the window. Any attempt to read or concentrate on anything was in vain. The intense anxiety that something terrible had happened in the idiotic car chase gradually habituated, giving way to a nagging worry that gave him a tedious stomach ache. Drinking did not help because he had already drunk enough to make himself feel sick. Her absence made him feel terrible, but feeling so bad, what made it worse was her careless failure to phone. Unless of course she couldn't phone, because she was in hospital, in a coma. Then the sense of panic would return, and the itching desire to pick up the phone and start calling the police in case there was some news. Or perhaps he should phone the casualty departments of the hospitals. But which ones? Where had they been racing off to? He had absolutely no idea. He did not know in which county to start. If only she would phone, or better still, turn up.

He went into the kitchen and idly made himself a sandwich. He put on the nine o'clock news on the Home Service. Nothing but news about the scandal. Nothing else was going on in the world except that. Miss Ashcroft's life history was being raked over in great detail to an appalled world.

Then there was an interview with her about her recent trip to Spain. She spoke in a breathless, baby doll voice. "We had only enough money to buy petrol and children's sweets. I didn't know that the police were looking for me. When I heard that the police were looking for me I went straight into a police station and said, 'I am Miss Ashcroft.' Then the Consul came. Then I came home."

He switched to the Light Programme. Benny Goodman, wonderful, but far too pleasing for the frame of mind he was in. He switched to the Third Programme. "Semper Dowland, Semper Dolens" That was more like his mood. He settled down to a dolorous evening on his own.

The evening lengthened out miserably and interminably. As it dragged its weary way towards midnight he became more and more concerned. If only there would be that simple turn of the door key, then all the agony would be over. But it was not to be. After midnight his despondency became desperate and his alarm became frantic. It was now too late to phone anywhere. He could not phone the police, they would want to know what his relationship was with the missing girl. He could not say in what manner she had gone missing, nor could he tell them who she was. Try as he might, he could not absorb himself in the book he was reading, concentrating as he was on every little sound, in case he could hear her footstep coming up the stair. Was there someone out there step-stopping? No, it was nothing.

At some point, he had no idea when, he must have dozed off in a chair. He jerked awake suddenly in a state of extreme anxiety. It was six in the morning. His mouth was dry and furry, and he felt nauseous and sweaty having slept in his clothes. He went into the kitchen to make himself some coffee. There were still two hours to go before he could reasonably phone Eaton Square. Idling with the radio, he came upon the World Service. He could not believe it, even they were dealing with the scandal. It was ridiculous, was nothing else happening out there in the world? Again, that breathy voice of the delectable Miss Ashcroft. It was unbearable. He switched it off at once.

At last he felt he could phone. To his joy and infinite relief, Clelia was there.

She was sweet but unconcerned. "Where on earth were you?"

"Oh, it was alright, Guy brought me back."

"But I was so worried."

"Yes, he does drive rather fast. But he seems to know all the by-ways and short cuts of Berkshire, so we easily got away."

"When are you coming here?"

"I can't come, I'm meeting Guy for lunch at Claridge's. You want me to meet him and get on with it, don't you?"

"No, I damn well do not. If you don't come here at once I shall come over there and get you."

"Well, I will come, if you agree that at one o'clock I can meet him at Claridge's. It was only on that basis that he – "

"Come here at once, and stop making excuses."

When she arrived, she could see at once the terrible state he was in. He was still slumped down in the chair he had slept in, still wearing the same clothes, looking haggard and drawn. He was unshaven and unwashed. The jacket he was wearing looked grey and crumpled. Nigel himself looked unkempt and ragged at the edges. There was no trace of his usual smart self. She had never seen him look like this. The word "*trascurato*" came to her mind. But worst of all was the accusing way he looked at her. There were dark rings under his eyes and the bloodshot eyes themselves looked bitter and unforgiving.

"Where did you go?"

"He took me home."

"Why didn't you at least phone?"

"You had seen the state we were in when we left. I didn't think – "

"No, that's it. You never do think. You have no care for the pain and anguish that you cause me. Didn't it ever occur to you that I would be worried? Of course I saw the state you left in, racing off like demons in an insane chase to shake them off. Imagine how I felt after that when you failed to get in touch. I thought anything might have happened. The least you could have done is phone me. But you didn't. I have passed the worst night in my life since my parents sent me off, alone and miserable, to prep school at the age of seven. I've never had such a night as last night."

"But darling, I thought – "

"You didn't think! That's how you are, careless and shallow. Really shallow. All you want to do is enjoy yourself and have a good time. You have no concern for those around you, you have no concern for me!"

All dolled up and ready to go to lunch, she looked particularly beautiful in a pale ochre silk skirt with a matching elastic off-the-shoulder top which clearly indicated that she was not wearing a bra. She kicked off her high heeled slingbacks and minced across the carpet towards him, pulling down the elastic top as she moved. Then she hitched up the skirt as she climbed on top of him, gently massaging him until he was rigid enough to slip inside her. Moving slowly up and down, she leaned forward and smothered his sour, turned down mouth with kisses. "Don't think this makes up for it," he said, leaning back and relaxing, and coming in a sudden rush.

She remained there for a while, leaning on him and kissing him.

"So you don't wear any under wear."

"You've torn most of it, I don't have any left."

"Do you really have to go? Can't you phone him and cancel it?"

"And undo all the good work you've been ordering me to do?"

"Well, maybe all that stuff is not such a good idea."

"But it's too late to choose anybody else."

"Yes, that is true, I suppose you'll just have to stick to him, at least for the time being."

But when Clelia walked into the restaurant at Claridge's it was not Guy who was waiting for her at the table but Rupert. He was very smartly got up, and came forward to meet her. He was very grown-up and formal.

"Will Guy be coming along?"

"No, he can't come. Papa ordered him back to Malplaquet. He said that it was very urgent."

"Do you know what it is?"

"Some business he wants to send Guy on. Actually," he dropped his voice confidentially, "He said that if Guy doesn't stop jaunting about, he'll stop his allowance. Guy has to go there to beg him not to. He said that I should entertain you. I've already ordered lunch. Lobster and champagne." He said it all so seriously that she couldn't stop herself laughing. Rupert laughed as well in his sweet, innocent, sincere way.

As the sommelier arrived with the aperitifs, Rupert took her hand. "I have to convince you that you should marry me. Guy's life is going to be all service and duty, politics, the House of Lords. It will be irredeemably dull. Mine, by contrast will be delightfully normal. No absurd duties, no sense of guilt for all the duties not fulfilled." His happy smile radiated into her face. "After lunch, we'll go to an art gallery and wait for news of Guy, but I really don't think Papa will allow him to return to London this weekend."

"Does he allow you?"

Rupert laughed out loud. "Don't you see, the rest of us don't matter. We can do as we like, up to a point. All the burdens and obligations fall upon the heir, the first born. He carries all our burdens for us, and as far as Papa is concerned, he is certainly heavily laden. Also in Guy's case there's another thing. I don't like to say it, and I've never told anyone, but I think there's a certain amount of jealousy mixed up in it. Guy is far too good looking, and he always gets the girls. I think Papa finds it very hard to take."

Guy quite confidently assumed that there would be absolutely no problem with his father about getting engaged. In fact, he was quite sure that his father would be only too delighted that he was settling down at last. With this in mind, he arranged to visit James at Farringdon, where the Osbornes had very kindly invited him as a house guest. It was a discreet address, known to very few, where James and Veronica could hide out and escape the frenzied press attention until the scandal had blown itself out. Guy arranged to go down on Friday night where, as a guest of the Osbornes, but without them or members of their family being present, he would have a private dinner with James and Clelia in order to make arrangements for her future. On his arrival after the long drive, he was exasperated to discover that Nigel was joining them for dinner.

They sat down in dinner jackets at an elegant table in the lower dining room. A few moments later, they all leapt to their feet as a vision of loveliness in one of Veronica's more daring creations swept into the room and joined them at the table.

"I'm sorry I'm late," cooed Clelia.

"Yes," said Guy, "you had much further to come than I did." They leaned towards each other and kissed.

"Enough of that!" cried Nigel sharply.

Guy groaned inwardly. "I can see it's going to be one of those evenings," he thought. "I wonder if I'll even get five seconds alone with Clelia."

James beamed amiably at everyone. He was blissed out on gin and tonic, and had probably also taken some of those tranquilisers that his doctor had recommended, and which he had specifically advised should not be taken with alcohol.

The waiters started to serve dinner. As long as they were walking about serving the dishes or pouring the wine the conversation was stilted and formal, but as soon as the waiters and butlers retired in between courses, the knives were out, to be hastily replaced under the napkins as soon as the waiters returned with the next course.

"James, you remember when I called upon you for drinks, and you were delighted that Clelia and I were engaged."

James tucked into the lobster bisque. "Absolutely, absolutely," he beamed.

"James," said Nigel imperiously. "You remember when you signed the documents drawn up by Sir Charles Hunter appointing me as Clelia's legal guardian."

"Yes, of course, Nigel, I have absolute faith in you, you know that, I've always accepted your advice in relation to Clelia's education."

"So you accept that it's up to me to assess any possible suitor."

"Absolutely, absolutely."

"You're not suggesting that I'm in any way unsuitable?" demanded Guy.

"Whether you are a suitable suitor or not is for me to determine," said Nigel decisively.

"So is this an interview?" cried Guy in alarm.

"Enquiries will have to be made."

"You want references from me?"

"I'm sure they'll be required."

"Who is supposed to supply them?"

"Anyone and everyone who knows you."

"This is intolerable!" cried Guy, leaping to his feet. "Surely it is for Clelia to choose, and James has already sanctioned our engagement."

Nigel stood up to face him across the dining table. "If only you would understand that it is not up to you to get engaged to a minor, who requires the consent of her guardian." They were now shouting at each other.

"Surely you give your consent," shouted Guy. "You know it's what Clelia wants."

"I know nothing of the kind. She is far too young to make a decision like this without guidance."

"And I am the one to give her guidance," cried Guy.

"I hardly think you are in any position to do so."

They might have come to blows at this moment had not the waiters entered the room with the baron of roast beef, so they quietly sat down and chatted about the new line of elms that had been laid out in the park.

James was very impressed by the elms, and joined in the conversation.

"You'd like Clelia to live in a leafy environment, wouldn't you, James, so you'd love her to live at and be mistress of Malplaquet."

"Mistress, yes, delightful," beamed James.

"That's it, Guy, isn't it, you want her for your mistress," Nigel snapped.

"How dare you twist my words round, you know what I mean." Again he leapt to his feet, the waiters having retired. "Are you determined to play games with me?"

Nigel, too, was immediately on his feet. "You seem to think that since you are the eldest son of a duke you have the right to demand that I give my consent, whether you have shown yourself to be a fit husband for Clelia or not."

"Not at all. I'm not the kind of snob who imagines that everyone is desperate to climb their way into the English aristocracy. I spend most of my time trying to climb out of it."

"Have a care you don't accidentally fall out of it," said Nigel charmingly. "Now sit down and let us get on with dinner."

Guy appealed to James. "Is there any reason at all you can think of why he should stand in the way of our happiness?"

"You don't just think you're in love with her because she has a pretty face. There's much more to marriage than that," cut in Nigel, sharply.

"I made the mistake," said James sadly, "of falling in love with a pretty face. I seem to have thrown away my whole life as a result." He lifted up the glass of russet Beaune wine that they were drinking, and gazed at the candle-light illuminating its pellucid surface as it flowed about the glass. "Nigel, you are too much perturbed upon the tempests of the wine dark sea. You must not fear that Guy, the helmsman of his barque, who has safely steered it into the calm waters of Clelia's heaven-haven, is insensitive, or is attracted only by a pretty face." The mouths of his listeners were already open since they were eating. Had they not been, they would have all fallen open. They remained gaping in wonder at him. "Guy knows that Clelia is an intelligent, well-read woman, that's what he's looking for, not just a pretty face. He's far too intelligent just to want to marry a girl for her looks. He's aware of her intellectual qualities, they match his own. She's going to Oxford, she's going to study, they won't marry before she gets her First." They all knew that James was very drunk. He gazed again into his glass, as if it gave him inspiration, and then said, "Am I looking for truth at the end of the glass?"

Clelia opened her beautiful green eyes extra wide, and gazed into the amazed blue eyes of Guy. "Is it the unfortunate Mr Marmeladov?" she whispered.

"Is it the truth at the end of the bottle?" he whispered in reply.

"What are you doing talking about marmalade in a bottle, and why are you both being so deeply disrespectful?" said Nigel crossly.

Clelia immediately apologised, while Guy remained staring silently at James.

After dinner, James and Guy sat drinking in the drawing room while Nigel took Clelia aside for a private talk in the Babbington Room.

"You know I'm totally against this engagement," said Nigel.

"But you told me to do it. In fact you ordered me to do it. You told me to pick up the phone – "

"Yes, yes, yes. That was then. At that time – "

"But things haven't changed. The scandal hasn't died away. If anything, every day things get worse. You've seen how eagerly the youngsters here gobble up every last detail in the trashy newspapers over breakfast every morning. Then there's that awful silence every day as I come down to breakfast, and the way their eyes linger pityingly upon me before they silently slink away, always leaving the crumpled up papers lying open all over the place. I'm not suggesting it's in any way malicious, I think they are genuinely fascinated by the remarkable antics of the elegant Miss Ashcroft, as is the rest of the country. If you don't allow Guy to be engaged to me, I don't think anyone else will ever come forward. I shall be a permanent object of pity. Not that I care!" added Clelia defiantly.

"It is true that things haven't died away. That's why I'm allowing this engagement to go ahead."

"Thank you, darling."

"But you know my view about it. You're not to regard it as real. And there is to be absolutely no hanky-panky. You are to remain a virgin, as James has always taught you, otherwise he will never respect you. He is so dissolute. He strikes me as just the sort of boy who will demand to go to bed with you, and then abandon you. I don't regard him as genuine at all."

"Nothing will happen before we are married."

"If you are married. Make sure he knows that you believe in no sex before marriage. Tell him that you intend to remain a virgin. Keep him at a distance. If you don't promise me this, I won't consent to any engagement at all."

"I do promise you this, really, darling, I do." She leaned up and kissed him tenderly.

"You are to love only me."

"I do love only you," said Clelia.

Finally they returned to the drawing room, where James was describing in great detail his triumph over a minister whom he particularly disliked in a cabinet meeting.

Nigel had been present at the time, and joined in the laughter, but he didn't think that James should be recounting the story at all. But it would have been churlish to say so, and he could rely upon Guy's discretion not to repeat a word of it.

"So what have you determined?" asked Guy, rising to greet them.

"With James's permission –"

"Absolutely, absolutely."

"I take the view that although I don't approve of this engagement, perhaps I am not wholeheartedly against it."

"So I'm sort of on probation?"

"You might put it like that."

Guy gave a whoop of delight and grabbing hold of Clelia, kissed her firmly on the mouth.

Through Radcliffe, his father's personal private secretary, Guy had made an appointment with the Duke at eleven thirty on Tuesday morning. As he walked towards his father's study, he found Rupert nervously hanging around in the Long Gallery.

"Papa's in a belligerent mood," Rupert warned. "It's nothing to do with you, but I fear that he will take it out on you. It is to do with the death of John Adams, a drunken carrier, and the family of the carrier are threatening to sue him for permitting the man to drink at work, and thereby contributing to his death."

"Wasn't there that business of the epitaph on the tombstone, mocking at him?"

"Yes," laughed Rupert, "but you are responsible for that. I don't know if Papa knows about that. For all kinds of reasons, it would be just as well not to supplicate him today, I don't think he's in the giving vein."

"I'm not a supplicant, I'm not asking him to give me anything. I just want his consent to my engagement. Then it can be announced in *The Times*. Then all the moths hovering around her can buzz off."

"I don't think moths buzz, but Papa is about to roar. He's in the cantankerous and irascible mode this morning, I advise postponing this interview."

"I can't, I've waited a whole week to get it, I don't know when he'll be available again."

He tapped politely on the study door, and waited. After a silent wait of a full two minutes, an irritable voice inside called out, "Oh do come in, will you?"

Guy crept quietly inside.

His father sat at his desk, frenziedly wrestling with pieces of paper. The furious face glowed red, the dark coal-fire eyes glowered. "Oh, it's you," he said irritably. "What do you want? I'm very busy. I'm not increasing your allowance, don't even bother to ask."

"I wasn't going to ask for anything like that. I just wanted to ask for your consent so that I could get engaged and make an announcement in *The Times*."

"Engaged to do what? What is this?"

"Engaged to be married."

"Where? With whom? Why? When?" His father looked startled. "Not that bloody Gloria, is it? I've already seen her off. Bloody little gold-digger, she is, but artful, hmm, and not bad looking. I can see what you saw in her."

It was Guy's turn to look startled. He had not heard of any of this, but he thought it was a can of worms he would rather not open. "No, it's with Clelia, you met her when she came here for various weekends."

The Duke groped about in the recesses of his memory. There had been so many girls, it wasn't easy to fit a face to a name. "That very beautiful blonde, who amazed us by coming down to dinner in a red basque? She looked as if she had forgotten to put her dress on." He reflected appreciatively. "She had forgotten to put her dress on. I remember how you thoughtfully placed those beautiful, almost naked bosoms next to me." He floated off into a reverie.

"So it had worked," thought Guy. "Now it will all be plain sailing."

"Wait a minute!" The old Duke jerked awake. "Isn't she the daughter of that wretched minister who's trying to bring down the government? You know who I mean, that dreadful Foreign Minister of ill-repute, whose scandals are daily reported in the newspapers." He looked hard and furiously at Guy. "You know who I mean, you know." He gestured wildly with his hands, frenziedly raiding the old lumber room of his mind, and throwing out old bits and bobs along the way. "To cap it all, he's a ruddy foreigner, who's come here and brought with him all his filthy foreign habits, you know who I mean!"

"Sister, not daughter."

"Yes, that's it, I'm right! Though she seemed perfectly English, and very well-educated, told me she was going to Oxford. I've never met him, thank God!"

"But, Papa!"

"Don't you Papa me, young fellow! I've already got you out of one scrape with bloody Gloria, getting her pregnant, or so she said. I'll be damned if I let you leap immediately into another scrape with another disreputable young woman from an impoverished background who's only after you for your title and money. That's all these bloody foreigners come to England for, twerps like you!"

"Papa, you can't blame her for something her brother has done, she is in no way involved."

"Oh yes she is, she's his daughter. Like father like daughter. No, thank you very much, none of them, please. And didn't I see you on the television the other day with the same disreputable minister going to the races?"

Guy was amazed. "I did go to Ascot. It was with the Queen Mother. I didn't know it was on television."

"And that you didn't!" sneered his father, "There's a lot a naïve young rake like you doesn't know! The Queen Mother can't be blamed for being in the company of one so disreputable, how can she know, God bless her! As for you, you knew damned well what he was up to, probably went along for a bit of the same yourself! Well, I won't put up with it, so there! I won't have you seen in public with someone so disgusting, and I certainly shan't allow him to marry his offspring into our family!"

Guy was so astonished at this outburst that he was unable to move.

The beady eye of his father remained fixed upon him. It was almost as if his father suddenly realised who he was. "You!" he shouted.

Guy leaped to his feet.

"I've been hearing some very bad reports about you! Maybe you've got your ideas from this fellow Crespi, that's his name! Debauchery, that's what it is! Where's your mother, she has to be here for this!" He reached behind the desk for the bell-rope and tugged upon it violently, all the while screaming, "Your mother! Your mother!"

The butler hurried into the room looking very alarmed.

"The Duchess! The Duchess!" he shouted.

"Yes, Your Grace," said the butler, and hurried away.

Guy gazed on him in silent alarm. "Is it a heart attack or a fit?" he wondered.

The Duchess came hurrying along the gallery and ran into the study. "What is it? What is the matter?" she cried in alarm.

The Duke rose heavily and portentously to his feet. "This is your son!" he boomed out, "Sift him! Sift him!"

Guy and his mother turned towards each other and their mouths fell open in amazement.

"Sift him!" screamed the Duke, "Sift him! A prodigal sifted and found out in his several debaucheries! Get on with it woman, sift him! No more indulgence to our graceless son, Let's sift him, woman, to know what he has done! Then sift on, wife, for it must be known how he has spent our money, not his own."

Attracted to the room by the noise of his father's shouting, Rupert stood in the doorway with mouth agape.

"This is most unmannerly, husband," protested the Duchess. "You hardly ever see your son, you can't be this unmannerly towards him!"

"And why is it that I hardly ever see him?" shouted the Duke. "He's too busy in his debaucheries, he only ever visits if his gambling losses and debts require to be paid!"

"I never go gambling!" protested Guy.

"Liar!" screamed the Duke, "You just told me yourself you went to Ascot, and in the company of a notorious whoremaster and profligate!"

"John, really, do stop it!" cried the Duchess, visibly distressed. But there was no stopping the Duke when he was in full gallop.

"Inconveniences and trains of evil attending idleness, tippling, gaming and drunkenness being a short view of the present shame, future misery and final end of ungovernable youth in their drunken excess. What we must do," he said, spitting out the words, "is pass this prodigal through the sieve. Then your bad habits will be seen by the objects that we see falling through the sieve!"

"Papa!" protested Rupert, "How can you be so cruel! Don't sieve him, please don't sieve him!"

The Duke, exhausted, slumped back into his plush velvet

armchair. "We would see dice, tobacco, a wine glass, fancy clothes and," he paused for dramatic effect, "a tennis racquet."

"Thank God for that!" said Rupert sotto voce. "It could have been much worse!"

They all exchanged anxious glances, and looked towards the Duke who was lost in a reverie and gazing at the angels of dust dancing in the shafts of sunlight. The butler came and brought him his brandy, and he indicated for Guy to come and sit near him. He dismissed the others with a glance. There was a long silence.

Guy suddenly became aware that his father was speaking to him.

"The fact is, young fellow, that there is no prospect of your being permitted to marry before the age of twenty-five. That is the tradition in this family. When you do become engaged the name of the happy fiancée in question will be communicated to you by myself and your mother. At your age I once made the mistake of falling for a pretty face, and did as you have done, requested permission to become engaged to her. My father treated me to a very sound thrashing, and I did not make that mistake again. My offer to sieve you is mild by comparison with my father's treatment of me. My father was right. Neither I then nor you now had the slightest idea as to who would make a suitable wife, to work hard, breed children and manage the household. A beautiful young thing intelligent enough to go up to Oxford will certainly not desire an occupation like this, that your wife will be destined to undertake. Think no more about marriage, and get on with your studies, otherwise I promise you, I shall take you away from Oxford, revoke your allowance, and set you to work in the farms of Rhodesia. And you won't return to Malplaquet until I allow you!"

Guy assumed that this was finally the end of this horrible

encounter, and was about to slink miserably away but his father restrained him with a gesture.

"You must understand," he continued, "and I'm sure I've said it to you before, but you're a damned casual fellow who never does listen, this ancient family has always lived with the tradition of service. Service to the family, service to the country, service to the Church, service to the Royal Family, service to the Empire. We're not here to have a good time and enjoy ourselves. We're here to give something to others, to serve the nation in Parliament, to help form and lead governments. The English aristocracy is the backbone of the nation. You can't go around just thinking of yourself, you have to think of others, and when called upon, make sacrifices for others, even if it means laying down your life for those less fortunate than you. I've made sacrifices in my time. I've seen active service in war, and cared for the men under my command. On my return I married the woman my father selected for me. That's your mother. Of course I didn't love her, but I did my duty. You will do yours. Now you are dismissed."

Guy dragged himself out of the room.

Rupert was waiting for him in the gallery, and helped him up to the nursery where Mrs B. comforted him.

"It's so beastly unfair," groaned Guy. "He's never like this to you."

"That's because I'm not the eldest son," commiserated Rupert. "He has to put you under tremendous pressure as you are the eldest son and heir. He's determined to mould you to his will. You're the one who has to run the estate and carry on all the antique traditions. It's not so important in my case."

"You're so busy charming him he never has time to tell you off."

"You've been away a bit, but I can tell you, it's pretty bad with Cedric. He spends all his time screaming at him. I don't think Papa would dare to beat him, he knows Cedric would kill him if he tried."

"Thank God someone has the guts to stand up to the bully, I certainly can't."

At times Clelia found it quite comforting to return to her room in Somerville and find Henry waiting there for her. He was devoted to her, and would sit and read while he waited for her, and then welcome her on her return. But she began to feel that his presence was sometimes intrusive, particularly when she had the odd impression that he might be looking through her letters while she was out of the room. Returning to her room on Thursday after a music lesson she was very surprised to find Henry there, since they had not arranged to meet. He was sitting in the gloom, having only put on the bedside lamp, seemingly engrossed in a book. She felt uneasy about something, but could not quite identify what it was.

They chatted generally about various things and after a bit, Henry said casually that there was an envelope for her on her desk.

Clelia immediately went to find it. It was a small envelope of Florentine writing paper which, although closed, was not sealed. She quickly opened it. Her heart missed a beat as she read the message. "Walton Street, tomorrow, at six. I have missed you so intensely, angelic being, I am longing for you." She turned away quickly from Henry as she read it, so that he would not see the intensity of … the pleasure that suffused her face. In the darkened room she was sure that he had noticed nothing. After all, wasn't he busy reading a book?

But while giving every impression of appearing to be

engrossed in his book, Henry was watching her particularly closely, and in the mirror had seen the intensity of the delight that her face had betrayed. He tried to see where she was busy trying to conceal the note.

Then she bounced happily across the room and came to sit beside him, and chatted happily about where they would go for supper.

"We'll have Sunday lunch together, of course," he said.

"I'm afraid I can't, I've arranged to do something."

"Dinner on Saturday night, then."

"Actually, that's a bit difficult, too."

"Sunday night dinner?"

"Henry, it's a bit awkward, but just on that night – "

"You're not going away for the weekend, are you? You know it's completely forbidden in term time."

"Of course I'm not, it's just that I've arranged to meet various different people at different times, and …"

"Then we'll go out together on Friday night?"

Clelia paused and looked at him.

Henry looked at her questioningly. "You're busy on Friday too?"

"It's just that – "

"We'll have tea together, let's say, four o'clock?"

"Yes, that's fine."

The following day Henry called round at Somerville at four o'clock. He idled about in her room, picking things up, examining them and putting them down, and seemingly constantly busy, but constantly watching her closely. He noticed that she had stuffed some things into a bag, and he was trying to get near it in order to examine the contents, but Clelia placed it down on the floor at the side of the bed. They went down to the common room for tea. Henry bustled about to bring the tea and toasted tea-cakes.

Each time he went away to get something, Clelia allowed free range to her state of nervous excitement, which she had to bottle up and conceal every time Henry came back. He went away to get the strawberry jam, and Clelia found herself in a wonderful, fluttery, anxious state of anticipation. She lost all interest in the tea-cakes, and could barely manage to sip her tea with a trembly hand that caused the cup and saucer to rattle.

Henry missed nothing of this, and watched with interest as she refused any crumb to eat. "But you asked for them, I especially went to get the jam."

"Please, don't make me, I can't."

"They are very fresh."

"Yes, I can see how delicious they are."

"That's a ridiculous thing to say. You can't see how delicious they are. That's what's known as a category mistake."

Clelia found it difficult to continue the conversation. She was far too agitated. The butterflies continued to fly about in her stomach, and she knew she had never felt so distressed and so happy at the same time.

"You're not even having your tea."

"No, I'm sorry, I can't have anything. Now I really have to go."

"I'll accompany you."

"Really, you don't need to."

"I'd like to."

"Please don't."

But Henry insisted on following her up to her room where she seized the bag, and he insisted on holding the umbrella over her head as she walked in the drizzly rain along Little Clarendon Street to reach Walton Street near the Oxford University Press buildings.

"Thank you for coming with me," said Clelia in a very formal way, "But now you are not to come any further."

"Are you going away for the weekend?"

"Of course not."

"Then why are you taking that bag?"

"It doesn't contain anything."

"Let me see it then."

"Of course not. Now you must go back. I shall be very upset if you don't."

"Why should I go back? If you have nothing to hide – "

"I have absolutely nothing to hide, but there is no reason for you to stay any longer."

Henry handed her the umbrella and said goodbye. He walked off with the drizzle pouring down on his head, but waited until she was distracted and looking elsewhere, and watched her carefully from a safe distance. He saw a large black limousine draw up, and Clelia got inside. It glided silently away. Henry moved back into Walton Street to watch it go. Long after it had disappeared from sight, he stood with the rain pouring down his face watching the spot in the road where it had last been.

As happened from time to time, when they were all going to a particular dinner, they all gathered in Clelia's room prior to going out together.

Guy, looking elegantly beautiful in full evening dress, was stretched out languidly at full length on the bed. Caroline was very excited because Nigel was there, Matthew and Jeremy had joined them, and Henry was looking particularly smart.

Clelia came running in from the bathroom and sat down at the dressing table to fix her make-up. While she was looking at herself in the mirror and dabbing eye-shadow on her eyelids, someone suggested that Henry should read to them some of the poems that he had recently published in *Isis* that were making quite a stir in Oxford at the time.

Caroline handed Henry a copy of the magazine. He started to read. Everyone listened with rapt attention.

Clelia, sitting at the glass with her back to the assembled company, was busy applying her mascara.

He was reading about the poet's experiences as he went around a wind-swept ice-cold Oxford of the mind. Then he read:

She walks beside me though she is not with me,

She has already left me, and is already with him in their world.

The fine spray of the ever-increasing rain has washed me into a feint ink stain that barely remains beside her, and that as she walks away, will obliterate down to nothingness.

She steps into the large dark limousine.

There was a momentary pause in the reading. Henry was looking fixedly in the glass, where Clelia's hand had frozen halfway between the mirror and her face.

I stand alone on the rain-darkened pavement.

I have missed you so intensely, angelic being,

I am longing for you.

Remaining completely frozen, she looked into the mirror and their eyes met. Clelia bit her lip very hard. Everyone in the room remained completely silent, all lost in their own innermost thoughts.

Henry continued to gaze deeply into the mirror long after Clelia had hurried away behind the wardrobe door to slip into her slinky evening dress.

As they all set out together to walk towards St Giles, Nigel spent his time trying to avoid walking next to Caroline and trying to walk next to Clelia on her own. Walking together in a crowd, this was somewhat difficult. He wanted to pull hold of Clelia by the arm, but he could not do so in front of the others. He could see that she was avoiding eye contact with him. Finally he managed to get near to her out of earshot of the others. "Who is the man in the large dark limousine? Where did you go with him? Tell me, tell me."

"You don't really think it's anything to do with me, do you? It's just a poem. Henry is always writing poetry. It's just his vivid imagination."

"You mean there never was such an incident as he described?"

"Only in his imagination. Besides, what would it have to do with me?"

"The way he read it, I suppose, the way he looked at you."

"How could he look at me, I had my back to him the whole time. Besides, I wasn't really listening, I was doing my make-up."

Since he didn't know what to think, Nigel let the matter drop. In any case, it wasn't something he could talk about in front of the others.

"So you do go through my things and read my private letters." Clelia stared at Henry.

"No I do not. I don't care if you go around deceiving and tricking Guy, he couldn't care less anyway, he's far too busy even to notice, but I'm damned if I'm going to let you deceive me." Henry stared back.

"I'm not in a relationship with you, so how can I deceive you?"

"Who are you in a relationship with? Who is that man? You left Oxford quite illegally and went off and spent a weekend with him. Who is he?"

"It's absolutely nothing to do with you."

"You refuse to sleep with me, even though I love you, but you sleep with him."

"No I do not, how dare you! You don't know any such thing, how dare you say it!"

"What else do you do for a whole weekend. He's as desperate for you as I am."

"How dare you read my letters, and then quote them in your publications. Have you no sense of privacy?"

"And have you no sense of decency, deceiving me and lying to me."

"How dare you go following me about and spying on me?"

"I'll forgive you everything if you sleep with me. Don't pretend you haven't already done it."

"How dare you! How dare you!" Clelia became very angry, and ordered him to leave her room.

"I know you have, I've seen the pills in your sponge bag."

"That doesn't mean anything. Girls have them for all kinds of reasons. It just proves that you go spying on me, which is unpardonable."

"They only have them for one reason, if you would only admit it. Surely you know how much I love you, I've published my love for you so that the whole world can read it, doesn't my agony have any effect on your heart?"

"I've never misled you. I never pretended that I had feelings for you that I didn't have. I always said that we were friends, and I've always said that we should be very good friends who studied together. You are destroying the relationship by trying to take it further."

"And by the fact that you are so obviously in love with someone else."

Clelia turned sharply away from him. She bit her lip very hard, and twisted her handkerchief tightly in her hand.

"You're carrying on a clandestine affair," Henry continued. "I always thought that it was with Nigel, but I'll admit that I was wrong, and thought unfair thoughts about him which I now disavow."

Clelia took a very deep breath, and recovering her composure, said very firmly, "I'm not having an affair with anybody."

"Are you still engaged to him?" asked Nigel.

"I suppose so. You ordered me to get engaged to him, and I did as you said. You said it was desperately essential, and I obeyed you."

"Well, now I'm telling you to call it off."

"Why?"

"Because he's thoroughly disreputable, and if you're in any way associated with him, you'll get a bad reputation."

"But I don't do anything with him."

"I should damn well hope you don't," he said fiercely.

"I didn't mean that, of course I don't do that."

"I should hope not, he'd really despise you if you did. I've heard some very bad things about him."

"What have you heard?"

"His rooms in Christ Church are completely stuffed with women."

Clelia turned away to laugh.

"So you think it's funny?"

"No, it's just the way you said it."

"Did you know they were there?"

"I'm afraid I did."

"Why did you never tell me?"

"It never came up in conversation. We never talk about him, it has nothing to do with us. Everybody knows what he's like, he's very open about it, he doesn't try to conceal any of it, girls know they can just go to his room and tap on the door and get welcomed in."

"Aren't you offended?"

"It doesn't have anything to do with me. I hardly ever see him anyway, I'm too busy working."

"I'm told that he spends the allowance his father gives him on throwing wild parties, which sometimes get completely out of hand, and then he bribes the scouts or the bulldogs to take no action against him. As a result the proctors never get to hear about it. He's suave, louche, and always surrounded by a bevy of adoring, beautiful female admirers. His boast is that he's slept with every girl in Oxford, including all the secretaries and girls at the polytechnic – "

"Especially the polytechnic, and all the language schools."

"And now he's on the second time round. So you do know all about it."

"Everybody does, and just in case I didn't, Henry is always busy filling me in on the latest escapade."

"Why didn't you tell me? Doesn't he have a moral tutor?"

"I'm sure if he did he'd bribe him as well."

"The worst of it is that everybody also knows that you are his fiancée."

"I'm not officially engaged to him, it was never announced in *The Times*. His father has forbidden him to get married before he's twenty-five, so I don't think you need to worry."

"You wear his ring, I've seen you at parties wearing it, and whenever I come near, you hide your hand or take the ring off. Are you still thinking of marrying him?"

"I don't think about it at all."

"Why don't you just call it off, send him back his ring and have done with it. If you're nervous about saying it to his face, just send him a letter, put the ring inside and have it delivered by a scout. The ring is very valuable, you couldn't send it through the post."

"There's no need to do any of this since the question doesn't arise. It's completely otiose. The problem arises out of the fact that you were so upset about what was happening to James that you ordered me to go ahead and get engaged, quickly, before the scandal broke, and before any of us had had any time to do any research on his character. He just happened to be the only aristocrat in the list who I had actually met. There were a lot of others in the list, but I hadn't had time to meet them, and you were worried that as soon as the scandal broke, I would immediately become a social pariah, and be unable to go into society. In a way, that has been the case, and I've kept a very low profile socially, as you advised me, and I spend all the time in the library. The only person I ever see is Henry, we work together."

"He doesn't make improper suggestions?"

"You seem to forget that he is also an aristocrat, though his title isn't as antique or as famous as Guy's. Should I get engaged to him instead?"

"Has he suggested it?"

"Yes, he keeps telling me it's what I have to do. He's always telling me what a worthless, feckless, effete character Guy has, how he swaggers about with all his girls, fancying himself, that he's a complete narcissist and he thinks he doesn't have to do anything, he just has to be."

"That certainly is my view of him. What has Henry said to you?"

"Just that."

"But is he in love with you, or something?"

"He says so."

"You don't – ?"

"Of course not. I know what you said to me, I haven't forgotten it."

"What was all that stuff about the poems he wrote in *Isis*?"

"I don't know anything about it."

"Don't lie to me, he was reading it out to everyone in your room when I arrived last week."

"I think I wasn't there at the time, I was changing."

"Well, you did come in when he read the most poetic bit about somebody, presumably you, the loved one, going off in a limousine in Walton Street, while he, the abandoned poet, was left alone standing in the rain, watching the limousine draw away. I remember that you denied it, but everyone in the room assumed that he was writing about a real experience, and that the poem was addressed to you. In fact, now I think about it, Guy actually asked you who was the man in the limousine that you went off with."

"It's all a figment of Henry's fevered imagination. You know that works of art are created in the imagination. He just wanted to write some tragic-sounding poetry, and just because he and I work together people jumped to the absurd conclusion that it had happened. He's become famous all over Oxford, and people go around thinking it is life when it is in fact art. You shouldn't regard the woman he writes about as being me. He isn't writing to an individual woman, he is writing in a universal theme, like Byron in 'She walks in beauty like the night,' which is universal, it is about all women. By the way, at dinner tonight, there are a number of things he wants to ask you."

"What do you mean, 'at dinner tonight'? I thought it was going to be just us at dinner tonight," he said in astonishment.

"I thought you knew. It's dinner at Balliol tonight, then it's the meeting of the Cerberus Society. Sir Roy Harrod is speaking. He's a student at Christ Church. A number of friends are coming. Caroline especially wants to sit next to you."

Nigel looked astonished. "I thought we were going to have a quiet dinner together, and then go to bed early."

"The last time you spent a weekend in Oxford when I didn't tell anybody, I was accused of being extremely selfish. You're very popular, Nigel, everyone complained to me that I'd hogged you to myself."

"But I only come to Oxford to spend the weekend with you! Next time I'll insist we stay in a bed and breakfast at Little Tew or Milton-under-Wychwood. Is anyone else coming to dinner tonight?"

Clelia lowered her eyes. "Guy is coming."

"Oh no!"

"He asked very nicely if he could come, he wants to talk to you about some new ideas."

"Why does he have to talk to me?"

"He respects your views."

"Well, I don't respect him. Do I really have to see him? After all I've heard about him, the very idea of him makes me feel sick. Why does he have to be part of our circle? If you would only break with him we wouldn't have to see him at all."

Later, that evening, they all gathered as usual in Clelia's room in Somerville. They all wore evening dress and were particularly smart. Caroline was very attentive to Nigel, which made him feel very uneasy. Guy was his usual elegant self and looked especially ethereal that night.

As they set off to walk towards St Giles, Guy naturally walked beside Nigel, and they immediately fell into a serious conversation about Hobbes. It suited Nigel to continue this conversation on their arrival at Balliol, not only in order to avoid the attentions of Caroline, but also because he was intensely interested in what Guy was saying, and the sharp and awkward questions that he was raising. They sat together at dinner, and spent the whole meal in a world of ideas, completely cut off from the rest of the company.

As Clelia lay in Nigel's bed at the Randolph Hotel later that night, she asked him what he thought. "I'm stunned, I just find it remarkable, Guy has a brilliant mind and an original way of thinking. It forms such a contrast with his dissolute, rakish behaviour. He was deference itself towards me, he couldn't have been more polite, and listened politely to everything I said even where he disagreed with me, and then quietly and decisively defeated me in argument. He is one of those extremely clever people who is capable of making a very clever or subtle point with a series of very simple but completely incisive questions. Does he spend any time at all studying?"

"He thinks a First is his given right, it will come naturally to him."

"He's making a terrible mistake. I can't understand how he doesn't realise this."

"Did you tell him this?"

"No, I couldn't, we only discussed ideas, it was impossible to raise anything personal. I had to put out of my mind all those things we talked about before dinner, otherwise it would have been unbearable for me. In any case, the person I was talking to seemed like a different person. How do you explain that?"

"Sometimes he behaves like that, sometimes he behaves well. He's perfectly capable of it. It's just that he doesn't do it very often."

Following that weekend Clelia saw very little of Guy. She spent all her time working and studying. Henry was her permanent companion in the Bodleian Library, and they spent much of their time together. They were very good friends, except in the moments when Henry couldn't restrain himself from begging her to sleep with him. This always made her very cross, and then she would refuse to talk to him until he apologised. His argument always was that they were going to get married anyway. Clelia would always counter this by saying that she didn't intend to marry anyone, and was determined to pursue her own career.

But with various changes taking place, and the pressure of work making it difficult for Nigel to visit her as often as she would have wished, Clelia found that Oxford could be a very lonely place. Everyone around her seemed to be happily set up with friends. For personal reasons and because of pressure of work, Clelia had no desire to go out and look for friends. The permanently cold and drizzly weather also had the effect of making her feel isolated and depressed. She knew that she wasn't abandoned, and letters did something to alleviate the sense of loss, but there was always that underlying sense of sorrow and distance that she could never quite overcome. There was no family to visit, and since his disgrace and public humiliation, James was a shadow of his former self; she had almost lost all contact with him. He lived forlornly in the countryside, she was never quite sure where, moving about dolefully as a mendicant house guest, almost living on the charity of friends, nervous about showing up at his country estate, since the constant antics of his former mistress kept his name almost permanently on the front pages of the trashy newspapers.

This particular feature of affairs was another reason for Clelia to hide herself from the public gaze. Most people were unaware of her connection with James, but unfortunately, a number of people at Oxford did know about it, and it was yet another reason for keeping a low profile. She could never know, each morning as she went out and walked past the newsagents on the corner of Little Clarendon Street, whether or not her eye would fall upon a newspaper headline detailing in all its gory exultancy yet another arrest or trial or misadventure of the ever more scantily clad Miss Virginia Ashcroft or of her ever more outspoken and revealing call-girl friends.

The famous nude photos of Miss Ashcroft were on display everywhere, and James's name was always dragged into it even when the story had nothing to do with him, and was something new that Miss Ashcroft had invented as a folly of her own in order to receive payments from journalists to meet her constantly rising legal expenses. In the photographs, Miss Ashcroft always looked stunningly lovely, in direct contrast to the mad and foolish conduct of her life, and in interviews with journalists always maintained that she personally had been responsible for creating swinging London and the swinging sixties.

One Sunday afternoon, when the weather was extremely chilly with an overcast sky and a biting wind, Clelia conceived the mad idea to go and call on Guy at Christ Church. She was feeling particularly depressed. She walked through an ice-cold and deserted St Giles and Carfax where the infuriated wind flailed the harassed shreds of rubbish and newspapers that were trying to crawl out of its persistent swirl and huddle together for warmth in the gutter. Everything was very quiet at Christ Church as she passed under Tom Tower, walked across the quad and entered the building. No-one noticed her as she approached Guy's room and tapped quietly on the door. The noise coming from inside meant that no-one inside could possibly hear her, and she had to knock much louder to make her presence known. Suddenly the door burst open and the jolly red face of a young man appeared before her.

He was just about to welcome her inside when he suddenly realised who she was. A look of shocked horror flooded his face, and he moved back sharply and tried to close the door in her path.

Clelia's initial reaction was to try to push her way inside, but she immediately desisted when she heard Guy's voice asking who it was, and the stunned silence from all the inhabitants as soon as they were told. She waited quietly in the deserted corridor.

Eventually, the door opened and Guy came out, carefully closing the door behind him. "Matthew is away this weekend, we'll go upstairs to his room." He led her up the narrow staircase at the end of the corridor.

As soon as they got inside Matthew's room, he immediately began to kiss her and pull her clothes off.

She tried to resist at first but it was very difficult.

"Tell me what's the matter," he said, looking at her miserable face.

"I want you to give me some of that stuff you take."

"I thought you could get your own dope, you always have plenty."

"Of course I do. I don't mean that, I mean the white powder. What is it, is it coke?"

"Whatever it is, I'm not giving you any. It's not suitable for you. Why do you need it?"

"I need it, please give me some."

"No, I wouldn't dream of it. You don't need it and you're not going to have it. What's wrong with you, anyway?"

"Nothing, I'm absolutely fine."

"Then why do you want it? We took some very good mescalin the other night, why didn't you come then?"

"You didn't tell me. Why didn't you invite me?"

He had pulled off her black mohair sweater and was now removing her bra. "Because you're so completely stuffy and proper. You probably would have refused to come if I'd invited you. It's all this ridiculous business about insisting on remaining a virgin, as if anyone does that nowadays. I suppose you see the idea of hanging on to your virginity as a vital part of your freedom and independence. You behave as if you believe that to yield to a man would limit your independence or freedom. You ought to know that with me it won't." They were lying together on the bed and he was caressing and kissing her. "Make love to me, don't hold me off like this. Can't you see what it means to me?"

"You've got all those girls downstairs. You don't need me."

"If only you could understand, you're the only one I do need. I don't want any of them, I want you. It would make an enormous difference to my life, can't you grasp that?"

"I don't believe it for a single minute. Now give me some of that white powder, I'm sure you give it to them."

"No, I don't." He reached into his jeans pocket and pulled out a screwed-up piece of silver paper. "Here, you can have this."

Clelia grabbed it and jumped up from the bed. She felt contaminated by being in the same room with him. She quickly pulled on the black mohair sweater and made to leave the room.

"What about this?" He dangled the white bra from his hand.

She snatched it from him and ran out of the room. As she ran down the narrow staircase she screwed up the bra in her hand. She ran quickly past the door of Guy's room and along the corridor. As she turned the corner she almost ran straight into Henry whose eyes fell immediately upon the bra in her hand. She immediately put her hand behind her back, and searched vainly for a pocket into which to stuff the bra.

"Come and have tea," said Henry.

She followed him into his room, and sat in the seat in the window embrasure that looked out onto the ever-darkening quad.

Henry busied himself with boiling up the water on the little gas ring and getting out the cups and saucers. "Toasted tea-cakes?"

"Yes, I'd love them."

In order to toast them on a toasting fork at the gas fire, Henry was obliged to light the gas fire.

"Aren't you freezing in here without the fire on?"

"No, I'm very used to the cold. At my parents' house we don't have any heating."

"Even in the depths of winter?"

"If it's really cold, we are allowed to make a coal fire in the hall. If you spend all your life like that, you get used to it. We don't have any modern form of heating at my parents' place, and the buildings are far too old to have any installed." He smiled happily at her. "Strawberry jam?"

"Yes, lovely."

They cuddled together in the window seat, enjoying an intimate tea together.

"I know you didn't come to see me, but it really doesn't matter. You see what we have to put up with on this corridor."

"Is it always like this?"

"Yes, all the time, Guy doesn't do any studying. One of his tutors has sent a number of notes to him, asking him why he hasn't turned up at his tutorials. He proudly showed them round the college, but he hasn't done anything about it."

"What will they do if he doesn't respond?"

"They'll discipline him, he won't be able to take his finals."

"Isn't he worried about that?"

"Far from it, he just mocks them. He was very upset that his tutor in Political Theory at Balliol arranged that his tutorial would be at nine o'clock in the morning. Not his favourite time of the day."

"But did he go?"

"Matthew and Jeremy were detailed to drag him out of bed and send him on his way. When he got to Balliol, all drugged-up and hung-over, his tutor thought he looked so dreadful that he made him a coffee!"

"No!"

"Yes! He had to do something to wake him up! The next week he looked just as bad, and he even told the tutor that he'd been up all night, and again the tutor made him a coffee! Imagine! Then, the third week, Guy staggered into his tutorial, slumped himself down in an armchair, and said to the tutor, 'Where's my coffee?'!!"

"Wasn't the tutor amazed at this dreadful behaviour?"

"He was so utterly amazed that he went and made the coffee!"

They both laughed. Henry stroked her golden hair and nuzzled her. Soon they were kissing and his hand was caressing her inside the sweater.

"You know I love you. Do break off with him, being connected with him only does you harm. Become engaged to me." Being with him was warm and comforting. He was very sweet, and he obviously loved her. Allowing him these personal intimacies made her feel so much better. "Let me take you out to dinner tonight, we can go to the Elizabeth. Let's go back to your room, and you can change into a beautiful sequined décolleté evening dress."

They set out happily to spend the evening together.

While Clelia was slipping into a slinky dress, Henry lolled about in her room and entertained her with the latest stories that were going around Oxford. There was the perennial story about Guy refusing to have a green light attached to his car.

"But why are undergraduates obliged to have a green light attached to their car? I've never understood the reason for it."

"So that law-abiding citizens can get out of their way, I suppose. Dangerous by day, and drunk by night, or in Guy's case, drugged by night. So that the police can monitor them more efficiently, I suppose. Guy regards it as demeaning that he should have to be identified as an undergraduate, and he completely refuses to do it. He risks getting punished for it if he gets caught, though, but apparently, if he does, he plans to say that it's not his car, it's not registered in his name, and he's only borrowed it for the day. Otherwise he's worried that they'll drag him up in front of the beaks and endorse his raincoat. There are various places he has where he hides the car from the prying eyes of the Bullers who go around at night trying to spot students' cars. One of them is with Mrs Butterfield at Elm Farmhouse just over Foley Bridge."

"But it would be demeaning for him to have to go around with a green light on his car. It's like a leper going around ringing a bell and shouting out, 'Unclean, unclean!'"

"I think you're right," laughed Henry. "That's exactly what Guy should go around shouting about himself! There should be a government health warning attached to him! The main thing about Guy is that he has always regarded himself as above the law or above any rules. If there are to be any rules, which he denies, he invents them for himself. You know that big sign up on the wall of the Bodleian, the one in Latin, '*si movet, impregnate!*'

You must have seen it."

Clelia laughed.

"Well," laughed Henry. "That slogan, or exhortation, is widely attributed to Guy, since it embodies his philosophy. Not that he actually wrote it there himself, of course not. But having inspired it, he incited someone else to paint it up there. He would far prefer to let someone else risk being run down by the Bulldogs and get rusticated than run the risk of doing it personally himself."

"But he's not a coward, you told me that."

"Far from it, he's always been prepared to take the most amazing risks, even where his own personal safety is at stake. He personally organised and supervised the raising of that Mini Minor onto the roof of the Clarendon Building in the middle of the night. Imagine the organisation involved in that! They could have been caught at any moment, and if they had they would all have been sent down. But the consternation the next morning when the car was spotted up there was wonderful! It was a real triumph!"

"But you told me about another boy, what's happened to him?"

"Oh yes, Ian Flintoff at Trinity."

"Tell me about him."

"Well, it's hilarious. For the whole of the last year he's had a girl living with him in his room in college. All her things are kept in a trunk. Imagine how careful and tidy they have to be! If the scouts or cleaners go into his room, everything has to be completely hidden away, otherwise, if he's found out, some terrible retribution will fall upon him."

"Is she a student?"

"No, she works in Oxford, and she goes to work every morning. Imagine that! For a whole year she goes to work every day, and she can't go out each morning past the porter's lodge, every morning she has to leave the college by climbing over the wall. She must be very athletic!"

Immense excitement surrounded the advent of May Day. It was a very important celebration, comparable only in importance to Suicide Sunday in Cambridge, which occurred later in the year, after the exams. Invitations were flying everywhere for students to go to balls and parties. There was fierce competition for the few available girls.

Guy was anxious to invite Clelia, but Henry was determined to have her with him on that night. It would, of course, be a long night, because it would continue right through until the champagne breakfast in Magdalen at five thirty, and the ritual gathering on Magdalen bridge at six to hear the choir boys greet May Day morning with their piping strains of May Day carols from the top of Magdalen Tower. Usually the wind was high and the voices drifted off into the stratosphere, unheard by those below, or it rained. Guy was planning to spend the night with friends on Angel and Greyhound Meadow by the Cherwell. They would have fun lighting bonfires and roasting sausages and potatoes. Then they would cross the pontoon of punts under the bridge in order to go for breakfast in Magdalen. The bonfires would be needed because the night promised to be freezing.

Clelia, got up in her finery, was wearing little enough as it was without spending the night in a dank meadow in the mists and marshes, and after a lot of tussling, Henry managed to persuade her that if she did go there she would catch her death of cold. Instead she consented to dance the night away with him. He was overjoyed at his success.

Guy and a whole crowd of friends set off with hampers and

satchels stuffed with goodies and lots of wine, and Henry's voice ringing in their ears as they departed: "And the best of British freezing luck to you! Don't leap into the river, every year people jump from Magdalen bridge and drown. Not the same people," he hastened to add.

All the girls were wearing very thin ball dresses and rickety high heels upon which they tottered around the soggy marshes. The boys instantly set about lighting the bonfires and scavenging for twigs upon which to roast the sausages. As the fires blazed up, they stuffed the potatoes into the hot charcoals to roast them. Bottles of wine were uncorked and all the little groups of happy party goers were soon busy enjoying themselves. Excited boys and girls ran from group to group, swapping hints and stories, borrowing wine glasses or packets of salt and butter, or huddling under shawls at the side of a thousand blazing fires that dotted about the meadow and sparked up delightedly into the sky above.

The cold wind whistled across the meadow and the dank mists wafted through the night as the punters on the river gradually steered the punts into place along the Cherwell. They had to take care because the water was very high and flowing faster than usual after days of excessive rain. Guy had arranged with his friends that while the supper was cooking, they would bring into place just beside Magdalen punt station three punts which had been lashed together and upon which had been secured an upright piano. The idea was that during the course of the evening, Patrick, wearing dinner jacket and black tie, would sit at the piano and regale them with his selection of Twenties and Thirties tunes. It was a very delicate job manoeuvring the piano into position against the flow of the current, and then it had to be wedged into the pontoon of punts, so that while entertaining them with "My Blue Heaven," Patrick did not absent-mindedly drift away down the Isis to a watery inferno.

When Patrick was well set up and bashing out the numbers, Guy and the others returned to the task of cooking round the fire. The smells of roasting meats wafted across the meadow, and jolly shouts of laughter and banter echoed across the water. It was clearly the duty of the boys to forage for wood, which was mainly torn off the hawthorn bushes by the water margin. They had to cook the supper and drink all the wine. It was the girls' task to look decorous and huddle together under the shawls, freezing to death and complaining at how long the roast potatoes were taking.

Barnaby excitedly handed them a twig spiked with scorched sausages, the first thing he had ever cooked in his life, which they eagerly grabbed and started to eat. "Ugh!" they cried, as they realised that the sausages were burnt on one side and raw on the other. Barnaby apologetically took them back and promised to do better, stuffing them quickly into the fire.

Peter ran across to another group to borrow the mustard which his crowd had forgotten to bring, but decided to stay there when he realised that their feast was far better organised. The girls became desperately impatient when the potatoes took all night to roast, and they never seemed to get offered a glass of wine which the boys were busy hogging to themselves. The party had reached the raucous laughter stage, and some boys fell down in the mud in hysterics. The freezing girls became ever more disgusted with the whole procedure, and some of them decided to leave.

"But you can't go yet, we haven't had supper," cried the boys.

"And we aren't ever likely to," cried the shivering girls.

The boys were very distressed at the idea that the girls they had fought so hard to convince to come were likely to go off when they had made such an effort to make the party a success. And the real events of the night hadn't even started, it was all too bad. Finding one's way about in the dark on the meadow was not easy. The main orientation as to where the water was came from the strains of the piano, with some of the sounds lost in the night air. Some of the girls took pity on the boys' efforts, but some just could not stand it a moment longer. Someone announced that the choir boys were going up the tower, although it was still quite dark, but in the drunken enjoyment everyone had lost all sense of time.

There was an enormous surge of everyone on the meadow to rush across the pontoon bridge to get to the tower side, and in the mad rush the sheer weight of numbers caused the punts containing the piano to plunge into the water, causing their precious cargo to sink to the bottom of the Cherwell. A terrible scream went up as the punts began to glide beneath the surface of the water, and everyone fled to the bank as fast as they could.

Patrick, who had been in mid chorus of "I'm Forever Blowing Bubbles" was very miffed as he was obliged to swim for it. "Damn!" he shouted, "We're not supposed to jump in until after they've sung, and then only from the top of the bridge! Just as well," he muttered to himself, "That I'm a wet-bob, and that the first thing I ever did was to pass a swimming test in flannels at the St. George's Baths."

Girls in lovely chiffon skirts were dragged screaming from the icy waters, and torn stockings were wailed over at the muddy banks.

Guy watched mournfully as the piano bubbled down under the waves, and plans were immediately put in train to rescue the drowned instrument. By eight o'clock that morning the waterlogged piano had been dredged up to the surface by a group of saturated students, their clothes wringing wet. It was manoeuvred slowly and laboriously up the ramp and brought out into the road where the Morris Dancers were performing their

May Day dances on the bridge. By twelve o'clock it had reached the High Street. By two o'clock in the afternoon it had arrived in Broad Street outside Balliol. There were no further sightings.

It was very early on Sunday morning. Clelia lay asleep in her room in Somerville. She moved about uneasily in the bed, troubled and worried. In that strange state of half sleeping, half waking she suddenly had the odd sensation that there was someone in the room. "I must have slept badly, I'm having delusions," she thought, but she lay very still and held her breath and listened for any sound. Suddenly she became fully awake, and sat up in bed. There was a dark shadow over by the window. Someone was there. She was just about to leap quickly from the bed when he came across the room and grabbed her, pinning her to the bed.

"I thought we had a lunch-time appointment, not a breakfast time one," she said angrily.

Henry held her down hard.

"How dare you come into my room at this hour. How did you get in?"

"You left the door open, I suppose you are expecting someone, at any moment he will walk in."

"I did not leave the door open. No-one is coming. Tell me how you got in."

"I walked in, the door was deliberately left open by you."

"No it was not. Leave at once."

"So I don't catch you with whoever it is you are expecting?"

"I'm not expecting anyone."

"Is it the man in the limousine?"

"You have no right to go around spying on me. I dislike it intensely. We could have a very good relationship if you didn't do that."

"Let's have the relationship anyway."

While still holding her down, he tried to pull off her nightdress. Clelia resisted with all her strength but the nightdress got torn. They were both very upset at this.

"Why do you make me do this?" he groaned miserably. "Why don't you just consent. You know I want you, I can't live without you, I'll take you on any terms."

"What on earth does that mean?" she wondered to herself.

Henry continued to tussle with her, and she determinedly fought back. Finally, still clinging to her, he lay still. They lay in silence for a while.

"Let me persuade you to give this up. Let me get up. We can go for breakfast together. We can still be friends."

Henry was in a very bad temper but he eventually allowed her to get up and dress. Although he was still very grumpy, he agreed to go out for breakfast.

Winding her arm through his, she dragged him along St Giles towards Boswell's. It was only just eight o'clock.

"Shall we go to the cafe in Boswells? Is that where you would like to go, darling?"

Henry considered. "It's alright for breakfast," he conceded. "But I just want to be with you, and if we go there we shall have to be civil to all those Balliol men sitting there taking breakfast in their elegant silk dressing gowns. They use it for breakfast as if it's their own private restaurant since it's just across the Broad."

"Surely they won't be there this early on a Sunday?"

"I don't want to risk it. I'd rather go to the Cadena."

"Because Auden held court there?" laughed Clelia.

With their arms round each other they wandered off down Cornmarket. They had only gone a few steps when they found themselves in front of the shop windows of Muspratt and Ramsay, the photographers. They looked in to see the latest photos. Right in the centre of the central window was an enormous blown up photo of Guy proudly standing there in his cricket whites, ready to go out to bat.

Henry was astonished. "What on earth is he doing there?" he protested. "It's enough to make anyone throw a brick through the window at that smarmy, triumphant face. Don't they realise what an invitation it is to his enemies to lob a cricket ball at him?" To Clelia's amazement, he let go of her arm and started scouring the gutters for the stray, abandoned beer or wine bottle casually left lying about by the drunks of Saturday night. He seemed serious, too. Clelia was forced to grab him by the arm and drag him on.

At last they arrived at the Cadena and went inside. They sat down together and ordered coffee and toast.

Henry was still obsessed by the offending photo. "When there are so many intellectuals at Oxford, I can't understand why they would choose to advertise their wares by a photo of an obnoxious cricketer. And do you know, Mrs Ramsay is the widow of Frank Ramsay, the brilliant Cambridge logician so worshipped by Wittgenstein, so admired by Keynes. What an inappropriate choice to adorn her window. Frank Ramsay died tragically at twenty-four. If only we could be sure that the insufferable cricket captain would meet such an early fate!"

"Really, Henry, don't say that!"

"I mean it!" said Henry defiantly.

At that moment the door of the cafe opened and a great blast of cold air flooded the room. Henry was about to get up to close the door when he realised that the whirlwind bursting through it was Guy, wearing a full-length trench coat and with his hair soaking wet. This was no early bird, it was clear that he had been up all night.

He flung himself down at their table. Their faces registered their utter astonishment at seeing him out and about so early on a Sunday morning. He laughed at their amazement.

"Janet!" he shouted right across the restaurant. "Bring me masses of black coffee!" Turning to Clelia and Henry he explained, "I have masses of studying to do today – two essays to write – I'll never get through it."

Clelia was very distressed at his soaking hair. "In this cold weather you'll catch a terrible chill." She went in search of a dish-cloth, and came back and dried his hair.

"So where did you two spend the night?" He leered at them.

"Not together."

"So how come you're here together so early in the morning?"

"We arranged to have an early breakfast so that we can spend the day studying. We're very keen not to lose time."

"I just wish that Henry wouldn't spend so much time hanging around you."

"What on earth's it got to do with you, you don't spend any time with her."

"You seem to forget that she's my fiancée. If you want a woman, go and get your own, don't try and take mine."

"But you don't give her any attention, you're far too busy with all your floosies, and whoever it is you spent last night with. You've obviously been up all night with your latest whoever they are."

"None of this, true or false, gives you the right to imagine that Clelia is planning to go off with you. Whenever she needs me she comes round to see me, like she did the other day."

"But what good does it do her when you can only manage to tear yourself away from all your other guests for only a few minutes, and she can't even get into your room because it's so stuffed up with disreputables. What on earth is the value of a relationship like that? You surely can't imagine that it's what she wants?"

"Perhaps she'll tell me what she wants rather than having you as her representative speaking on her behalf."

They were standing up shouting at each other across the table, and it looked as if at any moment they would start fighting.

Clelia was desperate to fling herself between them in the hope of stopping it, and she was assisted by Janet, the waitress, who was determined that nothing bad should happen to Guy.

Janet anxiously took hold of Guy and started to steer him away from the table. "Please, darling, come away, he looks horrid," she begged.

"Ah!" cried Henry in triumph. "Another of your women, even in this cafe. I might have known that's why you came in here this morning."

"How dare you!" cried Janet, and slapped him hard in the face.

"Oh, very nice, Blandford, now you get your women to attack me," shouted Henry, "Too cowardly to do it yourself, you set your women on me."

"If you don't get out at once, I'll call the police!" cried Janet furiously.

Guy was deeply embarrassed at the idea that a female had marched forward as his champion and assaulted his rival on his behalf. As he tried to stutter a protest he heard Janet shouting, "And you can take your fancy woman with you!"

"No, no, Janet," he called out. "That's not his woman, that's my fiancée."

Janet looked at him in total disbelief. "But Guy, I had absolutely no idea that you were engaged!"

"Of course you didn't," said Henry gloatingly. "From the way he behaves how could anyone know that, least of all a woman who – " He was just about to say something really nasty when Janet, glaring at him, moved towards him with her hand raised, ready to clock him another one. He eyed her warily.

"Yes," said Guy. "I assure you, this is my fiancée and he's trying to steal her, that's what it's all about. Let me introduce you."

Janet was very impressed, and wiped her hand on her apron before shaking hands with Clelia.

Henry was astounded to see Clelia, Janet and Guy deep in conversation, and all three of them totally ignoring him.

"Oh yes, that's the picture book about my ancestors, you always liked that book. It's in the library, I'll go and get it for you."

Guy set off down the long corridor for the library.

Mark trotted along behind. As soon as they went inside the library, Mark flung his arm round his neck and tried to kiss him.

Guy flung him furiously away. "Don't ever do that again!" he snarled.

"Nobody else is here."

"You're lucky they're not. If you did it in public, I'd kill you!"

"You said we'd always love each other. You even promised, don't you remember, when we sat on that wall, that you'd love me forever."

"Don't ever refer to that again. I've already told you, I'm engaged to be married. That was all a long time ago, it's all in the past, it may have a meaning for then, I'm sure it does, but it's all over."

"It has a meaning for me."

"Yes, you've told me, among your souvenirs, and that's where it has to remain, locked up tight inside your souvenir box, never to come out."

"Like Pandora's box."

"No, no, never to be opened!" He looked at him in fear. "So you intend to open it, like Pandora's box?"

"It depends on what you do."

"So you're threatening me?"

Mark sat down on a chair and smiled at him.

"What are you planning to do?" asked Guy, uneasily.

"Why don't you sit down, perhaps we can talk about it. I came here so that we would be friends, I don't want to upset you."

Guy became very worried. "Mark, I have to explain to you, whatever hopes you have, it really is all over. You've got lots of other friends. I wish you would realise, the past is the past. I don't do that anymore. I know it was fun and enjoyable and everything, but we all have to move on. It was difficult for me at first, too, and some friends had to help me – "

"Yes, I remember all about that, and how you deceived me, that Christmas – "

"I didn't deceive you, it was just the process of growing up and moving on to the next stage. You just didn't want to do it then, and I see that you don't want to do it now."

"We could do it in private."

Guy jumped up in fury and shouted, "No, no, no! Don't you understand what I'm saying? I invited you down here because I thought you understood! I invited your friends here so that you could have companions, if you needed them, and to make sure that you wouldn't consider me! Surely you realised this?"

"But I only love you." He looked at him plaintively and pathetically. "I've never loved anyone else. Of course, I go about with them. I can't be alone. Since you've rejected me, I have to have someone. But I don't really want them, I want you."

Guy sat down in front of him and looked at him. "We were very good friends."

"We were more than friends."

"I admit that, but that was then. Can't you tell the difference?"

"I don't want to. Don't make me. Don't be so unkind, it's not like you, it's not in your character. Remember how nice you were to me, you used to do my construe for me, you were happy to look after me. It's not friendly to reject me now."

"I'm not rejecting you, we can still be friends, I'm very keen that we should be friends, as long as you understand that all the rest is over. Adolescence is very beautiful, even if it is very painful. Saying goodbye to it is terrible, it's like a terrible wrench, leaving behind that golden glowing time of our youth. In my case it was just as painful to leave all of that behind but I had to do it. You have to as well. Do you understand?"

"I accept that," said Mark, and cheerfully held out his hand to Guy, who gratefully took it and held it tenderly. "As long as you stick by the rules," he said.

"I will," replied Mark, smiling.

"Promise not to say a word to my fiancée."

"I haven't met your fiancée."

"Well, don't. Can I trust you?"

"Yes, as long as you remain my friend."

Guy wasn't quite sure what this meant. "No overt acts of affection in public."

"Just a few in private."

"I thought I said – "

"Just a few. Don't be mean. Something symbolic when no-one else is around. Just to show that you care about me and that you haven't forgotten everything."

"It's better to forget everything."

"It's easy for you. For me it's more of a problem."

Guy decided to let the matter go as he wasn't getting anywhere and Mark was determinedly persistent. He would just have to avoid him as much as possible during the course of the weekend, and never invite him again. There was something about Mark's attitude that he didn't like, and underneath it all lurked the unsavoury smell of blackmail. Somehow he didn't fully believe it, but it could never be totally ruled out. Wherever he went during the weekend he felt that Mark and his friends were watching him closely, and it made him feel uneasy. For the moment, things were going very well with Clelia, and he didn't want anything to be ruined. He had to use all his ingenuity to make sure that they did not meet each other, but fortunately, there were a lot of guests around, and so Guy made sure that there were lots of games and activities to keep everyone busy all the time.

It was an intense relief when Sunday evening came to a weary end, and Mark and his friends prepared to set off on the drive back to London.

Guy went down to the courtyard to see them off. He could tell by the glint in Mark's eye that he wasn't going to be let off lightly. Mark must have been counting on something, and he obviously wanted to do something in the presence of his friends to illustrate his intimacy with Guy. Guy approached him warily. Politeness forbad him from just letting them leave without a word of farewell.

Mark was leaning against the car waiting for him, smiling that awful, knowing smile he had so recently taken up.

Guy found it intensely off-putting. He wished to God they would just leave.

"I've behaved myself, haven't I? I haven't done anything you didn't want."

Guy glanced at all the friends silently staring at him. "Just don't kiss me in front of everybody," he said.

"Why not? They all know."

"If only it could be over and done with quickly," thought Guy. He glanced up at the dark clouds rolling across the sky. They all ducked at the sudden crash of thunder, and the large drops of rain that started to slosh down in sudden dollops. As the water splashed down Mark took his chance and grabbed hold of Guy in a sudden embrace.

Guy tore himself away and ran through the pouring rain back into the house. Finally they had gone.

It was Saturday night. There was a feverish party under way in St Hugh's, where the music was far too loud and there was far too much beer.

After much reluctant refusal Guy had eventually agreed to play, and had brought a bass player and a drummer with him. Guy had even persuaded a trumpeter friend of his to join them, and while the drummer was setting up his drums, Nick was practising his Satchmo riffs and cadenzas. Gerry Mulligan meets Thelonious Monk was the theme of the evening. Guy had only been finally persuaded because it was a girls' college and there would be lots of talent, he had been assured. On arrival, he wasn't so sure because there was an enormous crush of men. Crowds thronged all the rooms and staircases, and there was dancing in the hall to the juke box. It was quite late before Guy and his friends got up to play. By then, Felix, who had organised everything, had become delirious with happiness and intoxicated with wine. He ran around helping to organise the sound system and wiring up the speakers. The riotous party continued until well after two o'clock in the morning.

Felix and his friends stood in the silent, darkened street

outside the college.

"What would you like?" asked Felix.

"What have you got?" asked Robert.

"Everything. Charlie, Henry, you name it."

Robert considered for a moment. "Henry," he said.

Felix reached into the right-hand pocket of his elegant trousers, and brought out a selection of neatly wrapped twists of silver foil. "How many would you like?"

"I'll take three."

"Do you want to pay me now or later?" asked Felix. As he said these words he became aware of a police car cruising gently along the kerb towards them in the silent night. He watched horrified as the police car stopped, and an officer got out and started to walk towards him. "Quick!" he said to the others, "Run to the car." They ran to the car and jumped inside. Felix immediately drove off, the police car in hot pursuit. As they raced away, they were aware of the flashing blue light behind them.

Felix was at the wheel and he drove like a demon along the Woodstock road.

"Faster, faster," said Gordon, "they're still on our tail. Put your foot down and we'll get away." Racing like a madman, the car hurtled towards St Giles.

Looking back for him, Robert shouted, "Don't slow down, there's nothing coming from the Banbury Road." The car raced along St Giles.

"Which way, which way?" shouted Felix as the car sped past St John's.

"Straight on through Cornmarket!" shouted Gordon.

"Go left at St Mary's!" shouted Robert. "Don't you know? Left here, left here!"

Felix swung the car violently to the left at the Martyrs' Monument, and raced along the narrow lane at the side of Balliol.

"Where now?" he screamed as he got to the junction with Broad Street. "Left or right?"

"Left!" screamed Robert.

"Right!" shouted Gordon.

Felix was already turning the car to the left as Gordon screamed, "Right, right!" Making an enormous effort to swerve back to the right he took the turn too fast. Unable to swing the car fast enough to the right he lost control, swung too far across the road and saw the enormous glass window of Boswells rear up before him. Slamming on the brakes, he wrenched the car to the right, but the steering wheel was on full lock. It was too late and the astonished car leapt through the glass window, which shattered before it. The car juddered to a halt as it embedded itself in the shop front. The sound of crashing glass gave way to silence. The shocked boys listened as, in the distance, the distinctive sound of the police siren wailed ever nearer.

"Quick, get out, run!" cried Felix. He wasn't sure what happened to the others or how he had got out, but without a backward glance and before he was aware of it, he was streaking down Cornmarket, running past Carfax, past the Town Hall and arriving at the part of the wall of Christchurch that was the regular route for those returning to college after midnight. Risking everything but unaware that he was risking it, he leapt over the wall, and fell down the other side, almost impaling himself on a nine-inch metal spike designed to discourage such incursions. He raced in the darkness across the Quad and hurtled down the corridor arriving breathless and in panic outside Guy's door. He tapped frantically on the door. There was no response. He tapped again, louder. Still silence. He tried the handle, and to his amazement, burst suddenly into the room.

"Guy, Guy, you have to hide me!"

"Thank God it's you," said Guy in annoyance, getting up

naked from the bed. The naked girl in the bed covered herself hastily with the sheet.

"I thought for a moment it was the Bulldogs or one of the Proctors. What on earth do you mean by bursting in on me like this giving me a shock."

"It's my father's car," said Felix. He looked around the room. "What have you got to drink?"

"The party was at St Hugh's," Guy reminded him, "You didn't tell me that the return match was here."

"Quick, quick, give me something to drink." He scrabbled around the room grabbing anything he could, and started biting a packet of nougat, not even bothering to take off the silver wrapping paper.

With a look of annoyance on his face, Guy handed him a glass of water.

He downed it in one and immediately held out the glass for more.

"Well?" said Guy irritably, "What have you done with your father's car? Have you drowned the bugger in Mercury?"

"No, I've embedded it in the front window of Boswells."

Guy looked impressed. "How did you manage to achieve that?"

Felix was unable to answer at first because he was so busy chewing at the sticky, gooey nougat through the silver paper.

"Do you think they will trace it back to me? My parents are away in Rhodesia. If the number plates got crushed, I'm alright. If they were to trace it to the house in Gloucester, do you think the housekeeper would tell the police I was here? My father doesn't know I borrowed the car, I don't have a licence."

"But you weren't driving the car tonight," said Guy. "It was taken and driven away by an oik from Blackbird Leys, who scarpered as soon as he realised that Boswells was closed for the night and he'd have to get his scrip from an all-night chemist."

"Then how did it get to Oxford in the first place?"

"Some yokel in the countryside needed to get to an urban centre in a hurry for a quick fix. He'd heard there was a lot of stuff available in a student centre like Oxford, so he drove it here. The housekeeper doesn't drive, does she, so she never noticed when it went missing from the garage. It could have been at any time. You've been in college lately, haven't you, so you have an alibi for all of them." He refilled the glass with water, and Felix downed it desperately. He noticed Guy starting to get dressed.

"What are you doing?" he asked worriedly. He became even more worried when Guy left the room. He looked at the girl huddled under the sheet. "Do you mind turning round," she said. "I want to get dressed."

"Oh. Yes." He continued foraging in the room. He found an orange and bit directly into it. While he was absentmindedly munching it, and worrying about what to do, Guy returned to the room, followed by a group of friends who had all hastily dressed.

"Where is it? Is it really in Boswells?" They were all terribly excited and very congratulatory.

"What are you all doing?" cried Felix in alarm.

"We're going to see it!" cried Guy, putting his shoes on. "Come on, darlin'," he called to the girl, who hastily slipped into an impossibly high pair of luscious red stilettos.

"She'll never get over the wall in them!" cried William.

"You haven't seen our Betty!" laughed Guy, "That's how she came in, and that's how she's coming back in afterwards!" They all laughed. "Shshsh!" cautioned Guy. "We can't all go over the same wall. Some of you go round the back, we'll meet up at Boswells."

It was about three o'clock in the morning when they arrived at the corner of Broad Street and Cornmarket. An enormous crowd had gathered. Late party goers and Hearties and Bloodies on their way back from a drunken dinner at the Bullingdon Club, still in their elegant if somewhat dishevelled evening dress, were enjoying the scene immensely. They were joined by intellectuals on their way back from dinner after a debate at the Arnold and Brackenbury Debating Society. There were three police cars, their blue beacons still flashing, and a fire appliance with its amber beacon lighting up the night. A line of police did their utmost to keep back the excited crush whose numbers swelled every moment as the news spread.

A tow-away truck arrived and slowly forced its way through the crowd. Every time the police moved into the shop to try to attach the steel tow-away hook to the back of the Ford, the Hearties and Bloodies shouted out in chorus, "Heave!!!" The police didn't know whether to be furious or amused. Instead, they were embarrassed, and wished the crowd would go away.

Some journalists arrived and pushed through the crush, anxious to get a photo before the car was extracted from the window.

To Felix's chagrin, the car, sitting neatly in the window, proudly displayed its clearly legible and undamaged rear number plate. Guy, with his arm tightly round Betty's waist, and with Felix miserably in tow, moved about in the crush looking for friends. He soon came up against the Balliol men, standing there in their pyjamas, silk dressing gowns and slippers, smoking their cigarettes from their long, indolent cigarette holders, all highly amused and exchanging witticisms with each other.

They were delighted when they saw Guy. "Anything to do with you?" they mused.

"Well, you know that the murderer always returns to the scene of the crime," he beamed. "I'm amazed you lot had the energy to come down. The others have got a ring side view from the windows."

Felix looked up. All the windows of Balliol were wide open, and thronged with cheering onlookers. Felix tugged anxiously at the sleeve of Guy's jacket.

Followed by Felix and his Balliol friends, Guy wormed his way as close to the police as he could. In a very loud voice, while purporting to be chatting to his friends, he said in his most aristocratic accent, "It's these fellows from Blackbird Leys. They will steal a man's car. But instead of hot-rodding it in their own high street, into their own shop windows, they will try it out for size in the Giler. Bloody good shot, of course, to get it into Boswells first go!"

"Are you suggesting this was intentional, Sir?" asked a very surprised police inspector.

"It's obvious," replied Guy. "They steal a car to hot-rod it for drag racing. But they have to try it out first. If they don't like it, and obviously they didn't like this one, they slam it into the first suitable shop they can find. You'll probably find they chose Boswells so they could make off with all the items in the drugs cabinet. But if the police were as efficient as they usually are, they would have got here too soon for these fellows to take anything." He smiled sweetly at the police inspector. "Don't you think so, Inspector?" The Inspector did not know what to make of him. He could not decide if he was being ragged or not.

Felix, standing at his elbow, nearly fainted, and had to hold on to Guy's arm for support.

Guy retreated slightly from the front ranks, and was soon engaged in noisy banter with the Balliol men who were leaning out of the windows. As the ripostes on either side became more and more ribald, the police inspector threatened to arrest him for indecent conduct. There would have been no way that he could have reached Guy to do so in all the jostling crush, and there was a risk if he tried that it would have provoked a riot. It was bad enough holding off all the Hearties and Bloodies who, amused at the total inability of the police or the firemen to move the car, were offering their leading rugby toughs to go in there and bodily pick up the car, and carry it off as a trophy. In their riotous drunkenness they hardly seemed to notice the danger of the remainder of the plate glass window shattering down upon them.

"If we keep the party going much longer," said one, "Alastair will turn up with his guitar and sing us one of his tuneless protest songs."

It was absurdly hot. The sun glinted infuriatingly on the turrets of all the glistening spires, making everything seem even hotter. Mark wandered along disconsolately with his jacket draped over his shoulder, sweating soggily under the armpits, as he followed them along the dusty path that led from the meadows, past Broadwalk and towards the Botanic Gardens. The way had never seemed so arduous, dry and dusty in the past, why did it seem so unbearable today. He followed their jolly voices and silly screaming past Corpus Christi and Merton. Other people were wandering by, so he could conceal himself to some extent behind them, but the noise they were making was so loud that he wouldn't have lost them even if he had had to trail even further in the distance to avoid detection. But there was no prospect whatsoever of his being noticed. Guy was far too busy shouting and laughing with the girls to be aware of anyone else on earth. And why did Guy need so many girls? Surely three or four would be more than enough. And what about the other boys, the ones who were carrying the drinks and the picnic hamper? Did not they feel left out, with almost all the attention being given to

Guy? Why on earth were they traipsing so far in the heat to the Botanic Gardens, when they could just as easily have had their picnic in Christ Church Meadow? If they were doing all this in order to take the punts from Magdalen Bridge, they could just as easily have taken punts from Christchurch.

If they did intend to go off in punts, then Mark would be unable to follow them further, and his day would be wasted. "I shall have wasted all that money on the ticket from London," he thought, "though I've wasted the money anyway. With all that crowd around him, there's absolutely no hope of approaching him at all." But he couldn't persuade himself to leave, however painful it was to continue to observe Guy enjoying himself and having such carefree fun with so many careless friends.

He watched from a distance as they settled themselves in the grounds of the Botanic Gardens on the soft green mossy bank of the Cherwell. The boys were busy setting out the tablecloth and opening up the hamper, and popping the champagne corks while Guy rolled on the bank with all the girls fighting to get on top of him. They were all screaming and frolicking and in great danger, at one moment, of all rolling down the bank into the water. When they all actually realised this, they all screamed even louder, and enjoyed the moment immensely, narrowly escaping a ducking.

While all this foolish adolescent behaviour continued, Mark, lying on the grass, gradually wormed his way forward. Other students were lying about on the grass, dotted about here and there, so his presence would not be noticed. Not that anybody was looking anyway, but just in case. They were now all shouting and telling each other jokes and tucking in to the lunch. Mark could hear some of the words, but not whole sentences because they all shouted across each other, and kept roaring with laughter. Apart from feeling extremely lonely, Mark suddenly felt terribly hungry. He felt inside his pocket. A half melted Mars Bar, but nothing to drink. Lying full in the hot sun, he felt dreadfully hot and thirsty. If he went off to try and get a drink, they might finish their lunch and then move off, and he might lose them. He couldn't eat the Mars Bar without a drink, and anyway it felt unappetisingly squashy and macerated. He lay there watching them, digging his nails into the turf and pulling at the grass. What a gulf now existed between him and Guy. How had it become possible? How had they once been such inseparable friends, and now he was reduced to the position of an unwanted outsider, a bug, a mere insect lying in the grass, who no longer existed as far as Guy was concerned.

The raucous sound of their voices faded slightly, and Mark mused to himself. He remembered one hot summer afternoon being taken to the Palazzo Maroncelli, where he had been shown some wonderful apartments decorated by Sebastiano Ricci. The ceilings in particular had impressed him, and one especially. Craning his neck and almost lying on his back he had looked up to a scene in which the young post-adolescent Eros, wearing nothing but a magnificently swirling rose-coloured cloth that only just hid a certain part of him – the best part, naturally – flew expansively above some disconcerted women who gazed longingly up at him.

Eros, beautifully painted and fully stretched out above them, with a blindfold tied lightly round his eyes and his quiver of arrows lightly slung round his shoulder about to empty all its contents upon the earth beneath, was utterly distraught by the fact that his magnificent wings were being assailed and ravaged by a horrible winged being that flew above him and was in the process of tearing out his feathers. The lips of Eros were parted in agony at the torment to which he was being subjected, his outstretched arm failing to ward off his assailant. Two horned Pan-like satyrs hovered menacingly below, waiting for the moment when, his feathers all plucked out, Eros would crash to earth into their power. The title of the painting was *La punizione d'Amore*. For what offence was Eros being punished?

And why was he, Mark, also being subjected to such a cruel punishment? After all, his only crime had been to fall in love, something he couldn't have helped, and over which he had had no control. He hadn't committed any other offence at all save that he had been constant in his affections. Why was such a hideous punishment being meted out to him? The desirable figure of Eros resembled that of the young Guy as he had been when Mark had first met him, and at that time he, too, had been unjustly punished.

In Guy's case perhaps it had resembled more the punishment of Tityus, where a powerless man, enchained and overwhelmed with love, was punished for a love that was too audacious. Guy's audacious passions and his provocative celebrations of them had provoked his enemies to an outrageous and savage punishment of him, even as the vulture had torn at and macerated the flesh of Tityus.

But the brutal plucking of the feathers from the wings of Eros much more closely resembled Mark's own fate when God had taken back from him his golden voice, and he had been dashed down to earth, condemned to grub about on its dusty surface as a mere mortal. Was it fair, then, that he should be punished twice, by also losing the love of the one and only being on earth whom he so constantly adored?

Mark remembered what they had told him at that time about the artist, the impetuous, fiery creator of this desirable Eros. Sebastiano Ricci had led such an ardent, passionate, turbulent life in his youth that he was obliged to flee from Venice to Bologna after committing a crime of love, *un delitto d'amore*. But they had never told him what it was. Then again, later, for another illicit love affair, *per altro illecito amore*, he had been obliged to escape to Turin. Mark imagined these broken hearts following him all over Italy. Angry and confused as to his own situation, his mind burning, Mark's attention was drawn again to the jovial picnic crowd, whose noisy rioting broke into his distant reverie.

As he started again to worm slightly further forward, he glanced through hooded eyelids to notice that they were finally packing up the hamper, and getting ready to leave.

Guy and the girls were all slightly tipsy, and staggered about even more foolishly than before as they began the long dusty walk back to Christ Church. Guy and the girls walked slightly ahead along the hot dusty path, laughing and tickling each other and messing around, and occasionally leaning on the iron fence, laughing and exhausted as they waited for the boys with the hamper and other items to catch up with them. The girls were jostling for the position of being the one in Guy's arms, and Guy was enjoying the situation immensely. They were pulling him this way and that, and at one moment were shrieking with pleasure as they undid his shirt and tried to pull it off.

In order not to be noticed by them, Mark had to keep pausing by the side of the railings, pretending at one moment to be examining his nails, which he noticed to be completely filthy and muddy, and at another time pretending to be tying up his shoe laces, or examining the contents of his empty pockets. He came across the Mars Bar again, this time completely melted, and irritably flung it away across the railings into the park, but not without some of the sticky contents remaining on his grubby hands. He then had to strain through the railings to reach some grass on which to wipe away the sticky goo.

The boys with the hamper eventually walked past him and joined the jolly crowd of Guy and the girls in front of him, and they finally returned along the path to Christ Church.

Mark noticed that everything was being set up for a cricket match. Obviously Guy was going to play, and in all probability was the captain of the team. Mark mingled among the crowded audience and was soon rendered invisible. He sat among the crowd knowing that now there was no chance whatever of Guy noticing him. He was right.

It wasn't long before the two teams arrived at the pavilion, and Guy, having changed into his elegant cricket whites and with his golden hair slicked back, led out his team to field, having won the toss and put in the team from Wadham to bat first. Of course Guy was doing all the bowling. At first he lulled the other team into a false sense of security by allowing them to score. Then he really hit them when they least expected it.

Mark had never seen him bowl so magnificently, even in his most glorious school days, nor had he ever seen him show off quite so outrageously.

Every time the ball hit the middle stump Guy would scream "Howzat!" loud enough to wake the sleepers in Duke Humphrey's Library, and leap high enough into the air to win the high jump.

His fans and admirers leapt into the air screaming, and the general level of behaviour was disgraceful.

The Wadham team was so demoralised by the deadly accurate bowling accompanied by the ferocious and triumphalist screaming that they were soon bowled out, and miserably went to take their tea in the desperate hope of better luck in the second half. But it was not to be.

Mark, who hadn't dared to go forward to join the crush taking tea, despite being starving and

desperately thirsty, but had skulked alone in the garden, now watched in amazement at the cocky way in which Guy then strutted out as he led his team out to bat.

Already demoralised, the bowlers of Wadham had tried to

keep their end up, manfully bowling at Guy with all their skill. But every time he hit a six, and almost knocked their heads off, and screamed in the most appallingly boastful way imaginable, they almost retreated before this physical and psychological intimidation. Despite their hopes and intentions, they practically conceded the match.

After Guy hit the winning six, the whole audience irrupted in cheering and screaming and streamed onto the pitch.

Mark was shocked at Guy's ecstatic celebration of his victory and his shamelessly arrogant triumph over his enemies. He watched as Guy was immediately surrounded by women jostling and flinging themselves into his arms, kissing him and hugging him, men straining in the crush to reach him and pat him on the back in heartiest congratulation.

It was Guy's apotheosis. Hailed as a god, he was swirled away in the joyous crowd, sweeping in through the great portals of Christ Church. Swelling with the rhapsody of flamboyant triumph, his supporters bore him like a river god riding the tide along the corridor and into the great courtyard.

Mark watched the excited cortege move away. He followed them only as far as the first alleyway, and then as they swept away to the left, he watched as they receded into the distance. He then turned right through a little wooden door into the Fellows' Garden.

How gloriously silent it was after all the racket and cheering. And how bejewelled and sparkling green the manicured lawn where even the angels of Christ Church Cathedral dared not tread. The banks of flowers were bursting with the most glorious blossoms of roses, begonias, hollyhocks, pinks, carnations of every colour and hue. The perfumes were overwhelmingly lovely. "It must be the most beautiful garden in the whole of Oxford," thought Mark, his grubby hand reaching out softly to stroke and caress the flowers as he felt no-one would ever again caress him. His hand glossed over the blue globe-like dome of a glorious bloom when he heard a voice say, "Enjoyed the cricket match?" and in shock his hand closed suddenly upon the globe, accidentally breaking it off. As he turned in surprise to face the speaker he held the guilty hand that had broken the blossom behind his back, crushing it and crumbling it in his nervous hand.

The man who stood before him was smiling at him quizzically. "Good cricket match, didn't you think?"

"Oh yes, absolutely." The remains of the crumpled flower floated to the ground behind his back.

"Like some tea?"

"Yes, I'd love some."

"Let's go and get some, then."

Mark trotted along obediently behind him.

"Studying at the college?"

"Yes."

"What's your subject?"

"History."

"Ah! That explains why I haven't seen you before. I'm Herbert Spurway, I teach Physics."

Mark followed him up a narrow staircase until they reached Herbert's rooms. "Aren't we going to have tea in college?" asked Mark.

"It's too late for that, they'll have finished serving. We'll have it here, do come in." He ushered him into his rooms. "Perhaps you'd like to wash your hands." All attempts at concealing the grimy fingernails from Herbert's hawk-like gaze had failed. Herbert followed him into the bathroom and handed him the nail brush. "Have a good scrub with this," he instructed.

When Mark had finished washing his hands, face and neck, he felt much better and returned to the sitting room where the tea was ready. He was ravenously hungry, and wolfed down the bread and butter and toasted tea cakes.

Herbert was highly entertained. "So what do you think of our Captain?" he asked.

"Most appalling show-off!"

"You speak as one who knows him."

"I was at school with him. He never behaved as bad as that there."

"Oh, I see," said Herbert gazing long and hard at him, and Mark felt furious with himself that he'd betrayed himself so thoughtlessly.

"You've had a long hot day," said Herbert solicitously. "Would you like to take a shower?"

The beautiful dark eyes shot suddenly at Herbert, quite unnerving him. "Well, yes, I would. Would you mind?"

"No, go right ahead, let me get you some towels."

Standing under the shower was so intensely refreshing. He watched all the shame and agony of the day swirl away down the drain along with the grime, sweat and pain. He soaked his long dark locks thoroughly, and made another determinedly furious effort with the nailbrush to brush Guy out of his fingernails along with the remainder of the mud from the meadows. Finally he wrapped the towels around him and returned to the sitting room, dripping water all over the expensive Persian carpet.

"Let me dry your hair," offered Herbert.

"No, I'll do it," said Mark, seizing the proffered towel roughly from Herbert's hand, and furiously rubbing his long hair with it. As he did so, the towel around his waist slipped accidentally to the floor and he made no effort to retrieve it. He sat down in the armchair with his legs spread wide, and looked directly into Herbert's eyes. "What do you want me to do?"

Herbert quickly looked away.

Now completely naked, and still rather wet, Mark walked slowly into the adjacent bedroom and extended himself languidly along the bed. Still looking directly at Herbert, he said, "How much will you give me?"

"Twenty pounds," said Herbert, opening his wallet and taking out the money, which he stuffed into the pocket of Mark's jacket, and followed him into the bedroom. "Do you mind if I draw the curtains?" he asked.

Mark looked at him. "One of them," he thought, as he lay face down on the bed, waiting to be pierced by Herbert who obviously did not wish to be seen in the act.

It was all over very quickly. "Mark," gasped Herbert. "I want to do this again later, in a more leisurely way. Let me take you out to dinner. Will you stay the night?"

"Are you sure?" asked Mark. "If I stay the night you'll have to pay me more."

"Another thirty pounds?" Again he removed the money from his wallet and quickly placed it in the jacket pocket.

Mark reclined back languidly on the bed, his arms folded behind his head.

Herbert's eyes ranged greedily over the voluptuous body displayed before him.

"You'll have to set the alarm clock for very early tomorrow morning," said Mark.

"You don't want to be seen leaving my rooms."

"I have to catch the ten to seven train to London tomorrow."

"When are you coming back to Oxford?"

"Whenever you want me to, as long as you pay."

"So, you're not a student here?"

"No, I have to work in a bank in London. I must get into the bank tomorrow, I can't risk being late."

"Tell me about your time at school."

"No. I know what you want me to talk about, but I don't want to talk about it. Some other time, perhaps, but not now. Would you like me to kiss you? You have to tell me what you want."

"No, you know I can't. Just do it."

It was very misty the following morning as Mark hurriedly walked to the station. He had to stand in the queue with the usual commuters and buy another ticket since the half stub of the day return of the previous day was out of date and invalid. But at least he had the money for the ticket.

"Change at Didcot," said the inspector as he clipped his ticket at the barrier.

"I'll have it here," said Mark softly to himself. "At least I'll get to Paddington by eight thirty, and I should get to the bank by nine fifteen if I can fight my way onto the underground in the rush hour."

By nine twenty he walked into his office.

Ian was already at his desk. "Successful day? I made a good excuse for you, they believed me. You might have phoned. Did you get to speak to him?"

"No, but I spent the day trailing about after him, which I suppose is the next best thing. I got picked up. Look at this." He proudly displayed the money in front of Ian, spreading it out like a fan. "What do you think of this?"

Ian was very impressed. "Just one night?"

"Yes, just a few more regulars like that and I could quit this tedious job. I'm no good at banking, I'll never get to the stage where I earn serious money. I don't want to plod along all my life, and yet these punters aren't reliable either. What if they get arrested? What if they pick up a prettier boy, then they'll drop me like a hot potato!"

"But at least you've learned your lesson about Guy, you're going to give up on this obsession of following him around."

"Who on earth said so? Why should I? If this don goes on paying for me to visit him in Oxford, it will pay for me to go wandering around checking up on Guy."

"But to what end?" asked Ian seriously. "What's the purpose of it all, if he spends all his time enjoying himself with other people?"

Mark's sweet face became immeasurably sad. He sat down silently at his desk.

Ian hovered solicitously nearby.

Mark's face was turned up sadly to gaze into the concerned look of Ian moving towards him. "You think I should give it up?"

"For your sake, I really think so."

"That's because you have never walked in the red hot fire of passion, your life is dull and colourless, you have no conception of the unendurable suffering that I am daily going through. If you had any idea at all …" His voice trailed off, he hung his head down and turned his tormented face away.

Henry was recovering from flu, and lay in bed in his room in Christ Church.

Clelia came to visit him, and was reading to him. She was sitting some distance from him. The curtains were closed and Clelia was reading by a small yellow lamp. Henry had his eyes fixed upon her.

Suddenly and totally unexpectedly Guy came marching into the room to ask Henry if he could borrow a book. He was unaware that Henry had been ill, and totally unaware that Clelia was in the room up until the moment when, in total panic, and gathering up a garment, she fled out of the room past Guy and raced on down the corridor. Guy was amazed. "What were you doing in here?" he accused.

"Here I am dying, what could I possibly be doing?"

"What was she doing?"

"Reading to me."

"So why did she run out like that? Where has she gone? Why was she undressed?"

Henry didn't reply.

"What was she doing? What were you doing?" Guy shouted at him. In her flight, Clelia had left the door open and boys in the corridor could hear Guy shouting. Since Henry wouldn't reply, Guy seized him fiercely by the throat and started shaking him violently all the while screaming at him, "Tell me what you were doing! Tell me what you were doing!"

The boys at the door immediately raised the alarm and an enormous crowd gathered while a number of them pulled off the infuriated Guy and clung onto him tightly to restrain him. They all shouted to each other to go and get Matthew, the famous Captain of the School, from school days, who was believed to be the only person on earth who could exercise any form of control over Guy, and who was the only member of Pop for whom Guy had ever had any respect.

Clelia, now dressed but without her shoes, hovered inconspicuously and nervously at the back of the crowd that had gathered in and around Henry's room and blocked the corridor.

The members of the college always found Guy's activities highly entertaining, and no-one wanted to miss the show. They all gathered expectantly, and made way for Matthew to push his way through the crush into the room.

"Control yourself, Guy!" he immediately ordered as soon as he entered the room. "Tell me what happened," he commanded, turning to the others.

"He's trying to kill Henry," a chorus of voices shouted.

"You can't kill Henry, he's ill," said Matthew in amazement. "You can't kill a man who's ill."

"He's not ill," shouted Guy furiously. "That's just an excuse so that he can screw my fiancée. He's always trying to get her, and now that I've caught him, he tries to pretend he's ill."

They all looked at Henry, who was still lying in bed. "It's all untrue," he protested.

"Then what was she doing naked in your room? You didn't expect me to come in, did you? You thought you could get away with it because I never normally come to your room."

"No, you're too busy screwing girls in your own room to visit him!" shouted one of the boys. The others laughed.

"Let him have one girl," said another boy. "You have so many. He never has a girl, it's not fair."

"He can have any girl he likes, he only has to ask me, there are always spare girls," said Guy magnanimously. "He can't have my fiancée and he knows it. I've told him before. Now he has to be punished."

"We're not still at school," commented Piers, who had been at Eton with them. "You have no right to punish him, Guy, you never made it to Pop anyway, you'll have to challenge him to a duel."

At this the whole crowd became extremely excited, and began to discuss how it would be fought and what weapons would be chosen. Many of them were in favour of it being a drinking duel, to be staged in a "War and Peace" Hussar style standing balanced precariously on a window sill at the top of the college. Whether any of them had ever read the book was uncertain, but they had all seen the recent film. They were animatedly discussing where the best place to stage it would be, and who would take the bets as to who would win.

Robert, who was studying Zoology, suggested an anthropomorphic explanation. "The idea is taken from the deer in his father's park," he announced as he began his disquisition. "Guy, who has corralled all the female doe in his rooms, is facing up like a young buck to his rival antagonist, ready to lock antlers with him and rout him from the field. The young aggressive male, in the rutting season," the boys all just fell about in hysterical mockery at this, "has to rout all other rutting or would-be rutting males, who, once defeated by superior force and strength of antlers, are left without any females at all, and are forced to content themselves with playing with each other."

There was enormous merriment from the boys, and furious rage from Guy, who wrestled ferociously with those restraining him, and tried to get at Henry and Robert.

"Just because everybody else finds it so amusing doesn't mean I'll let you get away with it," threatened Guy.

"Whatever you do, do it quickly," mocked Albert. "Remember, Guy, the doe – oops, sorry, the girls in your room – are getting restless."

"There are no girls in my room," said Guy furiously. "I'm busy working."

"Must be the first time this year," said another boy.

"Bring the girls here," suggested another voice. "Bring a few here now, to Henry, he'll give you back your fiancée, and the case will be solved."

"Yes, how about that?" mocked some of the boys in chorus.

"Henry needs them," said another boy. "Bring him some, you said he can have some."

Henry's eyes narrowed in fury, and he spat fiercely at Guy. "I won't let you get away with this, Blandford."

"And nor will you!" cried Guy furiously, again desperately trying to shake off those restraining him in order to lunge at

Henry. They held on to him as tightly as they could, and Matthew placed himself in between.

"Now, how did you describe the fiancée, Henry?" asked Albert mockingly. "'A kite torn to pieces by fauns' was it, if I remember correctly?"

"Or was it, 'A candyfloss floating in the wind,' I think?" mocked Piers, and all the boys roared with laughter.

"Go on, someone," said Albert. "Get the latest copy of *Isis*, let's read the latest love poems to the fiancée. The poet ought to be allowed an audience, don't you think, Guy, and here we all are. We'll judge who is more poetic, and hence more fit to have the delectable fiancée."

"And guess what," cried Piers. "Henry's poems are deemed to be of such high quality that Walters are planning to include them in their series of Walters' Guide to British Institutions in the Oxford Man's Shop, Ten the Turl! I'm sure the next edition will also include a cartoon of this very encounter we're all taking part in!"

All the boys thought that this was hilarious. Both Guy and Henry found the ridicule intolerable, and as their school-mates knew, it was always the best way to end their frequent squabbling.

Finally everybody went away. Guy alone remained, standing in the empty corridor and looking out of the window into the grey quad, where the ice-cold rain was sleeting down.

Clelia stood nervously some distance away.

After a while Guy turned to face her. "There are no girls in my room. Will you come there?"

"Not there, somewhere else."

"When?"

"Tonight."

"Will you?"

"Yes."

He remained where he was, leaning against the window.

She moved slowly towards him and put her arms round him.

"You see how much trouble your behaviour causes me."

"I won't do it again."

"Will you give up Henry?"

"I never took him up in the first place. We only ever studied together, that's all, and he really is ill at the moment, it's not an excuse. I like him but I've never loved him, and I've never led him on. He knows I don't love him, I've always told him that."

Guy looked at her rather severely. "I suppose you'll always do things your own way."

She smiled sweetly. "Yes."

"So we'll meet tonight?"

"Where will it be?"

"I have a friend who has a house in Jericho. I'll arrange it with him. We'll have dinner together, but it will have to be rather rushed as I have so much work to do. I'm much further behind than I realised. I'll have to work very intensely to catch up. I'll call for you at Somerville at eight."

Clelia was ready with her overnight bag when Guy arrived. There was very little time to eat, so they went to a small cafe in Little Clarendon Street. They then walked to the Hart Street house in Jericho where Guy's friend was waiting for them and offered them his room.

Guy's plan was to be very sweet and loving and tender, but when it came to it he was so overwhelmed by passion and desire that he was unable to restrain himself, and could hardly wait for Clelia to get her clothes off before grabbing hold of her and seizing her very roughly. Considering how many women he usually had, Clelia was overwhelmed by his intensity, but she was surprised at how soft and sensual he was. It was certainly something to do with the intense physicality of his beauty, and she did feel at certain moments that it was like making love to a masterpiece of Praxiteles carved lovingly in Parthian marble, with the added advantage that he was surprisingly sensitive to her feelings and concerned that she should enjoy the experience as much as he undoubtedly did. Clearly, as he had boasted to her, he was an absolute expert, and he knew exactly where to touch, caress, kiss, suck and lick every part of her in order to bring her to orgasm many times. She looked up into those amazingly lovely blue eyes gazing lovingly down at her, and, in the midst of all the intense pleasure, was genuinely puzzled. Did he love her? Was he capable of knowing what love really was? Was she? The pleasure was so intense, did she need anything more than this? Was there something else, could there be?

He woke her up several times during the night to continue the process of pleasure, and they were both exhausted when the sunlight began to filter into the curtainless room. Guy held her very tightly. "I've never passed such a naked night. We'll do it again tonight. But we have to get up now because there are so many things I have to do today."

"What are they?"

"The men are coming from my father's estate to throw out everything from my room. Today and tomorrow they are going to spend decorating the room, and then they are going to bring some furniture that I've chosen to refurnish it. In the meantime Matthew has said that I can study in his room until my room is ready." Clelia gazed at him in wonder. "You're amazed, aren't you. You didn't believe that I could change, did you?"

"But what about when all the girls start knocking on the

door?"

"Last night I left a notice on the door to say that I would not be receiving any visitors. For the next few days I won't be there, so they are sure to give up. They'll soon get the message."

While they were hastily dressing, Guy asked casually, "Is Nigel coming up this weekend?"

"Yes, he's coming on Friday."

"Could we have dinner with him Friday night?"

"Yes, why not?"

"You'll be seeing him before dinner?"

"Yes, probably."

"Do you think you could ask him if he would have time to tutor me for Schools?"

"Do you think you need it?"

"I know I need it."

"What about your tutors?"

"I can't really go to them. I've behaved very badly towards them. I know they're cross with me. I can't even do a normal tutorial with them now, I've fallen out badly with them. Anyway, leaving that aspect aside, they have nothing they can offer me. That's basically why I was never enthusiastic in going to them. One of them was hopelessly confusing, another one smoked all over me."

"Really?"

"Yes, you know what Stephen Leacock says about it. He says the hideous truth about the tutorial system is that what an Oxford tutor does is get a group of students together and smoke at them. Men who have been systematically smoked at for four years turn into ripe scholars."

Clelia laughed.

"But darling," said Guy taking her hand, "what I really need is some very intensive tuition from someone really brilliant like

Nigel. He hasn't forgotten anything about his studies here, and he has an original and well-trained mind. In fact, he's a person of quite exceptional originality of mind. He's highly sophisticated, enigmatic, subtle, penetrating and stimulating."

"Do you really think that?"

"Yes, don't you? I remember you saying that he helped you enormously with your A Levels. Individual tuition is so important, we always had it at school where we could choose our own tutors in the subjects we selected, and you always had a very close rapport with your tutor which encouraged you and helped you to work well. I have never established that sort of rapport with my tutors here, and my awful behaviour has just pissed them off. It's difficult, well-nigh impossible for me to get in touch with them now for the sort of intensive tuition that I need. Also I like to think that Nigel and I get on quite well, despite our obvious differences and his general disapproval of me. Perhaps you can tell him of my plans to change, if you think that will help."

Clelia had managed to find the books that Guy needed, and took them to Christ Church to give them to him. As she walked along the corridor of the House, the boys who happened to be there stared at her. As she arrived at Matthew's room, the group of boys studying with Guy all fell silent, and stared at her. Nature abhors a vacuum, and so did Guy, who used the opportunity to run forward, seize hold of her and kiss her violently on the lips. This made the boys stare even more.

Clelia drew him outside into the corridor in order to escape from this oppressive scrutiny. She knew that it wasn't in his character to keep a secret, but she could not have imagined that he would have gone around the college telling everyone of their passionate embraces. Later she was to discover that with his closest friends he had gone much further than that, giving them a far more intimate account of everything that had transpired between them in their nights together, describing his feelings and emotions and analysing them in detail. It was almost as if he were trying to discover why it was so different from all his earlier encounters, and why everything mattered so much more to him than at any earlier stage in his life.

To leave the college, Clelia hurried through old passages, old staircases, old chambers decorated with old portraits, in the midst of which she walked as it were in the early seventeenth century. It was dark and there was very little light, and she was hurrying along in a daze, worried about whether Guy would ever be able to study enough to catch up. A dark, slightly bent-over figure was shuffling along the corridor near the beautiful old hall, clutching books under his arm and muttering to himself. Hoping that the dusty darkness made her almost invisible, she tried to glide past him unobserved. She had almost achieved this when the sharp claws that he stuck into her side made her shriek with terror.

The eyes pierced her equally hatefully. He clung on to her forcefully, his books gliding noiselessly to the stone floor. "He's told absolutely everybody. Everybody knows what a slut you are. You didn't bargain for that, did you?"

"Please let me go, your nails are hurting me!"

"He's also told them every single detail of everything. I see why you're trying to sneak out unseen. You can't face anyone here, or anywhere else. They know every last detail about you. They all know you're a whore, just like all the other slags who threw themselves at him, and were then discarded by him. You liked to think that you were superior to them, but in fact everything shows that you were worse than them."

Clelia froze in horror at these words, and the hateful way

they were spat at her.

"You did it all to spite me, didn't you?" he went on, relentlessly. "You did it to show your contempt of me! You didn't do it for any feelings you have for him, I know you have none, you couldn't care less about him. You did it to show your contempt for me!"

"No, no, no!"

He was gripping her very tightly. "Tell me, then," he said with icy coldness. "Tell me why you did it, after everything we'd talked about, after everything you always said about saving yourself." He gazed into her face, as though he were trying to read an ancient manuscript. "Tell me, I really do want to know. You constantly refused me for higher motives. You said that you had to preserve yourself. So why did you do it with him?"

She looked at the tortured face that was turned towards her, the twisted, agonised mouth that could hardly articulate the words, the expression that told her that at any moment he would crumble and collapse.

"I wish you didn't hate me quite so much," she said softly.

"I don't hate you," he said bitterly, turning his face away so that she could no longer see his feelings, all too painfully revealed in his expression.

"Let's go somewhere, then I can talk to you."

"No, there's no point. I don't want to talk to you. I really don't have anything to say to you, and anything you would say to me would not be the truth. It never has been. That's how you are." He bent down wearily and scrabbled about trying to pick up his books. "I suppose you did it to help Guy get through his exams, but it couldn't have come at a worse moment for me. I really don't know how I'm supposed to concentrate on my work with every conversation in college turning on what you're like in bed, and who thinks he's going to be next as soon as Guy moves on to the next girl and you become generally available."

Clelia looked aghast. "It can't really be like that, can it?"

"You didn't think about any of this, did you? Callous and careless, that's all you are. Now you've lost everything, and," he mumbled as all the badly balanced books fell to the stone floor again, "so have I." He finally managed to bundle the books together, and slowly continued on his way.

Clelia snuggled down in Nigel's bed in the Randolph Hotel. Nigel had tuned the hotel radio to the Third Programme and they were listening to a delicious performance of Brahms's Violin concerto.

"The Romantic Movement taught us that music is by far the greatest of the arts. It has the power to transport us from our dull earthly bodies away into the stratosphere, it transforms and transcends all that is merely mortal, passionate, corporeal into something, somewhere, above all these; it is otherworldly, divine!" said the presenter.

Clelia was going through her usual summary of the week's events, and, in her inimitable style, making it, as always, witty and humorous for Nigel's amusement. She was mocking very slightly at Guy's character, but trying at the same time to convey the impression of how he had changed so radically that she could lead up deftly to the idea that it would be suitable for Nigel to tutor him, when she suddenly heard herself saying, "but that all happened after I slept with him."

Nigel leapt so violently from the bed that Clelia gasped in surprise. He turned the radio off so fiercely that the knob broke off in his hand. "What did you say?" he said to her so aggressively that she immediately feared for her own safety. He launched himself at her and seized her ferociously by the shoulder, gripping her hard. "What did I hear you say?"

Clelia tried to pull herself away from his grip, but he held her tight.

"Perhaps I mis-heard. Perhaps you didn't say it." He placed his face very close to hers and glared at her with an expression that she had never seen before and that was deeply menacing.

She began to feel very sick and realised that her face was wet with tears.

"Perhaps you said it but perhaps you didn't do it. Tell me you didn't do it. I can't believe that you did it."

"Nigel, please, please," she pleaded with him, desperately trying to pull away.

He held her in a vice-like grip as if he would break her arm. "I can't believe it, you didn't actually do it? After everything we talked about? Not with him? Not with a total, utterly – " He groped about, stumbling, seeking for a word, but was unable to find one. "Tell me you didn't, I don't believe you could have done, you utterly despise him, as I do. Tell me it isn't true."

She desperately wanted to tell him that it wasn't true, but she knew with regret and bitterness that she could not.

He looked at her soaking wet face with a puzzled expression. "So you really are a callous, careless little tart! That's all you are! Why on earth am I wasting my time on you? And I thought I was going to marry you." He quickly got off the bed and started to dress and pack methodically, speaking in a bitter, controlled and chillingly cold voice. "You realise that you have totally destroyed our relationship, you do realise that? It is as if you had taken it up between your careless little hands and torn it into a thousand little shreds of – of – " Once again he was stumbling, almost collapsing, unable to find the word.

"Nigel, no, no!" She tried to grasp hold of him but he pushed her roughly aside.

"You do understand that this is the end? And, I am, perhaps, the only person – "

"Nigel, please, you are the only person – "

"Of course, you understand that he will despise you as much as I do? You do understand that you have compromised yourself for ever, with anyone of quality?"

"Nigel, please don't leave me!"

He was moving off towards the door with his suitcase in his hand. "We won't see each other again," he said dramatically as he opened the door, preparing to sweep through it. The sound of voices in the corridor and people walking by caused him to step back sharply into the room and close the door. He leaned heavily against it, still clutching the suitcase, and this gave Clelia the chance to run to him and grab hold of him. He looked dazed and shocked.

"I swear I'll never do it again! Don't be so unrelenting with me. I don't quite know how it happened! It won't happen again!"

"You think that makes it all better? What a total swine he is! And as for you!!"

She could see that his anger was beginning to flare up again.

"I just don't understand you, after everything we said!"

"It was something to do with getting him to change and sit down and study and get on with his exams."

"But what on earth has that got to do with you?"

"There was a very bad argument between him and Henry, at his college."

"Oh, and I suppose that you slept with him too?"

"No, of course not."

"Really, you surprise me! What held you back?"

"His studies for his exams are going all right."

"Good, I'm glad to hear it. Anyone else in difficulty?"

"Guy really is in difficulty. He wants you to tutor him for

Schools."

At this Nigel really did explode. He flung down his suitcase, tore off his jacket and looked at her in total disbelief. "You aren't really telling me that after behaving dishonourably towards you, and insulting me, he actually expects me to help him with his exams when he has been too feckless to bother to study for the whole year?"

"Nigel," said Clelia quietly, while looking at him intensely. "He doesn't know anything about us. How can he possibly? Nobody does." She pulled him down onto the bed beside her. He looked very surprised. She was rationalising after the event, and trying very hard to cover up for her disastrous gaffe. "No-one even suspects about us. But in view of the closeness of our relationship I felt that I had to tell you about the situation with Guy. Now it will make him calm down and get on with his work. But he can't do it without your help. He's really relying on it. Only you can save him."

"You're not in love with him?"

"You know I'm not. I never have been. You know that."

"Then I don't understand any of it," he said weakly.

"I don't quite know how it happened. I don't have a relationship with him. I hardly ever see him."

"So did you both just stumble into bed with each other by accident, each thinking it was someone else?"

"There was an argument between him and Henry."

"I don't want to hear about that. They are perfectly good friends. I know that there was an intellectual rivalry between them when they were at school, but that's perfectly normal. It's all about who comes first in Final Order. In my case too there was always someone who thought that he should beat me to being first in Final Order, but he always failed."

"But this time Guy has to get a First in Schools, which Henry is bound to do anyway."

"And he has to get you."

"No, that really won't happen again. But you have to help him. He's going to discuss how you will tutor him at dinner tonight."

He gazed at her in amazement. "You really have got such a bloody nerve! I suppose you've already promised this to him?"

"Darling." She put her arms lovingly round him and started to kiss him. She knew what he liked, and thanks to George, she knew how to give it to him.

At dinner that evening at the Elizabeth they all looked the ultimate in elegance, the men in dinner jackets and black ties, and Clelia in a dark green and amber sequinned dress.

Guy was politeness personified, listening attentively to all Nigel's advice about how to prepare for the exams, and calling him "Sir" on a number of occasions.

Henry was polite but pointedly distant as far as Clelia was concerned, addressing not a single word to her save where good manners could not avoid it, and studiously avoiding eye contact with her. He also listened attentively to the advice about the exams.

At the end of the meal they were obliged to sit together in silence while Nigel took Guy to another table for a private talk. Nigel ordered brandies, but it wasn't certain if they were to steady his or Guy's nerves.

"I want to know if your intentions are honourable," he said very severely.

Guy was completely taken aback. "But of course they are, Sir, you know they are, we're engaged, James gave his consent, you remember."

"You are not married yet. You can't behave as if you are. Your father has specifically refused his consent, and said that you can't marry before you are twenty-five."

"I wish you'd go and speak to him, Sir, once the exams are over. Of course, James can't go and speak to him, that's the reason for the refusal."

"I hardly have time in my busy schedule to give tutorials to you, and I certainly don't have time to go and have a wrangle with your father. While you're preparing for exams you have no time for any extra-curricular activities, and they are to cease at once. Is this understood?"

Guy lowered his eyes under this withering glare and murmured, "Yes, Sir."

As they were leaving and getting their cloaks, Guy, bending over Clelia as he adjusted her long black velvet evening cape, murmured in her ear, "Why on earth did you tell him? He didn't need to know. Now he's forbidden it. What are we going to do?"

"We can't do it anyway while he's in Oxford," she whispered back. "He's determined to keep a close watch on us while he's in Oxford, you know what these old fuddy-duddies are like. If you don't have a moral tutor, at least I do."

"Was he angry with you?"

"Yes, completely furious, so we had better be careful until the end of the weekend."

That night she was particularly loving to Nigel as they lay in bed at the Randolph Hotel. No mention was made of the earlier scene, and Clelia was desperate that they should resume the smooth-running nature of their relationship.

Nigel was deeply disturbed, but more amazed with himself at how badly he had reacted. He had no idea that he had been capable of such insane jealousy. He was also surprised that one thought kept going round and round in his mind. "When he has so many women, why does he have to steal the only one that I have?"

The following morning, at nine o'clock as arranged, Nigel attended Guy's rooms in Christ Church. He was pleasantly surprised by the new decorations, particularly the ornate pelmet and the golden damask curtains draping down to the floor, the rich silk fabric interwoven with designs and figures picking up the brilliant morning sunshine that streamed into the study. Word had got about that Nigel was holding a tutorial, but this was widely interpreted as though it were a seminar. All those in college who heard about it and who were facing Schools were anxious to come along and take advantage of Nigel's skills and knowledge.

As he entered, Nigel found Guy sitting ready at his desk, holding his essay, and an eager gathering of a number of young men who wanted to listen and then participate in the discussion. He recognised some of them. Henry was included in the number.

Nigel settled himself comfortably in the red velvet antique high backed armchair that had been brought from Malplaquet, and invited Guy to read his essay.

Guy read the essay carefully and thoughtfully, and then waited politely for Nigel's comments.

Nigel paused for a moment, and then started a series of questions, simple and innocuous at first, but gradually building up in intensity, complexity and power.

Guy weathered the initial questions well enough. As the bombardment continued he took a deep breath and braced himself for a lengthy session. Nigel's tone, initially methodical and enquiring gradually became more searching and probing.

Having established the basis and groundwork of his cross-examination, he began to step up the pace and intensity with piercing precision.

He moved on expertly in the interrogation, catching Guy out here, luring him into traps or illogical arguments there, with all the skill of a practised inquisitor.

As Guy squirmed and shifted uneasily in his chair the pace continued relentlessly. Guy remained polite throughout even as Nigel's style and manner began to shift from the interested and enquiring to the harsh and condemnatory. The questions he now asked were sharp, incisive and lethal.

Nigel was sneering, contemptuous, even, of Guy's essay, almost, those in the audience felt, as if he had deliberately set out to humiliate him before the others. Even though the other students thought his answers were good, even excellent, Nigel picked fault with them, belittled them, diminished them and by implication, castigated Guy for failing to study properly and read widely. At each answer that Guy gave, Nigel would deliberately quote an author that Guy had not mentioned, and by implication, had not read, thereby underlining his lack of study and general ignorance.

Guy was forced more and more onto the defensive, and was forced to retreat more and more into the darker recesses of his mind where all his schoolboy reading was stored, and pray it in aid. He defended himself valiantly, although as the attack increased in ferocity, he became ever more disconcerted. He was concentrating very hard on the cut and thrust of the interrogation, but his mind was also ranging wildly as to precisely why Nigel was subjecting him to this particularly humiliating form of torture, humiliating enough as an intellectual exercise had they been doing this alone, but even more devastating in its destructive power by the fact that Henry and the others, having come, as they thought, to learn from Nigel, were witnessing the total degradation of their colleague and school-mate.

Henry and the others, as they looked on and listened in amazement, could only puzzle at why Nigel was behaving like this. As it continued they were forced to admire Guy's perseverance under fire, and his courage at fighting back. Henry, clever as he was, did not believe that he himself would have been able to withstand such a withering, oppressive assault, but Guy rallied manfully, and after the initial shock and retreat, was now beginning to fight back, and give as good as he got, but politely, and without any sense of acrimony.

The battle persisted a little while longer, and then Nigel seemed to change his mind. He started to make constructive criticisms, and the whole mood in the room began to change. They began to discuss the subject like equals.

Guy made suggestions that Nigel acknowledged as good. The audience felt that they could breathe more easily for Guy's sake. Guy's hot, red, sweaty face looked less frantic, his tense body less taut. He concentrated more on the argument now, less on Nigel's motives for seeking to crush him so devastatingly.

Then, at a certain moment, Nigel became silent. He sat there in deep thought. They imagined that he was concentrating on dreaming up a really difficult question, and all craned eagerly forward to hear what he would say next when he shot his next barbed arrow. But he seemed to be away from the scene in a sort of trance. The room was pervaded with silence.

Guy strained forward, his eye fixed on Nigel's face. Great Tom boomed forth that it was one o'clock.

Called back to earth from his reverie, Nigel announced in a matter-of-fact voice that it was lunchtime, and said that he would return at two o'clock. When Guy, relieved that there was to be a break in the ordeal, said that he, too, would go to lunch, Nigel retorted very sharply, "Certainly not! You don't believe for a moment, do you, that you have got time for lunch? You'll spend the lunch-hour writing an essay for me on: 'Was Hobbes the first political scientist?' When I get back from lunch, you'll read it to me, and we'll discuss it." He then left the room.

Guy almost collapsed onto the bed. The others all crowded round him, congratulating him on his courage under fire, and saying how well they thought he'd done. As Giles mopped his brow with a flannel, and offered to bring him lunch on a tray, Guy asked anxiously, "Do you think it will be the same this afternoon?"

"No," said Richard. "I think he's shot out all his spleen, and taught you a lesson about the folly of not studying and leaving everything to the last minute. Now I think he'll get down to the real business of cramming into you as many good ideas as possible to prepare you for the exams. But he won't respect you at all if you don't get on with the essay."

Giles went off to get lunch for Guy, and the others went off for lunch in hall.

Henry remained. He was deeply curious as to the meaning of what they had all witnessed. He also felt a strange, inexplicable need to rally round and help Guy, particularly in view of the savage battering he had received. They sat together plotting out the essay, and Henry had some very useful suggestions to make, while Guy discussed them and made notes.

When Nigel returned at precisely two o'clock there was a buzz of excitement among the enlarged audience in the room. The word had spread about that morning's flaying, but the audience mainly consisted of serious students who really wanted to avail themselves of the chance to learn from someone as brilliant and knowledgeable as Nigel.

The afternoon settled down to a long and serious debate about the subject. Nigel and Guy discussed the subject as equals, fulfilling their roles as master and pupil. There was no repetition of the morning's duel, nor even as much as an echo of it.

The debate continued until late in the afternoon, and the other students all participated in it, with great profit for all of them. It was agreed that they would all assemble the next day, but Nigel firmly rejected the suggestion that another student could volunteer to write the essay.

He insisted that it should be written by Guy, regardless of how late it required him to stay up that night. Looking round at all the straining, eager faces, and speaking like one of his own and their severe school masters, he said, "And don't think I don't know all about that business of another student writing the essay and giving it to Guy to read. I've heard two essays by Guy today, and I shall know at once if you try to palm someone else's essay on me!" He looked at Guy's exhausted face. "You can have dinner tonight. I'll take you out to the Fitzherbert Rooms." He was amazed when all the boys cheered.

After Nigel and Guy had set off for dinner, boys ran around eagerly in the corridors. "Did you witness the flaying of Marsyas?"

"Yes, it was quite remarkable. Why did Nigel do it?"

"It was merciless. Did he do it because he tried to sing better than Apollo?"

"Did he do it to shame him because he knows he hasn't studied all year?"

"Guy appealed to him to help him, because he's hopelessly behind with his work, and maybe Nigel felt that it was the only way of bringing it home to him."

"But Guy knows that anyway, it didn't have to be demonstrated quite so publicly, and in some a humiliating way." They were all impressed with the courage with which Guy had handled it.

Henry listened to these debates and took part in them. He knew Nigel well, and was genuinely puzzled by the fact of Nigel behaving so totally out of character. He wondered whether it fitted into a private theory of his own, that he had thought for some time in relation to Clelia and the recent events. Did it mean that Nigel also knew all about that, as did the whole of Oxford?

Patrick called in on Guy and admired the transformation of the room.

"You've done wonders here. But there's something I don't understand. I gather you're actually working."

"It's about time, don't you think? Schools is in three weeks' time. I'm determined to get a First. I always intended to do that."

"So why didn't you work before?"

"Madness not to."

"I hear you've got a private tutor."

"So you heard that story, how he flayed me alive, like Marsyas."

"It's gone all round Oxford." Patrick laughed.

Guy looked chagrined. "I suppose everyone's heard it."

"But why do you need to work?" asked Patrick. "I don't."

"Of course you do, don't pretend."

"No, I don't, even though I'm doing two degrees."

"You can't be, it's not allowed."

"Yes it is, you just go and sign up for another degree."

"What did you sign up for?"

"Modern Greats!" said Patrick portentously.

"As well as History?"

"Yes, now I'm doing both."

"But how can you study for both?" asked Guy in amazement. "There isn't time, I'm having a problem studying now just for PPE."

"But it's easy. For Economics, I read *The Economist* each week so that I'm fully informed on the up to date situation of the economy. For Politics, I read *The Times* every day."

"Not the court columns, I hope."

Patrick laughed and replied, "No. For Philosophy, it's just plain common sense."

"You must be joking. What about all the great thinkers from Plato and Aristotle onwards?"

"Guy, the great advantage for both of us is that we studied a lot of these thinkers at school, and certainly all the Greek thinkers in Classical Studies. If you'd decided to read Greats you would have walked through and got your First without any of the bother of studying."

"That's precisely why I chose to read PPE. I wanted to pit myself against something new, and study in depth a number of the thinkers we had mentioned in school. The Classics would have been far too easy."

"Well, it's the same with me, I've got enough background in Philosophy to sit the exam, all the rest is common sense."

"What kind of degree do you expect to get?"

"It's not the kind of degree that matters, you get a degree anyway here. If I get a Third in History, it's just as good, even a Fourth isn't a failure."

"For me, anything less than a First is a total failure. If I don't get a First, I'll kill myself," said Guy earnestly.

"What about your beautiful fiancée? "

"If I don't get a First, she won't want me."

"Has she said that?"

"No, of course not, but I know I won't be worthy of her, and I'll kill myself anyway." He looked at Patrick whose face bore that usual mocking glow. "You don't believe me, do you, but I assure you that I cannot, cannot, live with a Second, and if I do not get a First I shall commit suicide!"

"How will you do it?" came the sneering reply. "Run through the Meadow and leap fully clad in ermine and coronet into the Isis at the boat station? You swim too well, you'd never allow yourself to drown."

"You're so busy mocking, you never take anything I say to you seriously."

"It's you who never take anything you say seriously, that's the problem! The whole of your conduct this year has shown that you turn recklessness into a philosophy of life. You spent the whole year assuming that you are entitled to a First, and supposing that you'll get an alpha on every paper just out of sheer brilliance. You turn recklessness into a life style, an art form, passing the whole year as a sybarite, without once even opening your books, without ever doing a shred of studying, imagining that you'll swat it all up in the last few moments. And now, when it hasn't worked out quite in the way you intended, you behave as if life truly was absurd and as if suicide really was a serious option. With everything you have going for you, it really is rather ridiculous. Apart from the academic point of view, it really doesn't matter what degree you get. After your behaviour this year, nobody really expects you to sit the All Souls exam and continue with an academic career. They'd be amazed if you even contemplated it at all."

"But that's exactly what I have to do," said Guy desperately. "I have to stay at Oxford in order to be with my fiancée, otherwise

Henry, who, naturally, is bound to get a Congratulatory First, will snap her up, and I can't contemplate any future of any sort anywhere without a First." "Desperate words, what does it actually matter, especially to you. You've got everything anyway, to commit suicide would be truly absurd."

"You obviously don't understand how important it is to me. All you chaps at Magdalen, you think it's so easy being born the eldest son of a duke."

"But the only point of being at Oxford is to complete our education. We are expected to become gentlemen. Don't you love the way all the notices in the colleges always start, 'Gentlemen will dine in hall, gentlemen will wear dinner jackets, black ties, white gloves …' When we come down, we're all going into the City to make money, what else is there in life?"

"I'm not, certainly not," said Guy.

"You don't need to, you're going to inherit the money."

"I'm going to inherit the responsibility, I don't call that fun. I'm not going into the City because I have other things to do with my life, but I can't do any of them if I don't get a First. None of you chaps ever considers what it's actually like to be born the eldest son of an aristocrat with all the attendant burdens and expectations that are fastened irremovably like chains round my neck at birth, and which nothing but death can untie. It commits me inexorably to a certain kind of life that doesn't accord with my aims or personality in any way whatsoever. Of course I concede that there are advantages, and anyone not in my position wishes that they were in my position, but that's because they are totally unaware of the intense pressure that my father has always exerted on me to make me live up to a certain historical role."

"All right, enough of this, come and have dinner," invited Patrick.

"That's the one thing I can't do. Haven't you noticed how

thin I've become. You'll have to excuse me. Now I really have to study."

Patrick really was amazed when Guy persisted in his refusal of the invitation to dinner, and sat miserably working at his desk until late into the night.

Guy sat in his elegant room, beautifully redecorated with pelmets, drapes and brass bed, walnut desk and Louis Quinze easy chairs. They all gathered round him.

"Don't look so miserable," said Matthew.

"No, it's right," groaned Guy wretchedly. "I have no idea what I'm being viva'd for. It could be for a Second."

"Can't you ask a tutor?"

"With my relationship with my tutors? You must be joking!"

"They'll think you're calling round for another coffee!" laughed Jeremy.

"At least you should pity poor old John Kemp," said Martin.

"Why, whatever happened to him?"

"Well, they were viva-ing him to try to save him from a Fourth."

"Nobody gets a Fourth!"

"He did!"

"It's impossible, you'd have to work very hard to get that. You actually have to be clever to get a Fourth. Anybody can get a Third but you actually have to work hard to get a Fourth. How did he manage it?"

"At the viva they tried very hard to help him get a Third."

"What subject was it?"

"History. They asked him to list the Kings and Queens of England, but he was unable to do so, so they gave him a Fourth."

Everybody laughed.

"What college is he?"

"Balliol."

"No," said Guy, "it's impossible. Balliol has the highest academic record. Christ Church may be very ancient, grand and magnificent, and a beautiful college, but it's not known for its high academic standards." He paused. "And I," he continued sadly, "have hardly improved them if I really am being viva'd for a Second."

"No, you can't be," said Henry, not unkindly.

"It's alright for you," said Guy. "You've got your Congratulatory First, and so have Edward, George and Adrian, all of whom were always behind me in class. I can't understand how it happened."

The others in his room exchanged glances.

"Of course, you do know," said Patrick, "that vivas are public."

"Of course they're not," said Guy crossly.

"Yes," persisted Patrick. "It's a public examination. It's called the second public examination."

"That's its technical name," said Guy testily. "It doesn't mean it's public."

"It is," insisted Patrick, "and I'd like to see how you exhibitioners, who study, perform."

"You can't come, nobody ever comes to a viva."

"But the examination is public," said Patrick.

"And so is the written, it's called the first public examination. People don't come to the written exam, it would be absurd, what would they look at?"

Patrick smiled mischievously. "But wouldn't it be fun to come to the viva, and hear what you had to say."

"I'm sure your malicious presence would put me right off my stroke."

"Just as an experiment, I'd like to know if it makes any

difference whether you study or not. In my case, I'm going to get two degrees without any studying at all. I really do want to come along and see what you've got to say for yourself."

"I'd like to come," said Matthew, "but in my case it would be to give you support."

"I'd like to come too," said Henry but he didn't add a reason.

"Me too," said Jeremy.

"Well. you can't," said Guy, "the examiners wouldn't let you in. I'm sure it's against the rules to have outsiders there."

"I'll apply to the examiners for permission," said Patrick.

"It has to be three weeks beforehand and in writing, so you're too late."

"You just made that bit up."

"Well, nobody goes, it's unknown. Why would they go?"

"I'm definitely going, I've decided," said Patrick.

"But listen, Patrick," said Jeremy. "What if you do put the poor fellow off?"

Patrick smiled gleefully. "Far from it, I'm sure he'll do far better if there's someone there to report to everyone else how well he did."

"But what will they ask me?" wailed Guy. "What if I fumble about for an answer? I've never done an oral exam before, there's no tradition for it. In some countries, on the continent, for example, all doctorates are examined orally."

"Here too", said Henry. "If you ever get to the doctoral stage."

"Yes, that's right," said Patrick. "After you've written your thesis, you have an oral examination on it, and that definitely is public. In fact, I remember reading in the histories how Gladstone did his viva in the Sheldonian, and people leaned over the rafters and the balconies and applauded at the brilliance of his answers."

"There was a tradition of oratory in those days," conceded Guy "It's died out since then. Nobody does it any more. All that stuff is left to the university orator, and he only does it on formal occasions, and then only in Latin."

Henry laughed. "I hope they don't ask you to be viva'd in Latin!"

"You've forgotten, Henry," said Jeremy. "If they did, Guy would do pretty well."

Guy said sadly, "In Latin I wouldn't do too badly, I remember all my Latin. I did very well in those days." He looked wretchedly miserable. "I'll have to start studying again, but how many days do I have?"

At that moment Clelia came running into the room, shouting excitedly, "I've spoken to Nigel and he's agreed to come. He's cancelled all his appointments and taken a week's leave so that he can coach you."

"Does he think I need it?" asked Guy, looking even more despondent.

"He wants to make sure you'll do very well. He's convinced you're being viva'd for a First."

"Can he at least find out?"

"Yes, I'm sure he can, as soon as he gets here. He's coming this evening."

Patrick was as good as his word and set about making enquiries from the examiners as to the possibility of attending Guy's viva. Although no-one ever did normally attend, the name of the examination was "Public Examination Number 2." As their name indicated, they were theoretically public, the prelims being "Public Examination Number 1."

The examiners were very surprised that anyone would, indeed, want to attend, but said that it was perfectly alright provided the candidate himself did not object, and there were not too many people, since the examination room was rather small.

The candidate himself was never asked as to whether he objected or not. The matter was simply never raised with him. Besides, he was far too busy studying, reading and practising being cross-examined by Nigel.

The idea that people would attend Guy's viva started to circulate around Oxford. Guy, cloistered away in the House and studying very hard, was entirely unaware of this. Gradually the idea expanded, and as Patrick spread the news that an audience would be admitted, more and more people decided to attend. If nothing else, it would certainly be entertaining, and there had not been a publicly attended viva with an audience for more than half a century. Guy's tutors decided to attend on the grounds that during the whole of his three years most of them had hardly ever seen him, and his moral tutor was determined to go since it presented a chance finally to meet him, or, at the least, see what he looked like. Guy's school friends were determined to go because they knew that any public event in which he was involved was sure to be entertaining. His enemies were keen to go and mock at him in the hope of doing him down or, by their very presence, making him feel ill at ease and therefore less likely to do well. His friends would be there to give him moral courage and support. As news of their excitement spread abroad those who only knew of Guy's reputation decided to come just for the amusement value, and such benighted students as there were who did not know him and had never heard of him decided to come as it promised to be a fun occasion and definitely not to be missed. When the news spread that it was to be the first public viva for more than half a century, local journalists decided to come and cover it for the Oxford newspapers and Radio Oxford.

Guy, entirely unaware of all this frenzy of agitation that was taking place around him, arrived very early at the Examination

Schools looking handsome and striking, smartly dressed in sub fusc. At first he had absolutely no idea that the excited crowds waiting there had anything to do with him. Accompanied by Nigel, he tried to enter the committee room that served as the examination room, but they both found it completely impossible to force their way through the crowd.

The committee room was already full of excited spectators, and the clerk to the examiners was nervously running around like the White Rabbit trying to calm the audience and close the doors, indicating that there was no more space for the agitated crowd outside.

"But the examination is public!" shouted a number of protesting voices.

"You have to let us in!" shouted the boys from the newspapers. "Freedom of the press!"

"The press! What on earth has the press got to do with it? This is an examination!" cried the White Rabbit, running anxiously to and fro. There was a delay while he went off to consult the examiners. Since Patrick had alerted the examiners to the fact that at least some people would attend, it was impossible to go back on that now, and ask the crowd to go away. It was feared that any attempt to do that would have caused a riot. It would have been equally unfair to announce that a small number could attend in the committee room, and the rest not. It was feared that any attempt to do that would have provoked even greater unrest.

After a hurried consultation it was decided that the only fair thing to do at that stage was to transfer the examination to the main hall of the Examination Schools. As soon as the White Rabbit announced this, the entire crowd flocked joyfully along to the main hall and settled down expectantly.

Guy stood at the front, waiting for the examiners to enter and call him forward. There was an intensity in the waiting as the silent seconds ticked by.

Finally there was a great crash at the door and the seven examiners came marching in bedecked in their magnificent academic robes and bonnets. The colours were magnificent as this parade of peacocks, as at Encaenia, ostentatiously processed by. Brilliant emerald-green trimmed with ermine was followed by shimmering scarlet trimmed with sable, glistering gold trimmed with mink and eternal sapphire trimmed with fox. The audience fell silent in amazement.

Guy gazed at them in awe. The White Rabbit cleared his throat and called out Guy's name in a sing-song voice. Guy stepped smartly forward. Everyone expected there to be a cushion for him to stand on. He waited, attentively.

The first examiner leaned forward and pierced Guy with his dart-like gaze. "What is the most serious criticism you could level at Kant?" he said.

This was a very easy question for Guy, and he was able to hold forth eloquently and at some length. They all nodded as he wound the answer to a close.

The second examiner then asked, "Tell us about Benjamin Constant, the concept of liberty between the ancients and the modern."

Guy paused for a moment, and then began to answer the question. But as he started to speak, he began to stammer and hesitate.

The hall fell into a deathly hush. Each person present was hanging on to his every syllable with every fibre of their being. All eyes were fixed upon Guy who, now stammering and stuttering, had suddenly become completely pale and silent and looked as though he was about to faint. Was he about to fluff the whole viva?

Sitting near the front next to Nigel, Clelia dug her finger nails hard into her hands and willed with all her strength that he would recover and reply.

Perhaps it was only a matter of seconds, but it seemed like an eternity. Not a soul moved. They hardly dared to breath. Even his enemies seemed shocked and upset.

Suddenly Guy seemed to make an enormous effort and pulled himself together, and began his answer, gradually improving, finally starting to think again, and getting back into his stride.

"All this without notes," murmured one of the astonished boys.

Sir David Butler leaned forward and asked, "What use is it knowing what Locke said if we want to know whether or not to join the Common Market?"

Guy was now fully in control of himself, but he paused for an instant to reflect, "This is either a very clever question or an incredibly idiotic one." While this thought was going through his mind, Professor Plamenatz exploded with rage at the question.

"Really, David, this is a completely ridiculous question to ask of a first class student at a viva, particularly at a public examination which has never before excited so much attention or drawn such an interested and attentive audience. Ignore the question, my dear young man, ignore it."

At this insult, a very lively debate broke out noisily between Sir David and Professor Plamenatz, which became so heated that the audience became involved and the continuation of the viva was seriously in doubt. Everyone was delighted at the anger and the throwing of insults, so that finally Sir Adrian Derby was obliged to call a halt to the duel of wits, and order the examiners to return to the examination.

Guy was now very relaxed and in excellent form, and he sensed that the audience was definitely on his side, and that it was his duty to entertain them as much as to cross swords brilliantly with his examiners. The next question was about

Hobbes and Guy answered it brilliantly. The audience murmured its approval, and settled down expectantly for the next.

One of the examiners asked him Isaiah Berlin's famous question, "Are there two concepts of liberty and does it matter?"

Guy replied immediately, "No, there are three." The audience fell about with laughter, and when they finally calmed down enough for his voice to be heard above the din, Guy, speaking loudly, clearly and eloquently, launched on a learned disquisition on the concept of liberty from Theognis of Megara through the Greeks, the Romans, the French, the Italians and the Germans before starting an analysis of liberty as considered by those writing in English in his native land. The disquisition was so eloquent and so perfectly paced that it was remembered for years afterwards as a symphony of colour, harmony and sound. As his voice rose and fell and as the originality of his own interpretation intermingled with the classic presentation of the ideas and authors, the examiners and audience alike sat back to enjoy the lecture they were suddenly being treated to. Guy finally arrived at Isaiah Berlin's own writings, and spoke with great knowledge and appreciation of them to such an extent that Isaiah, later having heard of this famous event, regretted that he hadn't had the good fortune to be present at it. Guy gradually wound his peroration to a brilliant, climactic finish.

As he stopped speaking, an outburst of applause burst from the audience who clapped, stamped, shouted and whistled. The applause was uncontrollable and continued for some time.

Guy was called to the table where Plamenatz grasped hold of him and shook him warmly by the hand. The other examiners were very anxious to congratulate him, and Guy could clearly hear them saying among themselves that it was a pity that Oxford didn't have a Congratulatory First as some other universities had, and how amazing it was that such an outstanding student hadn't been awarded a Formal First automatically anyway. The tumult of the audience continued to rise, and Guy was seized by his friends and supporters and swept along into the High Street on a wave of euphoria.

The crowd swelled out into the street, stopping the traffic from flowing in either direction and requiring the police to come rushing along to order the crowd to move along.

On the pavement an old, retired professor, walking along with a stick, came up to Guy. "You've just done a viva, have you?" he asked.

"Yes, Sir."

"I used to examine them. Did you take History?"

"I took PPE."

"Ah yes, Politics. What did they ask you?"

Despite all the insane jollity and rejoicing going on around him, Guy stood there politely and modestly answering the old professor's questions, in no way stating or even implying that it had been an outstanding personal triumph, and in no way seeking to explain the noisy shouting and wild activity of his supporters swirling around him that the old professor seemed unable to notice.

Curiously enough, even though he had achieved his Congratulatory First in History, Henry hadn't stopped working. He was now busy writing a paper on philosophy, about which he thought he knew everything. He was anxious to finish it and send it to Stuart Hampshire for his approval. and for his comments before publishing it in the *Philosophy Journal.*

Everyone else was falling about in exhaustion now that Schools and the vivas were over. If they could manage it, they would stagger off to parties, or picnics by the river. It was very difficult to prise Henry out of the Library, and take him on a punting trip with a hamper for a picnic lunch by the water's side.

Clelia was anxious that he should come with them in the vague hope that he and she might be reconciled in some way. The summer weather was glorious, with the early morning sunlight sparkling the waters, and the heat haze over the river gradually building up to scorching brilliance.

Henry only finally agreed to come when it had been made clear to him that Nigel was also spending the day with them, and he brought his paper with him so that Nigel too could give his comments upon it.

The day was gloriously fresh with dazzling sunshine and not a cloud in sight. It was that time of day when everything still bore the signs of glistening life, after the dawn was over but before the day had fully settled into heat and heaviness.

Nigel had brought a hamper from Fortnum's and some bottles of chilled champagne. He was very happy to celebrate the triumph of his pupil, though doubtless he wasn't so keen to celebrate the success of his rival. At least chatting with Henry about philosophy would keep his mind off other things.

They took a punt from Magdalen boat house, and Guy, resplendent in striped blazer and straw boater, punted along the narrow waterways past the banks of the botanical gardens, gliding silently past the dream rushes in their deep green watery stillnesses. The flickering light caught the surface of the water and echoed to the deep silences of the darkness below.

Nigel regarded him with interest from the punt. "I always had the idea that you were a dry-bob," he said.

Henry looked up from his reading. "I'm sure you know," he muttered, "that Guy is as ambidextrous in every field as it is possible to be."

The object of their attentions studiously ignored their comments. Guy glided the punt expertly to a grassy bank slightly out of the way of the main stream, and they all scrambled to the shore.

Clelia organised the smoked salmon and game pie for lunch while Guy elegantly opened the champagne as though he were still standing in tails at the bar in Tap. As they lolled about on the bank enjoying the delicious lunch, Henry, coldly ignoring Clelia but being perfectly affable with the men, discoursed upon his philosophy paper.

"I take the view that Oxford philosophy at the moment is shallow, trivial, arid and inconsequential, if it is possible to be both arid and shallow at the same time."

"Did you send the paper to Stuart Hampshire?"

"Yes."

"What did he say?"

"He wrote me a very nice letter. In fact, he was very diplomatic. He said that if one wished to argue on such important matters it was very essential, in order to support one's argument, to have a thorough knowledge of the subject. He sent me a reading list. After I've read all the books, I intend to study philosophy with him. I think it's the most important subject there is."

Guy looked at Henry. There was no denying that he was extremely clever. Even in their school days he had always been under intense pressure from his father to do well, and he studied far more hours than anyone else. Guy remembered when they were preparing to sit the entrance exam for Christ Church, how Henry's father had rung up the college just to make sure that they knew precisely who it was who was applying, and to make sure that they gave him the top scholarship. In the event, Henry won the top scholarship from sheer genius alone, so none of the other boys felt bad about it, since apart from putting intense pressure on Henry himself, the conduct had not unduly influenced the examiners. Now Henry was changing subjects so that he could face something even more challenging, something that now seemed to him to be far more important.

From a deep blue sky the intense heat bore down on them as they lay on the bank in the shade of a weeping willow. There was no breeze to alleviate the oppressive heat.

Clelia served the strawberries and cream and they drank champagne. The liquid light merged with the liquid stream. A perfect, crystalline silence descended. Not a sound could be heard. They gazed into the shadows and reflections of the stream. Suddenly Clelia could resist no longer, and tearing off her clothes she jumped into the cooling water.

Without hesitating for an instant Guy tore off his clothes and followed her. They screamed and laughed like children as they splashed about together, spraying water over each other and trying to duck each other under the surface.

"Bloody exhibitionists!" growled Henry, "Of course he always was like that."

"Was he like that at school?" asked Nigel.

"Yes, you know he was. Terrible show-off. Just because with your help he's finally pulled through doesn't make him in any way responsible or likeable. If you had any real sense of responsibility as her guardian you would call this whole business between them off. Anyway, it's totally fake because his father won't let him marry her, he's made that absolutely clear."

"Is that because of the scandal with James?"

"You know it is. He's a terrible snob. He doesn't want his family to be tainted with scandal. He says awfully harsh things about James whenever the subject comes up."

"But how can he blame Clelia for any of that?"

"It's called contamination by association. Guy deceives

himself into thinking that sooner or later it will all blow over. But then Guy deceives himself in lots of things."

They both leaned forwards to feast their eyes on the frolicking couple, who were excitedly messing around and splashing.

"It's not Parson's Pleasure!" Henry shouted at them crossly. He didn't feel nearly as cross with Guy as he did with Clelia. He did not feel that Guy had betrayed him in the way that she had. The intensity of his bitterness and hatred was mingled with the overwhelming sensation of the beauty of her body as it rose and fell where she bounced around in unconcerned joy in the grey-green waters. He hated the carelessness with which she had rejected him, and matched this with the utter casualness with which she had given herself to Guy. Indeed, it was that very casualness, as indicated in the public descriptions that Guy had given of it that convinced him that it hadn't been the first time. And if it hadn't been the first time for her when she gave herself to Guy, why had she so resolutely and selfishly refused to give herself to him? After all, he was in every way more worthy of her than Guy, more studious, more clever, and deeply and selflessly in love with her in a way that was entirely outside Guy's comprehension.

Now if ever seemed to be the moment to revenge himself upon her. In the depth of his agony, all his sufferings seemed mocked at by the easy happiness that she enjoyed with Guy. Guy could easily play about and behave like an idiot, he had always done so, but it was unbearable for her to do so as well. Had she deliberately invited him out today so that she could mock at him by disporting naked with someone else in front of him? Did she have so little imagination that she would not realise that the sight of her naked body flaunted like this in front of him but eternally denied to him would not drive him to distraction? Was she doing it on purpose? Then he would revenge himself by telling everything to Nigel, and utterly destroying her reputation with him. He felt such a malicious hatred of her that he could barely control it. Nigel was watching them too. But perhaps he had drunk a lot of champagne, since he seemed to be in a dreamy, blissful state, his eyes following their movements, but not, somehow, taking in the full significance of what was going on. And then there was all that business of the famous tutorial, where Guy had been flayed alive. Different witnesses at the scene had offered different interpretations, but listening to them in silence, and mulling over their ideas in solitude later on his own, Henry had often wondered whether the intensely personal nature of Nigel's attack upon Guy hadn't resulted from the profundity of his own affections for Clelia, now blighted by the dominance of a younger, handsomer, jollier rival. If that supposition was right, by unburdening himself of all his miseries, he would only be inflicting further suffering upon the already deeply disappointed Nigel. If the theory was correct, Nigel was already suffering as much as he was.

He turned towards Nigel, beginning mumblingly a sentence that would indicate that he knew a lot about life at school, and that he could, if he would, tell Nigel a number of things about his rival's misdemeanours, but Nigel dismissed it with the phrase, "Young males are usually boisterous," and sank back into his indolent state.

Finally the nereid dragged herself out of the water and pulled herself up onto the bank. She did not look at Henry but she made no attempt to cover up her nakedness.

Guy followed her slowly, and dabbed at her with his shirt to dry her, which he then wrapped round her.

They were so idyllically happy together that it made Henry want to drown both of them in the river. He felt his blood boiling with fury, but he knew he had to control himself. He got out a paperback that he had in his pocket and tried to read it, forcing himself to look at the book and not at them.

He heard Nigel telling them that they had better get dressed in case anyone carne by and saw them and then complained to the Proctors. "You don't want to ruin everything by getting sent down at this stage."

Messing about and being completely stupid, they did finally get their clothes back on.

"Perhaps it is because they are drunk," thought Henry. "Getting drunk doesn't help me, it doesn't make me jolly." He was so absorbed in his furious thoughts that he did not realise that Nigel was talking to him.

"So you are going to sit the All Souls exam for the Prize Fellowship?"

"Yes, I shall have to study for it, there will be a lot of competition for it."

"You'll get it," shouted Guy in the background. "No question of it. You always live in fear and dread that you won't be top, but you've always proved that you will be."

"I wasn't in Final Order."

"That was the one and only time, and then you only missed it by two points. You'll never, ever let that happen to you again. I'm not going to sit the exam because you're there."

"There are two fellowships," said Nigel.

"Neither is for me, but one is definitely for Henry," said Guy magnanimously.

Eventually, they climbed back heavily into the punt, and Guy glided the punt skilfully along the rivulets and waterways, expertly avoiding the dangerous parts where less practised puntsmen were likely to get their heads knocked off by overhanging branches, or the punt pole caught in the reeds. The punt floated gently amidst deep shadow and sudden shafts of light darting among the overhanging leaves.

Clelia, reclining at full length, trailed her hand in the pellucid waters, sometimes raising it slightly to allow water drops to fall, sparkling, into the stream.

"And I," thought Henry, watching her closely, but pretending not to. "I am a mere water drop that falls unconsciously and uncared for from her hand, when instead, I should be to her a pearl of great price that she should grasp forever in the palm of her hand and never let me go."

Nigel also was musing on life at Oxford. "You know, Henry, it is amazing how things at Oxford have changed since my day. As far as the undergraduates are concerned, they are much more powerful intellectually. The students now are a lot more able, more hard-working and more serious. But in my day there was much more spirit. There were aesthetes, and all those sort of no good people, who were brave, and knew that they would be sent down in the end, but they had a lot of spirit, a lot of fun, some of our coterie were totally abandoned, and they created an atmosphere which had an intense excitement. The clever ones were cleverer than they are now, the brilliant ones were more brilliant than they are now. The top was better and the middle was worse. Is there still that air of excitement now? I think it is lacking."

"Ever since he's been up, Guy's been trying to recreate that air of excitement, of risk, of utter abandonment, of being in imminent danger of being sent down, of challenging the authorities, of daring them to try to tame him, to take him to task. He did it at school, where they always try to dampen down a spark that's a bit too bright, and he's certainly been trying to do it here. He's always dicing with being set down."

"All right, that's enough," said Guy while continuing to punt.

"You see," continued Henry. "At school he couldn't stand the idea that there were rules."

"I couldn't stand the idea that they were always telling you to do this and not do that. I couldn't accept it at all," said Guy.

"So," continued Henry, "he would break every rule there was. But my favourite memory was when the House Master, P.S.H Lawrence – or Wetty Lawrence, as we called him – put up a notice in college which had at least ten important do's and don'ts, the final one of which was, 'And no boy shall be allowed to deface this or any other notice.' As soon as Guy saw this, he took out his cigarette lighter, which he wasn't supposed to have since smoking was forbidden as well, and immediately burned the whole of that last restriction from the notice!"

Nigel and Clelia laughed.

"Enough of my misdeeds!" cried Guy, still punting and carefully watching the water, the banks and the overhanging branches.

Clelia looked mischievously at Nigel. "Are you telling us that you never sang the Gordouli song?"

"I might have."

"Do you claim that you never shouted 'Bloody Trinity!!!'"

"Well, it's some time since – "

"It's still a regular post-prandial activity," laughed Guy, "and they still sing the Gordouli song, we heard it the other night." They all laughed." I suppose," added Guy, "that you will deny that you were a particularly riotous member of the Annandale Club, and that you wrought havoc with the college crockery in ritual waterfalls down the Hall steps after dining rather than debating!" They laughed again.

"Certainly the main feature about Oxford is that year after year there is this extraordinary tidal wave of nice, intelligent, enthusiastic, interesting people," said Nigel. "My friends who stayed on as dons always tell me this."

Guy was gently directing the punt to Magdalen bridge. A large number of punts were being returned at this time, and so they had to wait an unconscionable time while the boatmen stacked and arranged them, and hired them out again to the waiting line of customers. They all lay in the punt as it gently rocked to and fro on the light waters underneath Magdalen Bridge. The sunshine, reflected from the water onto the upper part of the stone arches under the bridge, shone a phosphorescent, permanently sparkling metwand of light that spangled, sparkled and kept in perpetual motion a thousand dazzling suns. They were caught up in this luminescent glimmering and glistening, which dazzled as they looked at it, and yet hypnotised them and prevented them from looking away.

"They are the thousand spirits of the departed souls," said Henry. "They have not become the spirit of an anemone, nodding at me and greeting me as a breeze moves it in Long Meadow, but here, these spirited souls, all scintillation, fulguration, luminescence together, sparkling just for me, there she is, my grandmother, her spirit returned as a lambent flame of light."

Finally the boatmen came and pulled in the boat, and they scrambled over the other punts to reach the shore. A boy in cricket whites had been sent down to fetch Guy, and remind him that he had to hurry back to Christ Church for a cricket match.

Nigel excused himself by saying that he had to lie down and rest in his hotel room.

Clelia and Henry walked slowly up the High. He had not addressed a single word to her the whole afternoon. When they arrived at Queen's, Clelia started to climb up the stone steps.

"Where are you going?"

"I'm going to visit someone here."

"Another of your lovers?"

"No, not at all."

"Another poor, suffering, unrequited wretch like me, then?"

Clelia looked at him. She scraped the ancient stone of the college wall with her nail. "Please, Henry, can't we be friends?" she pleaded with him.

"Either we're lovers or we're nothing. You choose."

She remained silent.

"I know you don't really care about Guy, but if you're worried that he'd find out about it, I can be very discreet, unlike him. He would never need to know."

Again, Clelia remained silent, frowning and looking down.

"Very well, then! " said Henry bitterly, and turned away to walk up the High Street. He did not look back.

She watched him walk away. She had never observed his gait before, but now she saw slightly hunched shoulders, a sort of rolling way of walking from side to side rather like a sailor, and a dragging of the right leg, something she had never noticed before, that almost amounted to a slight limp. She allowed a number of people to fill in the space on the pavement between them, and then followed at a distance, watching his odd way of dragging himself miserably along, until he reached All Souls, where he turned to the right into Catte Street to approach the Radcliffe Camera. As soon as she was sure that he had gone, she ran lightly to Carfax, turned into Cornmarket where she hurried on through the crowd to the Randolph Hotel. She ran quickly up to Nigel's room, where she found him lying in bed waiting for her.

"Too much naked disporting," he said, "You have got me very excited. Now you'll have to disport for me."

Henry isolated himself at All Souls, reduced himself to an atom, atomised himself. He was unable to account for how he spent each day. He obviously passed some of the time in the library, and a lot of the time at his desk writing. It was difficult for him since he hadn't studied philosophy before, but he persevered, reading as much as he could, and puzzling things out for himself. But wherever he was or whatever he was doing, it was always that particular moment of the day when the sun was hovering somewhere near the horizon, and was about to go down. Or at least, was indicating that it was about to go down pretty damn soon if you didn't do something about it. "But what am I to do," gasped Henry, "How can I stop it?" Staring at it didn't help, although he always thought it might, since it didn't move when you looked at it. The bright golden orb was somewhat more dimmed than usual, but soon enough it burned a cluster of purple circles centred with gold onto the backs of his retinas and he had to look away, blinded by the searing suns that swam about before his eyes. As soon as they began to clear away, he would look back, and still it had not changed. Today he would have some effect upon it, at last. It would remain with him, not desert him, not abandon him to the eternal dreary evening and night. He was distracted by something, and then suddenly remembered the sun again. It had moved on a bit. Staring had not helped. Again he turned to his papers. It was too late. The sun had set. The afterglow had not yet faded from the sky, but the sun had gone, it had abandoned him. He watched miserably as the last streaks of light in the sky floated away. The day was over. It was already dark.

Some of Guy's friends gathered in his rooms to take serious stock of what would happen to them now. The idea of going down was exciting to some, who regarded it as a liberation, but daunting to others, who had always relied on someone else telling them what to do and organising their lives for them. What would it be like when there was no-one to look after them? Some of them were going into the family business, others had already set themselves up with jobs in the City. Those who had, found themselves having to defend their choices against the more radical element who questioned their unswerving loyalty to capitalism.

"How can you justify joining the ranks of those who spend their time exploiting the masses and expropriating the fruits of their labour?" demanded Tom.

A furious debate broke out in which Tom tried to prove to them that socialism was scientific, and would surely overwhelm capitalism before too long.

"And the Soviet Union, is that the sort of socialism you want for us here?" retorted Patrick.

"That isn't socialism. The ideas of socialism have never been put into practice there. That's state monopoly capitalism, we are as much against that as we are against capitalism here. So far socialism hasn't actually been tried in any country, so you can't say that it would fail."

"Nor has Christianity," said Jeremy, who like the others, had been extremely impressed by Buñuel's *Nazarín* that they had just seen at the Scala in Walton Street.

Guy found that it had made quite a deep impression upon him, and they all fell to discussing it. While they were debating its implications, Tom suddenly said, "I might envisage a situation in which I would find myself with a rifle in my hand."

"Yes, in the cadets, or the territorial army," mocked Patrick.

"No, in reality," said Tom very seriously.

They gazed at him in amazement.

"I know our fathers still insist that we serve in the Territorial Army, and waste our weekends there, but all wars are over," said Guy. "In what circumstances could you possibly imagine you might find yourself taking part in a war? There are no more empires to conquer, at least as far as Britain is concerned."

Tom was enigmatic. "There are all sorts of struggles, my dear fellow, but you wouldn't know anything about them, Guy. You're basically on the other side. You've been born into the aristocracy and there's no way on earth that you could ever imagine what life is like from the point of view of someone who doesn't have titles, class, estates, money. And it would never occur to you to take the time to find out."

"If it's all that Marxist nonsense of yours, Tom," said Patrick mockingly." We've heard quite enough about that from you. We haven't had to read about the Russian Revolution, we've lived it through you!"

"But then they betrayed it," said Tom bitterly.

"We know that too, you've enacted the heroic defence by the sailors of Kronstadt against Trotsky's Red Army many times."

"No, no," said Patrick. "If you're going out there to fight for civilisation, you'll find that Guy is not on the other side. He is the civilisation that you are fighting to defend."

"I can see you don't intend to say," said Guy, "and I accept that certain things are better left unsaid, hidden in the darkness of mystery. But I can't for the life of me imagine what you can have in mind. Where on earth would you go to fight a war? Whose war, anyway? Why would you do it?"

Later, after Tom had gone, they discussed what he could possibly have meant.

Patrick said, "I think he's just saying it to sound romantic. It can't relate to anything. Where on earth would he go off to fight a war?"

Andre set off down Threadneedle Street to take the tube home. There was a dank, misty atmosphere that hung over the City in the darkened evening. It was dusk, and the murky dimness of the fading light gave the impression of walking in a foggy cloud. In the gloom he stepped suddenly aside as a shadowy figure almost walked into him. As it brushed past him, he looked again, uncertain. His heart almost missed a beat. He felt a sudden numbness. It couldn't be, could it? No, it was not possible. It must be someone else. But then again ... He ran back along the way the figure had gone, but it was nowhere to be seen. He hurried to the corner with Cannon Street, but the crowds of City workers leaving their offices and hastening to the station were everywhere around him, making hope of finding anyone impossible. He must have been mistaken, he considered, but why then had his memory chosen to give him such a sudden jolt at that moment?

Two weeks later he left the office to go for a late lunch at the pub. The entrance way was extremely crowded with drinkers who had spilled out onto the pavement, holding up their pint mugs, shouting and carousing. As he tried to push his way in he met the boys from his office trying to push their way out on their way back to work. "I'll only be ten minutes," he shouted at them above the roar of the voices. He tried to push his way through the throng at the bar to order a drink, but it was hard going. He turned to look down the long hall lined with oaken barrels to decide where he would sit. His eye fell upon a figure walking past him along the line of the wooden cubicles, glancing into each one as though seeking someone. It was the figure he had seen before in the street, he was sure of it. Before it could get too far away and vanish into the riotous crowd, he lurched forward, caught up with it and grabbed hold of the arm. The figure turned round and looked at him. Their eyes met. Andre gazed hard at him, not realising that he was still gripping him by the arm.

"It is you. I felt sure of it." He stared intently into that sullen face, at those sulky lips, that fractious expression that combined a curious mixture of smouldering anger and joyless dejection. "Let me get you a drink."

"No," was the despondent reply as he tried to pull his arm away from Andre's continued grasp.

"You will have a drink with me, surely?"

"Why should I," was the insolent retort, and again he tried to pull away.

"Something must be seriously wrong," ventured Andre tentatively.

"No it isn't, why should it be. Let me go."

But Andre became ever more determined, and noticing that a group of boys were leaving a cubicle to return to work, he dragged his unwilling companion past the roaring open fire and hogsheads of port into the seats that had been vacated. He called a waiter over to order drinks and sandwiches.

"Let me buy you lunch."

"You think I need it?"

"I didn't say that. I'd like you to eat something. They do very good sandwiches here."

"Don't you think I know?"

The elderly waiter wearing a long white apron wound many times round his dark green uniform waited patiently for the order.

Andre ordered smoked salmon sandwiches, pate and toast and beer. "I thought I saw you go by the other night."

"So what?" The words were uttered with such a gloomy dejection that a chill went through Andre's heart.

"Mark, don't talk like this. You never used to be like this. Something awful must have happened, tell me what it is." He had never seen him look so forlorn, his disconsolate mien manifesting to evident display the downcast manner of his movements and facial expressions. For a moment the dark eyes overflowing with sadness looked at him, but instantly looked down. Andre's soul trembled with the burden of this unknown sorrow. They remained in heavy silence until the waiter returned with their lunch.

"You know I work round the corner from here for Burg and Nathanson," ventured Andre cheerfully, after the waiter had gone.

"Yes, I heard you had a very good job, and that you were doing very well."

"If you knew I worked there why didn't you get in touch with me? I had no idea that you were in the City. I assumed you were at Oxford."

"I decided not to go."

"That's completely crazy. You had the offer of a place."

"Oh, you really think that I would be able to concentrate on study, and keep up with the intense pressure of the work, with him there ignoring me?" spat out Mark ferociously.

Andre was bowled over by the intensity of his anger. "Tell me what happened."

"There's nothing to tell. He lied to me. He betrayed me."

"Mark!"

"He swore to me we'd always be friends. He said he'd never abandon me whatever happened. Then he tricked me, and went off with girls. After that he has ignored me. He refuses to see me." The eyes blazed with an astonishing fire. They seemed to effuse a most fearful and preternatural lustre.

Andre had never seen anything like it. He tried to turn his attention to his lunch while Mark continued to glare at him. "But you still love him?"

"What do you think?"

"Please have some lunch."

"How can I think about lunch!" Mark almost screeched.

Andre felt his heart pounding as he looked at the haggard face, the hollowed eyes, the desperate expression that told him more than words could ever say. He saw before him someone whom he still regarded as a boy whose heart was bursting with love. It was impossible to tell upon what food this unrequited passion, deprived of its proper aliment, might prey; the impossibilities to which, like a famished garrison, it would look in its despair for its wretched sustenance.

"I'd like to do something for you," said Andre.

"There really is nothing you can do. You can't intercede for me. He wouldn't listen to you, he never did. Besides, he's far too busy with his endless stream of girls."

"Yes, I had heard that."

"Oh, it's famous!" sneered Mark contemptuously.

Ian's face peered anxiously in at the cubicle. "Am I interrupting?"

"Come in," said Mark airily, indicating a seat, and effectedthe introductions. "Andre thinks I ought to eat some lunch. He's very kindly bought me some." He thrust the plate in front of Ian who picked up a sandwich and started munching at it greedily.

"It's very good of you," said Ian hastily between bites. "He needs looking after. I can't do it much myself, he's always going off. I cover up for him as much as I can at work, but sooner or later ..."

"Mark, you can't risk losing your job." Andre was shocked to discover where Mark spent his time. "It's absurd to go following him about, you must stop it."

"That's what I'm always telling him. I keep saying how degrading it is to continue to follow someone about who has rejected you, but he never listens." He continued to wolf down the food as fast as he could, and grabbed hold of Mark's beer for good measure, drinking it fast and then waving the empty glass about in order to attract the attention of the waiter for a refill.

"It is not degrading to show loyalty and devotion to one who doesn't even know the meaning of the words, and who does not understand the concept of love," said Mark in a soft, melancholy tone. "Love is a very noble and exalting sentiment in its first germ and principle. We never love without arraying the object in all the glories of moral as well as physical perfection, and deriving a kind of dignity to ourselves from our capacity of admiring a creature so excellent and dignified. But this lavish and magnificent prodigality of the imagination often leaves the heart a bankrupt. Love in its iron age of disappointment becomes very degraded. It submits to be satisfied with merely exterior indulgences: a look, a touch of the hand, though occurring by accident, a kind word, though uttered almost unconsciously, suffices for its humble existence. In its first state it is like man before the fall, inhaling the odours of paradise, and enjoying the communion of the Deity; in the latter, it is like the same being toiling amid the briar and the thistle, barely to maintain a squalid existence without enjoyment, utility or loveliness."

They both stared open-mouthed at him in silence, bits of half-chewed toast falling onto the table from the astonished Ian.

As the silence persisted, Mark seemed unaware of their presence. "But I shall persist and persevere in this," he said. "I shall make him aware of the intensity of my feelings. It shall not go unnoticed."

"What on earth do you intend to do?" asked Andre worriedly.

Mark heard him, and turned his head and looked at him. A strange, bitter, mysterious smile spread slowly over his countenance. Andre found it distinctly unnerving as he waited for the answer. "You know me, Andre," Mark said with his sardonic smile. "I'm never at a loss for a plan."

Clelia was feeling unwell, and Matthew very kindly consented to escort her back to Somerville. They said a fond farewell and set off, walking through the quad and leaving by Tom Tower.

Guy lay in bed in the darkened room, the curtains closed to exclude the brightness of the light which hurt his eyes. A peaceful hush prevailed. It was so marvellous to relax and lie there doing absolutely nothing after all those weeks of frenzied energy, working ten, twelve, even fourteen hours a day, and sometimes staying up half the night in order to cram in all those things that he had so casually ignored for the greater part of the year. He was gradually drifting off into that silent, floating state that rests somewhere between sleeping and waking, *dormiveglia*, rocking gently along the pellucid waters, in the punt, the light shimmering and sparkling on the stones above the water under Magdalen Bridge … He didn't hear the door open silently, or the naked feet stalking noiselessly within his chamber, or the muffled rustlings of the bedclothes moving in the husky stillness, but he did instantaneously recognise the impetuosity of the movements, caressings and fondlings of the lips that were gripping fast hold of him beneath the silken sheets that were all that covered him. The passage of the years had dimmed nothing, and even now he could have physically removed and forcefully thrust away the intruder, had not all those years of delicious memory, in such sudden auscultation, been brought so forcefully and voraciously into the present. His will to resist was overcome in the instant and he lay back passively, allowing the eager, ravenous mouth to slake its thirst upon him. Satiated at last, and glowing with sweat and happiness, the cherubic face surrounded by soft, moist black curls finally made its way to the pillow beside him. It was doing its utmost to look as innocent as possible, but this was difficult considering how triumphant it looked. Guy leaned back on the pillow and gazed at the burning black eyes that blazed in ecstatic bliss back at him.

"It was my voice that first attracted your notice, my countenance that fixed it, and my manners that attached you to me forever," said the soft, clear voice of the former choirboy, "And I am two years younger than my noble patron, though the rest of the description doesn't quite fit, and you did feel for me a violent, though pure, love and passion, and you certainly love me more than any human being – " As the voice spoke faster and became more excited as it warmed to its theme, Guy, sensing the danger, tried to raise himself from the pillow, but Mark was too quick for him and flung himself violently upon him, pinning him down with all his strength, and saying excitedly and breathlessly, "I believe the only human being, that ever loved me in truth and entirely, was of, or belonging to – "

Before he could complete the sentence, Guy made an enormous effort and said desperately, "Don't say the verses, don't say the verses!"

"Do say the verses!" said Mark smiling, that naughty little look playing pleasurably across his face, smiling with delight at Guy's discomfort. He took in everything, and in particular the look of intense anguish that appeared on Guy's face.

"Do you realise what you are doing?" cried Guy in despair.

"I know exactly what I'm doing, and so do you." Watching his face closely, he pinned him down even harder. Then, holding him very tightly, he placed his lips as close to Guy's as he could without actually touching him. The hot breath fell upon Guy's lips, the eyes burned furiously in his face. Mark held this position for a dramatic moment, and then began, in a soft, melodic voice:

Ours too the glance none saw beside;
The smile none else might understand;
The whispered thought of hearts allied,

The pressure of the thrilling hand.

The kiss, so guiltless and refined,
That Love each warmer wish forebore;
Those eyes proclaimed so pure a mind,
Even Passion blushed to plead for more.

As the voice faded slowly away, the lips descended, and there was no denying the passion of the encounter both in he who gave and in he who received. Everything that Guy had denied to himself for so long came flooding back to him, and in the intensity of the encounter it really was as if they hadn't separated for a single day.

"Everything that you had always said to me," said Mark softly. "It really is true. I told you it was. You didn't believe me. You wanted to take me and throw me into the oubliette, let me crash down there, without a ladder, no means of escape, slowly starve to death, with no man to pity me or remember me, or even to say an orison over my discarded bones. You thought that you could evaporate the past, just by willing it to disappear. I knew that I had to demonstrate to you that this was not so." Fearful that he hadn't made the point fully or forcefully enough, he passionately embraced Guy in every way that he knew he liked, and was overjoyed by the gradually dawning realisation that he was meeting with no resistance.

It was several hours before even Mark was exhausted. Guy was groping around for a cigarette, and Mark immediately found one, lit it in his own mouth and then handed it to Guy.

"You should never have done any of this. I suppose you watched outside my door to see when the others left."

"I've been outside there or in the quad for three days. You've been very busy with other people. This was the first moment you were actually on your own."

"So you've been watching me all that time! Don't you have any realisation of what you've done?"

Mark smiled an extremely satisfied smile. "We love each other. You tried to deny it. Now you can't go on denying it."

"Why have you done this to me, why, why? Do you really want to destroy my life? You're always protesting that you love me but you came here deliberately to turn my whole world upside-down."

"No, I came here to turn your life the right way round, and to stop you denying to yourself what you are always denying to me. Now that you know what you want, you know that I am the person who can give it to you best. As long as you accept that, I won't interfere in any way at all with your life. I promise I'll never come over to Malplaquet, if you don't want me to, but if you do invite me there, I'll be on my best behaviour, and not do anything that would displease you, or that would give us away. But if you'd rather meet here, we can do that, or you can come to London where I have a very small flat in Wharton Street."

"Don't you share it with that jealous boyfriend of yours? I wouldn't fancy turning up while he was there, he might well try to injure me."

"No, he's not like that at all, he's very understanding where you're concerned. I've told him everything about you, he fully understands the intensity of my feelings towards you. In fact, if it hadn't been for him standing by me throughout this period when you've been rejecting me, I really can't imagine how I would have got by at all."

"Don't talk like that!" said Guy in an exasperated voice. "There was a long period when we didn't see each other at all. I only started to invite you again because I thought you'd finally got over everything, and that you'd settled down to life with him."

"That's your treatment for me, isn't it," said Mark bitterly. "Ignore me for as long as you can, and hope that I just fade away. Well, I don't, and I don't intend to."

For a while they lay there, quietly smoking. Mark produced some very nice pre-rolled spliffs in a butterfly shape made specially for him by one of his artistic friends. Gradually he gathered his courage again. "Guy, I beg you to admit that you love me. I know you do. Why won't you say it?"

Guy stroked his arm. "Listen," he said softly. "You got what you wanted. You want me to be in thrall to you, don't you, you want us to go back to how we were before. Don't ask for anything more. Don't ask me to talk about it, I can't talk about it." He paused, then asked, "Would you like me to take you out to dinner?"

"Would you?"

"If you promise to behave yourself."

"Then we'll come back here and spend the night together."

"Mark!"

"Well, you can't go to your fiancée, she's got her period, that's why she finally left you alone."

"So you were listening to everything?"

"Not at all, I was waiting for everyone to go. When they finally did go, I couldn't help hearing why they were going."

Guy gazed at him. "Did you really hang around here for three days?"

"I would have stayed a lifetime if necessary. I decided that I had to, I didn't have any choice. I couldn't write to you, you'd have thrown my letters away, I couldn't bear the idea of that. Will you write to me?"

"I can't do that, it's far too dangerous, you do realise this, it's all completely illegal."

"I thought they were going to change the law and make it legal."

"They keep saying that, but they haven't done it yet."

"You don't need to worry, you can rely on me."

"But can I rely on your friend?"

"Yes, really you can. Come to London this weekend and meet him. He really won't interfere with us, he'll let us be together."

Guy eventually allowed himself to be persuaded to visit Mark in London, and a series of clandestine visits were organised for weekends.

He felt very ill at ease with Ian, Mark's friend, whom he recognised as one of the least pleasant of the group who had visited Malplaquet.

Mark would insist that Guy spend the weekend with him but the relationship was strained by the invidious, brooding presence of Ian. In any case, there was something about the relationship that was disquieting, as Mark tried to enmesh Guy deeper and deeper into the lives of his London friends.

"Mark, I know you like them, and they mean a lot to you, but I have nothing in common with any of them, and I know that Ian resents my presence. It would be better if I came here less."

Mark was very alarmed. "Where can we meet, then? You don't want me coming to Malplaquet and interfering with the rest of your life."

"For the moment, it will be alright if you do come. Clelia is going away to do voluntary student work overseas, helping the impoverished, and my father has ordered me to spend the summer with him in Rhodesia. It will only be remotely bearable if you come out there with me, and provided you behave yourself, nobody will notice anything. Can I rely on you?"

Mark was so insanely overjoyed at the idea that he flung himself rapturously into Guy's arms. "We'll have a wonderful summer together, I promise you. I'll behave impeccably as long as you arrange that we share a room and spend every night together. Your father knows me from school days, he won't suspect a thing."

"Let me go, now, I have to get back, but I'll tell you when you can come."

"No, no, don't leave me now, you promised you wouldn't go back 'til tomorrow, I find it unbearable every time you leave. Each time, it becomes harder to take."

"But we'll spend the summer together, a month, maybe six weeks. Ian won't be jealous, will he?"

"Yes, he will be, he can barely tolerate the situation as it is, but I don't care, I've put up with all these people because of your erstwhile indifference to my very existence. Let me come with you now, don't abandon me to them, I'll stay quietly with you until we're ready to leave."

"That's completely impossible! Nobody knows I come to visit you. You have to stay here until I've sorted things out, got your ticket and all that."

"Until your fiancée is quietly out of the way, you mean."

"You know what I mean."

Guy found it very difficult to understand how he had got himself into this remarkable situation. Whereas he felt that he was making the decisions, he recognised that everything he did was in reality being directed by the invisible hand of the being who now controlled him. When Clelia had told him that she wanted to spend the summer doing voluntary work overseas, he had received the news almost with a subconscious sigh of relief that there would be no witness to his clandestine way of life. However much his father agreed to taking Mark with them to

Rhodesia, he was determined that Clelia should never find out about it.

"But I don't understand. How can you possibly want it to be known about? It must be the most private thing there is about a man, how could he ever want people knowing it about him?" said Guy.

"It's not quite as private as you think. All my friends know about it, for a start." Mark smirked.

"Oh that, that's different."

"What makes that different?"

"Because they all do it themselves anyway."

"And what about at school, when you wanted the whole world to know all about us?"

"That was youthful romanticism, and insane egoism. I can be forgiven for changing my mind since then. Besides, in those days school was the whole world, one couldn't imagine anything else that mattered so much."

"No, it's more than that. You were very proud of our relationship, it was very important to you that everyone should know about it. Now that at last we've gone back to that original relationship, why shouldn't you feel the same way? What makes you want to be secret about it, hide it under wraps?"

"Apart from the personal side, it's completely illegal. People get disgraced and sent to prison. Do you want that to happen to us? Would that be a fitting way of declaring one's love? But even if it were legal, even if it were decriminalised, as they say it's going to be, I still don't understand why we would want anyone outside your immediate circle to know about it. I certainly don't want anyone in my circle to know about us. I always made that clear to you, and you gave me your promise. You can't go back on that now, can you? I would find it unbearable."

"Why are you so fearful?"

"Because discovery would be a disaster for me, and you know it. Surely you wouldn't want to do that to me, would you, after everything that's happened between us?" He looked at those sharp, little eyes that cut through him, and lacerated his brain, causing him a severe pain at the back of his head. "Surely he can't be wanting to do this, can he? What on earth would it prove?" he thought. Again he saw the look that shredded his brain. His throat felt strangely dry. "Mark, tell me, what is it you want? Don't you think I do enough for you as it is?" The fragmented shards of broken glass glinted at him, and gritted oddly in his mind. He felt peculiarly off-balance and hastily sat down. "I can't really believe this is happening. Mark, tell me it isn't true. You don't really want the world to know about us, do you?"

"You could be a bit less cowardly about it," came the unnerving reply. "After all, you're in a privileged position, you could take a lead on this, nobody would want to touch you."

"The law is no respecter of persons, they'd be down on me like a ton of bricks. Don't you know how many people of our sort have been arrested, and been given horrible jail sentences. When it comes to people with titles they can be especially ferocious, just to prove that they don't take our side and are not letting us off too lightly."

"Oh, that's in public order offences, guardsmen, I'm not talking about that. This is completely different."

"The law makes no distinction, I assure you."

"What then," said Mark, drawling out the words, "if we were to agree that we won't do anything right now, but that if the law is changed, when it's changed …" He hesitated for maximum effect.

"What, what?"

"Then we announce it, when it's all perfectly all right and lawful."

"What are we supposed to announce? It's not something you announce. It doesn't mean anything to anybody else. If it has any meaning at all, it means something to us, in private."

"I hope it does mean something to you, I intend it shall."

"What is that supposed to mean?" Guy asked in alarm. The words seemed oddly threatening. Again, somewhere in the back of his mind, the worrying idea appeared again. Was this some form of blackmail? But surely it couldn't be. He looked at the innocent face, the bee-sting lips, that had expressed, indeed, demonstrated so much passion for him, contorted now in an insolent grimace. The jagged eyes sharply cut him again, then he saw Mark leap to his feet.

"I'm going out with Ian tonight," he announced in a nonchalant tone of voice. "He's not frightened of acknowledging me. Oh, didn't I tell you I was going out? I thought I had, careless of me."

"You're not leaving me here alone, are you?" asked Guy, in considerable alarm.

"It's what I have to put up with when you go away," said Mark casually.

Ian appeared at the door, leaning on the doorpost. His expression was more than usually impertinent, even slightly threatening.

"Had he been listening to the whole conversation?" thought Guy in some alarm. "Is it something they've hatched up together?" A menacing silence prevailed.

"Mark, I'd like to speak to you alone," Guy blurted out.

"You can do that when we get back," said Mark insolently. Watching Guy very closely, he linked his arm through Ian's and they both left the flat.

The flat fell silent. Guy wandered morosely around. He glanced idly at the magazines. Not a single book in the place. He went to his bag, and sifted through the books he had brought. He took out Plato's Socratic Dialogues, and sat down to re-read the Symposium, but the words swam before his eyes, and he found his mind returning again and again to the dreadful scene. How had it been possible? How had they dared to treat him like this? He was unable to stay in any one place, and wandered about disconsolately. He wondered whether to eat something, but he didn't feel hungry. He looked miserably at the food in the fridge, the filet steak and fresh vegetables which he had made an effort to get and which would now go to waste. He certainly didn't feel like eating on his own. How could they permit themselves to behave to him like this? It was all so unlike the earlier passionate intensity that he was used to with Mark. Of course, he could leave, he could go back to Oxford, but it was rather late for a long drive. At any rate, he could go over to the house in Charles Street. He hadn't told the servants that he was coming, but that didn't matter, he could still go there. It would serve Mark right if he came back and found him gone. But somehow he found himself unable to drag himself away.

The night was wearing on. Surely they would come back soon, they wouldn't stay out all night. Musing, dreaming, falling into bitter thoughts of self-recrimination, he found it impossible to fall asleep, and equally impossible to stay awake. Underneath it all was the knowledge that there was nobody he could talk to, nobody he could tell about it without shaming himself.

He suddenly woke up from a doze and looked at his watch. It

was a quarter to four.

The door burst open and Ian and Mark noisily entered the room.

Guy pulled himself together and looked at them. "Had a nice evening?"

"Yes, thank you," replied Mark. They stood together by the door.

Ian put a proprietorial arm round Mark. "He's spending the night with me," he announced, darting a nasty look in Guy's direction.

"No," Guy managed to gasp out, suddenly feeling terribly sick. He appealed desperately to Mark. "You can't do this, I've been here the whole night waiting for you. I waited here especially for you to come back."

"Why, were you thinking of leaving?" said Ian acidly.

"Of course not."

"You don't know how to treat him well, you don't look after him, that's why he wants to be with me."

"What do you mean? I do everything he asks."

"No, you don't. You haven't done anything about getting that flat decorated, it was only a question of painting it, and then he wouldn't be living here in all this squalor."

Guy had a terrible sense of feeling that he couldn't comprehend what was happening to him or how on earth he had managed to allow himself to be caught in the trap that was now threatening to spring shut upon him. The situation was surreal. Was it a delusion? They both stood close together, watching him intently. "If they kiss each other," he thought to himself, "I'll go completely mad." He turned his face quickly to the window, so as not to see.

"Don't say you've given up lots of things for me, you haven't given up anything for me, that's the one thing you won't do," said Mark viciously.

Guy gazed at the beautiful, cherubic face, the mouth distorted by its harsh, bitter utterance. He couldn't believe what was happening. Once again he felt that familiar, sickening knot tightening in his stomach, the chill rising from the base of his feet, up his legs, up his spine, the sweat breaking out on the back of his neck. He lurched towards Mark, trying vainly to grasp at his hands.

"Darling, angel, tell me what you want me to do."

"I told you earlier in the evening," replied the cold voice. "But what you said then didn't make sense."

"Because you're so effortlessly superior to him," cut in Ian swiftly. "You don't think anyone else's ideas are valid, or have any worth. You don't even consider his idea about how important it is to be open in a relationship, to be honest both to others and to yourself."

"It's alright for all of you, that's all you do, but you know all too well that my situation is totally different from yours. For me it would be a complete disaster. Is that what you want?"

"That's because you're in such a completely dishonest relationship with that woman," said Ian.

"What woman?" asked Guy in amazement.

"Your fiancée, of course. You want all of your passion for Mark to be completely hidden from her, don't you. You don't mind deceiving her. You don't even seem to realise how thoroughly dishonest you are being."

"But she wouldn't marry me if she knew any of this."

"You don't think that you are planning to enter into a totally dishonest arrangement with her, and she seems to be quite a nice girl, too." Ian flung himself down on the sofa. "I can't quite understand why you're bothering to get married anyway," he continued. "Women going into an emotional or sexual arrangement carry far more emotional baggage than men do. 'Women are not compris'd in our Laws of Friendship: they are ferae naturae.' I can't imagine why you would want to be involved with them."

"So it was blackmail," thought Guy, turning away to the window to prevent their intrusive glances from penetrating his bitterly disappointed face. "And they are planning to destroy me, as I always feared, and tell Clelia." But despite all of this there was only one thing uppermost in his mind, that gripped him with its intensity and dominated his whole being. He moved slowly towards Mark and took him by the hand. He gazed lovingly into Mark's face. "Angel, darling, you must spend the night with me. Tell me what you want me to do, I'll do anything you want, but you must spend tonight with me." He kissed Mark gently on the face.

Every time he tried to kiss his lips, Mark turned his face resolutely to the side, but did not pull away.

"You may make a promise now, but how is he going to hold you to it later?" asked Ian. "After you've got what you want, there's no way he can enforce it."

"Mark, you know you can trust me."

"So you'll make our relationship public?"

"Only when it becomes lawful to do so." At that moment Guy would have promised anything, his very soul to the devil, just to catch Mark by the hair and plant a passionate kiss on his bright red lips. "It's very late, let's go straight to bed." He pulled Mark down onto the sofa, narrowly missing falling onto Ian, who got out of the way angrily.

"Well, if you sleep with him, that's up to you," shouted Ian crossly at Mark. "He'll promise you now, and tomorrow it'll all be different, you'll see." Seeing that they were continuing to embrace each other, Ian stormed out of the room, banging the door loudly as he left.

As soon as he was gone, Mark relaxed and smiled, and seemed like another person.

Guy started to tear his jacket off him.

"Look out, don't tear it, it's the suit you bought me from Savile Row. If you ruin it, I'll make you buy me another."

As they lay in bed together, Guy felt all the happiness flooding back to him. He knew that it was all insane, but he couldn't remember a time when he had been quite so deliriously happy. It had been an agonising wait, but this moment with Mark was the only moment he lived for.

The grey light was beginning to creep under the dirty, bedraggled curtains as they fell asleep. But Guy didn't sleep for long. He woke feeling wretched and sweaty. All the daytime noises of the street irritated him. He gazed in wonder at the quiet, smooth, unbroken breathing of the creature who lay so untroubled beside him. The lips were parted, and Guy placed his own lips above them so that, the sleeper undisturbed, he could feel the soft breath gently upon his face. He stayed for a long time in this position, until the pins and needles all down his side forced him to lie back down. He wanted to touch Mark but he was also determined not to wake him. He tried to go backwards in time to work out how it had come about that he had become so enthralled, to the point of such degradation and destruction. "Last night they set out on a deliberate course to humiliate me. I've never, ever had to beg for someone's love before. He really got me to grovel for him. I would have been prepared to do anything for him. I still would. Something terrible has happened to me. What on earth did that sentence mean, 'emotional baggage'? My emotions are deeply tied up with a worthless creature who is manipulated by that shallow wretch who is bent on my destruction. Doesn't Mark realise this? If our relationship is made public, we'll both be destroyed, but the damage for me will be far, far worse. Worse than any court-martial. What a vile wretch Ian is. Does he think that men's emotions are less profound than those of women or that men care less? It's as idiotic as those men who claim that women don't have deep feelings of sexuality, that only men do … Gide's claim about his wife … absurd … it didn't matter to him that he married her and never, ever slept with her, because, as we all know, women don't have sexual feelings, only men do. And then he had the nerve to have a child with another woman, claiming all the time that he never loved anyone as much as Madeleine …" He gazed again at the beautiful boy dreaming sweet dreams, his limbs uncovered, unashamed. "He ought to be ashamed, exploiting me like this, playing with my feelings in this heartless way. I just can't understand this manic desire to tear my world apart. And yet, however hateful he was last night, I can't imagine being without him, I couldn't bear to be parted from him. If I were to break with him, he'll appear on my doorstep ready to tell everyone, if I don't pay. What then, I'll be destroyed. So I'm trapped, whatever I do. I think this must have been what was in the back of my mind when he approached me all that time ago at Malplaquet, and I rejected him out of hand. I feared him then, and I fear him even more now. If only I could get up now and sneak away." He imagined himself doing this. "But then, how would I see him again?" he wondered. "Do I really have to go on sharing him with Ian? Of course I do, unless I set him up in that flat, but that would only be to court disaster, unless I went to live there with him, and that would only be worse. I'd have to go there to stop him having all these revolting hangers-on there, but that wouldn't stop them, he'd invite them in anyway, and they'd all live there at my expense."

Guy was strangely struck by the contrast between the sublimely decadent beauty of the boy lying beside him and the heartless, manipulative behaviour that he had exhibited so callously just a few, short hours previously.

"Of course I know he doesn't intend to make our relationship public, it's a threat he can use against me, to control me, manipulate me, blackmail me. I've fallen in love with an ideal, a dream. See how innocent he looks, his limbs uncovered, unashamed."

He tried then, at all costs, to put Mark out of his mind. The days were spent plunged deeply in his work, forcing himself to read, study and write. Clelia was his shining example, spending most of the day in the Bodleian, in Duke Humphrey's Library. Casually, and without making a special point of it, he engineered that they spent each weekend at Malplaquet, so that he simply wouldn't be free to succumb to temptations in London. He was getting on well with his thesis, and hoping to tear out of his mind the recent past by stuffing as much cotton wool into his head as possible. The days were interesting and filled with intellectual achievements, the evenings with a whole series of magnificent concerts in the college chapels, music rooms and the Sheldonian.

A number of operas were put on by a travelling company in the Warden's Garden at New College. Guy and Clelia were invited and spent a wonderful evening at dinner with Sir William and Lady Hayter in the oak-lined dining room of the Warden's lodgings before moving out into the warm, star-lit night in the Warden's Garden. There, surrounded by the perfumes of flowers and to the accompaniment of the fountain in the waterlily-covered fish pond, they listened to the delightful music of *Così fan tutte* until late into the night. Returning to the lodgings for drinks and coffee well after midnight, they all took part in an animated appreciation of the costumes, the sets, the acting and the music.

It fell to Clelia to initiate a heated discussion on the relative fickleness or constancy of men and women, both in life and literature, hotly contested and stoutly debated on all sides.

Guy was immensely proud of the way in which Clelia argued and defended her position, particularly against a freckled, red-haired, bespectacled young don from Peterhouse who was on a visit from Cambridge at the time, and who, when he found himself losing the argument, finally said angrily, "Oh, what is the point of entering into a debate with women, they are simply incapable of logical reasoning!" He became even more angry and continued, "When women argue, they are over-emotional and unable to think properly. When men argue it is crystal clear that they are eminently logical and reasonable."

Guy and Sir William found this immensely amusing, and congratulated Clelia for having trounced this obnoxious young don, who was so cross at being laughed at that he swept out of the lodgings in a huff, not even pausing to say goodnight to his hostess.

As they were leaving, they paused in the drawing room to admire a fine drawing in an oval gold frame. "What beautiful long golden curls, what beautiful girls!" cried Clelia.

"Except," said Lady Theresa Hayter. "One of them is not a girl. The most beautiful with the loveliest curls is Hastings Rashdall when a child. Lovely, isn't it."

"Do you know," said Guy, "in the Charles Street house, there's a framed portrait of me like that, about the same age, with long golden curls."

"Hmm," sighed Sir William. "Pity you don't have them now!"

The following Friday they went for a quiet study weekend at

Malplaquet. After dinner they went to sit on the terrace to read. In the fading light Guy became aware of someone lower down in the garden trying to attract his attention. As he went forwards to see who it was, he realised with shock that it was the same boy that Patrick had pointed out in the pub.

The boy had thin, straggly, light greasy hair, an emaciated, mean, discontented face. He spoke in a low, rasping voice. "He's waiting for you at The Old Cloud. He's there now." He stuck out a filthy hand and Guy immediately gave him all the loose change from his pocket. The boy disappeared silently into the shadows of the garden.

Guy felt a terrible sense of foreboding corning upon him. Was there really no escape? He moved close to Clelia, bent in deep concentration over her book. He stroked her golden hair, as if it would somehow work as a talisman against the impending catastrophe that was about to overwhelm him. He placed his lips close to her ear and said softly, "Listen, darling, I'm just going out to get some cigarettes. Don't stay out here too late. Go up and wait for me in the bedroom." He kissed her softly, and then with a heavy heart set out across the terrace, through the house, across the courtyard and down the long gravel drive to the main gates. Halfway down the drive he became aware of a magnificent amber fox striding confidently across his path. He paused to allow the fox to go by. It trotted confidently along, turning its head to throw him an untroubled glance and then hurried on through the leaves and into the gathering darkness. Guy continued his anxious walk towards the village. He finally arrived at The Old Cloud. Mark was standing in the street smoking a cigarette, watching him as he approached.

"Is Ian with you?"

"He is, but he's not here at the moment. You haven't been in touch for ages. Have I offended you?"

"Where are you staying?"

"We thought we'd stay with you." Mark looked at him keenly.

Guy turned sharply away and leaned on the wall of the pub. "What do you want? I'll give you whatever you want, as long as you stay away from me."

"For a start, I think you ought to pay him," said Ian, emerging from the shadows at the side of the pub.

"How much?"

"£500 to begin with."

"I'll go to the bank tomorrow, I can't possibly give you a cheque."

"That's fine, we'll spend the night at your palace. There's always lots of room, you're always having guests to stay," said Ian.

"I've got some nice stuff," said Mark. "Lots."

"I suppose that will help," said Guy. "But couldn't you stay at The Old Cloud, I'm sure they do rooms, I'll pay for you. Coming to the house is really quite awkward at the moment. You didn't give me any warning, I – "

"Oh don't make such a fuss," said Ian. "Your palace is enormous, no-one will notice us. Put us in the East Wing. I remember staying there once, miles and miles of empty corridors without a footman in sight."

"Do let us stay," wheedled Mark. He was in the ingratiating mode. He placed his arm through Guy's arm and Ian immediately took hold of Guy's other arm. They led him along through the village towards the great iron gates of the main entrance of the palace. As they moved into the dark shadows of the enormous beech trees Guy stopped them.

"Listen," he said urgently. "This isn't a good idea. There are all kinds of reasons why it would be better if you didn't come."

"The fact is," said Ian relinquishing Guy's arm. "I've been

having this debate with him all the way up here. Whatever I said, he was determined to come here even though you hadn't invited us and he'd promised not to come."

"Don't say this!" screamed Mark, clinging wildly to Guy's arm and looking as though he were about to have a hysterical fit.

"The truth is," continued Ian, trying not to raise his voice above Mark's anguished screaming and clasping of Guy's arm. "He's completely obsessed with you, and desperately upset that you're obviously trying to break with him, although you've never actually said so."

Fearful that Mark's screaming would attract the attention of the village bobby, and genuinely anguished at the terrible state into which Mark had suddenly fallen, Guy did his utmost to soothe him and with Ian's help dragged him into the estate through the great wrought-iron gates. They started to pull him along the drive towards the palace when suddenly Guy's soothing words and gestures had a remarkable effect on Mark, and he became sweet and compliant. As they walked along the drive he chatted happily about different things of no consequence, and when they arrived within sight of the palace he effused enthusiastically about the beauty of the grounds and the architecture now bathed in the light of a low moon, as though he hadn't been nearly on the point of death a mere five minutes before. Apart from all the other things, he really did seem to be genuinely happy to be with Guy, and he made Guy feel responsible for maintaining that happiness.

On arrival at the main door they all became silent, and Guy sneaked them into the East Wing without encountering anyone along the way. He installed them in adjacent guest rooms and remained only long enough to ensure that they had all the things they needed.

Mark happily purred over the monogrammed towels and silk

dressing gowns and pyjamas that were laid out on the beds in preparation for guests. The others had to tell him to make less noise.

Guy hurried away to his own bedroom in the central part of the palace.

Clelia was lying in bed reading by the light of a small bedside lamp.

"Why did you take so long?"

"I went to the pub to get cigarettes, and some locals there saw me and offered me a drink. It would have been churlish to refuse. Now put that book down and let's go to sleep. You've done enough studying for one day. Tomorrow I'll test you on it." He took the book away and turned out the light. They cuddled up together, and gradually began to fall asleep. Guy waited until he could be sure that the soft rhythmic breathing indicated that Clelia really was asleep, and then silently slid out of the bed and hurried quietly out of the room. It was a long walk along silent moonlit corridors past the suits of armour, display cases of weapons and brooding portraits of the ancestors before he eventually arrived at the East Wing and approached the guest bedrooms. The doors of both were open, and all the lights were blazing. The creaking of the wooden parquet floor alerted them as to his presence and they both looked up.

They were sitting together in Mark's room and Ian was organising the lines of coke. They invited Guy to join them and have some, which he was only too ready to do.

"I thought I'd given up taking this," he said as he snorted it.

"You thought you'd given up taking him, too, didn't you," said Ian.

Mark and Guy looked at each other. Mark looked very fetching in the silk pyjamas. He slid onto Guy's lap and became very childish in his happy prattle. "I always only ever wanted to be your teddy bear," he said softly. "I want you to take me around with you. I won't impinge upon anything else you do."

"The ideal thing would be to set him up in that apartment," said Ian. "I don't know why you don't just get on with it. He'll live there quietly, he won't bother anyone, and you can visit him whenever you want to without fear of discovery. He'll be very discreet. He's decided to give up on this business of declaring your love to the world, he realises how dangerous it is."

They all looked at each other and a silence fell. Ian was the first to break it. "Mark was terribly badly affected by what happened to Jeremy. He was very fond of Jeremy, as we all were, and he admired his daring and decadence immensely. He found it unbearable that such intolerance and spite should have driven him to such despair."

"I found it totally unbearable, someone so talented, so brilliant," said Guy looking keenly at Ian. "The KGB caught him, they took photos of him, and then they were in a position to blackmail him. He wouldn't stand for it, so …" A silence fell.

Finally Mark said, "You mustn't think that we … I mean … all the things I said then …"

"No, I don't," said Guy.

"That's why we came," said Mark very softly. "We didn't want you to think … The KGB did it out of hate, everything I've ever done or said is out of love."

"You don't think the effect is similar?"

Mark looked shocked. "How can you think that? You don't think that, do you? Tell me you don't."

"No, no, of course I don't."

"You really don't think that we – "

"Of course not."

Mark happily accepted this and put his arms round Guy's neck.

Ian wanted to avoid another argument and quietly withdrew.

Mark looked triumphantly into Guy's face, and gazed into his eyes. In his sauciest manner he said, "Why sit we musing, such sweet delight refusing? Shall we play barley-break?" He knew the offer was irresistible.

As soon as they were in bed Guy became concerned about waking up before dawn since they didn't have an alarm clock.

"You don't have to worry about that," said Mark, "You always wake up well before dawn so that you can sneak out on me."

"That's because I'm always so worried about you. I'd better go and get an alarm clock." But things were already starting to happen, and there was no turning back. He would have to stay awake all night to make sure that he didn't oversleep. In any event, there was hardly any time left for sleep and he slept very little, and eventually crept out of the room to return to his own bedroom. He slipped quietly in beside Clelia hoping that she had not noticed his absence during the course of the night. Worried and exhausted, he soon fell fast asleep.

Waking up late, Guy found himself unwontedly alone. Hastily leaping from the bed, he grabbed his dressing gown and ran downstairs. Running into the dining room he was horrified to find Clelia and Mark sitting together, laughing and joking.

"I'll get you some coffee," said Clelia as soon as she saw him.

"No, I will!" cried Mark, leaping up and going off.

"Why did you always tell me that you didn't like Mark?" whispered Clelia, "He's terribly sweet and entertaining, if somewhat silly, and he's over the moon that you invited him down to stay."

Mark came hurrying back with the coffee, and sat down at the dining table facing Guy. The sharp black diamond eyes were telling him not to worry, nothing had been said.

Guy was in such a state of panic that he was simply unable

to follow the jolly, bantering conversation that then resumed between them. He felt himself frantically waiting for the moment when Clelia would go to the library and resume her studies.

Suddenly she turned towards him and he heard her say, "Darling, you look very tired. Why don't you go back to bed?"

"A very good idea," said Mark solicitously. "Let me take you upstairs. And we'll all meet for lunch!" he announced happily. There was nothing for it but to allow himself to be led away. Mark flashed him a wicked look of triumph, and led him away to his bedroom in the East Wing. "Ian's asleep, we won't wake him," said Mark as he locked the door and started to arrange the coke in lines on the table.

They lay down together.

"I didn't say anything, and she doesn't suspect a thing, so you can take that worried look off your face," said Mark.

"But you could say anything at any time," thought Guy. "And you could ruin me at any moment, and you know it."

They lay together in bed with their arms round each other.

Mark smiled serenely. He was enjoying the exercise of absolute power over Guy.

It had all happened before, and as they lay together in a drug induced haze, the details of it crept again from the far distance, past the river, over the meadows, across the stone walls and through the courtyards into the deepest recesses of Guy's mind, where it had all lain hidden for so long. He had been perfectly happy studying very hard each day during Michaelmas Half with Geoff Miller who came to his room every afternoon where they prepared their construe of Greek and Latin together, and went through all the other subjects cross-checking each other's work. Guy had been perfectly happy with Bennett, who kept the room tidy, handed them the enormously heavy dictionaries whenever they needed them, brought them all the other reference books as and when they were needed, and made the tea and crumpets. Guy and Miller studied until late into the night, and when Miller went off wearily to his own room, Bennett would be happily waiting for Guy in bed. It was all very domestic, private, and no-one would ever have considered giving them away. After all, Guy had learnt his lesson about privacy the hard way, and would never have considered risking any of that again.

Somehow or other they knew Mark, but as he was in Oppidans they didn't see much of him. They all remembered his superb voice as a choirboy, no-one could ever forget the exquisite power of that almost ethereal sustained solo top E, but after his voice broke he had rather faded from prominence. At about this time he used to call round at Guy's room with various messages, or to deliver books or sports equipment. From time to time, although he was studying very hard, Guy would notice Mark doing domestic chores around the room, especially when Bennett wasn't there. He never gave it much attention, he was far too preoccupied, but he did remember a time when Mark served them a very nice tea, with special biscuits and toasted tea-cakes, slightly earlier than was usual, and Bennett had come into the room, had been amazed that the tea had already been served, and had remonstrated furiously with Mark. The row had been so heated that Guy had been forced to intervene and enquire what precisely was going on.

Miller had shouted at them to shut up so that he and Guy could get on with their work.

Bennett had been reduced to tears and had left the room.

Mark had happily thereafter continued to pour out the tea and serve the biscuits.

While continuing to study, Guy had noticed out of the corner of his eye that Mark was continuing to tidy up, and at one point was to be seen changing the sheets and making the bed. It was much later that evening, when, tired and exhausted, Guy was getting ready to retire to bed, that he had realised that the person waiting for him in bed was not Bennett, but Mark.

"You must tell me what's going on," he had said. "Where's Bennett?"

"He's not coming back," had been the confident reply. And then a very soft hand had insinuated itself around his neck, and a very soft white cheek had placed itself close to Guy's unshaven cheek, bright red lips had placed themselves close to his ear, and a musical voice had murmured, "I'm much better than he is. Let me show you." And then it had, indeed, been completely different from any other previous experience that had ever happened to him or he had ever imagined might happen within the confines of the school. The passionate actions had been accompanied by very passionate words, such as Guy had never heard before. "I've seen you a lot in the school, and it's not just a schoolboy crush. I really am in love with you. If you have any idea what it means you should take it seriously. Don't tell me I've been reading too many romantic novels. I've hesitated a long time before doing anything because I know you've been with Bennett. But that's been going on for far too long, he can't have you all the time. Now it's my turn."

They also formed a very close friendship. Mark shared his love of mocking at the authorities, and had a wicked sense of parody. He was able to take off all the beaks, and many of the well-known senior boys. Instead of studying, he spent his time in class doodling or sketching on his books or notebooks, which were filled with caricatures of masters and boys and other grotesque faces. The caricatures were very life-like, and the best ones were passed around the classroom during the lessons, causing great merriment to the boys but fury to the masters. However much they threatened to punish Mark, they never had the heart to do so because he was always so innocent and charming. He was able to get away with things that no-one else would have dared. He had discovered, at a very early stage of his time at the school, to his amazement and disappointment, that he knew much more and indeed was much cleverer than most of the masters. He was certainly much sharper and definitely more crafty. He almost went too far when, asked to give the main aims of the French Revolution, he had stated that there were four aims, *Liberté*, *Fraternité*, *Egalité* and *Sodomie*. But before the startled History master could smash down his cane and admonish him, Mark had saved himself by moving very swiftly and elegantly into an eloquent discourse on the fact that the slogan now attributed to the French Revolution of 1789 had not, in fact, contrary to popular belief, existed at that time, but had been invented in France in 1848 at a later revolution, but that historians had attributed it back in time to the revolution of 1789. Nevertheless, he had continued, without pausing for breath, the idea of *fraternité* had been present in the thinking of the revolutionaries of 1789, even though the famous slogan had not existed at that date. And to show that he was not being disrespectful about sodomy, he continued to point out that since the French Revolution, sodomy had never been regarded as a crime in France, whereas by contrast it was illegal in England, and he was well aware of that and naturally obeyed the law. He then sat down to a round of rapturous applause by his class-mates.

The History master, the wind taken out of his sails, was unable to make any comment.

The class-mates were able to bask in the irony that far from obeying any law, Mark was the first to break each and every law, the law against sodomy being the one he most frequently and publicly broke at every available opportunity. His charming smile and the naughty little look that so frequently illuminated his face were like a talisman against all harm.

Now this beautiful, exciting, refreshing young soul had made a pitch for Guy. He had planned his campaign very skilfully. He had carried out his research well. He had spent time gathering up all the useful information he would need. He had made a careful study of the strengths and weaknesses of Guy's and Bennett's characters, and the relationship that they had, and had calculated the chances that Guy might well be bored with Bennett, but too busy with work to look out for a replacement. With care and tact he had insinuated himself into their domestic arrangements, and arranged for his friends to waylay Bennett at the crucial moments of each day so that he could substitute himself for him. With Guy and Bennett so totally unsuspecting, it had all worked like clockwork. When the moment had come to give Bennett the push, he had carried it out with ruthless ease, and disposed of him swiftly, ferociously threatening him with all manner of dire consequences if he dared to set foot in Guy's room again. He had even pre-empted any possibility of Bennett making a direct appeal to Guy himself, and with the help of his friends had ensured that Bennett would be unable to return to Guy's room on that crucial first night that would seal his fate. If he performed well that first night, he knew that Guy would no longer want Bennett to return, so that any appeal would be useless. "Guy, you must understand, eventually I had to come here. I couldn't stay away. I've adored you from afar, but my feelings have finally overwhelmed me. I'll look after you and do everything you want." Mark had the ability to anticipate all Guy's needs, and save time for him by preparing everything for him. He very swiftly made himself indispensable, and Guy couldn't imagine an existence without him.

Shortly afterwards, Guy confided to Geoff, "I'm very concerned about him. How can he be out of his room each night without it eventually being discovered?"

But Mark, ever resourceful, and having planned the whole exercise like a military campaign, knew at precisely what time in the early morning he could climb the appropriate wall without fear of discovery, or cross the appropriate courtyard with a legitimate excuse. He adored the plotting, planning and intrigue of it all, and the skilful way in which he could manipulate the feelings, vanities and insecurities of all those involved within the web of power that he had contrived. He was masterly at reading other's characters, and always knew whom to cajole, wheedle, flatter or threaten, and the precise moment at which to do each or any combination of these.

Not long after this, Guy and Geoff sat together at the burry studying intensely. Guy broke off to light a cigarette. He always smoked although it was strictly forbidden. Mark had taken to lighting Guy's cigarettes in his own mouth and then passing them to him, already lit. At this moment Guy had sent him to get some more cigarettes. "There's something I have to tell you," he said to Geoff.

"Can't you tell me later. We've still got eight pages of Sallust to construe."

"I have to tell you now."

"You're just going to rave on about Mark, and how utterly exquisite he is."

"It's more than that. It's this terrible sensation that I get, I feel as if I can't breathe."

"Then smoke less."

"It's not to do with that. I've lost my appetite, I can't think straight, I keep feeling as if I'm going to faint."

"You keep thinking about Mark."

"Yes! That's the terrible thing! I can't concentrate and I can't think of anything else. I think about him all the time. I've never been like this before. What do you think I can do about it?"

"Retire to bed early, or take a cold shower!"

"Oh, you're no help, you don't understand anything, you've obviously never been in love."

"Love has to wait until eleven o'clock, now get on and work."

Later, Guy was so distracted that he gave up studying and went out to have a bath.

Shortly afterwards, Mark came into the study. He was very distressed to see that Guy was not there.

"He hasn't gone to see Bennett, has he?" he asked in panic.

"No, don't get so worried."

"Well, I do get worried. Perhaps you don't understand. Ever since I came here I've been feeling really strange. I can't describe it. Palpitations, I can't breathe. I have this awful feeling of sickness in the pit of the stomach. I can't eat anything, I've completely lost my appetite."

"What is this?"

"I don't know. Can't you tell me?"

"Guy described similar symptoms to me a short while ago, I think it's called *folie à deux*."

"Did he really describe the same symptoms?" Mark was ecstatic.

Soon after that Guy returned to the room. "Where on earth were you? I was very worried that the beaks had got you."

"You sent me out to get cigarettes."

"But look how late it is. I was terrified that you'd got caught."

Guy sat in his chair, but turned his back towards Geoff, in order to face Mark, who sat on the corner of the bed. They sat gazing at each other and whispering. Mark took up the towel and started to dry Guy's hair in a very sensuous way while Guy caressed him.

Geoff tried to carry on working but it was very distracting. When it became really embarrassing, he thought he ought to slip out of the room, but he was unable to do so, since Guy's chair was blocking his path. There was no way of slipping out unobtrusively, and he was reluctant to disturb the scene of voluptuous pleasure, or even to remind the participants of his presence. The only thing to do was to get back to work or to cough very loudly. But they both seemed to be carried away in a charmed world of their own, unaffected by any outside influence.

Although he would never have said anything to anyone outside his own circle of friends, Mark had been secretly paranoid about the arrival of the first hair upon his downy cheek. He knew that his attraction lay in the soft whiteness of his delicate skin, and he dreaded that he would be perceived as less desirable once the stubble started to grow on his chin, and the necessity for shaving presented itself. He had seen the awful botched-up jobs that boys of his age always made of their faces in their first efforts at drawing a rusty blade across the stubble fields of their cheeks and chins, and how it was impossible to cover the red and raw gashes with lotions and potions and evil-smelling aftershave. He was determined not to end up like a ravaged radish at breakfast each morning. The fear of all this ugliness rushing headlong towards him had made him all the more determined to proceed with his plan for Guy, and then, having succeeded, to use everything within his power to grapple Guy's heart to him with hoops of steel.

Mark had never fully recovered from the loss of his beautiful voice. He had been a star choirboy of whom an enormous fuss had been made. He sang in the school chapel at evensong each Sunday, and was famous for the beauty of his high E in the *Miserere* by Allegri. Blessed Cecilia appeared in visions to him and gave him faculties and powers that were almost supernatural. During the school holidays he was in great demand to sing at Mass at the Brompton Oratory, where he always sang at the Midnight Mass at Christmas. On his return to school he was always teased as being a closet Catholic. But he had gloried in his voice and the power that it gave him over mere mortals. When he had first heard about the voice breaking he had asked a companion in panic, "What comes first, your voice breaking or hair growing on your face?"

"Your voice breaking."

"How do you know?!"

"Well, you've never seen a bearded choirboy, have you?"

The choir master had begged Mark to consider waiting for his voice to adjust, and re-join the choir as an older boy, but Mark would not hear of it.

He regarded the loss of his voice as a death of the spirit and the soul, and had a deep sense that at his tender age his life had ended. He was unable to adjust to the lack of attention, the lack of demand that he had become so used to, the loss of all that glory that he had basked in, the intensity of being the object of everyone's desire. It had almost seemed to him that God, suddenly jealous of that soaring, magical voice that reached the very heavens in all its glory, had seized hold of the innocent young angel and clipped off his bright golden wings. He had been cast down, to wander the gutters of the world with mere mortals. "Down, and arise I never shall," was all he could murmur in memory of Dowland. There had been no help for him, no comfort, no advice or counselling of any sort. Now, he faced the prospect of a second death, and he found it all totally unendurable.

Mark was very keen not to expose his weakness to Guy but in the intensity of his concern he was unable to prevent the subject from coming up.

"I promise I won't love you any the less when you start shaving, don't worry about it so much, it really doesn't matter. It doesn't have the momentous significance you think it has."

"It does, my face will be all stubbly, and the worst of it is, I'll appear to you less feminine, less soft – "

"Not in any way less desirable, I absolutely promise you."

He looked at the anxious white face that was upturned towards him. Whereas in public Mark never presented anything other than the happy, smiling face of radiant joie de vivre, there were moments in private, together, when, albeit rarely, Mark had accidentally let slip the mask, and someone else had peered through. It had happened only for an instant, once or twice, and Mark had immediately recovered, but it had not escaped Guy's notice. In his arms lay a nervous, trembling figure, looking up at him. "Mark, I swear to you – "

"Guy, I know why you love me now, but when I am altered, almost beyond recognition – "

"No, no, darling, you exaggerate, I assure you, it isn't like that. You can only become more desirable to me, every day you become more so."

Mark brought out the tenderest feelings in him, all his protective instincts, and the strongest desire to care for him. But life with Mark was always very dangerous. There was always the fear of discovery. Not that Mark deliberately courted it, but he lived his life always balancing on the edge of the volcano. He didn't go out of his way to make enemies as such, he was far too clever for that, but his ruthless pursuit of his own ends always meant that those in his way, if not always handled delicately, might return with the desire of getting their own back.

The other realisation that crept more slowly upon Guy, but somehow began to form in the back of his mind, at first inchoate, but later beginning to take on a shadowy, ghostly form, was the fact that every so often something would happen from which Mark required to be rescued by Guy. Some altercation, some scrap, some challenge, some ill-considered word or deed … or had it been so ill considered … Mark wouldn't do any work, but he was clever, he tended not to make mistakes … perhaps they weren't mistakes … attention seeking perhaps? But in a way in which he always had to be rescued by Guy, and in circumstances in which the nature of their closeness was revealed, in a way that subtly revealed Guy's attachment to Mark, almost like a declaration of love for him that had to be made almost publicly. Most dangerously, it was also almost as though Mark was determined to display to others the control he had over Guy's heart. The danger lay in the fact that all these incidents became the subject of intense gossip. The more Guy allowed Mark to do it, the more Mark was driven to continue it, to the extreme danger of both of them. Of course, if they both got expelled, they would be together. Otherwise, Guy would leave school two years before Mark, and then what would happen to him, without his friend and protector.

"I sometimes wonder whether you aren't trying to get us both expelled," said Guy to him once.

"How can you say that, of course I'm not, that would be insanity."

"Perhaps it's a form of insanity that appeals to you."

"No, because whereas it wouldn't matter to me, it would be devastating for you."

"Well, I'm glad you realise that. It would be total death for me. I have to go to Christ Church and get a First, I hope you realise that. Why do you think I spend so much time studying for A Levels?"

"You're lucky, you've got your whole future career mapped out."

"You could too, if you'd only concentrate on it. I'll help you, but you've got to get on with your academic work, you can't just rely on being brilliant at cricket."

"You always have, that's why you're so popular."

"But I spend all the rest of the time madly studying, you know I do. And no love letters, you know how dangerous it is. If they got intercepted, there would be written evidence against us. You do realise how risky it is. But the problem with you is that you love the risk, you thrive on it."

"I assure you, I'm not like those tarts who go around school advertising the fact that they have a protector who adores them and will look after them. I don't do that at all."

"Not half you don't!" thought Guy. "Where, I wonder, will it all end up!"

"Although you know that Elspeth Astell came on Wednesday and took Giles Redhead to London with her in her limousine. He told us that they went to lunch in the Savoy."

"Yes, everybody knows that."

"And that last week she took him to a hotel in Windsor, and they spent the night there."

"Yes, I know that. What are you saying? You surely can't expect me to take you out of school during Michaelmas Half and spend the night with you in a hotel? Have you gone completely crazy?"

Mark smiled. "At least you could take me to the Savoy."

The next thing he heard was that Robin had written a play on the theme of homosexuality which Mark circulated in the school among his friends, and from which they performed a number of scenes. They gave readings of the play to select audiences and it was very well received.

Mark decided to give a series of private lectures to select audiences of aesthetes on the history of Italian Renaissance art. He astounded his friends by announcing that he would not lecture on Giovanni Bazzi, popularly known as Sodoma, whom they had all assumed was the object of his intentions and the raison d'être of this series of lectures. He announced that although he preferred the lifestyle of Sodoma, he preferred the paintings and drawings of Luca Signorelli, and in particular the Martyrdom of Saint Sebastian at Città di Castello. He produced a very beautiful reproduction of the painting which his audience admired. "We are not so concerned here with the figure of Saint Sebastian in the upper part of the painting," he said. "The object of our interest is in the lower part of the painting, and the lower part of the anatomy of the archers who turn their backs to the audience and bending over away from us, and exposing their buttocks towards us, strain upon their cross-bows in order to re-load them and fire their sacred flowers upon the body of the martyr." He then continued to discourse upon the artist, his paintings, frescoes and drawings, and the paintings in the Cathedral at Orvieto. These lectures were very well received among his select group of friends, and once again, word of them spread about the school. He read out to them extracts from *The Stones of Florence* by Mary McCarthy where it was noted that in 15th century Florence, "the well-turned, sturdy male leg and buttock cased in the tight hose of the day is always painted with a flourish; this leg is seen from all angles, in profile, in demi-profile, full on, and perhaps most often from the rear or slightly turned, so that the beauty of the calf can be shown."

A series of lectures that he gave to a far more select group of friends and acolytes included the readings of a series of letters written by Francesco Vettori, Florence's ambassador to the Papal Court, to Niccolò Machiavelli in 1523.

Machiavelli had expressed his concerns about his son Lodovico's intimacy with a younger boy.

Vettori recommended indulgence recalling their own youthful experience, and in a message which Mark considered more than appropriate for the beaks, delighted in reading it out. "Since we are verging on old age," (he regarded all beaks as unendurably antique, even those still in their thirties), "we might be severe and overly scrupulous, and we do not remember what we did as adolescents. So Lodovico has a boy with him, with whom he amuses himself, jests, takes walks, growls in his ear, goes to bed together. What then? Even in these things perhaps there is nothing bad." Mark debated whether or not he would put this letter forward as a defence were he and Guy ever to be directly discovered. He maintained that whatever happened he would on no account be forced to leave school for the usual reasons, and he equally had no intention whatsoever to be swished for it.

Guy from time to time patiently managed to dissuade him from being too actively forthright on the subject. He also restrained himself from spending too much time growling in Mark's ear, although he did complain that Mark spent a bit too much time growling in his ear when he should have been at his construe.

Patrick and Tom came round to call on Guy. "Jeremy's coming to All Souls tonight, would you like to come? He's home on leave from Moscow for a couple of weeks, he'll have lots of exciting stuff to tell us. They're trying to persuade him to take up a fellowship at All Souls."

"I think they might desist when they see the state he's in," said Jonathan. "He drinks an awful lot, and he's very predatory these days."

"Won't get far with us," laughed Tom.

"Don't be so sure," warned Jonathan. "He watches you like a hawk, and then takes his chance to pounce. Things are too restrictively controlled in Russia, he simply has to burst out of his chains on the rare occasions when he comes here. He's pretty uninhibited anyway, but when he's drunk he can be rather menacing."

"Maybe it will be a chance to see Henry," mused Guy, "he's really rather isolated these days. He doesn't come out if you invite him, you know that, Jonathan."

"I don't think he'll come," said Jonathan. "He hated Jeremy, he is still furious for that letter he wrote, and bringing the school into disrepute."

"That was ages ago."

"He might come as a sort of revenge visit, to vent his spleen on Jeremy."

"And on you, Guy," added Patrick. "Is he still angry with me?"

"Don't you know? Henry is very unforgiving."

Jeremy's impending arrival brought up the memory of Spicer, who, having gloriously won the high jump by leaping 5.5 metres into the air, went off to celebrate his triumph by taking a junior boy into the forest to … The boy must have complained. By next morning Spicer had been expelled from the school.

There followed drunken evenings with Jeremy, on home leave from Moscow, who drank enormous amounts, and was constantly on the prowl: they had to watch him closely all the time, to see when he would pounce. Clelia wanted to come but they told her that it was impossible, no girls were invited.

Jeremy regaled the boys with tales such as the one about the members of the Communist Collective who had set up a watch committee – or "commyitttee" – of public safety to intercept any big boy trying to grab hold of or ravish a small boy against his will. He expounded on the desperate needs of the older boys suddenly becoming aware of the intensity and uncontrollability of their sexuality, the intensity of the attraction of these beautiful young thirteen-year-olds, with their soft skin, representing the feminine in a world totally shut off from women or girls: the older boys kept trying to pounce, and grab hold of, and cuddle the younger boys.

His senior officers had fallen in love with him when he'd gone to do his national service. He had to avoid their attentions, which was difficult. On New Year's Eve in Washington, Sparrow, the spy, seeing the light on in his room, had invited Jeremy to spend the evening drinking with him, and tried to inveigle him into bed. Later on, the spy's wife had seen Jeremy at parties, very drunk, menacing, and self-destructive.

Giles brought up the party that gone to Austria: an older boy arranged that he would spend the night in the same room, as a younger one. The next day all knew what had occurred in that room.

"How can you still have the same girlfriend after a week?" said Jeremy, distractedly. "How terribly predictable, and boring; to do the same act in the same way. Every time you do the act, it must be different, fresh, unique, special. If you are always with the same person, how can you be different, or do it differently? Quite frankly, masturbation is cheaper, quicker, and you meet a better class of person."

At All Souls, in the morning, they all fell in love with a blue-eyed, golden-haired boy, who had to walk around the breakfast table with his plate over his front, and defending his rear. They prowled, got nearer and nearer, and pinched his bottom.

Guy wanted to invite Henry to dinner.

"It's nice of you to invite me, but I can't come, I'm preparing a paper a seminar."

"Come when the seminar's over, what shall we say, next week?"

"The seminar's in six months' time."

"What! You can't mean that you won't come to dinner for six months!"

"You don't understand," said Henry wearily. "I've got six months to prepare the paper I am going to give. The whole of Oxford will be there. If there is the slightest flaw in my argument, someone will pick it out. If they do so, I shall have to have a reply ready, so I have to anticipate in advance any objections to my argument that anyone might make. I have to be prepared for anything that they might object to. Basically, I have to anticipate anything that might be said about it, so that I can refute whatever they say."

"So really, it's rather like a chess game?"

"Yes, philosophy is like that."

"And you really need six months to work all this out?"

"Actually, six months isn't long enough, but it's all I have."

Henry declined to come to dinner, or even meet for lunch. He worked obsessively on his theory, since he was determined that it should be a success.

Guy had the impression that he was living the life of a recluse at All Souls, seeing no-one, hardly ever going out, and working all day and all night. In an attempt to break through this, he persuaded Jonathan to invite him to dinner in college.

"He'll have to learn to cope and persevere in life." Jonathan advised.

"But it would be friendly to invite him out once in a while," said Guy.

Jonathan agreed to send the invitation. He then received a reply which he showed to Guy.

Dear Jonathan,

It is very kind of you to invite me, but I am afraid I must decline. I would love to come and have dinner if it could be ensured that I would spend the evening talking with you. However, were I to come and have dinner in hall, I would run the risk of having to talk to other people. On this basis I cannot accept your invitation.

As ever,
Henry.

Henry lay in bed in his rooms at All Souls. Somewhere in the back of his mind, in the far distance, he could remember how it had once been with Clelia. They had been such friends. They had studied together, confided in each other, helped each other understand what they were studying, argued together, debated the important issues of life. They had agreed on so many things, they had held so many opinions in common. They had mocked and despised Guy together, both of them, he had believed, holding the same low opinion of him. Where had it all gone wrong?

He longed for her, he dreamed of her at night, he fantasised about her. He could never understand how she had gone with Guy instead of with him. How could she possibly have done it? It was all incomprehensible, and unbearably painful. He knew that she was continuing her studies at Somerville. He knew that she knew that he was now at All Souls, having been awarded a top fellowship after sitting the exams. His success had been published in the *Oxford Gazette*, everyone had seen it. The physical distance between them must be less than half a mile at most, but they might have been living on different planets. He never saw her. He never tried to phone her, and she certainly never phoned him. He wondered if he might write to her. Perhaps he might drop her a note. But what on earth would it say? Should he try to invite her out to dinner, as they had so often gone out together in the past? Perhaps that was a bit elaborate. Maybe he could invite her to tea? She might refuse to spend a whole evening with him, she would be too busy working, and simply not be able to spare the time, but she couldn't refuse an invitation to tea, could she? Maybe she would. What would he do then? He would feel even worse than he did now. He got up and lit a candle. He sat at his desk and took out some special Florentine note paper that was only used for special circumstances. He opened the silver ink well, and dipped the pen in the ink. Draining off the excess ink on the blotting paper, he started to write:

Darling Clelia,

We haven't met for such an age, don't you think we ought to see each other? Would you like to come to tea in my rooms on Friday at four o'clock?

Love,
Henry.

He addressed the envelope, and sealed the note. Blotting it carefully on the blotting paper, he carried it carefully down to the lodge, forgetting completely that he was walking about the college at night in pyjamas, moth-eaten camel-haired dressing gown, slippers and nightcap.

"Put this in the university mail, will you, Bill."

"Very good, Sir. Goodnight, Sir."

Feeling less wretched, Henry returned to his room, and got back into bed. But he was unable to fall asleep. After wasting an unconscionable time trying, he again got up, again lit the candle, and tried to read a book. Eventually, at about three in the morning, the book slipped from his hand and he dozed asleep. He must have been asleep for about a quarter of an hour when he experienced the distinct sensation that a breath had breathed across his lips or as though the feather of a wing had lightly brushed his mouth. He jerked awake immediately. By the candlelight he could see nothing in the room. Perhaps it was a moth that had casually brushed by, or a nocturnal butterfly, or just the light breeze of a draught in these damp and dingy rooms. Worried that he had dozed off with the candle burning, he hastily blew out the candle and fell straight back to sleep.

But the following night, just as he was about to fall asleep Henry experienced the same sensation. If anything, it was slightly more distinct. Instead of sliding immediately from his lips there was a distinct sensation of something resting on his lips, albeit for the briefest space of time possible. Somewhat surprised, if not alarmed, he immediately put on the light and glanced about the room. But there was nothing to be seen. Nothing was flying about in the room, though moths and may-bugs did often buzz about in the room and slap against his pillow. Slightly perturbed, but not overly worried, he went to sleep, but slightly less easily than was his miserable wont.

On the third night the sensation on the lips was sufficiently perceptible for him to recognise it for what it really was. There was no denying it, it was a kiss. It was a kiss that came out of the darkness itself, and attached itself imperceptibly yet certainly to his lips. It was as if the darkness itself concentrated itself into the passion of a kiss upon his lips. And yet there was no possibility that it could be the darkness that was giving him this kiss, there could be no doubt that it really was a kiss. He felt hot and sweaty, feverish perhaps. It was probably the projection of all his passionate secret desires, a hallucination of all his hidden imaginings and longings about Clelia, and the hope that she would come and visit him at night, kiss him and make love to him. Perhaps, too, it was the answer to his note. Perhaps, somehow, she was there, with him in the darkness, sneaked into his room in answer to his prayers, in the way he used to sneak into her bedroom in college, and wait for her, breathe in her air, her clothes, her perfumes, and leaf through her correspondence with secret lovers. Now she was perhaps in some mystical union in imaginary contact with him. His desire for her was so intense that he was convinced of it. Overwhelmed, disconcerted but delighted by the delicious sensation, he lay rigid as a log in his bed in the darkness, anticipating the intensity of the pleasure of the next longed-for and eagerly awaited kiss.

Trying desperately to imagine what she might really be like, Henry spent some nights in the frantic effort of trying to grasp within his arms the body of the being whose lips caressed him. But try as he might, in ever increasing despair, the ethereal being evaded his grasp. Should he try sleeping with the light on, he wondered, then he might see her. But might the presence of the light impede her from approaching his lips? Whenever he lay there in the darkness, and received a passionate kiss, he would quickly turn on the light and look about the room, only to be met with the spectre of nobody.

Night after night as he lay in his bed the kisses became more frequent and more substantial. Yet try as he might, he could never quite reach or locate that female mouth from which they sprung. He noticed that there was something arid about these kisses, passionate though they were, that did not savour of the moist sweetness that he dreamed about, or imagined that he still remembered from the sweet mouth of the woman who so ignored him and had it seemed, yet again failed to respond to him or his note. But maybe this was her response. After all, was she not nightly here in the room, in some ethereal form, spending her nights smothering his lips with breathless kisses?

When he least desired to spend any part of the evening away from his room, Henry was invited to dinner with the Warden. "You know these people, you've been here before. They are dreadful. Sooner or later they will have to go, and you will have to let them go!"

"But it's not up to me to let them go."

"Nevertheless, you will haveto let them go!"

The Warden regarded him keenly, and then continued, "You are not to see Tom or sit next to Tom. You are to sit next to me!"

"I can't have a drink with Tom?"

"Certainly not. What do you think of these people, tell me frankly."

"Really, Warden. It's not up to me to say, I am only a junior research fellow."

"But I'm asking you!"

"How can I say?"

"But I'm asking you!"

"It would be grossly improper of me to say."

"But I'm asking you! You have to say!"

It was late before dinner ended, and even later before dessert of port and nuts had wound to its weary close, with all the old stories, anecdotes and dangerous double entendres.

"I really do wonder what he wants of me," thought Henry wearily. "I don't in any way resemble any of those beautiful young men with Greek profiles that throng about in Oxford and that he's always got his beady eye on. His eyesight can't be that bad, can it? At breakfast this morning was a brilliant young fellow with blonde-red curly hair, tall, elegant, fresh freckly bespeckled face, stunning blue eyes. They all eagerly followed him around the breakfast table. He had to keep his plate in front of him and his hand on his rear to protect himself, in case they all had a good pounce. Why on earth didn't they insist that he came to dinner? They wouldn't have got anywhere with him, but they could have had a damn good try, at least they would have had some fun, and they could have left me out of it." He was desperate to go back to his room. Throughout the evening he had found the Warden's attention oppressive and his conversation relentlessly trivial. He found himself constantly thinking about returning to his room. Perhaps this time she would really be there.

Finally Henry managed to slip away, much to the Warden's annoyance. In hurrying down the narrow staircase in the dark, and having had much too much port unwillingly thrust upon him, he fell and twisted his ankle. It was only one of a number of incidents and accidents that he had experienced lately. He had had a whole series of events in which inanimate objects had assaulted him. Whilst going through a doorway, the door handle had caught him savagely in the elbow. That very evening, on moving from dinner to dessert, while going through an antique archway, a marble floorstone had risen up and struck his foot, causing him to stumble and lose his balance.

It had given the Warden the opportunity of seizing him by the arm, with the admirable excuse of having saved him from falling. Still clutching him by the arm, and looking hopefully into his face, the Warden's comments had been most unwelcome.

Despite this, Henry had been obliged to thank him for saving him from a fall, and hadn't had the courage to shake away the offending arm. The memory of it upset him intensely. Too many things were conspiring against him. Now even the stairs were crippling him. He limped miserably back to his room, and quickly got into bed. Throughout the night the pain in his ankle was assuaged by the passion of the kisses that forced themselves upon his lips.

By dawn the kisses vanished, and he felt their absence all the more keenly as the swelling in his ankle now dominated his nerve endings. He was unable to get up and lay there miserably. Finally in despair he summoned his scout, who arranged for matron to attend him and bind up his ankle with a bandage. She did this in an expert way that held the ankle tightly, but left the toes uncovered. "Now I can't do anything," thought Henry desolately, "So I won't."

When he failed to turn up at both breakfast and lunch, the Warden became concerned. He sent his valet along to visit Henry and report to him about the problem.

Before Henry was aware that anyone was approaching, the door was opened quietly, and throwing an imperious glance into the room, the Warden entered. His black hair was swished back from his forehead in its usual smart style. "Stuck down with Brylcreem, only gentlemen didn't wear anything quite as cheap as Brylcreem. In which case," thought Henry to himself, "it definitely is Brylcreem since the Warden is no gentleman."

"Three o'clock and you're still in bed!" proclaimed the Warden. "What is this young generation coming to?" He flung himself heavily into the easy chair beside the bed, and looked with impolite interest at the extended leg and bandaged ankle. "Wounded!" he cried, "and not even walking wounded! It's a stretcher case!"

"No, no, I'm fine," protested Henry, realising to his chagrin that he was well and truly trapped. He glanced uneasily round the room.

The Warden followed his glance. "Who have you got here?" he demanded. "Got a woman under the bed?"

Henry looked at him with an astonished face. The fact was, he almost felt that he had. For all he knew, he probably did.

The Warden stared at him, equally astonished. "You have got a woman here," accused the Warden, and bent down and peered under the bed. They again looked hard at each other. "I really believe you have," said the Warden. "Where have you hidden her?"

"Who?"

"The woman. You know you can't have a woman. This is an all-male college, it has been that way for seven hundred years, and will stay that way for the next seven hundred. No wonder you were so anxious to leave the dessert last night. In your rush to get back to her you busted your ankle. That's the fate that befalls all men who chase women." He began opening the wardrobe and rummaging about in it. "Come out!" he cried. "You can't hide in there any longer." He stood back a bit to allow her to come out, and he and Henry both stared at the wardrobe, expecting a woman to climb out from it. Curiously enough, they were equal in their determined expectation that a woman would really emerge.

"At last," thought Henry, "I shall finally see who it is who has so passionately assaulted my lips these many long nights. If anyone can give her a physical form, it is the imperious incantation of the Warden." The minutes passed in silence, and as they did so, Henry felt a curious sensation invading the toes of his foot that emerged from the bandage. The Matron certainly knew her job, but perhaps she had tied the bandage just a little too tight, because either he was losing his sense of feeling in his toes, or the being who caressed his lips was now being equally familiar with his naked toes, despite the fact that it was daytime. Perhaps she really had emerged from the wardrobe. As he experienced the curious sensation he suddenly heard a voice say, "What adorable little toes you have." He looked down with utter horror to see the Warden leering at him and caressing his toes.

"What on earth do you think you're doing?" he cried in frustrated fury, jerking his foot brusquely away.

The Warden looked at him oddly. "Who did you think it was?" he asked archly.

Tears of impotent rage formed in Henry's eyes as he dragged himself across the bed as far away from the Warden as possible. The Warden watched him closely, and he did his best to avoid the Warden's searching eyes, as he tried vainly to find something to dry his own.

"You did expect this woman to be in the wardrobe, didn't you?" said the Warden mockingly.

"Of course I didn't!"

"Where do you normally keep her?"

"I don't. There is no woman."

"Then why did you ask 'who?'" The Warden's hand was moving dangerously back to the naked toes.

"Don't you dare touch me!" screamed Henry.

"What will you do?" mocked the Warden. "Will you scream rape?"

"Yes, yes," screamed Henry hysterically. "I'll scream rape!"

Henry spent time considering his days. Was he the same person as the day before? Would he be someone else tomorrow? If he would be someone else, would that person have any connection with the person he had been before, the day before yesterday? What was the self? Was it someone else? What was the personality? Did he have one? What was the person? Who was he? Was there such a thing as the self? Who am I? What did I do yesterday? Was it I who did it yesterday? Could it have been another I? What did the I do? All the I does is connect. The I is the connection between all these various experiences. There is no such thing as the self, the person, the personality. It is just a construction. It is just a series of connected experiences.

It was one o'clock, time for lunch. Henry went to the fellows' dining room. He always found lunch a very awkward occasion. There were two long tables that were stretched out, with benches along either side of them. It was hard enough climbing along the benches in order to reach a place at the table, but in addition, the benches were very awkwardly set back against the low walls, so that you felt as though you were being forced to lean forward over the table. It was impossible to sit upright. It was also impossible to have a proper conversation. He sat next to John and Alastair, who were entertaining each other with their witty, elegant table talk.

John, tall, freckled, handsome, was describing a seminar he had attended at the Jowett Society.

Alastair, with his black hair, raffish poise and foxy profile, indicated that he knew the person who had presented the paper. "Thoroughly third-rate mind!" he chortled.

"I agree with you," said Marcus Dick, a guest who was sitting opposite.

Henry said, "I think philosophy is the search for the absolute."

"Good God!" cried Marcus Dick. "Have a glass of gin."

It was rather early in the season, but strawberries were being served. They were not entirely ripe, and some had ends that were still white. The talk turned to Wittgenstein and mathematics.

"The trouble with old Witters," said Marcus Dick, "Is that he didn't know any mathematics."

Henry, unaware of the presence on the table of sugar and cream, or spoons, ate his strawberries with his fingers.

Alastair, who had helped himself to lashings of sugar and cream, watched him with a bemused look on his superior face.

"Why are you eating your strawberries so parsimoniously?" he asked.

Henry looked up to see them all looking at him. He was surprised at himself.

"By contrast," Alastair continued, "John here makes them as thoroughly distasteful for himself as he possibly can by squeezing lemon juice all over them. He forces himself to eat them like that. Then when he can't stand it anymore, he smothers them in sugar." As he spoke, he anticipated John's hand reaching out for the silver sugar bowl. Just as John's hand approached it, Alistair swooped, and scooping up the silver sugar bowl, he placed it well out of John's reach. "You stuck the lemon juice on them," he crowed. "Now eat them like that!" Alastair then turned his attention to Henry.

"I don't understand about your friend Blandford," he said. "He's easily brilliant enough to get a fellowship here. Why didn't he accept the offer?"

"He's too undisciplined to follow the studious, monastic, rigid way of life here."

"Do you find it so rigid?"

"If it is to be of any value, it requires to be absolutely rigid."

"His watchword is austerity," said John. "He won't find favour with the Warden with that."

"The last thing I want," said Henry, "is to find favour with the Warden."

"But Blandford was thinking of accepting," said Marcus Dick, "As far as his academic career was concerned, he spoke of it as a foot in the door."

"Or a head in the cupboard," said Henry to himself, not realising that he had said the words out loud. He suddenly saw them looking.at him with total amazement on their faces.

"This austerity business, you know," said Alastair. "It can be taken a bit too far. Why don't you let me come up to your room and play you some songs I've just written. I'll bring my guitar."

John groaned. "Oh no, not that again, sub Bob Dylan. There are other things you're better at, why not give up on the songs."

"Don't you like the songs?" asked Alistair. He looked rather miffed.

"And if you don't like the songs," John warned Henry, "He won't give up, he'll try and convert you to ley lines."

Henry walked along the High Street towards Carfax. He walked down Cornmarket. At the Martyrs Memorial he ran into Jasper Griffin on his way to Balliol.

Jasper was his usual affable and jovial self. He looked at Henry's hangdog face and wanted to cheer him up. "Have you heard this one?" he said as he loomed above him:

The philosophy of Norman Coles
Is putting pegs in little holes,
And when he's filled up lots and lots
He goes and shows them all to Potts.

"Ah yes, Timothy Potts, yes, their philosophy is a bit finicky. But did I not read that in the Balliol Record?"

"Ah, then you're not quite as out of touch as they say."

"Is that what they say?"

"You're not in circulation much. Don't you have a need to discuss and debate all this philosophy you're formulating? Why don't you come to dinner tonight in Balliol?"

"Tonight? No, not tonight, it is not possible." He hurried away as fast as he could. Crossing the road he turned into Beaumont Street and walked the whole length of it until he reached Worcester College. He walked through the quad, down the stone steps, through the college and out into the gardens. He moved across the lawn towards the lake. The early spring flowers were just beginning to arrive. There were clumps of ice white snow drops trembling under the trees, and in front of him where the lawn rose up into a mound, the grass was covered with a carpet of crocuses in a wild blaze of colour. They were golden, purple and white. Further along where the grass was green grew a single anemone. It grew alone. Henry saw it and stopped. There was not the slightest tremor of a breeze. All was silent and still, he was sure of this. The pinkish purple anemone began to nod at him. Who was it? Should he nod back? Was it impolite not to nod to the anemone? All his senses were heightened as he looked at the anemone and communed with it. He was convinced that there was no wind or breeze of any sort, and yet the anemone continued to nod at him. There was no doubt that it was saluting him. Was it his grandmother? He thought it might well be. What was she saying to him? She continued to nod at him. He knew that Proust said that those departed could return to us in the form of a leaf that floated down, a feather that wafted on the breeze, or a poppy that nodded at one, and admonished one as she had in life.

He recalled a conversation he'd overheard during his first year at Oxford.

"Whatever happened to Middleton, didn't he go to Hertford?"

"What's Hertford like as a college? Is it any good?"

"It's an impoverished, low and backward place."

"Is it really that bad?"

"It's alright, I suppose. Rather poor, bit obscure. When you're in outer darkness there are no degrees of outer darkness. But then I would say that, wouldn't I? After all, you are talking to a Balliol man."

Henry sat at his desk. He was looking at the letter that he had written the dark watches of the night in a moment of frenzied loneliness.

"I have to write to you, with words that are wrenched from my heart. Leaving you that night was truly unbearable. I have always adored you ever since I first saw you. Perhaps I meant nothing to you then. Perhaps I mean little to you now. Over all this time I have loved you We had gone our separate ways, alas. Perhaps it had to be. But now, now, when such happiness is within our grasp, must it be taken from us?"

Even as he wrote, he found it difficult to distinguish between the reality of what he did and the imagination of what he wrote. It was real that he was writing. But did the words that spluttered inkily from the pen represent anything that really was the case, or had ever been a reality. It had seemed so then in that dark hour in the night, in that obscure, narrow chamber. But in the daylight, if he read it then, as he read it now, would he not crumple it up, and tear it into pieces?

The door burst open, and the Warden flung himself inside the room. He was very smartly dressed, very dapper, the dark hair spruced down, the sharp, beady eyes taking in everything at a glance.

Henry leapt to his feet, and tried to conceal the crumpled letter behind his back, but the Warden was on to it like lightning.

"Love letter to the woman in the wardrobe?" he mocked. "Trying to entice her to come out by correspondence?" He tried to seize the letter, but Henry stepped back smartly.

The Warden flung himself down on the bed. "I'm off to London!" he announced, "Like to come?"

"Why are you going to London?"

"So that I can catch the overnight to Inverness!"

"Can't you get a train from here?"

"Got to go to London to pick up the guardsman."

"What guardsman?"

"The one travelling with me in the sleeping compartment to Inverness."

"Who is he?"

"Oh, I don't know, I haven't met him yet! Fancy coming along, a threesome would be nice."

"Do you have to go to Inverness?"

"You mean, you would come if it were somewhere else? If that's the case, I'm perfectly prepared to change the destination. Where would you like to go?"

"I'm not going anywhere."

"You mean you'll do it here? I thought you'd eventually come round to my way of thinking. You know, doing it with women is thoroughly disgusting!"

"Don't you need to catch your train?"

"Not if I can catch you." The sparkling eyes leered at him.

"I'm afraid I must get on with my writing," said Henry.

"That's the problem with you. You're interested in posterity, but I'm only interested in posteriors. Wearing your trousers the wrong way round won't help you, in that regard. I've spent all my life pinching posteriors, I know all about it. Bum bandit, that's the life!"

"It's a subject upon which I'm prepared to remain ignorant."

"That's a pity, because tomorrow night, when I get back from Scotland, a very nice, hairy chested young revolutionary who has been stirring them up to mutiny and excess at the Town Hall will be joining us for dinner. Would you care to come?"

"Yes, thank you, I will."

"Thank goodness I've managed to tempt you with something! Now I must be off."

Henry felt a sigh of relief as the Warden departed on his cross-country Odyssey. He sat at his desk, his fragile personality dangling between life and death. His soul shattered and in torment, he felt his physical and spiritual strength were weakening under the insupportable weight of his grief and boundless anguish. A terrible trembling overtook his hands and he could no longer hold the pen. The paper crumbled from him and floated down to the floor.

Guy was asked to give some tutorials while one of the Dons was ill. The students were always very polite, and always knocked on the door before entering the room. One afternoon, he sat there listening to one boy reading his essay on Spinoza while another boy listened and prepared to comment.

Suddenly the door burst open without anyone knocking. Mark came charging into the room. "You'll have to give me some money!" he shouted.

Guy was amazed. "Excuse me. I'm teaching. We can't talk about it now."

Mark reached inside his jacket pocket and pulled out a letter.

"Look, the bank sent me this letter. They won't honour my cheques. There's no money in my account! You have to give me some money!" His voice rose almost a scream. He seemed to be totally unaware of the presence of the shocked students.

Guy was acutely embarrassed, and started sweating. "It's my brother," he faltered, "He gets like this. You must excuse him. Perhaps you could wait for me outside." He hastily ushered the astonished boys outside. "Mark, you can't come in here and do this!"

"Give me the money and I'll go!" cried Mark.

"I don't have any with me."

"Give me the money!" screamed Mark furiously. He noticed Guy's jacket lying on the couch and seized hold of it. A quick rummage through the pockets disclosed an empty wallet which he threw onto the floor in disgust. "What am I supposed to do?" he cried desperately.

"Have you ever thought of getting yourself a job?" asked Guy, nervously.

Mark made a furious sound through his clenched teeth and violently kicked the coffee table over, shattering the mugs which crashed to the floor. "Don't you dare say that to me!" he growled. His eyes ranged wildly around the room.

Guy nervously followed his glance. At the same moment their eyes fell upon the mantel piece where stood a number of ornaments including a round Japanese doll in a silk kimono and an elaborate golden antique clock modelled on Tom Tower. "You can't touch any of those, they don't belong to me. This isn't my room, you –"

"I know that," said Mark superciliously. "I don't even have any money or cigarettes."

"Here, have these." He handed him the packet.

Mark snatched it from his hand. "Your bank is in Cornmarket, isn't it?"

"It's in Market Street."

"You can finish your tutorial," said Mark magnanimously. "I'll wait for you at the bank." He swept out of the room and banged the door loudly.

Guy decided that he would apologise to the students and postpone the tutorial. Although doubtless they had heard the sound of the breaking crockery, he didn't want them to go away with the image of actually having seen it. He went out into the corridor. "My brother is rather ill, I have to go and look after him. Could we meet again tomorrow at the same time, and I'll give you a full hour."

"But I thought your brother was Rupert," said one of the boys.

"Yes, he is, but you know I have lots of brothers and sisters. Unfortunately, this one is ill. Please don't tell anyone, it's a misfortune the family has to bear."

The boys looked sympathetic.

Guy hurried away to Market Street, where Mark was waiting for him in the bank.

He was smoking and reading the paper, which he threw down as soon as Guy walked in. Mark lounged next to Guy as he stood at the counter and withdrew three hundred pounds.

He gave two hundred to Mark.

They walked through the covered market. All the game birds were hanging on wooden racks, pheasant, quail, woodcock … They went to Mrs Palms and looked at all the exotic foods from all around the world … near the exit to the High Street was a rough café where tea was poured from enormous brown teapots which seemed to have been brewing for months. They sat down in a desultory way and Guy ordered tea.

Mark said very little. He seemed to be absorbed in his own thoughts.

Guy was wary about entering this private world, he sensed the danger of it, and the risks to himself that it presented.

"Are you still with your fiancée?" asked Mark as if it did not really matter to him.

"Yes, we're still together."

"In that house in Park Town?"

"No, she's studying very hard, and she has a private tutor, so she's back in college at the moment." He was careful not to say the name of the college, and hoped that Mark did not know it.

"So can we go there then?" asked Mark.

Guy hesitated. "Sometimes visitors come there."

"You could always say you weren't in."

"Not if it's my fiancée calling round." Guy sensed that Mark was very miserable, and desperately wanted to put his arm round him and comfort him, but he could not possibly do so here, in public, in the covered market. He noted distinct signs of change in Mark's demeanour, and his face had a desperate, almost haunted look about it. The corners of the beautiful mouth were turned down in a sour grimace.

"Can I order you something to eat?"

"No. I don't want anything."

"Have you eaten today?"

"What's it to you? As if you could care."

"But I do care about you."

"Then why don't you give us that apartment you promised? You don't care if we live in squalor. It's the same as this." He pushed the tea roughly away from him, causing it to spill in the saucer and on the plastic table top. "You would bring me to a rotten place like this. If your aunt came to tea you'd take her to somewhere genteel in the High Street, or The Nosebag in St. Michael's Street, whereas you bring me to The Nag's Noose instead."

Guy couldn't help laughing.

Mark laughed too, which eased the mood a bit. But Mark continued, "It's that business of taking telegraph boys to the Café des Fiacres, I suppose, or people who are out of fashion to little hidden-away places, so our society friends don't see us consorting with them."

Guy was impressed. He nodded with approval.

"There you are!" cried Mark mockingly, but also laughing. "You agree that's what you're doing!"

Guy smiled, totally forgot where they were, and stretched his hand forward and caressed Mark's hand. When he realised what he was doing he immediately withdrew his hand, and forced himself not to glance guiltily round to see who might have seen him.

Mark eyed him merrily.

Guy picked up a doughnut with a hole in it. Before he bit into it, he said, "These are sometimes stodgy. You can't tell just by looking at them. It all depends on how long they've been standing there." Then he bit into it.

Mark watched him. "How long has it been standing there?" he asked.

Guy chewed appreciatively for a few minutes. "About two months," he said. He threw it down on the table. "Quite a vintage one."

An old woman hobbled over and wiped the tea from the plastic table top with a dirty rag.

"All right, we'll go to Park Town," Guy said.

"Not if it will create difficulties for you. Why do you never write to me?"

At this, Guy became concerned. Why did Mark always ask him this? How could he possibly write to him?

"Just the odd letter," continued Mark, "Just a nice word from time to time."

"A sonnet or two?" queried Guy. "A love letter, perhaps?"

Crowds of Oxford people were wandering by with bundles of shopping, vegetables, fish, groceries,and there was a general noise of jolly conversation, bustle and racket.

"I say it to you often enough, I don't have to put it in writing," murmured Guy. He was wondering how he could stop Mark from bursting into his tutorials without sending him a regular banker's draft, which would be traceable back to him.

"We'd better go, but let me phone first to make sure no-one's there." They went to look for a phone booth, and Mark crowded inside it with him, pushing himself up against Guy, making it awkward for him to dial.

After a long, dreary walk they finally arrived at the Park Town house. They sat in the conservatory. Mark ordered white wine.

"You had something to tell me."

"Yes, I'm in a spot of bother. Either you consent to hide me, or you have to get me out of it."

"What is it?"

"There was that boy who used to come round, you remember."

"I never liked him, why did you let him come?"

"He paid us so that he could use the place. We never had much money, so we needed whatever he gave us. You didn't give us anything. Anyway, he's been arrested. There's stolen goods involved, and other substances. To try and get himself off the hook he's named names ..."

"Yes?"

"And made allegations. Ian thought it better to disappear for a while, and I've come to see you."

"Thank you, very nice of you."

Mark looked at him archly, and savoured the wine. "This is a very nice Orvieto, why didn't you offer it to me before, instead of that rancid tea?" They contemplated each other in silence. "Of course, that boy is very dangerous," said Mark.

"And you're not," thought Guy, waiting for Mark's next communiqué.

"All things considered," said Mark, looking round appreciatively. "It would be better if I don't go back to London for the time being, and you'd be better off if you stay here with me."

"Of course, that horrid boy knows where I live, you once took him there."

"But he's unlikely to remember."

"I'm sure the police will help to jog his memory, if they wish to do so."

"Then we had better lie low here, don't you think?"

"Is there nowhere I could send you off to?"

"I don't think so, I think I'm pretty well set up here, wouldn't you say?"

Istanbul was a blur, as they went through the souk, the covered market, bargaining for things over glasses of coffee, seeing the sights of Haghia Sophia and Taksim Square, and rushed about in a *dolmush*, a shared taxi.

The hotel room was unbearably hot and Guy was very anxious to leave. He was very concerned not to miss his appointment with Ali.

"Do let's go," he said irritably. "What on earth are you doing? Don't put make-up on, you never wear make-up. If you have to put it on, you can do it afterwards. I can't miss this appointment, I can't be late."

"Who are you going to meet anyway?" asked Clelia.

"I told you," said Guy crossly, "the doctor is on holiday and he very kindly agreed to see me before he sets off to his country estate. He won't wait for me if you go on messing around."

"I'm almost ready, I just have two last things to do, just wait."

"But you're making me late!"

"Why do have to see this doctor?"

"I told you, I have this infection on my foot."

"Show it to me."

"Certainly not, you don't want to see it."

"Are you sure it's on your foot?"

"What the hell is that supposed to mean? Where are you suggesting it is?"

"I wasn't suggesting anything."

"Well, will you hurry up. What are you doing now? You're not even dressed. Just put on a cardigan. Why can't we leave? This is becoming unbearable."

Clelia still hadn't brushed her teeth, but she saw that he was desperate and she would just have to go as she was, otherwise he would go without her.

"Hand me that blouse."

"Hurry up, can't you?"

She grabbed her handbag and hurried out of the room after him.

Guy was striding off down the street, and she had to trot at quite a pace in order to keep up with him. It was very difficult to force her way past the crowds of people swirling about in the hot street. She constantly had to step aside to avoid being struck by bicycles, motor scooters and vans forcing their way through the crowds of pedestrians, and every time she did this she could see Guy striding further and further ahead. He was clearly visible since he was head and shoulders above everyone else, but keeping up with him was almost impossible. At every turn the crowds blocked her path: mothers struggling along with young babies and bundles of groceries, young men pushing past them carrying crates of fruit and vegetables, boys running by with trays of coffee in small glasses, bakers striding along with enormous trays of freshly baked sweetmeats carried high above their heads, and cyclists forcing their way through everybody else while projecting great paniers of freshly baked bread strapped to the front and back of their bicycles. The streets were so narrow that it was almost impossible to push one's way through, but at least the narrowness of the streets and the high buildings meant that the intensity of the burning sun couldn't bear down directly onto one's head. But running and struggling along made her feel intensely hot and sweaty, and she felt her makeup gradually melting down her face. Guy never once even as much as glanced back over his shoulder to see if she had managed to keep up with him, and each time he turned yet another sharp corner she was convinced that she would lose track of him. Just when she thought that she had finally lost him she turned a corner and almost bumped into him. He was talking to a tall man in a shabby suit.

"This is the bakery I told you about," said Guy, leading her into a delicious smelling bakery. All the shelves were covered with freshly baked sugary sticky sweetmeats, cakes, brioches, buns, rolls and breads.

"What would you like to have?"

Before she could reply, he immediately started ordering the smiling, obliging baker woman to place various croissants, brioches and sticky cakes onto a tray. As he did so, he proudly said to her, "This is my wife."

"How lovely, how lovely," nodded the charming baker woman, "So young, so beautiful!"

She handed Guy the tray and he swept out of the bakery to the cafe next door. He led Clelia to one of the tables on the street, and placed the tray down.

"This is very good, this is excellent," he cried. "Sit here while I order the coffee."

A waiter with a thick black moustache and slicked back hair immediately appeared before them bowing, and wiping his wet hands on the enormous white apron that was wound many times round his enormous girth. "The English Milord," he said very proudly to the other cafe sitters who were smoking and reading the cafe's newspapers which were attached to thick wooden sticks.

"This is my wife," Guy said, equally proudly.

"So young, so beautiful, stupendous!" cried the waiter, bowing low. All the cafe sitters turned towards Clelia and had a good stare at her over their glasses and over their newspapers. The waiter ran off to get the coffee.

"I'll be straight back," cried Guy, and disappeared off down the street.

She did not see where he went, he suddenly wasn't there. The cafe sitters returned to the perusal of their newspapers, and Clelia sat in silence drinking in the fumes of the trucks and lorries that deliberately idled their engines in front of the cafe and belched forth great clouds of black soot. As the sweat and the heat and the soot mingled together on her face, and as the makeup melted down into all three, she regretted most the failure to have remembered to bring her fan, so that she was obliged to sit in the noise and sweltering heat slowly melting. She felt so miserably abandoned by him but at the same time she felt that it was unfair of her to insist that they leave the city. He was right to say that there were still lots of museums and monuments that they hadn't yet visited, and a number that he had enjoyed so much that he was desperately keen to return to. He was also right to say that if she was so keen to read, she could read as well in the city as on the beach. To her protest that the city was unbearably sweltering, and at least on the beach there was the possibility of a whisper of a fresh breeze, he would constantly offer to move from the rat-hole where they were staying to a fully air-conditioned hotel, however much it cost. Clelia knew that it would be expensive, and that it would mean asking his father for money, and since she wasn't supposed to be with Guy anyway, it would probably be a mistake. She knew that she couldn't ask Nigel for any more money.

He was willing to spend any amount of money on her if she went off on holiday with him, and he was prepared to take her anywhere she would like to go. He was very annoyed that she had gone off with Guy, even though he had generously given her money to get by, but only on condition that she also spent some part of the summer with him. He couldn't understand why she wanted to spend any part of the summer with Guy.

"I don't know how clearly I should speak out," he had said.

"You don't need to tell me," she had replied.

"Well, if you know, why are you going with him at all?"

"He's rather insisting that I do."

"So that you can sit around and look pretty, and attract young boys."

"No, of course not!"

"Then what are you hanging around with him for? You have nothing whatsoever in common with him. You were nice enough to him to help him through his exams. Now that's all over, why don't you just say goodbye? He doesn't need you, there are at least ten or twelve other girls all anxious to take your place, and you don't even really like him, you've told me so many times."

The memory of this conversation came buzzing back into her ears as she sat in the boiling heat and sweated rivers inside her blouse. She woke up as the waiter unctuously served the coffee with a grand flourish.

Guy suddenly appeared at her side, smiling happily. "Delicious breakfast!" he cried happily as he seized at the cakes and croissants and started to wolf them down. "I told you the bakery was wonderful, didn't I, and the coffee here is marvellous, isn't it!" He tucked in happily, chatting away as he ate. "We'll leave the city as soon as you like. As soon as we've had breakfast, we'll go back to the hotel and pack our things. I'm sorry I had to hurry you, darling, but he was about to leave, and I had to catch him. Everything's fine now. You do like these cakes, don't you."

"Yes, they're delicious, but we need some more coffee."

"Yes, of course, darling."

After breakfast he linked his arm through hers, and together they forced their way through the crowds in the street to return to the hotel. The room was unbearably hot, and they had to take their clothes off at once.

Guy immediately switched on the fan, but it didn't help. Someone had thoughtfully wedged open the window with a broken plastic plant pot.

Clelia leaned out into the courtyard until she suddenly became aware of all the neighbours peering out of their windows at her, and she immediately withdrew into the hot room.

Guy was busy zipping up the suitcases. He flicked through the guide book. "Look," he said, showing her the pictures, "Topkapi. We have to go there. We've got time. Let's go. After that, there'll still be time to catch the bus to the sea."

They set off for the museum.

"It's one of the greatest museums in Turkey. They have the most wonderful things." He was very excited, and they walked about in the cool museum, looking at all the artefacts, and reading the labels in detail. Very few visitors were wandering around, and they had the feeling that the museum belonged to them. Guy particularly enjoyed the section on illuminated manuscripts, and they then drifted into the section of sculptures. As they entered each room Guy would read from the guide book as he led them round the exhibits. In one large room an enormous carved wooden door from the sultan's palace was displayed. Standing in front of it and gazing up at it was a young man.

"You see that the carvings on this door are all representations of non-figurative motifs," explained Guy.

"Yes, you know that it was forbidden to represent any forms of living things, humans, beasts or birds in art," replied the young man.

"Leaves or flowers?" queried Clelia.

"Only geometric patterns, but some of them extremely intricate and convoluted," the young man replied, and took them on a guided tour of all the intricate patterns carved on the door. From then, it seemed only natural that he would take them on a tour of the remainder of the museum, pointing out all his favourite things and giving them delightful and personal accounts of the things he showed them. He introduced himself as Güner.

Guy introduced Clelia as his wife.

Having spent several hours in the museum, Clelia was exhausted and wished she hadn't worn high heeled shoes. She felt as if he had walked herself off her feet, and had to go and sit down.

"You must rest," Güner told her, "let me invite you to lunch." He took them to a small restaurant by the waterfront.

Everyone was asleep in the intense heat of the day, but the waiter leapt up as soon as they entered the ice-cold interior of the cave-like hostelry, and showed them to a table covered with a clean white tablecloth and already set for lunch.

They all sank gratefully down into their seats, and while they sipped the ice-cold yoghourt, Güner told them about his family and his ambitions. "I'm studying at university now, but I very much hope to continue my studies at Oxford, only I wouldn't know how to go about applying."

"Don't worry, I'll help you," said Guy. "It won't be a problem."

"We have a house by the sea. The family will be going to stay there soon. Meanwhile, you can come and stay in our villa just outside the city. That way we can spend the mornings visiting the museums and mosques and churches, and in the afternoons we can relax in the cool rose gardens. We also have a very splendid library that I think you would like, and I can teach you Turkish in exchange for English lessons."

"Your English sounds very good to me, you don't seem to be in need of any lessons."

"I've never been to England, I've only studied English at school and by radio."

The waiter brought the lunch to the table.

"After lunch we'll collect your things from the hotel."

"Are you sure your parents won't mind?"

"Of course they won't, I've often invited friends to stay. I love meeting English people so that I can practise my English."

Güner insisted on paying for the lunch. He then drove them to the hotel where they collected their luggage, and they then drove to his family villa, situated in a beautiful road just outside the walls of Vespasian.

The family was very welcoming, and Güner's sisters were very excited at the idea of Clelia staying with them. They excitedly watched her unpack all her things, and examined everything closely and with intense interest. They all sat together on the bed and watched everything she did. They then sat together with her and taught her the words of various household objects in

Turkish, laughing uproariously as she repeated the words back to them. "Tomorrow we go swimming," they announced to her, suiting the action to the words, in case she hadn't understood the few words of English they knew. They were particularly excited by her ring, imagining it to be her wedding ring, and spent hours trying it on and admiring it. They thought the idea of Guy and Clelia together on their honeymoon unendurably romantic, and enthused and swooned over them. They were terribly proud of Güner for having found them and brought them to the house.

Guy spent the cooler hours before dinner closeted in the library with Güner, looking at his father's magnificent collection of miniatures, manuscripts and antique books. They quickly realised that they had an enormous number of interests in common, and were soon swapping stories and anecdotes, and arguing about their favourite philosophers. Guy had always thought that he was well-read, but he was amazed at Güner's erudition.

"I have nothing else to do but read," explained Güner. "Apart from the cinema, the swimming pool, and sport, there's very little for young people to do here. I really want to get away to England, but I can't do it until I graduate."

At dinner, the family was extremely hospitable. Children ran around the table and were shouted at by their somewhat elderly father and kissed and caressed by their remarkably young and fine-looking mother. The types of dishes were many and varied, and there were delicious vegetable dishes that the guests had never come across in the street cafes they had frequented. Some of the pepper dishes were remarkably hot, and the children roared with laughter as their guests coughed and spluttered and loudly shouted for water.

"I've never eaten anything so spicy," spluttered Guy, coughing and choking with tears pouring down his face. "Why didn't you tell me?"

"We did, we did, we said it was hot!" shouted a chorus of laughing voices.

"You'll soon get used to it," said Güner, merrily enjoying their discomfort. "Here, have some raki," he offered, smiling.

"Definitely not," said Guy. "I've had that before, it's worse than ouzo. It's like drinking methylated spirits."

"Soon you'll like it," encouraged Güner.

Clelia bit rather too hard into a sweetmeat that was full of pistachio nuts.

"Be careful," laughed Güner. "The last time I did that the pistachio nuts quite ravished my tooth."

While Clelia was chatting with the mother she made the terrible mistake of admiring the bracelet that she was wearing. It was amethysts and lapis lazuli set in silver and fastened curiously with a silver pin.

The mother insisted on giving it to her as a present, and despite Clelia's protests that she couldn't possibly accept it, the whole family insisted that she did. It seemed only too appropriate that the family should offer a wedding present to this handsome young couple who had chosen to take their honeymoon in Turkey.

The girls then joyously escorted Clelia and Guy up to their bedroom, in happy excitement as though it was their wedding night, and hung around shyly while they got ready for the night, reluctant to leave them and say goodnight.

"They're very keen for you to go swimming with them in the pool tomorrow afternoon. They can't go swimming on the beach. Girls aren't allowed to, and nobody does. It's so different from Greece, where everybody does. Will you go?" asked Guy.

"Yes. What will you do?"

"I'll spend the time with Güner in the library. He's going to teach me Turkish. There's no point coming here and not learning the language. In the morning we'll go to the church of Saints Cosmas and Damian, and we'll come back here for lunch."

The following morning they set off early for the church of Saints Cosmas and Damian, which they found in a derelict part of the city, surrounded by excavated sandpits and building works.

"They don't care about it," Güner explained. "They don't realise its importance and they don't appreciate its Byzantine beauty. For me the whole city is a work of art, I love the Byzantine presence as much as everything else that was built later."

After lunch Clelia set off with the joyful girls and spent a giggly and intimate afternoon with them in the swimming pool.

On their return they found Guy and Güner again closeted in the library, fiercely debating the interpretation of Greek texts as seen through the eyes of their rediscovery at the time of the Renaissance. The debate was so furious that they could hardly be dragged out of the library to attend the family dinner.

Guy then spent the remainder of the evening entertaining the young boys of the house. They ended up playing hide-and-seek and running around the whole house screaming and laughing until they were finally caught and ordered to go to bed. "The two boys who are eight and nine are coming up to the time when they have to do their circumcision, when they are ten or so, sometimes earlier. The very idea of it makes me extremely ill, I dread it for them, but Güner assures me it is the tradition. I have to blot the whole idea of it out of my mind." Guy lay down on the bed exhausted. "Tomorrow he's taking us back to the Yerebatan Saray, I want to spend some more time there, and in the afternoon the girls are taking you out to tea with some friends of theirs."

In the following days Clelia found her programme arranged for her, and the days passed very pleasantly. She also found that she had much more time to read, as Guy became less and less visible.

The day came for the family to prepare themselves to set off for their house by the sea in Anatolya, and there was mad excitement and packing and running about all over the house looking for things. The children always wanted to take the most improbable things. They kept running up to their mother and demanding permission to be allowed to take this and that, and their mother had to smilingly say no on each occasion. It turned out that the children regarded Guy as the ultimate arbiter on each of these frequent occasions, and he had to be dragged forward each time, and appeal to their mother on their behalf as to whether yet another unlikely item might be included in the enormous amount of baggage that the servants were preparing to pack.

Naturally, Clelia and Guy had been invited to join them at the sea. Guy spent some time trying to persuade Clelia that she should go with them now, and that he and Güner would come along a few days later.

The girls also spent some time trying to persuade Clelia to come with them, and were very sweet about it. They were not entirely unaware of the neglect she now suffered, and wanted to entertain her.

Clelia patiently explained that she was very happy to spend her time lying in her room reading, even though Guy was elsewhere.

In a ceremony of great laughter and jollity, three cars containing the family, the luggage, and all the necessary servants finally set out from the courtyard of the villa. For quite some distance as they drove down the road, the sound of chattering, laughter and the chirpy sound of all the children chorusing "Goodbye!" could be heard echoing into the far-flung distance of the sky.

A sudden silence descended upon the house.

Guy paced up and down edgily in their bedroom, while Clelia lay on the bed reading.

"This is an extremely exciting part," she told him. She was reading *The Brothers Karamazov* and was perfectly contented to spend the time in the room reading. "I have a whole pile of books which I brought out with me. Really, I'm perfectly happy. It's wonderfully cool here, I don't need to be by the sea, I assure you."

He continued to stalk about the room, looking at her and then looking away, never making eye-contact, always about to say something and then never quite saying it. "You'll get bored," he groaned, "Wouldn't it be better …"

"No, no, I'm absolutely fine."

"But Güner and I have many things to do."

"I won't disturb you. I promise you. I'll stay here in the room. I have lots of reading that I'm very keen to do."

After that she hardly saw him at all, and then, only briefly, when he came into their bedroom to throw a closely written completed notebook into his bag and grab out of it another empty notebook.

Güner felt that they were deserting her too much, and when he failed to prevail on Guy to make a visit to her in the bedroom, he would sometimes drop by himself just to make sure that she wasn't getting too lonely. "You can go to the sea at any time," he told her. "I talk to my mother every day on the phone. All they have to do is send the car for you. The girls would love to look after you."

"I do like them very much, but I had intended to spend a lot of this summer reading. Look at how many books I brought with me. I've still got all the rest of Dostoevsky to read, and it's so marvellous that I don't want to read it too quickly. You really don't have to worry about me."

He looked at her closely. "You don't mind, do you? I know you're not married, Guy told me. I like you very much. I find it strange that Guy neglects you quite so much."

"It really doesn't matter."

"We're all having supper together tonight, so we can talk about things."

"I don't think Guy wants to talk."

"No, I don't think he does. But he does an awful lot of writing. Do you know what it is?"

"He made me promise that I wouldn't read any of his notebooks."

"Have you read them?"

"No, I wouldn't dream of it."

But as soon as Güner left the room she couldn't resist stretching her hand out slowing towards the leather bag, and slowly and silently undoing the zip. Listening very attentively for the sound of anyone approaching, she slid her hand inside and carefully extracted the first notebook she came across. The handwriting was neat and small, and covered every inch of the page. She began to feel the sweat creeping along the back of her neck as she read the minute detail with which each intimate, intricate encounter was recorded, and the care with which the feelings, passions, sensations and pulsations were analysed. It wasn't so much the content that shocked her, after all, she was only too well aware of what was going on, as they all knew, but the intensity of the involvement and the psychological skill with which it was all approached, carried out and then dissected, from the point of view of both participants. She suddenly heard the sound of voices, and footsteps on the stair, and hastily shoved the notebook back into the bag, straining desperately to do up the zip, which was very awkward from that angle. She quickly lay back in the bed as the two men came in.

Guy flung himself down onto the bed beside her.

Güner went and stood by the window.

"You loved it at Impos, didn't you. Güner is suggesting that we go there."

"Would you like to?" enquired Güner casually.

At that moment there was a tap on the door, and a servant came to tell Güner that his mother was on the telephone. Güner went off to take the call.

"The fact is that for some time now he's been asking me if he can sleep with you."

"Would that be a problem for you?"

"That's what I don't know."

The room became strangely silent. She listened to the breeze softly blowing the blossoms against the window. She considered the situation. "What would you like me to do?"

"I don't know. He insists that I should agree, on the basis that I should offer to him whatever means the most to me, as a symbol of the strength of our friendship. On the other hand, I'm very concerned as to how it will affect his relationship with me. Should I be jealous that he wants you?"

"Instead of wanting you?"

"Not instead of. Along with." He paused. "The fact is that when you went swimming with his sisters he ordered them to observe every detail about you, and then describe it to him."

"Did they?"

"He's obsessed by the idea of having you. He says it won't make any difference to us."

"In other words, he won't want you less?"

"So he says."

"Can I believe him?"

He looked at her. "Of course, you'll enjoy him immensely. He's very good."

"Better than you?"

Guy laughed.

"Tell me what you want me to do." She stroked his hair. He looked worried and concerned. "I'll do whatever you want me to do."

"Will I be jealous?" he asked her.

"Of whom?" she queried.

"That's what I don't know."

"Do you want to wait until afterwards to find out?" she asked, smiling mischievously.

Guy suddenly panicked. "You haven't been reading my notebooks?" he enquired suspiciously.

"Of course not," she replied sweetly, gently stroking his hair.

He leaned over and started to kiss her.

Güner entered the room and watched them. "Well?" he said, "Are we going to Impos?"

"If we go there, it will happen there," Guy whispered into her ear.

"You have to decide," she whispered back.

They went downstairs for a languid supper, waited upon by the household servants.

During the course of the meal Güner realised that he would have to make the decision. He announced that they would leave the following morning.

"Aren't you being rather hasty?" asked Guy plaintively.

"We have to leave tomorrow. If we don't, my mother will insist that we join her, and that will spoil everything. If we go off to Erzurum, she won't be able to phone me up every day and give me lots of good advice."

Guy spent the remainder of the evening wandering around in an agitated way, and watching the others closely for any signs of a secret deal between them. Clelia and Güner were now discussing Spinosa. Guy very much wanted to join in, after all, it was his subject, but he felt too restless and contemplated the following day with trepidation. As he occasionally drifted nearby them in the cool night air, he murmured, "You would do better to debate Simmel, and his essay on numbers. He thinks that three is a particularly inauspicious number. Have you thought about that?"

"It may be something he considered theoretically," replied Güner confidently. "We don't have any evidence that he carried out any experiments in practice. His writing is all based on ideas and imagination. In those days they didn't do things, they thought about them. No-one was allowed to do any of that, they could only consider it in theory, or academic terms. Now, we've broken out of all of that. At last we are able to do things. Coming from England, you ought to know that, you gave us the term, 'Swinging Sixties from Swinging London.' There's even a song about it, 'London swings like a pendulum, Do!' They've been playing it here on the radio. Everyone is very excited, all my friends want to do it." He laughed. "They're not quite sure what it is, but we're all determined to have a damn good try."

"If only it wasn't with my fiancée," thought Guy doubtfully to himself. He was very concerned that the relationship wouldn't founder. Not that he thought it would, there had never been any suggestion of that. It was just that he was moving on to something new, and he couldn't quite see how it would work out. "What if they fall in love?" he thought. "What if they don't fall in love but still exclude me? Then we won't be a trio anymore but a couple and an excluded person. I can't contemplate being the excluded person, I would find it unbearable. Clelia can, she's strong enough to take it, but I can't, and I definitely can't contemplate being excluded by Güner. It would be absurd, why did I come here?" From the darkness of the distant terrace he watched them chatting and drinking and enjoying each other's company. "I could break it all up now," he thought, "I could insist that we leave first thing in the morning." But he knew that his relationship with Güner was one that he couldn't contemplate compromising, and in consequence was in no position to defend his vulnerability. He was drawn to them again to listen to their conversation. As he drew nearby, silently approaching them from the shadows, he was keenly aware of Güner's keen intuition as to where the balance of power really lay. "How is it possible," he thought, "that I always put myself in danger to take bread at their hand, and now they range, busily seeking with a continual change."

Güner smiled at him as he hovered nearby. "He looks at me as though he divines my thought."

Güner was telling about his father. "You know, my father thinks that all this permissive society is the beginning of the deterioration of the social order, and will lead to the breakdown of your society. A civil society is a very fragile thing. You couldn't allow that sort of permissiveness in this society, it would lead to total breakdown. But fortunately there's no danger of that here, we always have the army to hold things together."

Guy leaned forward and inhaled deeply on the reefer Güner was holding out to him. "We're not setting out for Impos tomorrow unless you've got lots of good stuff."

"I have."

"I don't mean this," he said, inhaling deeply again.

"I know exactly what you mean. Don't worry, I've got lots of it."

"Well, if you haven't, you'll be the one who has to go back for it."

"Can I have some?" asked Clelia.

"Certainly not," said Guy crossly. "It's time you went up to bed."

Clelia smiled sweetly, and went upstairs.

Guy and Güner sat in the quiet evening smoking together.

"I'm going to write a book of political definitions." said Güner. He read out, "A ne'er do well or failure: an individual with temporarily unmet objectives. A prisoner: a client of the correctional system." He was about to go on reading.

Guy interrupted him. "Do you love me?"

"You know I do."

"Are you saying it to get round me in order to have her?"

"You know I'm not."

"Won't it adversely affect our relationship?"

"Why should it? Our relationship is very sound, you know that."

"Then why do you need to have her?"

"I don't need to, I'd like to, and you would like to give her to me, wouldn't you."

"Would I? What makes you so sure?"

"Because you love me, and you want me to enjoy what you enjoy. It will bring us closer together, and that can only be to the good. It's what we both want, don't you think?" He smiled charmingly, and leaning out towards Guy, took hold of his hand and gazed sweetly into his face.

Güner came into the room with a look of anguish on his face.

"Guy tells me that you won't be staying with us for the whole of the summer."

"That's right," said Clelia.

"He said you're going to do some voluntary service overseas, it's called VSO."

"Yes, it's for poor people in the undeveloped world."

"Why don't you do it here, this is undeveloped, do it here if you have to do it."

Clelia laughed. "No, it's not like that. We go to special sites and build hospitals or clinics."

"You do building!"

"I don't personally, I mainly take care of sick children in orphanages, that sort of thing. It's usually the boys who do all the hard labour, although some girls do that too."

"Oh, so there are boys there, is that why you go?"

"Of course not, everybody behaves perfectly properly, nothing of that sort goes on at all."

Güner didn't seem to be convinced. "And where is it, anyway?"

"It takes place in all sorts of countries where they need extra help, and students from England are very pleased to offer their services."

He noticed that she was rather vague about precisely here she was going.

"We go where they send us, where the need is."

Güner was very disappointed. "This arrangement we have at the moment is absolutely perfect. It seems to be working very well. If we split up now, it will be very difficult to get it back together again."

"But Guy says that you are going to come and study in England, he's going to help you fix it up. Surely we'll all see each other then?"

He looked at her closely. "Do you want to?"

"Yes."

Güner had this strange, indefinable feeling that she was slipping away from him. "Something tells me that it's a big mistake to separate now."

"But you do, in any case, feel that our arrangement is inherently unstable. We often talk about how Guy is unhappy, and how he can't talk about it, or his feelings, and how he writes all the time, and although he tells us not to read it, he sort of leaves some of the pages about. It is, sort of, rather difficult."

"Ah, as I suspected, you are leaving because you think the situation is difficult. Perhaps you don't realise how unhappy you'll make Guy if you go."

"And yet I have a very strong feeling that he has an intense desire to be with you."

"But he doesn't in any way think you get in the way of that. Far from it. Perhaps it's his manner that you misinterpret, his moods, his grumpiness. Maybe deep down, you don't realise how important you are to him." He tried to get her to respond to this, but Clelia turned away.

Rupert hurried through the Long Gallery on his way to the West Wing. A shaft of sunlight flooded across his path, illuminating the antique silks and damasks of the chaises longues and couches along each side, and blinding him with its reflection on the polished wooden floor. He heard what could only have been the sound of a sob, and yet the gallery was empty. He stopped in his tracks. Curled up in a wing-chair, his face bathed in sweat, crouched Guy. Rupert had never seen him looking so ill. He ran to him and knelt down at his feet. He placed his hand gently on Guy's knee.

"You have to help me!" gasped Guy. "Can't you understand? You have to help me!"

Rupert gazed at him. Guy shuddered. Rupert put his hand on his shoulder to try and steady him, but the shuddering became uncontrollable. Rupert realised that Guy's shirt was completely bathed in sweat. "Let me help you to bed, and then I'll call Dr Vaughn."

"No you will not," snarled Guy. "That won't help me. I really need your help, but I don't need a doctor. Anyway, he's not discreet." He broke off sharply, and made a grimace of silent pain as he clutched at his stomach and clawed at the green and gold brocade on the eighteenth century wing chair. Gasping and almost crying with pain, he tried to speak, but his body shook so much that he couldn't get the words out. He had to pause and breathe very deeply for a while before he was able to continue. "I need help, but nobody in the family must know. And he mustn't know either."

"Who?"

"Him! You know. Rupert, we need someone to help us, there's only one person, you have to contact him." His teeth were chattering and he could hardly speak. "You have to contact him, I can't do it, he has to come, please contact him, but tell him that he mustn't say a word to Clelia. I've no-one else I can turn to, who has the authority, and and and ..."

"Yes?"

"Can get him to go."

"Where is he now?"

"I don't know, but I don't want him to find me. If he won't leave, I'll have to leave. But I can't look after myself, I'll have to be admitted some-where. Nigel will know where. He knows everyone in Oxford. He'll get me admitted to the Radcliffe Infirmary. I want to go there without any reference to Dr Vaughn.

He would immediately tell the parents. That's the last thing I want."

"While Nigel is coming here, let me take you to Park Town."

"No!" hissed Guy through clenched teeth. "I can't hide there! He's sure to come looking for me there. At least here I can hide from him, I can keep one step ahead of him provided no-one notices me." Again he paused to overcome the agony of the pain. "This is total hell, it's unbearable." He sank down on the chair, sweating copiously. His clammy hand clutched at Rupert. "Help me to the loft above the music room. He's never been there, he doesn't know about it. If you see him, say I've gone to London. Then maybe he'll go away." He glanced nervously up and down the gallery. "He's not here, is he? I thought I heard something. Take me there quickly. I'm going to be sick."

"Let me take you to a bathroom."

"No, there isn't time. Take me upstairs. Bring me some water."

"And some food?"

"No, idiot, a bowl to be sick in."

Guy spent the interminable day lying on a mattress hidden away in the amidst the bric-a-brac, while Rupert hastily made the arrangements. Every so often, when the coast was clear, he would run up to the loft and swab at Guy's forehead with a damp flannel moistened in icy water. "Look, I found this, a cologne stick of ice. Try it."

Guy irritably pushed his hand away. "Is Nigel coming?"

"Yes, but only after he finishes work."

"Then he'll be too late for a train."

"He said if it's too late, he'll drive up."

"I don't want him to have to do that," wailed Guy miserably.

"Try to sleep."

"Of course I can't, don't you know anything!"

It was late at night when Rupert led Nigel up the rickety staircase, ducking down to avoid banging his head on the beams.

"Can't we put a light on?"

"No, he won't allow it. He doesn't want you to see him."

"Does he look bad?"

"Pretty awful. You'll have a shock. You haven't told Clelia, have you? He'll go insane if she hears about it."

"You'd better get a torch, it's far too dark."

"It's here, only don't shine it on his face, or he'll go crazy."

Nigel crawled about in the low-beamed loft, carefully picking his way amidst the antique and broken furniture. He slid down gently onto the mattress.

"Not there," muttered Guy between clenched teeth. "I've been sick there."

Nigel moved further off. "I've spoken to friends of mine in the Radcliffe. Do you think you could get downstairs, then I could drive you there in the car. If we have to get an ambulance it'd be noticed and we'd have to give an explanation."

"There's no way I can walk, I can't even get up."

"Try to, Guy, otherwise someone will see you and tell Papa," begged Rupert.

"I can't, I can't, I can't even get up."

"Let's do it in stages," suggested Nigel. "Just a bit at a time. If we have to get an ambulance someone's bound to ask who it's for. Let us take you down this staircase to the music room, then we can rest there a bit until you're ready to go on."

"No, no, not the music room, he's bound to be there, then he won't let me go!"

"Who?" asked Nigel.

"There's nobody there," said Rupert.

"Have you seen him?" asked Guy anxiously.

"I haven't seen him all day."

"Who?" asked Nigel.

Guy's trembling clammy hand seized hold of Nigel's. "You have to swear not to tell her! Swear to me, swear you won't tell her! I'll go insane if you tell her!"

The clammy hand told him more than any words could have, and he realised the urgency of getting Guy to the hospital.

"There, there, in the darkness, is it him? Who is it?" cried Guy suddenly. "Who is it, Rupert, who is it?"

"It's just a rusty suit of armour, it's not him."

"Who?!!" asked Nigel.

"Perhaps there's someone we could ask to help us to carry him down," suggested Rupert.

"You couldn't trust them, you couldn't trust them, they'd tell Papa," said Guy desperately.

"We must try and carry him," said Nigel.

"Who?" asked Guy.

It was very slowly and with enormous effort that they managed to drag Guy down the first staircase to the music room, where they placed him on an ottoman and sat down to rest. By now Guy was delirious and rambling,

"If he goes on like that he'll give us away," said Rupert. "If anyone they'll catch us."

"Shall we all pretend we're drunk, and that we're staggering about at a party like in the good old days?"

"Except that nobody will believe it because Guy hasn't been drunk for so long."

"More's the pity," said Nigel. "I could do with a stiff whiskey right now."

"No, we can't stop now. Perhaps I could get John to help us."

"No chance," said Guy. "He really will be drunk."

They gazed at him. "Maybe Victor, then."

"No!" cried Guy in panic. "He'll go straight to Papa and sell him the story. He's always trying to blackmail me."

"You never told me that."

"There's a lot I didn't tell you, but you can't trust him. In fact, I think he's paid to spy on me."

"Surely not, Guy, you must be imagining things."

"I think you must get me out of here, I can't stand much more of this," groaned Guy. "Please get me out!"

They each placed an arm under his shoulder, and started to drag him along the corridor. Little children in pyjamas came running by at one point, and from time to time a servant was seen going by in the distance, and voices could be heard all over the place. But in the end they encountered no-one who paid them any attention, and they finally reached the courtyard.

As they were thankfully stuffing Guy into the car, Rupert noticed that one of the children, aged seven, had followed them downstairs. "Piers, what are you doing here? It's terribly late, you should have been in bed hours ago."

Piers' eyes opened wide as he gazed at Guy's head lolling back in the car, his face a greeny yellow. "Is Guy alright?" he anxiously asked Rupert.

Guy opened his eyes. "Who's that?" he asked.

"It's me," said Piers, leaning forward and placing his hands on Guy's face.

"I thought you said you didn't want anyone to see us."

"I'm hardly anyone," said Piers, stroking Guy's hair sympathetically.

"If I wasn't feeling so awful I'd give you a good chase round the courtyard, and up the stairs to bed."

"Please get better, Guy." He looked very anxious and stroked Guy's face.

Guy was immensely touched by his concern.

"Off to bed, young man," said Rupert, "And Piers, not a word to a soul."

Piers shook his head very solemnly. As the car drew away towards the drive, Piers stood alone in the centre of the immense courtyard waving sadly at them.

It was after midnight before they arrived at the Radcliffe Infirmary. Nigel drove into the courtyard, past the pond and parked in front of the main door. He immediately went inside to organise stretcher bearers to carry Guy upstairs.

Guy had again become delirious, and was rambling on noisily about a number of disconnected subjects.

Nigel's houseman friend came to organise everything, and Guy was soon installed in bed in a small room with an intravenous drip in his arm. The nurses were busy organising the tests they had to carry out, and the houseman was checking him with his stethoscope. They made notes in his file, and on his temperature chart. Nigel and the houseman stood in a corner of the room chatting quietly. Rupert stood next to the bed watching Guy anxiously and holding his hand. Guy was sweating intensely, raving deliriously and his face was all grey. Rupert felt the clammy hand clutch feverishly at his. While he saw them chatting in the corner, Rupert looked at the temperature chart and saw with alarm that Guy had pyrexia. A nurse came back into the room and began to swab him down, then re-adjusted the drip. Nigel and the houseman walked across to Rupert.

I'm not leaving him," said Rupert intensely. "I don't care what you say, I'm staying with him all night."

"But there'll be someone here all night," reassured the houseman.

"He's got terrible fever. I have to be here. Nigel, you do agree I must stay."

Nigel and the houseman consulted each other, and it was agreed that a bed would be brought into the room for Rupert.

"So that boy has gone?" asked Nigel.

"What boy?" asked Rupert nervously.

"You know, the boy who caused all the trouble."

"Please, Nigel, I beg you –"

"Rupert, don't worry, I'm not a fool, you know, and remember, I was in college too. Is there any danger that he'll come back?"

"Yes, he could turn up at any time, that's why Guy has to be hidden from him. He mustn't know he's here. If he were to find out – we must think of some way –"

"Would you like me to write him a letter?"

"Would you? Something stern and forbidding, telling him not to come back."

"You'll have to give me his details."

"Never tell Guy I told you."

"As soon as I've written the letter, I'll forget all about it, and blot it out of my mind."

"Thank you. Thank you. And by the way, erm …"

"Yes, what is it?"

Rupert's loyal eyes pleaded with him. "Guy adores Clelia, she must never know about this."

"Did she meet this boy?"

Rupert spoke guardedly. "Maybe, but I assure you she doesn't know. Basically, she doesn't know about these things. Girls don't. Clelia is very sweet and adorable, but she is very innocent in the ways of the world. She mustn't know, it would be terribly disconcerting …" His voice trailed away, but his sad eyes told everything.

Ian was sitting in the apartment drinking a vodka martini when Mark came in.

"Letter for you. Personal delivery. Must be important. It says private and personal on the envelope so I didn't open it."

Mark tore open the envelope. It was on Home Office notepaper, but a line had been scrawled through the address.

Ian looked over Mark's shoulder as he read it.

> Dear Mr Greville,
>
> I wish to inform you that Guy Blandford has been taken ill and has been removed to a sanatorium. He is now out of immediate danger, but in order to make a complete recovery he requires rest and isolation. I wish to make it clear to you that you are under no circumstances to call upon him either now or at any future time, nor in any way to contact him. If you make any attempt to do so, an injunction will be taken out to restrain you. I hope that this course will not be necessary.
>
> Yours sincerely,
> Nigel Rawlinson.

"Not to contact him even in any way!" whispered Ian. "Must be bad!"

"Who on earth is he?"

"Looks like someone important."

Mark clutched the letter in his hand. "How dare he, how dare he, whoever he is. This is absurd, of course I can see Guy. If he's ill, there's all the more reason for me to see him. They can't stop me!"

He reached for the telephone and immediately dialled the number of Malplaquet. "I wish to speak to Guy Blandford, please put me through."

"Who is speaking, please?"

"It's Mark Greville, put me through at once."

"I'm afraid I can't do that, Sir."

"Put me through – "

"I'm afraid he's not here, Sir. The fact is, he has been taken ill."

"Where is he, where is he?"

"I'm not at liberty to say, Sir."

"Damn!" cried Mark, and flung the phone down. He sat fuming, and staring furiously at the telephone. "Do you think he really is ill, or do you think it's an elaborate hoax?"

"Whatever it is, Mark, I always had doubts about this whole obsession with Guy. I always had fears and I often voiced them out loud to you that it would all end badly. The next thing we know is that there'll be a writ for possession of this apartment served on us, and we'll be back in slum-land in King's Cross."

"No, Guy will never do that."

"If he's ill, it's not up to him, someone else will do it. Like this Nigel Rawlinson, for example."

"Yes, who on earth is he? Perhaps I should find out."

"No, please Mark, enough is enough."

Nigel sat at his desk in his office, getting through a pile of papers in front of him. He was aware of someone coming into the room, but didn't look up. "Yes, what is it?"

There was silence. He looked up. "Yes, what is it?"

"Are you Nigel Rawlinson?"

"Yes. Who are you?"

"I'm Mark Greville. You wrote me this letter." He held up the letter clutched in his claw.

Nigel leaped up from his desk. "How on earth did you get in here?"

"I just walked in."

"You are not entitled to come in here, you don't have security clearance. You don't have an appointment. You must leave at once."

"You have to tell me where Guy is, I have to see him."

"That is absolutely out of the question."

"I have to see him." Mark desperately forced back the tears as he felt his voice rising. "You have no right to keep me away from him."

"Don't you realise that he is seriously ill?"

"That's all the more reason for me to see him, don't you understand."

"But it's because of you that he's ill. Don't you realise that he has suffered a severe nervous crisis that was brought on by you."

"What are you saying, this is completely impossible. I must see him." His voice rose almost to a shriek, and his face was red and bathed in sweat.

Nigel looked very hard at him. He was concerned lest the sound of screaming might attract unwanted attention to his room. He paused for a moment before he spoke. Lowering his voice he said, "Have you been supplying him with drugs?"

"No," gulped Mark.

"Do you know that supplying drugs is illegal, and carries a lengthy prison sentence even if it is supplied to friends."

"I haven't done it, I don't believe Guy would ever say that I had."

"Guy has been ill and delirious. You have no idea what he has been saying."

Mark looked very alarmed. "What has he been saying?"

"I think it would be most unwise for you to remain here. I'm not saying that I am going to call the police, but if I have to call the security guards to have you removed, I shall instruct them to detain you until the police arrive. You do realise that this matter is serious. Guy has been very ill. Someone is responsible for the state he has been reduced to." He looked very hard at Mark, who stood irresolutely before him, his lips parted nervously and his hand still clutching agitatedly at the letter.

"Mr Greville, I think that it would be better if you left now, and observed the terms of the letter."

Mark looked devastated. He seemed to take some time to take it all in, and appeared to be in a daze.

Nigel waited for a few moments, and then said softly but forcefully, "Would you like to be escorted out?"

At these words, Mark suddenly came back to earth, looked sharply at Nigel and swiftly left the room.

Nigel sat down at his desk. He realised that he was completely soaked in perspiration.

For the remainder of the week Guy was kept on the drip. As his condition began to improve he was able to take liquids, but it was more than a week before he was able to hold down solid food. He was very annoyed at the hospital's refusal to give him methadone. He had an angry row with a young doctor who came to his bedside.

"Why won't you give it to me?"

"You can get by without it."

"You don't know that."

"I believe you've got the guts to do without it. Besides, contrary to what all you chaps say, it's habit formingin itself, and soon creates dependency. It's given to weaklings or people we can't trust not to go back to smack. You don't need it and you know you don't. You've got a strong character, only you don't use it, that's your problem. Why did you go onto drugs in the first place?"

"It wasn't my fault, it was because of someone else."

"Everyone always has a good excuse to blame some-on else when they go on drugs. You weren't forced onto them were you?"

"In a sort of way, I was."

"I don't accept that for a minute. Anyway, I gather that all those circumstances have changed."

"Yes, thank God, they have."

"So can I have a promise from you?"

"It's pointless asking for it. I'll do what I can."

Rupert visited Guy every day. He would come into the hospital with his head held down, and a worried frown on his face, avoiding all eye contact as he hurried to Guy's room. He would then quickly go inside, determined each day to see for himself that Guy was getting better before he spoke to anyone.

"Piers hasn't said a word to anyone, but he keeps taking me aside and begging me to let him come and see you."

"Once they've taken the needle out of my arm and I look more normal you can bring him. He's very sensitive, I don't want him to have a shock."

Piers was eventually allowed to come, and sat on the pillow next to Guy, playing chess with him.

This was how Clelia found them when she made her visit.

As soon as Guy saw her he became very distressed, but he made an enormous effort to control his emotions in front of Piers, and went on with the game of chess.

Clelia smiled brightly and behaved in a completely matter-of-fact way, getting out fruit and books and arranging Guy's things.

Nigel arrived shortly afterwards, and chatted with Clelia about mundane things. "Does his family still not know he's here?" he asked her.

"Of course not, they mustn't know, they assume he's at Park Town working on his thesis. Anyway, they are far too busy with all their social engagements and the other children. They think he's a big boy now."

"His father doesn't."

"I actually think that's because he's jealous of him. He's jealous of his stunning good looks, and all the sensual rewards that they have brought him that his father wanted but never had. Guy's attractiveness to women is an essential and integral part of his very being, how he sees himself, his self-image. He has always projected himself in this way. As a result, a lot of people respond to him very negatively. Unfortunately, his father too has always responded very badly to that."

"Have you observed that?"

"Certainly, I think it's at the root of the whole problem between them. You know, darling, the father even made a pass at me."

"I'm not surprised. From what I heard, you went around half naked most of the time."

"That was to attract Guy, not his father." Clelia glanced at the bed.

Guy was deeply involved in the chess game with Piers, who was laughing and enjoying it immensely, boasting to Rupert that he was going to beat Guy.

Clelia surprised herself by finding the scene strangely touching. She always found herself impressed by the selfless enthusiasm Guy always showed when his younger brothers and sisters demanded his attention. They always knew that they could come and bother him, and drag him away from other guests or whatever else he was doing. Apart from the fact that he obviously enjoyed being with them and playing with them, it also occurred to her that he wanted to give them the attention that he felt his parents had always denied him.

Later, when Rupert had set off for home with Piers, and Nigel was consulting his houseman friend as to Guy's progress, Clelia said to Guy, "I'm glad that horrid boy has gone."

"Who?"

"The one with the straggly, dark hair and the sour, disappointed face who used to come to the house and demand money."

"Oh, him. Has he really gone?"

Guy was very unwilling to discuss anything about his present predicament with Clelia or Nigel, and seemed very resentful that Clelia had visited him. When questioned, he would only reply in monosyllables, or repeat the constant refrain, "I don't know."

There was a great deal of concern amongst all of them as to where he would go when he was ready to be discharged from the hospital. He would obviously require being looked after, but he was determined not to return to Malplaquet, which would have been the most suitable place. They were all sure that Mrs B would look after him, but Guy was adamant about not going back. Clelia was busy at her studies. The danger was that the whole of the burden of looking after him would fall on Rupert. No-one ever considered that Rupert too should be studying. Somehow this always got overlooked during the worried conversations that frequently took place.

The winder had broken on Guy's wristwatch, and he decided

to take it repairs to a tiny little watchmaker's shop on the High Street, tucked in between an antique book shop and a shop of precious stones. He left it there and was told to call back in three days' time.

When he returned to collect it he waited briefly. The shop was run by two elderly brothers with grey wispy hair. One asked the other for the keys of the safe to retrieve Guy's watch while the other, bent over his work surface and with a magnifying glass stuck in his eye, repaired a tiny watch. The shop was hung about with a magnificent collection of clocks of all different shapes and sizes, wooden, bronze, silver, ormolu, plain, patterned fancy spare; suddenly they were all chiming. The sound was magnificent. Guy was startled as the sounds burst out.

The watchmaker repairing the watch looked up from his work bench and laughed. Guy moved closer towards him and followed his movements. From a wooden box, with a minute pair of tweezers, he was removing screws that were tiny they were almost invisible, and with meticulous care, inserting them into the mechanism of the watch. As he delicately placed them there, he would then take up a miniature screwdriver and carefully screw them in.

"How can you possibly see them?"

"With this," indicating the magnifying glass, "I can see them, without it, not."

The other brother returned with Guy's watch.

Guy was unable to take eyes away from the delicate operation being carried out before him.

"You are interested in watch making?"

"It really is remarkable." He continued to be mesmerised by the tiny screws, and all the other miniature pieces of the works that were being so skilfully inserted back into the husk of the watch.

"It takes a very long time to become a watchmaker, it is a very complicated matter. You have to train for many years." He took down an old, framed photo that had been hanging on a nail on the wall between the clocks. "This is our grandfather, he founded this shop a hundred years ago. The shop front has not changed in a hundred years."

Guy gazed at the sepia tint photo of a young man with whiskers standing in front of the shop. On either side of him were wooden panels, like shutters, which contained displays of watches, clocks, a shelf of carriage clocks, and a row of golden fob watches.

"He founded the shop and our father continued it. We have worked here for almost fifty years, in my case forty-eight, in my brother's case, slightly less."

"And your sons?"

"We don't have sons, we each have two daughters."

"But they can learn watch making if you teach them?"

"You know what girls are like nowadays, they all want education, and then they go on to higher things. Watchmaking is an art, and in order to do it well you require imagination and fantasy. You have a watch and it isn't working, and you need to know why it isn't working. So you examine it, and try out various different things, and you think you've got it working again. You leave it for a few days and it seems to be getting along all right. Then it stops. You don't know why. You have to open it up and try again, you have to try something else. But you always know, inside that watch, that whatever screws you do touch, there is one screw that you must not touch."

"What is that?"

"That is the one screw that holds everything else together. That is the one screw that you may not on any account touch. Otherwise you will have destroyed the whole mechanism, the very essence of the watch's very being. It is a very delicate matter, it has to be approached with the utmost care. You cannot take a hammer to a watch."

Güner had never been to England before, and was very excited about his visit. He arrived at Oxford in a fever of anticipation, and was overwhelmed by the beauty of the city. The day was perfect, with golden sunshine bathing the pink and white stones in a translucent glow. He gazed in wonder at the gargoyles grinning down at him at Magdalen, and walked in the deer park as if in a trance. Having installed himself there, he set about exploring the High Street, and went into all the colleges along the way, admiring the architecture and statuary. He particularly liked the way he had to rise up the steps of Queen's College in order to enter the magnificent quadrangle, and then, crossing the road, he felt deeply moved as he stood and gazed at that anguished marble form in Shelley's monument. He remembered that he had heard no news from Guy, and returned to Magdalen to see if a note had come. There was nothing.

He set about unpacking and arranging his books, and familiarising himself with the intricacies of college life. He was diffident about entering the Junior Common Room, but summoning up his courage he took the plunge, and found himself being offered tea by a very jovial, tall, plump chap who, as soon as he heard that he was from Turkey, immediately started to speak to him in Turkish.

"That's not my main language," he hastened to add. "Well, it's pretty good to be going on with." Richard showed an immense knowledge of the classical world, and they fell into an easy friendship, and arranged that they would sit next to each other at dinner in hall.

"Something's gone wrong here," thought Güner, when again he found nothing waiting for him in his pigeon-hole. Guy had helped him make all the arrangements to come to England, and had stated that he would invite him round as soon as he arrived. He knew of the date and time of his arrival, but now seemed to be ignoring it. Of course Güner knew of the reputation the upper class English had of freezing you out when you had served their turn, but he honestly hadn't thought that Guy was like this. After all, they were good friends, although it was true that they hadn't seen each other for a while. But everything in Oxford seemed to be so beautiful, so perfect. Surely there was no reason for Guy to cold-shoulder him? "And if he doesn't invite me, I know that under English rules and customs it would be quite improper for me to invite myself. What on earth shall I do?"

It was a freezing cold dawn when he rose early and walked in the deer park. Güner felt deeply disturbed. A soft white mist rose from the earth and enveloped the garden, the trees and the white thorn in the meadow. Behind it shone a brilliant light obscured by the mist which covered the whole park like a blanket of cloud. As he moved forward towards the light he found himself face to face with a magnificent Stag. The first thing he noticed was the majestic horns that appeared suddenly from the mist like a medieval vision appearing before him. Then the soft brown eyes looked directly into his. The great stag remained still and silent. Güner half expected the crucifix of Christ to appear entwined in the enormous antlers as in the vision of St Eustache that he had visited in the Ashmolean. He and the deer both remained stock still as they regarded each other. The cold, misty stillness wrapped itself around him, and he felt as though he were part of a mystical experience that he could not understand.

Gradually the light behind the mist began to blaze through, and a blinding red sun shattered the vision. Before him he saw the snowdrops in the garden, the sweep of the river and the herd of fallow deer. Without a sound the stag had vanished.

During the following days Güner set about getting on with his studies, deeply perturbed that he had still heard nothing from Guy. Eventually he found the silence unbearable, and set off up the Banbury Road in search of address on the letter-head. He had to find Park Town, and he finally located this leafy grove and entered into its special private preserve. He approached the house with trepidation, and knocked on the door. A servant showed him into a large ground floor room filled with books, where at first he didn't realise that Guy was standing, consulting his books, and ignoring him. He moved forward to greet Guy.

As he did so, Guy glanced up briefly and said, "Oh, it's you," and returned to his reading.

Güner waited patiently, but Guy just went on reading.

"Aren't you going to say hello?"

"Yes, yes, hello," said Guy, absentmindedly. Finally he looked up at him, but still said nothing.

"I thought you would contact me as soon as I arrived."

"When was that?" He seemed cold and distant. There was a pause, and it seemed as if Guy would return to his work.

"Where is Clelia?" Güner blurted out. "I would like to see her."

"You can't," said Guy coldly.

"Why not?"

"She's gone."

"What do you mean?"

"Exactly that."

Güner found it unbelievable. "Guy, what are you saying to me? I was especially looking forward to seeing her and being with both of you. Tell me what's happened. Talk to me. Don't treat me like a stranger!"

Guy looked at him. "There's nothing to tell. She went away. That's all there is to say."

"But where did she go? When was this? What did she say? Did you have an argument? Is she coming back? Tell me, tell me!"

"When I know something, I'll tell you."

"You mean she just went off?"

"Yes."

"Where?"

"I don't know."

Suddenly Güner realised how dreadful Guy looked. Perhaps the darkness of the room had obscured the change in him. He stared hard at him as the awfulness of what he had said sank in. "Do you mean she left you?"

"I'm afraid so," said Guy getting up and walking about, as if to shake the awfulness of the realisation from him.

"When was this?"

"I haven't been counting the days," said Guy irritably, thereby indicating that he had.

"Have you no idea where?"

"None whatsoever." He came over towards Güner. "Let's go for a drink."

They set out from the house but after a bit Güner had the impression that Guy wasn't leading him anywhere specific but was simply wandering about in an aimless sort of way. He seemed to be entirely taken up with his own thoughts, and lost in a world of his own. The conversation, in so far as it existed at all, was desultory. They walked past the Eagle and Child but Guy refused to enter it. After tramping about aimlessly they finally came to the Lamb and Flag in St Giles and Güner persuaded Guy to go inside. They sat on wooden benches at a wooden table.

"Did you forget that I was coming?"

"Probably. You must have thought me terribly rude."

"I didn't know what to think. I had no idea things were that bad."

"You can see that I couldn't tell you." He appealed to him. "What am I to do?"

"You have to find her."

"I've tried that. She can't be found."

"Didn't she at least write a letter?"

"No, nothing. You're going to blame me, aren't you, you're going to say it's my fault, that she had good cause to leave me."

"I wasn't going to say that." He could see that Guy was dangerously unhappy.

"Well, you should say it. She wouldn't have gone if she hadn't had good reason." Again, he appealed to Güner, who was shocked at this open exposure of his vulnerability as he realised the full extent of the desperate emotional state he was in.

They sat facing each other at the wooden table. They hadn't ordered any drinks. Güner was worried about starting. He was fearful that it might get out of control.

Suddenly a young man came up to the table. Guy introduced Rupert. "Congratulations," said Rupert. "At least you managed to get him out of the house."

"Have you been staying at home?"

"He stays in all the time. He won't do anything or go anywhere. You've actually achieved something by getting him to come here. Not that this is necessarily a good place. It would be better if we took him to a restaurant."

"It's fine here," said Guy. "Why don't you go and get us some drinks."

"Because if you insist on drinking, you ought to eat something first."

"They have food here."

"Not what I would call food."

"Yes, they do, look." He waved airily towards the bar where there was a rack of hard boiled eggs and some sandwiches."

While they argued, Güner felt more and more concerned for Guy. He wondered whether he also was in some way responsible. Eventually, a waiter came by and took their order. The conversation was very difficult and stilted. Güner was very concerned to ask Guy if he considered him to blame, but he couldn't possibly do so in front of Rupert.

Güner sat in his room in Magdalen sorting out his books and trying to come to grips with his weekly timetable. He found his attempts to organise himself all the more difficult without the help from Guy that he had expected. He suddenly heard a terrible cry, and the door of his room burst open, and Guy flung himself inside screaming.

"Look, look, look!" he screamed, flinging a copy of *The Times* onto the bed.

"What is it?" cried Güner, leaping up in alarm and fearing that Guy was drunk, although it was only ten o'clock.

"Read it! Read it!" he screamed.

"What? Where?" He started to fumble through the newspaper, but Guy seized it from him, turned the pages, folded it roughly and then thrust it angrily in front of him. Güner stared at it. Before him he saw the wedding photograph of a very beautiful woman, with a handsome bridegroom and two bridesmaids in attendance. He was about to return the paper when his eye fell upon the caption, and he looked again at the photo. Clelia couldn't have looked more lovely. Güner was astounded. "Who on earth is she marrying?" he asked in amazement.

"Read it, damn it!" shouted Guy, glaring at him. He read

the caption. "This is all taking place in Rio de Janeiro. He's a politician. Do you know him?"

"Of course I don't!"

Two boys came hastily into the room to complain about the shouting and screaming. They were on the point of shouting at Güner to be quiet, but they restrained their protests as soon as they saw that it was Guy. They tried to look at the newspaper to see what it was, but Guy screamed at them to get out and stay out, and they scuttled away.

Guy started to tear his clothes off. "What have you got? You told me you brought some good stuff with you from Istanbul. You said it was particularly pure."

"Yes it is, that's why you have to be careful."

"Get it!" He tore off all his clothes and flung them on the floor. He lay on the bed glaring at Güner who was hurriedly looking through his things. Finally he found it and brought it out, fumblingly trying to bring out only a small amount, terrified that in his misery Guy would overdose, either deliberately or by mistake. "Have you been drinking?" he asked tentatively, fearful of the dangerous combination of the two. "This is very pure, you can't take much of it."

"I'll take as much as I want," said Guy fiercely, trying to grab the bag out of his hand.

"No, no, I'll do it," said Güner, trying desperately to stay in control. His hands trembled as he tried to remove the powder from the bag and arrange it on the table. He glanced over his shoulder to look at Guy who had unexpectedly gone quiet. He found it heartrending to see the intense concentration with which he was examining the photograph in the newspaper.

The silence of the room was broken by Guy barking at him to lock the door.

As he was returning towards the table he was surprised by the sudden violence which Guy used to catch hold of him, pull him down onto the bed and tear his clothes off.

"Don't do it so violently!" he gasped.

"Yes, do do it so violently," cried Guy continuing unabated.

The remainder of the day was spent locked in the room. Guy refused any attempts to let Güner go, or any persuasion to go out himself in order to get something to eat. He was overwhelmed by the intensity of his misery, and abandoned himself to grief. Incapable of making any decisions for himself, he resolutely refused to allow Güner to make any decisions for him.

In the late afternoon, one of the boys knocked on the door to tell Guy that there was a phone call for him at the telephone at the end of the corridor.

"You go," he told Güner.

Güner hastily got dressed, and went to find out who it was. He came back and said that it was Mr Rawlinson. "He says he must speak to you. He has spent ages tracking you down. He finally got this number from Rupert, who obviously guessed you must be here. Come and speak now because afterwards I have to phone Rupert to say you're here. He's clearly worried about you."

Guy was very reluctant to get up from the bed and he refused to get dressed or cover himself.

Güner eventually tied a towel round his waist and dragged him down the corridor. Güner was terribly embarrassed at the way all the boys gathered in the corridor and silently stared at them.

Guy was oblivious to all of this. By now everybody knew about the photo in the paper, and there was a lot of sympathy for Guy, particularly as many of the boys had known about his engagement, and a number had met Clelia, or at least seen her and admired her from a distance.

Güner didn't feel that the sympathy quite extended to him, and he had a strong feeling that he was regarded as a foreigner and an outsider. Many of the boys knew Guy well and some of them had been at school with him, so they were quite used to his antics, and although everything he did was of intense interest to them, nothing really surprised them. Everybody in the corridor listened silently as he spoke to Nigel, although most of the talking was done by Nigel.

"I've taken ages to track you down. Will you come with me? I've cancelled everything and I'm taking two weeks leave. I don't care where she is, I'm determined to find her."

"But will you bring her back?" asked Guy pathetically.

A tangible wave of sympathy swept round the boys in the corridor, all eagerly waiting for the reply.

"I've no idea. According to that report, she's married, so I doubt if she'll agree to come back."

"Then what on earth is the point of going there?" asked Guy in despair.

"I want to speak to her. I have to find out why she did this."

"She's very clearly told us by that photo in *The Times*. She probably arranged to have it syndicated to make sure that we saw it. That's her message to us, that's all we need to know."

"Please come with me, you'll feel better if you see her."

"I've seen the photo. She's told me everything she needs to tell me. There's nothing else to say."

Guy staggered back to Güner's room and slumped down on the bed. Some of those who knew him gathered sympathetically in the doorway.

Güner was terribly embarrassed at being seen in the room with Guy like this and wished they would all go away, although they were trying to be helpful. He found their presence and their intrusive eyes overwhelmingly embarrassing.

They offered to get Guy something to eat but he told them not to bother. No-one offered to get anything for Güner, who was feeling particularly starving, but knew that he couldn't go off to get anything for himself since he knew he couldn't leave Guy on his own, and did not like to ask another boy to stay with him for fear of what Guy might say behind his back.

Finally the boys drifted away and Güner closed the door.

Guy stretched out his arms to him, and he went and lay down on the bed next to him. Guy wrapped his arms tightly round him, and cried himself to sleep.

During the following days Güner was unable to get Guy to do anything. He became more and more appalled at the terrible deterioration that took place before his eyes. It was only when Guy had drugged himself into a state of stupor that Güner was able to leave the room, lock it carefully so that no-one else would come in and see what a dreadful state Guy was in, and hastily go the covered market and buy some ready prepared food for them to eat. These mainly consisted of a variety of pasties or pies, or rolls prepared at Mrs Palm's. Once he brought back a take-away curry, but Guy threw it furiously back at him, and he had to spend the evening clearing up the mess, along with all the rest of the mess that had accumulated in the room.

Whenever he did go out he tried not to meet anyone, but occasionally boys accosted him in the corridor and asked how Guy was. Güner immediately reassured them that he was absolutely fine, despite that fact that he felt he was becoming more and more desperate. When Güner felt that he was finally at his wits' end, a delegation of boys arrived at the door of the room and informed him that they had phoned Guy's brother who was coming in the car to take Guy home. Güner tried his hardest not to let the boys into the room, but they pushed their way in. They were shocked to see Guy lying naked wrapped in a filthy sheet, and immediately decided that when Rupert arrived with the car and parked it outside the college, they would all carry Guy downstairs. A boy went to his room to collect a clean blanket and they wrapped it round Guy to keep him warm and to disguise him. Two of the boys arranged that they would distract the porters in the lodge while the body was surreptitiously bundled by, lest there be any enquiries.

Rupert, waiting in the High Street outside the college, almost fainted when he saw the state Guy was in. He was so upset that he was unable to drive the car, and another boy had to take over the wheel. The rest of the boys followed in another car so that on arrival at Malplaquet, they could help to smuggle Guy into his room.

As they drove down the stately drive bordered by rows of magnificent elms with their cut-diamond leaves glinting and sparkling in the sunlight, Güner for a moment forgot all the agony of the last days, and gloried in the grandiose splendour of an aristocratic palace of such historic proportions. How could a man who was the heir to such a glittering patrimony permit himself to deteriorate into such self-destructive despair? It was incomprehensible. Of course, the cause of it was understandable, and he too felt the pain of the loss of such a woman. But looking around him at the elegance and opulence of centuries of aristocratic breeding, Güner was at a loss to understand any of it. How could Clelia have left a man who had all of this? And if she actually had, as clearly was the case, how could Guy permit himself to degenerate beyond the point where he could at least restore and comfort himself in the heart of so much pleasurable luxury. And after a while, when he had to some extent recovered, it was only too obvious that there would be crowds of girls at the gates queueing up to take her place. And surely, even though she was irreplaceable, at least among the hundreds of applicants there would be one or two who might just about tide one over for the time being.

Guy walked through the park towards the forest and paused at a small copse. As he stood still he listened to the sighing of the wind in the tops of the trees. He glanced up to their enormous height, stretching above him to the blue-grey heavens. The sun was a fiery yellow ball nestling among wads of orangey-yellowy cotton wool. Above, a great light bluey grey crocodile waddled along. But the sun was in no danger, the crocodile just drifted along above it, allowing its belly to be gently warmed by the brilliant orb. And the viewer was in no danger either. He could look at the golden sun as long as he wished without any damage to his eyes: no reflections within the eye, no thousand suns dazzling the landscape as he looked away. The sun was cocooned and swaddled in light golden frothy cloud. The distant hills stood out in silhouette, only the lines of trees along their surfaces were visible. The rest was a fudge of non-existent blue. The crocodile was fading. The hills were blobs of blue-mist water colour. The sun was moving away fast to his right. As it descended, it reddened and increased in size. Finally an enormous red pudding came to rest itself on the summit of a blue hill, where it wallowed and squidged, gradually widening itself and slurping its way down on the further side of the crest. It visibly slipped and sludged itself until it could sustain its shape no more, and disappeared into a reddish rosy gooey glow. Then it was no more. The faithful dog at his heels shot off into the meadow, where a frantic pheasant rose up, winging its way in an awkward arc along the surface of the earth until it disappeared into the marshy meadows on the other side of the stream. He whistled softly to the dog, and it came running back obediently to heel.

Guy spent his days lying in bed in a state of acute despair. Rupert tried to think of anything he could to drag him out of it. He came in with a new record he had recently come across.

"Guy, you must hear this, it's completely wonderful." He went across to the turntable and put it on. At first they heard the sound of a lute playing he introduction, then the voice of a counter-tenor:

> *O rosa bella, o dolce anima mia,*
> *Non mi lassar morire in cortesia.*
> *Ai lasso me dolente deco finire*
> *per ben servire e lealment' amare.*

It was sung so sweetly to the sound of the lute, a rebec, viol and crumhorn. Rupert, fairly swooning at the sound, cried out ecstatically, "Music like this gives you a reason for living."·

"*Non mi lassar morire,*" murmured Guy again and again. "Yes, play it again," he said, "It was written five hundred years ago expressly for me." As he listened to it again, he felt a desolating grief new born in him, like certain barely remembered pains of one's early infancy, pain in its pure state, against which there is no hope and no remedy. It was at this moment that he could now choose to sink down into the abyss of despair, and totally give up, and fall to that final resting place where all pain would cease, or by an enormous effort, make one last attempt to swim to the surface, and drag himself out of this terrible despair. "*Dolce anima mia,* that is what she is. I have to survive to see her again, however I manage to do it. But not as a supplicant, never, never as a supplicant, but as someone worthy of her."

Rupert became fairly desperate. He hoped that he could save Guy through music that he knew he liked. "Fats Waller!" he cried, putting the record on the turntable. The melodious voice sang out in its jolly tone:

Here we are, out of cigarettes.

"That's exactly the case, I am out of cigarettes. Go and get me some," shouted Guy. He leaned back on the pillows while Rupert obligingly trotted off, returning with a packet of Gauloises, which he handed to Guy.

"Revolting!" cried Guy, throwing it down onto the carpet in disgust. "How do you manage to smoke such filthy rubbish! Detestable! I'm sure you only do it as a pose."

"I quite like them," replied Rupert.

"Well I don't," shouted Guy. "They're disgusting. Get me something else and get it quick."

"They're the only ones I could find," said Rupert humbly. He brightened up and added, "I could run around and ask the servants for some."

"Certainly not, that would be degrading. I refuse to permit you to do it. I suppose I'll have to smoke this rubbish. Have you sent the car for Güner?"

"Yes, it's just gone."

"Phone him, and tell him to bring some of the cigarettes I like."

"I think he'll bring them anyway."

"Yes, so do I. He knows what I like, and he knows when to

give it to me."

Rupert looked at him.

"And you can go away if you disapprove," said Guy furiously, "You don't have to look at me like that."

"I'm sorry, I didn't mean anything – "

"Well, don't mean anything. And don't play any more of this jovial music. If you actually bothered to listen to the words you would realise how painful it is for me, how totally unbearable."

"I'm sorry, I'll go through your collection, and see if there's something better."

"Yes, you do that."

The furious storm that had been threatening for some hours could contain its wrath no longer, and lightening flashed, and rain came crashing down, soaking the windows in a sheet of water. The crash of thunder was so sudden and intense that all the glass in the windows shuddered ominously, and all the lights in the palace went out, leaving it in a pall of icy darkness. Hail stones flung themselves against the windowpanes like an angry tirade of bullets and the view of the whole park disappeared under a wash of water leaving hardly a trace of a grey smear behind, All the great trees became misty cloud-soaked giants gradually fading out of view. No-one had lit the fire in the great fireplace in Guy's bedroom, and soon the hail stones were falling in malevolent disapprobation down the wide-open chimney, striking the logs piled up there and bouncing with intense force all over the floor.

Rupert had hardly left the room before he heard the most heart-piercing cry, and immediately ran back to the room.

Guy had flung the casement windows wide open and was screaming at the rain and hail stones which were pouring in upon him.

Rupert tried in vain to restrain him, and had to call desperately for help before Guy could be dragged away from the window back to his bed. By the time this happened he was completely soaking, as was the carpet near the window.

Mrs B was summoned in order to dry him, but this made Guy even more furious because of all people, he did not want her to encounter Güner, who was due to arrive at any moment.

At last Güner arrived, and took over the task of drying Guy and calming him down. The rest of the servants retired, and Rupert watched Güner swabbing Guy down, and then starting to massage him with Californian oil of jasmine.

Guy noticed that he was still there. "You can go now," he said dismissively, "Begone!" He gave an imperious wave of the hand.

"Alright, I'm going." He continued to watch the increasingly intimate nature of the massage. "But just a word of warning. Mama might decide to pay you a visit."

"No visitors. I don't want any visitors. Go and find her and make sure she doesn't suddenly get it into her head to visit me. She won't get in anyway; she'll find the door locked."

"Better that she doesn't come at all."

"Too right, see to it, make sure you stop her. I only want one visitor, and he had better start visiting, so you had better go."

Thus dismissed, Rupert hurriedly left the room, carefully closing the door behind him. He heard the key turn in the lock on the other side.

"Why are you so unkind to him, he's really very sweet, utterly devoted to you, and always very concerned about you," said Güner.

"He has to learn to obey, and so do you. Now get on."

While Güner was moving about on the bed he noticed by the telephone the note with Clelia's address and phone number. Guy noticed him glancing at it. He immediately grabbed it. "Don't think you're going to get in touch with her behind my back," he shouted angrily.

"I've no intention of doing that. But I do think that one of us should contact her."

"Certainly not!" cried Guy furiously, "Why should we. She went off. She has to contact us first. You're not sneaking off to her behind my back."

"Of course I won't, but we ought to be in touch with her."

"She has to reflect on how badly she treated me. I'm not getting in touch with her, and I'm not letting you do so."

"She sent you a very nice book on the history of Brazil."

"Yes, to salve her conscience. If that's all she does, then too bad."

"Wasn't it accompanied by a message that you should get in touch with her? At least you ought to write to her to thank her for the book."

Guy became very angry. "If you don't stop talking and get on, I'll throw you out, too. You came here to make me feel better. Now get on and do it."

The blustery stormy weather started to blow over. The squalls and showers gradually retreated from the domain and drifted slowly away to lodge themselves on the distant hills. Despite the darkness of the day, a ray of light began to break through the bleak clouds.

Rupert was the first to notice it and hastened to open up the shutters. The feeble ray of light did its best to unravel itself from the grey sky and infiltrate itself into the bedroom.

"It's Spring!" announced Rupert excitedly. "A new beginning, optimism, something fresh to break out of this gloom. Outside the day is blue and gold." He looked at Guy lying in a bed that was covered with a mountain of books and papers scattered about, all within easy reach.

Guy looked up at him from the book he was reading. "'For us there is only one season, the season of sorrow. The very sun and moon seem taken from me. It is always twilight in my heart. Sorrow after sorrow has come eating at the prison doors in search of me. They have opened the gates wide and let them in …'"

"Oh stop it! Stop wallowing in it, Guy. You're not in prison. You're not even in the bin, which is where you most feared you would end up."

"Very nearly. 'She shows herself so pleasant to whoever gazes at her, that through the eyes she gives a sweetness to the heart which no-one can comprehend who has not known it: and it seems that from her face moves a sweet spirit full of love that goes to the soul with the word: *Sospira*.'"

Rupert went over to the bed and sat on the edge of it. He looked at Guy who spoke softly.

"'Alone and thoughtful, I go pacing the abandoned fields dusty deserts of the mind with slow, hesitant steps. I find no other defence that protects me from the open awareness of people; because they can see from without, in my actions bereft of joy, how inwardly I flame.'"

As they silently regarded each other they both felt the same emotions of love and loss sweeping through their hearts.

As usual, Rupert had gone out of the room leaving the door slightly open. He had also left the wardrobe door slightly open, so that from that angle, as Guy lay in the bed, he could see himself reflected in the mirror. A sudden shaft of brilliant sunshine burst through the window, illuminating the wardrobe mirror and reflecting from it onto the dressing-table mirror and thence onto the wall. He lay there looking at himself caught in the mirror in the reflected light. "If I just kill myself," he thought, "all the agony will be over. At least I won't have to suffer any more. I could go downstairs, get one of the guns, and just shoot myself. In one moment all this will be finished. It is an ignominious way to end, but at least it will be an end." He lay looking at the dazzling light that was painfully bright. "The light destroys my eyes, but if I get them to close the shutters, I find the darkness terrifying where I am alone with my thoughts, I stare failure in the face, and the barbed firebrands blister my brains to shreds. It is unendurable." His mouth and throat were constantly dry, every limb and every muscle ached. His stomach and guts were all knotted up, and the pain of it infected every fibre of his being. A sickly feeling pervaded everywhere, and would not leave him. He couldn't sleep at night, but then neither could he wake up in the day. At one moment he was so freezing that he ordered them to light the fire. Later, after tossing ang turning in a restless daze for a while he was so profusely covered in sweat that the sheets were soaking, and the burning fire made him freeze again. He had no desire to eat anything, and he couldn't stand the way they kept offering meals to him. The very thought of food made him feel ill. Above all, he wanted all of them to go away. If he could have had the strength to crawl out of bed, when even just standing up made him feel dizzy, he would have crawled away into the corner of the room into the little space between the wardrobe and the wall and remained there forever.

Finally, Guy was feeling well enough to be taken outside and placed in a chair on the terrace overlooking the park. There had been a raging thunderstorm the night before, and the ground was soaking wet. Guy sat in the weak sunlight wearing a quilted dressing gown. Mrs B had lovingly placed blankets over his knees and round his feet, and a shawl over his shoulder. Finally he was getting on with his thesis, and concentrating on something.

Rupert was very hopeful for a good recovery.

And yet Guy found it very difficult to concentrate. He gazed mournfully over the rain-soaked park at the torn-down shrubs and crushed carnations strewing the path.

An enormous mauve cloud in the shape of a giant mole straddled the sky amidst a gathering of murky grey and brilliant white clouds. The mole glided ominously along. There was a fear of a further downpour. The windy silence was broken by the creaking of shutters and the rattling of roof tiles, and the weary tossing of wet leaves in the trees.

Rupert came running out, wearing the anxious expression that had attached itself to his face ever since Guy's breakdown. "I tried to stop them coming in but you know what they're like, they just insisted, in fact, they practically – "

"Barged their way in!" said Mark triumphantly, hurrying hard upon Rupert's heels.

"You really shouldn't have come, you'll only make him worse," protested Rupert.

Mark went swiftly up to Guy and kissed him in greeting. He gazed into his face, examining it carefully.

"Changed?" asked Guy.

Mark glanced round at Ian who maintained a respectful distance, and then looked back at Guy. He considered for a moment. "No, I don't think so, not really. Of course, you don't look fully well, but you haven't changed."

"You didn't see the worst," said Rupert.

"But we did hear about it," said Mark softly. "You haven't forgotten that a lot of those Magdalen boys are contemporaries of mine: They told us everything. Afterwards, of course, not at the time. If I'd known at the time – "

"No, no, it wouldn't have helped, I assure you," said Rupert miserably.

"Well now," said Mark rubbing his hands together. "I think it's time to get the patient inside before we all get drenched by the next thunderstorm."

The sky had suddenly become very dark, and the mauve mole had settled ominously above their heads. The trees were waltzing rhythmically to and fro, and imploding upon themselves.

Mark picked up the books and looked at them. "Oh yes, Wittgenstein's *Tractatus Logico-Philosophicus*, and the *Philosophical Investigations*, I remember these."

"Most improbable," said Guy.

"Not at all," said Ian, coming up to the table, and picking up Popper's *The Open Society and its Enemies*. "He's not a slouch, he goes to Popper's lectures, and those of Lakatosh."

"Do you?" asked Guy in amazement, as they helped him to his feet.

"Never fails to amaze you, doesn't he?" said Ian, helping Guy with the blankets.

Mark took Guy by the arm to lead him inside. The wind was now very strong. "Come and live in London with me and we'll go to the lectures together. If you're studying him you might as well hear him. He's at the LSE."

"I know where he is."

"Come, then, and you can explain it to me. We'll study it together."

They all went inside and wandered into the Green Lounge. Mark looked around delightedly. "Remember this?" he asked Ian with pleasure.

"Behave yourself this time," said Ian curtly.

"Why, what is he about to do?" asked Rupert anxiously.

They arranged Guy in a propped-up position in a tall-backed arm chair. Mark helped him remove the quilted dressing gown.

"Not here, Mark!" hissed Ian furiously, as Mark quickly buried his face in Guy's lap.

"What on earth is he doing?" cried Rupert. "Anyone could come here at any moment!"

"Stop it, Mark, there are too many doors to close. His father could come at any minute."

Guy leaned back and relaxed. "It's not his father who's going to come at any minute."

Rupert looked particularly shocked and distressed.

"Don't you get your girlfriends to do this for you?" asked Guy in that awful nonchalant way he seemed to adopt whenever Mark was there. As Guy closed his eyes there was a great crash of thunder, and the rain burst against the windowpanes with a tremendous noise. Mark settled himself happily in the chair next to Guy and looked at Ian.

Ian looked back at him furiously. "He's totally out of control these days."

"Any more than in the past?" asked Guy.

"Yes, much worse. And he behaves very badly towards me."

"What does he do?"

"Shouting, screaming, hysterical fits. Complete fury if he doesn't get his own way."

"You don't need to say any of this," said Mark, but he didn't seem to mind at all.

"He's even attacked me, stamping on my feet. He nearly broke my hand the other day, he certainly tried very hard to."

"You exaggerate!" cried Mark. He got up and went to the record player where he put on the Mozart Clarinet Quintet. Ian waited for him to return to his place before continuing, "He can be intensely spiteful and manipulative." Mark just gave a smirk and waved his hand as though to dismiss the allegation. Rupert looked on in total disbelief. "And, continued Ian, "just to show that he's at the height of fashion he's taken up cruising."

Guy looked alarmed. "That's very dangerous, Mark. If you get arrested, it'll be very serious for you."

"I keep warning him, but he takes no notice. He says everyone is doing it, and he wants to keep up with them. He'll either get a black eye or be arrested. I keep telling him that police pose in public toilets, but he insists on going cottaging."

"I do not!"

"What was that long story you told me about an orgy in a public toilet, with people doing the most amazing things with total strangers?"

"I didn't say I was there, I said that someone told me about it."

"You did say you were there, and you described it in grotesque detail. You described what they were supposed to have done to you!"

Mark looked at Guy. "You were supposed to have gone out of my life," said Guy. They listened to the intense passion of the music. Mark cuddled up close to Guy as the swathes of sound swaddled them together against the chilling cold of the room. Guy knew that he had absolutely no defence against the sheer overpowering physical presence of Mark. Rupert felt an overwhelming sense of agony for Guy's weakness. Mark spoke very softly. "They told us all the details, all about your boyfriend." Guy tensed with alarm, and he sensed Ian straining very hard to hear what was said. "Is he here?" Mark continued.

"No, and you're not going to see him. Did you come because you were worried?"

"You don't need to be worried," said Rupert wearily.

"Really?"

Rupert shrugged his shoulders. He tried to sit as near as possible to Guy to protect him from malign influences. Ian, as tense as a taut piece of wire, moved nearer so as not to miss a word.

"But are you serious about him?"

"Oh God! Are you going to do something to him?"

"How can I, I don't know who he is."

"You know very well how to find out. Just leave him alone."

"That's the one thing he can't do," said Ian.

"Does he matter to you?" asked Mark.

"You know you're the only person in the world who matters to me," said Guy, and immediately dropped his eyes. No one said anything, and they listened intently as the beauty of the music swept about them, and the howling of the wind swept around the palace.

Reluctantly Rupert left them in order to telephone Güner to make sure that he did not turn up by chance. On his return, he discovered, as he had wearily anticipated, that they had all retired to the bedroom, and that Mark was busy organising that Mrs B would serve lunch to them there. Knowing nothing about the circumstances, Mrs B was delighted to see Mark visiting the patient, and warmly welcomed him on his return to Malplaquet, urging him to extend his visit in order to assist in Guy's cure. Mark exercised all his charm over her, and she was, as always, bewitched by him. Ian loved to see Mark performing his games of power play, and Mark loved to see Ian watching, and, as he imagined, admiring him. Guy watched both of them, and then, as he lay in bed, he saw in the mirror of the wardrobe, once again carelessly left slightly open by Rupert, the third person in the equation sinking irredeemably downwards, who knew whither.

"Soon, he'll insist on being left alone with me," thought Guy, "And I shall be sunk."

Guy read Nigel's name on the visiting card, and hastily went downstairs. Nigel was waiting for him in the West Drawing Room. They sat down together.

"How are you?"

"Much better, thank you. Did you see her?"

At this moment Mark swept into the room and came and sat down next to Guy.

"Oh, excuse me," said Nigel, looking very surprised, "I thought I might speak to Guy privately; I don't know – "

"Anything you have to say to him you can say in front of me."

"But you are –?"

"I'm Mark Greville. We met before, Mr Rawlinson, I called upon you in your office."

"Did you, Mark?" asked Guy in amazement, "When was that?"

"Ah!" cried Nigel, leaping to his feet. "That's who you are! What on earth are you doing here?"

"Why shouldn't I be here?" cried Mark, also leaping to his feet. "Guy is ill, he needs me here."

"But you – "

"Yes! You tried to get rid of me, didn't you? You refused to let me know where Guy was when he needed me. You thought I'd disappeared out of his life, and for a time I did. For far too long a time. Which means that I left Guy completely alone to be with his fiancée, and so he was, for quite some time. I wasn't around when she chose to leave him, so you can in no way put the blame on me, even though I think you would like to, in order to justify your action in getting rid of me."

"I can't understand why you're here now, and in any event, I really must speak to Guy in private."

"As long as you fully accept that I cannot in any way be

responsible for the actions of his fiancée, who I never even met." Nigel looked at Guy, who looked shocked and discomforted, but said nothing. Nigel paced about the room, with his back towards them.

"I'm not asking you to apologise to me, I'm asking – "

Nigel swung round to face Mark. "I don't intend to apologise to you!"

"I'm not asking you to. But you cannot put any of the blame of his fiancée leaving him on me."

"Very well," said Nigel. "And now I really must ask you to leave."

Mark paused for a dramatic moment, and then swept out of the room. Nigel looked at Guy's anxious face. "What on earth is he doing here?"

"I have been ill. Tell me about your visit." He couldn't bring himself to say her name.

"Forgive me, there is something I must ask you."

Guy looked pained. "Do you think you could ask me later? After you've told me about the visit. I'm much affected by the cold. Perhaps if you might ring the bell, we could order some tea." Nigel moved across to the fireplace and pulled the bell rope. There was a long awkward silence that seemed like an age as they waited for the butler, and then gave the order for tea. Nigel sat down.

"How is she?"

"The fact is, Guy, she's incredibly well, and terribly well set up."

"Is it a real marriage?"

"No, it's a marriage blanc – "

"So then," burst out Guy, "She's still available for me! Surely – "

"No, I'm sorry, you must let me explain," said Nigel in a concerned voice, "You must let me tell you. This Vargas, she's married –"

"He's famous, isn't he?"

"He's a relative of the former president, and he's a democrat. He's organising a democratic party to fight against the military dictatorship. For whatever reason, politics, I suppose, it was important for him to have a beautiful, personable wife to appear with him on platforms and in campaigns. Obviously, she's perfect for that."

"But what's in it for her? Why did she do it?"

Nigel paused before replying, and looked at the troubled, anxious face that turned pleadingly towards him, begging him for hopeful news. "She's there for someone else," he said softly.

"Who?!!" came the strangled cry.

"I don't know, I can't tell you," said Nigel softly, "But she's already carrying his baby."

"Already! How is that possible? Who is he?"

"She wouldn't tell me, but it must be someone who can't acknowledge her, so it suits her to appear to be married to Vargas, and no one will bother her as to the true father of her child. Maybe it's an important political figure who's already married, and she's the secret mistress. You know they don't have divorce in Brazil."

"So does that mean that even if I go there, she can't divorce Vargas and marry me?"

"They seem to have some form of informal separation, but the Church doesn't allow divorce. But you should go, she would love to see you. She was completely thrilled that I turned up. Perhaps she was feeling rather isolated and lonely. You should go."

"Absolutely not!" cried Guy ferociously. "She chose to go off. She also chose to do it in a particularly heartless way. Didn't she ever care to think of the devastating effect it would have on those she left behind, those she abandoned? How could she do it? How could she be so heartless?" He looked as though he were about to burst into tears but managed desperately to restrain himself. His furious anger got the better of him. "Let her rot there," he shouted, "She chose it, she deserves it. I'll never, never go and see her, however much she begs me to. Anyway," he calmed down a bit, "If she's having someone else's child, what on earth would be the point. You really have no idea who the father is?"

"No, she simply wouldn't talk about it, or where she met him or anything like that. Don't you think you might at least write to her?"

"Me write to her?" Guy shouted again. "To say what? To congratulate her on having someone else's child when she should be here with me having mine? How dare she even imagine I would." He paused and looked at Nigel. "She didn't write to me, did she?"

"No, but if you were to –"

"Ah! There you are! She doesn't write to me, but she expects me to write to her! Well, I shan't, and that's that." But he was unable to restrain himself from asking Nigel to tell him all the details of where she lived, what the house was like, how she had looked and what she had been wearing. He tried desperately to summon up a picture of what it would be like. Finally he asked Nigel, "In your honest opinion, is it likely to last?"

Nigel looked immensely weary and immensely sad. "There's no way that I can say. It's a question of time."

"If…if, somehow, it all went badly wrong, if…if somehow she realised that she'd made a terrible mistake, do you…do you think she'd be too proud to admit it, and come back?" He was so intensely hopeful. "Do you think that if I went there, I could persuade her to come back?"

Nigel shook his head sadly. "Don't you think that's what I

spent all my time trying to do?"

They sat in silence in the freezing cold room. The rain poured silently down the windowpanes. Where the shutters did not quite meet the wooden window ledges the water poured into the room and formed oozing puddles on the parquet floor. In the ordinary way Guy would have done something to mop up the water and adjust the shutters so that the wooden floor didn't get ruined, but in his desperately miserable state he was incapable of moving, let alone caring. He watched the ice-cold water ooze along the floor in a slow stream. They remained silent for a very long time, each entirely lost in his own thoughts.

Finally, Nigel felt that he must bestir himself, otherwise both of them must surely freeze to death before the oozing water actually drowned them.

"If there's any further news. I'll keep you up to date. Now that you know what the situation is –"

"Yes, it makes quite a difference. I have to make my own arrangements; I can't go on living in hope. "Nor should I, he thought to himself, continue to live in such unutterable misery. What on earth is the point in going on suffering?

The rain had stopped. An intense shaft of light burst through the window and illuminated one side of the room. The light was so bright that Guy couldn't believe what it was and went to the window to stare out into the park. He was at the same time soaked by the pool of water he wandered into as blinded by the intensity of the sun forcing its way violently through the clouds and through his eyes into the back of his skull. He stumbled from shock and Nigel thought that he was about to slip into the water.

"I'm fine, fine," he assured Nigel as he excused himself, and staggered off blindly to change. He returned shortly afterwards and suggested to Nigel that they retired to a room that had a fire. "You can understand the old pater not having much heating on, it costs a fortune to heat the place. He only does it when he's entertaining cabinet ministers." They walked down the corridor to the dining room. "It will be warm in here; they're preparing to serve lunch soon. You will stay for lunch, won't you?"

"There is something you must permit me to ask you, in view of what I intend to suggest to you as a future career."

"If it's to do with that young man, then I don't think you need to trouble yourself."

"Why is he here?"

"Just visiting."

"I had thought –"

"You mustn't allow yourself to have thoughts."

"Do you really assure me?"

"Yes, I do." The clear blue eyes looked directly at him. "On my word as a gentleman. You really shouldn't imagine anything."

"So that anything that I may have –?

"Nothing, it really is nothing." As he spoke, it did seem to Nigel as though the old, confident Guy had returned. He walked about in the garden whereas, earlier, he had hardly been able to get up out of his chair.

"Did Clelia never meet Mark? I thought they knew each other?"

"Perhaps they met at parties, I don't know. That whole period is very painful for me, I don't like to dwell on it, you must forgive me if I don't wish to talk about it."

"Of course."

"If you had any idea at all of how much I loved her, love her. I have behaved badly, I admit it, but I would be grateful if you wouldn't dwell on it."

"No, of course not."

"You mentioned that you had plans for me."

"I thought, perhaps, the Foreign Office."

"Would I get in?"

"With my recommendation. You'll have to sit the exam."

"And go to a villa in the countryside for a weekend of observations?"

"Not anymore. That was in my day. We had to go to Stoke d'Abernon in the county of Surrey and stay for two or three nights, and take part in exercises, be observed by psychiatrists, and have our table manners monitored. Nowadays you just go for the day to Savile Row. You do have to conduct exercises, act out hypothetical situations, solve logical problems, all under the watchful gaze of trained psychiatrists, but you can easily do that. I'll fill you in on what you have to do and prepare you for the exams. I'll also write a reference for you."

"Will you? I shall be so immensely grateful to start an active career. I can't sit around doing nothing, and in my present frame of mind, I simply can't concentrate on my academic studies. I could take time off from my thesis and continue it later."

"But you'll have to get on with it, the exams come up quite soon and there's only a very narrow time window. I don't know if you're physically or mentally up to it."

"I'll make myself; I'm determined to do it. If you back me, I'll be able to pull through."

Having persuaded Nigel to stay to lunch, Guy went in search of Mark to try to cajole him into good behaviour. He was only too well aware of the risks he ran. "If you don't behave well, you are going to ruin my future career. Either you let us have lunch separately, or you employ your best manners, and don't say anything compromising. Control your desires to show affection where it's inappropriate. As soon as lunch is over, he has to get back to London, and you can allow your passions free range then."

"You do realise that this is the man who threw me out of your life!"

"Someone had to do it, Mark," said Ian, "Perhaps you don't realise it, perhaps you are incapable of realising it, but your conduct was driving Guy to disaster. You say he is the person who matters most to you on earth, but your behaviour was destroying him."

It looked as if a terrible row was about to break out between them. Guy was determined to stop it and suggested that they had lunch elsewhere. Mark was determined not to be excluded, and to prevent them from discussing him behind his back.

"But you don't like him. What's the point of having lunch in his company?"

"So, he can intervene in your plans, and make life difficult for you," said Ian.

"Mark, it's in your own interests not to, because if he gets me a job in the Foreign Office, I'll be able to live in London, and we'll be nearer each other."

"Only if you agree that we'll live together. You'll give up your boyfriend here, and live with me, in the apartment we saw, or somewhere else, not in our slum, of course."

"Don't force him to make a decision now," cautioned Ian.

But Mark saw his chance. "Either you swear that we'll live together, or I'll go down right now and tell him everything. Then he'll know you're a security risk and you won't get the job."

"Are you really so determined to destroy me?"

"Of course, he isn't, he just wants total control of you," said Ian.

It was a dangerous game and there was an awkward stand-off. Guy paced about the room. "I want it in writing," said Mark. "You've made me promises in the past, and you've broken them."

"I can't put it in writing, you could show it to anyone, it's far too dangerous. It's like your mad scheme of proclaiming our love to the world, it simply can't be done."

Mark smiled a disconcertingly evil smile. "Don't you trust me?" he leered.

"He's waiting for me downstairs."

"Then decide."

"And you don't come to the lunch."

Mark smiled and shrugged his shoulders. Guy paused for a moment and then picked up the telephone. "Ashton, put me through to the Estates Bursar."

"Certainly, Sir. Line's engaged. Can you bear with me, Sir? Just putting you through now, Sir."

"Mason, that flat in Albemarle Street, is it available?"

"Yes, I think it is, Sir."

"I'm thinking of moving to London, could it be made ready for me?"

"I can't see why not, Sir."

"Last time I saw it there wasn't any furniture."

"It has been fully furnished, Sir."

"I'll square everything with Pap."

"Very good, Sir." He put down the receiver. Mark was overjoyed. "I want the lease put in my name," he demanded.

"That's not possible. These estates are all entailed."

"But you own it."

"No, we don't. I mean, we do, but it's all tied up in trusts."

"But you have to draw up a lease, to lease it out. A long lease, made out in my name, at a peppercorn rent. Otherwise, if I just have a licence to be there, you can throw me out at will."

Ian sat by, marvelling. He was very impressed. Mark was keenly aware of this.

"We'll see," said Guy decisively. "And now you must excuse me while I go down to lunch."

"We're coming too," said Mark, snatching up his jacket and

running out with him.

"But you said you wouldn't," said Guy.

"I'll be on my absolute best behaviour. You can rely on me."

Guy knew that it would be useless to try to stop him. Mark behaved impeccably at lunch, and no one would have imagined that he could have been the same person who had been so insulting to Nigel on his arrival at Malplaquet. By the time he was ready to leave, Nigel was overwhelmed by his charm, his polite and informed conversation, and his care and concern for Guy's health and future career.

As Guy walked Nigel to the courtyard where the car was waiting for him, Nigel was full of compliments for Mark.

"But in the past, Guy, when there was all that trouble, when you thought differently of him, it did then cross my mind… You do absolutely assure me, do you, that there really is nothing that I should be concerned about?"

"Nothing, absolutely, I assure you. Of course he is very pretty, but I pay no attention to that."

Nigel stared hard at him. Guy smiled and boldly held his gaze. It did seem to Nigel that at last, the Guy they had always known had returned to them. Nigel felt a great sense of relief as he rode in the car back to Oxford station.

Guy immediately returned to his bedroom, where he announced that he was better. Mark was excitedly making plans for their future, and instantly claiming the credit for Guy's cure. "If I hadn't come here two weeks ago and looked after you, you would never have recovered. Rupert should come and thank me for curing you. I know how to look after you, I always have done. Now you've got to arrange an interview with your father, move into the flat, and start preparing for the exam. I'll do everything else, just tell us when we can move in."

"No riotous parties with all your friends."

"Certainly not, just discreet soirées with you."

Everything worked well, and Guy was soon able to arrange for Mark and Ian to move into Albemarle Street. Mark insisted that on the day when Guy went to be examined for the Foreign Office in Savile Row, he should spend the equivalent time with Guy's tailor, naturally at Guy's expense. Guy was obliged to endure a long, arduous day at Savile Row, being keenly observed by a sharp team of psychiatrists, but his new enthusiasm carried him through, and the time he had passed being coached by Nigel had been well spent. Guy was overjoyed when the letter finally arrived telling him that his efforts had been successful, and that he was to report to the Foreign Office the next day.